VALOR
AMIDST
DECAY

Amongst Desolation
Book One

AJ SOMERS

Book Cover by Ashe Arends (@spookgeist)

Developmental Edits by Sarah Reside (@editsandrevisions)

Line Edits by Lindsey Clarke (@lindseyclarkewrites)

Blurb Edits by Jessie Cunniffe (@bookblurbmagic)

For the Neurodivergent reader

While some may see the world in shades of gray, we paint its colors.

CONTENT ADVISORY/WARNING

This book is not intended for anyone under the age of 18, as it includes themes and situations not suitable for children.

Some situations and themes in this book may be difficult for some readers. Please check out my Trigger/Content Warning on my website, which is linked below via QR code. While this book does not have more than one mild sexual encounter between the main characters, please keep in mind this series will progress to open door scenes.

It is okay if you need to step away due to the listed triggers. My main concern is that my readers are prepared and safe while reading, and I'd rather you put your mental health above all else.

https://ajsomers.com/trigger-content-warning/

Contents

Chapter One

Dahlia

Pulling my headphones out of one of my ears, I glance around, trying to see if anyone has gotten the okay to leave their seats yet. We landed over an hour ago but for some unknown reason, we haven't been able to exit the plane. The attendants have only walked by once, leaving us to stew. The pilot announced over the intercom that there had been a few minor delays, but we would be able to disembark shortly.

Clearly, those delays were more than minor. I internally roll my eyes. Although I still have a little bit of time, I need to be at work in a few hours. The longer I wait here, the more likely I'll end up late.

Not that I care about this job anymore.

A gentle tap on my shoulder has me glancing over to the window seat. I pull the other headphone out to hear what the elderly woman is trying to ask me.

"–by now?" She finishes, although I caught none of it since Atreyu was blasting in my ear.

Her hair is snow white, the color so many women would kill to have as they age. Her large, brown eyes are soft as she takes in my face, waiting for me to answer her question.

"I'm sorry, ma'am. I had my music on. Can you say that again?" I ask her politely, giving her a small smile, hoping I don't seem as awkward as I feel.

"Oh. I said, shouldn't we already be off the plane by now?" She repeats herself.

I glance back down the aisle in search of an attendant, but they're all still nowhere to be found. "We should be, but I'm not sure what's happening."

She mumbles something about missing her grandchildren, but instead of continuing to converse, she places her reading glasses on her face and returns to her novel.

The vintage cover is bright despite the book's worn appearance. On the beach, there's a shirtless man embracing a woman in an off-shoulder gown, completely transfixed in each other. I need to hold back the snicker at the thought of her reading a bodice ripper.

Damn, grandma.

The tropical cover has me thinking back to yesterday with my best friend, Meg. If she had been here, I probably wouldn't have been able to hold in the laugh.

"So, have you gotten a chance to meet up with Jax's friend?" Megan asks. She rolls onto her back and covers her eyes with her arm.

We're both lying on our towels in the sand. I usually prefer to enjoy the water, but if I want to catch up with my friend, I'll have to take the time to suntan. As if someone like me could tan. I only fry. I'm not overly pale, but my freckled skin isn't made for long exposure to the sun.

"Jerry?" I snort. "No. I'm not interested. Don't get me wrong, I'd love to meet someone, but he seems a bit, what's the word... boring? No, maybe just too formal? I don't know. I'm not into the rich, 'I went to Uni overseas' frat boy types. That's the vibe I get from him." I roll over onto my stomach and lay my head on my arms, facing Meg. "He's too pretty. Plus, he was wearing boat shoes when we met him, Meg. Fucking boat shoes." I laugh, genuinely wondering what Jax was thinking in trying to play matchmaker. I take a sip from the tall can while I ponder if I should tell her how crappy the last setup was.

Screw it, it's Meg. If I can't be honest with her, who the hell else can I be honest with? "Plus, the last date you set up for me was one of the worst I've ever been on. I don't think I trust you two to find love for me, okay?" Laughing again, I close my eyes.

"Honestly, I agree with you. I told them he wasn't your type, but we want to have a 'couple' friend, you know what I mean? Plus, I only want to see you happy," she says.

"Yeah, I know. And I appreciate you for it." A genuine smile breaks free. Without her, I don't know where I'd be right now.

"But I'm so sorry we can't find some tormented, broody soul for you." She snorts a laugh. I open my eyes to sneak a peek at her.

She stays silent for a while, taking longer sips from her fruity seltzer. "So, I know you've told me probably fifty times already, but seriously, when are you going to start dating?"

I almost spit out my beer as I hold back a laugh. Swallowing, I say, "For fuck's sake." I continue to laugh. She'll never let this go. I take another drink of my beer and sigh when she keeps giving me the 'well, come on' look.

"I've told you. I won't brush the idea off, but I'm not looking for anything. You remember the last time I tried to get serious with someone?" She hums in response before I continue. "Things were going well enough, and then he just ghosted me." I take another sip of my drink, thinking over that last experience. "Do you also remember how when we ran into each other, he acted scared as if the reaper would find him for only speaking to me?" As I think back to that day, I still can't figure out why he seemed so afraid of me.

"Anyways, the others who showed any interest were the goody two-shoe men who also wanted to go into the police force. I don't want to date cops. I don't even want to be one anymore." I let that thought slip, admitting it out loud for the first time. Meg, knowing me as well as she does, sits up, ready to ask me unending questions.

"Finally!" she exclaims.

"What the heck do you mean by finally? I ask her.

"I've been waiting for you to admit that already. I knew you loved the classes in school, but you never seemed a hundred percent into the actual job description. You hated when your dad was an investigator. And let's be real, you always preferred the dangerous sort. Bad boy stereotype seems to stick with you, my friend." She snickers as she throws her empty can into a bag and opens a new one.

She takes another tall can out, offering it to me before continuing, "I'm only half joking. Your track record just sucks when it comes to the bad boy type or, more like the crazy type. I'm glad that's finally behind you, though. I won't lie; I was worried about moving away and leaving you alone."

I chug the rest of my warming beer and take the offered one. "I'll be fine. You don't need to worry. It's been years since he's bothered me," I say as I adjust the headband holding back my messy, red curls.

Meg knows most of the story, but I never told her the full extent of it. I haven't told anyone. Since she was around for the beginning of that catastrophe, she knows how it began but never saw how it progressed other than the restraining order I had gotten. To her, he was a bad ex-boyfriend of sorts who had a problem with the word no.

"Anyways, I think maybe I want to go back to school. I have no clue what to do with myself," I mention, shoving the feeling of uncertainty back. I'm supposed to be relaxing, not stressing about how, at twenty-seven years old, I still have no clue what the hell I'm doing with my life.

Fuck, if my dad saw me now.

"You'll figure it out, Dahl. I wish you had more faith in yourself. You're one of the most capable people with a clear and smart head on your shoulders. You need to give yourself some more credit and be easier on yourself," my childhood friend says. Her bright smile is filled with so much love that I can't help but feel the gratitude warming me.

"Ma'am!" Startled, I whip my head around to the smutty grandma. "Are you going to get that, dear?" she asks, pointing to the phone on my lap.

Shit! "Thanks." I give her an awkward smile before glancing down at my chiming phone. I don't even need to see the screen to know who it is. Only two people would be calling me: my boss and Meg. I swipe across the screen, answering.

"You will not believe this shit storm, Dahl!" Megan says over the phone, jumping right into it before I can say hello.

Peeking over at the woman, I find her back in her book. Lowering my voice, I say, "Hey, is everything okay? What shitstorm?"

In the call's background, I hear what sounds like an intercom. "We had an emergency stop in Parowan, Utah." She pauses, speaking to someone else before returning. "There are no flights leaving this airport or any buses. Apparently, there are mass cancellations all over the States. I'm stuck."

That can't be good. I glance back down the aisle for what is probably the twentieth time.

Still no attendant.

What the hell?

"Girl, you there?"

Huh? "Oh, shit. Sorry, Meg. I'm wondering when the hell they'll let us off the plane. We've been waiting to disembark for way over an hour now," I tell her as I shove my headphones into my backpack.

Although I don't care about my job as a police dispatcher anymore, I can't help but stress about being late. My dad engraved in me to be punctual, and I honestly can't help but feel ashamed of myself at the thought of calling out.

He'd only be disappointed in you, Dahlia.

My friend's voice brings me back to the conversation. "I wonder what the heck is happening. It was like that for me, too. They wouldn't even tell us why we needed to land. By the time we got off the plane, all flights I could find were being delayed or canceled."

That's bizarre. "Have you spoken to Jax?" I ask her.

"No. They had a shift at the hospital tonight, I think. I left a voicemail. Hopefully, they can respond to me soon. I even tried the hospital reception but got no answer. It must be a busy night for them." She sounds worried, but knowing her, she'll find a way to get a hold of them.

"Shit, Meg, I'm sure Jax will call or text you soon. You're safe, though? You have a place to stay, at least for the night?"

A car honks in the background, briefly interrupting her answer. "Yeah. There is a motel I'm going to stay at for now. Looks like we'll all be giving this small town a bit of business tonight." Her chuckle sounds forced. "Anyway, I'm going to call Jax then. I just wanted to be sure you were good and vent a little."

I can't help the smile that curls my lips. I already miss her. "No problem. I love you. I miss you already," I say quietly into the phone.

"Miss you too, Dahl face."

Once we hang up, my chest tightens as if my heart knows something I don't, like a foreboding warning.

Chapter Two

Dahlia

Finally.

The captain finally gave us the clear to leave.

Everybody stands at once as if that'll get them off the plane faster, but it still takes some time for each row to slip out and grab their bags in the overhead compartments. Another twenty minutes go by before I'm finally moving.

Walking through the bridge towards the luggage claim and then the exit, I overhear someone arguing with an airport staff member.

"What do you mean you don't know?!" a short, stocky man exclaims.

"I am sorry, sir, but there have been delays with most of our flights, and we haven't gotten any updates regarding your flight's luggage quite yet. We will be able to inform you as soon as possible. We are estimating it to be about an hour's wait. If you would like, we can take your address and ship the luggage to you if you are unable to wait," the woman says patiently.

Damn. I guess it was smart to only pack a backpack.

I continue walking towards the exit as the man's voice grows louder, throwing profanity at the woman as if she purposely held their luggage to spite him. I roll my eyes. The poor woman is only trying to do her job. It isn't *her* fault his luggage is delayed.

LAX is usually a busy airport, but as I continue to walk, a sense of trepidation hits me. The airport that's usually bustling, even on a Sunday night, feels more like a ghost town in comparison to its normal crowd. There are still people, especially the ones from my own flight, but it's still strangely quiet.

I think back to what Meg mentioned. *Mass cancellations.*

Just how many would cause the airport to be this slow?

I almost run into a couple who stop in their tracks.

Seriously? Why the hell do people stand in the middle of the freaking walkway? For goodness sake.

Chill, Dahlia. It's not a big deal. It's just my nerves. Something about the silence is putting me on edge.

Although I was only gone for a weekend, I'm incredibly relieved to be home. My nerves feel shot, and I'm ready to be alone. I love spending time with Meg, but I'm just ready for some downtime. Not to mention, the thought of going back to work is already frying my already frayed nerves.

A jab to my back has me stumbling forward. I reach out. My hands hit the linoleum floor, and pain shoots through my wrists.

At least it wasn't my face.

"What the hell, man," I mumble.

The tall man in a rumpled suit runs away from me toward the exit. He doesn't even spare me a second glance. *What is wrong with people these days?*

I breathe in for a count of three to try to brush off my growing anxiety.

A group of people run by me and interrupt my exhale.

Why are people running? What am I missing?

A scream rings out behind me.

I scramble to get up while my eyes search frantically for the source.

Something feels off. There's no security around, and these people know something I don't.

A shrill scream has me whipping back around so quickly that I almost crash into someone else. There's nothing out of the ordinary other than a few people running in haste. Others are going about their nights as usual, although a few are also glancing around as curious as I am.

I turn back around and pick up my pace. Why hasn't security responded?

I need to get out.

Another inhuman scream pierces the air.

I come to a stop, but I can't pinpoint where it's coming from. It almost feels like it's echoing off the walls and surrounds me from all directions.

Chills crawl down my spine as I scan the crowd for the cause of the sound.

Panic is starting to fill the area. People are screaming, and some are looking around, worried or confused. More and more people run in my direction from further inside the airport, towards the exit.

What the hell?

I'm being shoved forward and almost trip.

The look of horror across a few faces has my adrenaline pumping and my heart beating out of my chest.

It's the blatant fear among some of the familiar faces from my flight that has me deciding to be a sheep and follow the herd. I turn on my heel and bolt towards the exit and the terminal parking structure.

I almost second-guess my initial reaction to follow everyone, but then that animalistic screech reaches my ears again. This time, it's accompanied by a wet gurgling sound and more screams behind me.

I make the mistake of looking over my shoulder.

A man, or what looked to be a man once, is on top of another person's back. He's violently ripping into the poor soul's jugular with his teeth. His skin isn't any natural color for a healthy person, but one I've seen on a corpse when I went on a tour at the LA coroner's office. He has a gaping wound on his forearm, but his blood is beginning to blacken. The sounds coming from his throat aren't anything I've heard a person make before.

My feet slow to a stop and root into the floor. For what feels like an eternity, I stare at the man shredding and *eating* the other man's neck and body as if he were a rabid, starved animal. Blood soaks into the patch of commercial carpet surrounding them, spraying and covering the attacker on the other man's back.

Some people freeze, shocked at what's before them, while others take their phones out to film.

Oh my god. Oh. My. god... What in the actual fuck?

Isn't this usually when the fight or flight is supposed to kick in? Isn't this when you should have some sort of reaction? Like maybe helping the person? Although I am pretty sure they would have already bled out as soon as the huge chunk got torn out of their neck.

Or maybe, you know, run. Run the fuck away from this horror scene straight out of *Train to Busan.*

The next person to shove me today, a willowy woman, breaks me from my stunned stupidity, and I finally get my ass moving back towards the exit. I try in vain to avoid the hurdles of people now shoving from all directions. As I run, more and more of that terrifying scream fills the airport.

Holy shit. I can't help but cast a last glance at the fallen man. Except, he's no longer down.

He's getting back up. Not just getting back up but running. Towards this direction.

I need to get the hell out of here!

It's like my feet can't run fast enough. I have no clue what is happening, but I keep running.

A cold sweat breaks out over my body. *This can't be happening. This can't be fucking real.*

The exit is just up ahead. I push myself harder, desperate to get out.

I'm barely through the exit when I'm faced with more chaos ensuing outside. An even larger mass of people are running in every direction in a flurry of panic. Further ahead, I spot the parking structure where my car is parked. Although there seem to be more people outside than inside, most are on foot. Not many cars are coming out of the structure. Somehow, those cancellations are working in my favor.

"Help me!" A voice to my right screams. I turn my head and stop in my tracks outside the exit. The bodice-ripper woman is crawling on the ground, trying to get back up. "I need help!"

Her slip-on shoe has fallen off, and her foot is a bloody mess. She struggles but manages to climb to her feet and slowly limps towards me. Behind her is another one of the attackers. *Crap.*

The woman follows my gaze while she attempts to move. She stumbles, unable to bear weight on her mangled foot.

It's on her before I can even blink.

"Please!" Her scream is a plea. She's fighting to keep the person's mouth away from her face. Their pale skin appears alien-like under the cast of the exterior lights.

Someone shoves me to the side, pushing me back a little further.

My heart feels like it's in my throat, choking me while I watch her struggle.

What should I do?

She tilts her head enough to meet my eyes while using all her strength to keep the person at bay. *Please*, her mouth words silently, tears falling down her face.

Her pleas echo in my mind, further escalating my need to panic. *What do I do? What the fuck do I do? Oh god!*

Swallowing, I take a tentative step forward but hesitate when someone runs into my shoulder. Before I can take another step, her arm slips.

The person bites down, tearing into her face.

Her scream pierces the air, shattering the last bit of resolve I have.

Bile rises to my throat. I spin around, sprinting hard toward the parking structure. Shame fills me, but I don't stop.

"Haruto-kun!" someone shouts. A woman, maybe in her late fifties or sixties, is yelling and reaching toward a boy who looks to have fallen in the chaos. She keeps getting pushed and shoved in all directions as she tries to fight her way back to the boy. The poor kid is struggling to get up as people keep stepping over him, sometimes on him.

I keep running, feeling bad for the poor kid but knowing I need to get out of here if I want to live.

I can't help anyone, even if I wanted to.

Hopefully, the woman can get to him before he's crushed... or worse.

He is slightly off to the side, but he's still in my general path. Maybe I can at least help him up before taking off again.

Flashes of the lady from my flight come to my mind. Her soft features now covered in gore.

There's nothing I can do. You can barely keep yourself together, Dahlia. You couldn't even help her up.

As I keep pushing forward, a break in the crowd opens around the kid. This allows the boy to climb to his feet, but that break also directs attention toward him.

I hear it before I spot it. And their focus is zeroed in on the boy.

It's a tall woman. A rabid, hungry look replaces what had once seemed to be a youthful appearance. She takes off at a sprint. Her pale, ashy-gray skin allows the blood on her body and beige sweater to stand out in contrast. She's fast. Fast as if she was running in the Olympics.

Fuck!

I speed up, trying my best to get to him before the creature-like woman does. Their number seemed to double in a matter of minutes.

She's close, so fucking close.

Wasting no time, I bend slightly to grab him around the waist. I throw him over my shoulder as if I'm some firefighter saving the damn day. I sprint towards the older woman, who's still trying to reach him.

When she notices me, she stops fighting the crowd, her relief palpable.

But then she spots it. Fear mars her face again.

The rabid woman is almost on top of us.

A growl-like sound rips from her throat before she shrieks.

I push my fatiguing legs harder.

Keep running.

Fuck. Fuck. Fuck!

Another fleeing woman crosses my path. She doesn't notice the thing behind me, and the creature-like woman tackles her instead of us. Warmth splatters across my cheek.

Guilt fills me with the relief that it hadn't been us, but I don't stop. I push my legs harder.

"The parking structure!" I yell, hoping the woman with the boy understands me.

Thankfully, she does, and she runs towards the lot. A few moments later, I'm behind her, running with the kid over my shoulder and using my left hand to grab my keys from my back pocket.

My legs are burning with the added weight of the kid as well as my backpack that has already felt like dead weight since I started running. My side cramps, not used to strenuous workouts anymore. I keep going, though, ignoring my body's way of telling me I should've drank less wine and got on a damn treadmill more often.

The inhuman screams are multiplying at an alarming rate. Sirens are wailing in the background. Gunfire is popping and echoing in the night. It's chaos.

What the hell is happening? Did I fall asleep on the plane and start dreaming of a freaking Stephen King novel? If so, I would love to wake up right about now.

People are dropping like flies. The pained screams are only growing louder.

My panic is threatening to overtake me, wanting to clutch its nasty claws into my chest and paralyze me.

I picture my dad as I run. What would Bradley Danaher have done? He would have told me what he always told me. *Just keep going, baby Dahl. When shit gets nasty, all you can do is keep going. The only way past it is through it.*

All I can do is put one foot in front of the other until we finally make it to the structure. The smell of burnt rubber permeates the air as the sounds of tires skid across the asphalt.

"Shit!" A white sedan comes barreling towards us.

I jump between the two closest parked cars. The woman yells for the kid again as the car passes. One of those raging people is clutching the front of the vehicle that narrowly hit us.

The kid's scream is loud enough to make my ears ring, but it acts as a trigger. My knees threaten to give out but instead, I push off one of the other cars and run.

Where did I park?! I frantically look around. Third row? Ugh, no! I think one more row over.

My panic is bordering on the lines of debilitating until I find it. My black and red 1978 Plymouth Trail Duster. I hurry to unlock the car door, my hand shaking violently as I frantically try to get the key into the lock.

Instead, they slip from my palm and clatter to the concrete floor.

"Fuck. This can't be happening," I whine. I put the shaky kid down so I can crouch to grab my keys.

The sounds surrounding us echo within the structure. The pressure to open the door is building.

A screech reverberates around us.

My hand is shaking violently. I try to jab my key into the lock, but I can't still my hand long enough.

Another scream pierces the air, as well as shouts from behind. It almost sounds like an attempted carjacking.

Come on. Come on.

Yes! I finally get it in and open the door.

I pick the kid up again and all but throw him in. He climbs into the back before I jump into the driver's seat, panting from my efforts. When I unlock the other door, the woman follows suit, climbing into the passenger seat.

I'm unsure if I should feel good that she's trusting me or if I should be more afraid to have two other people to worry about, especially since one can be no older than eight.

I pull out of the spot, trying to avoid hitting the people who have taken refuge in the structure.

More and more people are racing in our direction, making it harder for me to reach the exit without hitting them. We pass a few fighting over cars before those scary *things* reach the structure, causing them to run away with no success.

There! The exit.

Someone jumps in front of the car. "Shit!" I slam on my brakes and swerve to avoid hitting the man.

An officer.

I'm relieved for a fraction of a second before my mind processes what's happening. He's pointing a gun at me. The only barrier between us is the windshield.

Before I do anything else, another man slams into him, throwing them both onto the cement.

No, not a man.

One of those things.

"Oh my god," I whisper. I slam my foot back on the gas. I'm not stopping for anyone again. Otherwise, that could be us.

Was he trying to take the car? Did he need help? Shit, I can't let myself think about it now. We need to get out of here. I can try to dissect the guilt and reasoning later.

Outside, people are flooding the lanes. None care about the cars as they try to flee. The traffic in the few lanes is slowing to a stop altogether because of the people on foot.

The car to my right swerves and hits a woman running away. Those *things* are on her in a second.

The slowing of traffic has my nerves heightening. I'm surprised my heart hasn't beat right out of my chest at this point.

As we creep forward, the cars in front begin flooring their gas, disregarding people in the road, uncaring if they hit anyone trying to save themselves.

I hesitate before following suit, hating myself for taking advantage to get free. Yet, I'm silently grateful that I wasn't the one who needed to hit people.

Well... *first.*

Don't think about it. Don't think about— My car hits something solid, bringing my attention back to the fact those are people.

People.

Jesus. Tears stream down my face as I think about those poor people. *Oh god, I am no better than those things.*

My eyes fall on the kid in the rearview mirror. I think about the ones who are only trying to survive but are now getting run over. He's holding himself so small, wrapping his arms around his body. His dark hair partially obscures his eyes, but his bottom lip trembles as he stares out the window.

I steel my resolve. His life is reason enough.

I keep driving, grimacing but still trying to ignore the bumps in the road ahead of us and the thuds that follow.

The cacophony of noises surrounding us is as terrifying as the sight. Creature-like people screeching, the ones trying to escape screaming, so much blood and death.

Up ahead, a small barricade with police vehicles and special weapons and tactics officers are blocking most of the street. All the officers ignore the cars slipping by the only space large enough to drive through and are shooting at anything running in this direction.

More ambulances are arriving while some emergency medical technicians and paramedics are already stationed behind the officers' vehicles. They're near their rigs, waiting to be cleared to start triage.

My relief is so palpable that I can almost taste it. We'll be fine. The officers will contain this.

They just have to.

Chapter Three

Dahlia

We need to wait a few horrifying minutes as cars drive single file through the barricade while the officers continue to shoot. The SWAT team is pushing forward, trying to keep the attackers from the cars slipping through.

When we finally make it out, we all let out a collective breath of relief.

I relax in my seat a little more as we drive further away from the cluster fuck behind us.

We needed to wait, but if there were more drivers, I don't think we would have ever gotten out. Imagine if there hadn't been so many flights canceled. Holy shit, I would be dead.

"What was that?" the woman whispers. "Those people... were eating each other." The raw terror is evident in the slight tremor in her voice.

"I'm not sure." My hands ache from their vice-like grip on the steering wheel while I try to stop the trembling in my limbs. "I saw one inside the airport but then there were others. I honestly have no clue what the hell just happened. That noise..." Those screams will forever haunt me.

The woman appears to be in a state of shock but the whimpers behind me break her out of her reverie. "Haruto-kun. Are you alright?" she asks the boy, turning her body as far as she can in the seat.

He stifles a sob to answer her. "Yeah, Sayuri-san. I think so." His voice is so small. This poor kid shouldn't have to go through this. No one should.

After asking him a few other questions, and making sure he really is okay, the woman relaxes back into her seat.

The surrounding streets are calm except for the sirens racing towards the madness behind us. Everyone outside is going about their night as if everything is normal. It's surreal how calm this part of the city is now that we have made it out of the chaos. I hope the police can contain it.

Whatever *it* is.

My pulse is skyrocketing, and I'm beginning to get a little lightheaded. *What's going to happen if they can't contain it?* My panic is threatening to overwhelm me with the unknown of our situation. *What if the violence spreads?*

"Thank you," a small voice whispers.

In the rearview mirror, the boy's onyx, bloodshot eyes stare back at me. My heart shudders at the thought that he was moments away from being one of those poor victims. So many others ran around and trampled on top of him to get away.

People were going to just let him die.

I almost let him die.

"We can't thank you enough. Not only grabbing Haruto but also allowing us a ride," the woman next to me says.

Tears stream down her cheeks while fear is apparent in her eyes. That only breaks my heart further, knowing I almost left the kid. Whoever she is to this boy, it's obvious she cares for him, and she almost had to witness his death. Only because humans are selfish creatures.

I take a deep breath, trying to expel the knot in my throat. "You don't need to thank me. To be honest…" *I thought about running past.*

I try swallowing past the sudden dryness as I think back to that moment. The woman from the plane's face pops into my mind, accompanied by a tightening in my chest. *I did that. I almost let that be him.* The tears finally break free. My breath hitches, unable to get enough air. "You don't need to thank me," I repeat, unsure what else to say.

I turn my blinker on before I make a right turn down the city's street, heading to the nearest freeway.

I had been so lost in thought that I drove past the 405 freeway. Now I need to take the 105 instead.

Cars are all driving past, a few speeding, but nothing to indicate the shit-show behind us.

"You risked your life to stop," the woman persists. "We will never not be grateful for what you did."

I bite the inside of my cheek, trying to stop the tears from coming again. My heart aches so badly. Guilt for that moment where I wanted to keep running bombards my thoughts, but her face expresses nothing but gratitude.

"You're welcome," I say softly.

Reaching the 105, I merge onto the freeway, heading back towards my apartment in Willowbrook.

"I'm sorry. My name is Dahlia, by the way," I say, remembering I hadn't introduced myself yet. "Where would you like me to take you both? I was heading back home in a daze."

The woman gives me a soft smile. "My name is Sayuri, and this young man is Haruto. We were on our way to his uncle's house. I have his address in my purse here..." Her voice trails off when she doesn't find her bag near her feet. "I must have dropped it in the chaos," she says in disbelief.

"Well, if you'd like, you can come home with me for the rest of the night, and we can call his uncle." I frisk my pockets for my cell phone. "It's going to start getting late and to be honest, with what happened, I'm not sure I want to be driving in the dark much longer." Feeling it under my palm, a quick glance tells me it's dead. Just my luck.

"That would be wonderful. If you don't mind us intruding, we can call him when we get there and arrange for him to pick us up."

"Perfect. Do you mind if we stop quick? I want to grab a few things just in case," I ask her.

"That is fine," she responds.

My dad always taught me to be prepared, engraving into my head that I should at least have a change of clothes and a simple emergency kit at home or in the car. It led to me having a small bug-out bag in my car, and one at my apartment. Who knew I'd have reason to use it? I've had these bags for emergencies for years and only replace the food and medicine when they expire.

I can be a lazy person by default; well, that's what I call it, although it's not quite laziness as much as my anxiety having fun with me. Either way, my definition of lazy also reminds me that I would love myself later for being prepared and making my life much easier in the long run. This motivates me to get stuff done, and as it so happens, I create emergency packs for such an occasion. Granted, when I made these bags, I assumed they would be for some weird government shutdown, a California fire, or an earthquake. Not cannibalism on steroids.

Lovely, Dahlia. What a lovely thought. I blow out a breath as I pull up to the liquor store and park.

Once I climb out, I push the seat forward to make it easier for Haruto to get out of the car. He's shivering despite the blue thermal sweater and jeans. Reaching back into the car, I grab my black denim jacket.

"Are you cold?" I hold it out for him. "I have this if you'd want to wear it for a bit."

He takes it, and I'm a little surprised he's not more timid with me, especially after what we went through. No kid should have to see what he did. His adrenaline is probably crashing, and he's exhausted. Yet he's trusting me. I'm not sure how that should make me feel.

I close the door and lock it before I turn towards the store. There are only two other cars parked in the tiny parking lot. They both follow me in, the bell overhead signaling to the clerk that he has customers.

"Grab whatever you both need. Some snacks and something to drink," I tell them. Since Sayuri lost her bag, she most likely doesn't have her wallet either.

I don't have a lot of money by any means, especially after my trip, but if things happen to get worse, which I think they might, I'd feel better knowing they have some extra supplies, too. If things get worse, my debit card will most likely become useless for a while anyway, so I might as well not worry about the money.

"Dahlia-san, can I get this?"

I turn away from the selection of bagged chips to find Haruto holding up a container of Pringles.

"Sure, you don't need to ask. Grab whatever snacks you'd like, okay?" I tell him.

"Thank you." He smiles tiredly. "If you'd like, you can call me Ru or Haru. Most of my friends call me Ru-kun, but my family calls me Haru," he says while he grabs a second container.

My smile comes naturally as he talks. Even after everything, he seems okay. At least as okay as any kid can be, I guess. His friendly attitude lightens some of the darkness from tonight.

"Alright then, Ru. It's nice to meet you. Now, what do you say about some chocolate?" I look over his shoulder to Sayuri with an unspoken question.

"That's fine," she says before moving to the next aisle. Ru's smile lights up like a beacon at the mention of candy.

"We got the approval. Now, let's go raid the candy aisle. I would kill for a Twix bar right now," I say as we do just that.

Once we have our food, water, and other random finds at the counter, I noticed the news on the screen behind the clerk. The volume is on mute, but I can read the subtitles.

"...an emergency. People within a ten-mile radius of the Los Angeles International Airport are advised to stay indoors until further notice. Police have instructed to lock your doors and windows, keep your lights off, and stay inside. Homeland Security and local law enforcement are working together to identify the motive behind the riots. They've made no comment as to what caused the aggressive acts of violence but state they are continuing to work to dissolve the threat. Some are saying this is the worst riot seen in Los Angeles since the Los Angeles Uprising in 1992. Anyone outside of the ten-mile radius is being advised..."

"Ma'am?"

"Huh?" The clerk is staring at me expectantly. *Crap.* I got distracted by the news report. "Sorry," I mumble, typing my PIN before grabbing our bags.

"Did you see what they were saying on the news?" I ask Sayuri as we walk out the door.

"Yes, they think a riot. I do not understand, though," she says while we put the bags in the car and climb in. "Those people seemed normal one moment and then rabid animals the next. It's so bizarre."

I think back to the first person in the airport. With all the chaos and adrenaline, I never took the time to process what they actually looked like.

Human, yet not quite. It was surreal. No matter how impossible it seems, the same thought keeps flashing to the forefront of my mind. It's so ridiculous that I don't even want to entertain it.

"That wasn't a riot." I shudder. "That was a massacre."

I rest my hand on the passenger seat and back out of the parking spot. I'm ready to get home.

Tonight doesn't even feel real. It's like something we only see in fiction. My mind can't wrap itself around what those things even are. I wonder if there's a new drug being distributed to cause all this.

Could drugs have caused that, though? That man got back up after being attacked. I know drugs can do a lot of crazy things to our bodies, but he was... *dead*. Or he was incredibly close to death.

If not drugs, what other explanation could there be, though? It's the only thing that makes sense.

While attending school for my Criminal Justice degree, I took a narcotics class. We learned a lot about the different forms of drugs. Phencyclidine, or PCP, could do some crazy shit to the brain. I've seen a few videos, but one in particular, a man was shot multiple times and acted as if he was fine. He managed to drive down the block before succumbing to his injuries. I had even heard of someone who cut off their own arm and hadn't even flinched. It's an incredibly dangerous drug. I don't remember it causing changes in their physical appearance, though...

Despite drugs being the rational thing to believe, the same thought keeps coming back to me, no matter how ridiculous it sounds. It can't be possible... right?

They acted like *zombies*.

When I think of zombies, I think of rotting flesh, but they didn't seem that way at all. Their skin was a deathly ash-gray pallor. Their eyes looked as if all their blood vessels were blown, and some had pupils so dilated that no color was left other than the dramatic red against a yellowish-white.

Chills crawl up my spine as I remember the first man to be attacked. It seemed to be something spreading from person to person. Something causing the victims to get back up and attack.

They were also impossibly fast, which is making me second-guess my zombie theory. Well, that... and the fact it's absurd.

My chest feels tight just thinking about it. Images of the attack keep flashing in my mind with the echoes of their screams. I squeeze the steering wheel, trying to ground myself. I can't spiral now.

At least make it home first.

Chapter Four

Dahlia

I pull up into my parking spot in front of my apartment building. The drive was a blur of colors and images of the dead. I don't even know how I safely got us home at this point. It's like I'd been on autopilot.

My apartment building is small, with only a few units, but it's clean and has been recently remodeled to feel and look more modern than its original 1970s eclectic style.

We collect our bags, and my new acquaintances follow me into my home. I thought about leaving the bags in the car in case we need to make a quick getaway, but I haven't gone grocery shopping. If they get hungry, they need something to snack on.

As we enter, we leave the bags by the door, and I show them around the small space before I fetch my charger.

Once I find what I need, I take an empty pack from the tiny closet by the front door. Grabbing the liquor store bags, I return to where Ru and Sayuri are.

They're sitting at the small table against the wall in the back of the galley kitchen. Ru seems in a daze while he snacks on his Pringles.

"My phone should be charged enough to call his uncle in a few minutes." I plug my phone in and quickly stuff our purchases into the backpack. "For now, I can grab some clean blankets and such. I have an inflatable mattress I can put out. Might be a tad more comfortable than my old couch."

I take a second to appraise their appearances and realize they are as bad off as I am, with blood splattered all over their clothing and faces.

Damn, how did I not notice? I laugh softly at myself, remembering we went into the liquor store looking like we just about murdered someone. To top it off, the clerk didn't even blink an eye.

Hmm… maybe I shouldn't shop there anymore.

"I can also give you both a change of clothes. I don't have anything in your size, Ru, but I think at this point, anything clean would be preferable. You can wash your clothes in the washer once you've showered." I step away to grab everything they may need. I'm probably one of the few lucky souls in L.A. County with an in-unit washer.

Once I get fresh towels from the cabinet, I show them where the bathroom is and allow them to take turns showering and dressing before getting them settled in the living room.

I go through the apartment and start packing away any necessities or sentimental items in case I need to leave tomorrow. I also pull out the other emergency pack I have in my closet. This one has a few water bottles, a simple first-aid kit, some clothes, and some odds and ends. I'm not sure what the future holds for me, but the sinking feeling in my gut tells me I won't get to stay home for long.

Once that's done, I walk back to my closet and grab the shotgun stored on the top shelf. I can't remember the last time I used it, but I've kept it clean and functional. It had been my father's, and I couldn't bear to part with it. If shit goes sideways, a gun will most likely be needed. Meg used to laugh at me because I always took my dad's safety and preparation talks seriously, but now, more than ever, it paid off.

Meg. A sharp pang of guilt hits me. I need to call her to make sure she's safe. I wonder if she's facing the same thing.

Oh god… the mass cancellations. I hope they weren't related to this thing spreading, but I doubt it. It seems too much of a coincidence.

Back in the kitchen, I double-check my phone. It's a small relief when it turns on.

No texts from Meg or anyone else, but when I notice the time, I internally curse. *Fuck. I forgot about work.*

I shoot a text to my boss, letting them know I can't come in. I'll probably get in trouble, especially since I'm texting them and not actually calling, but I don't have the energy to deal with them. No way in hell can I function at work after tonight. However, if they know I was there at LAX, they may understand. I'd hope so, considering our line of business.

Meg is my next call, but it rings a few times before reaching her voicemail. *Damn.*

Sayuri walks in, brushing her hair with an extra brush I had. The overhead lights cast a soft glow, emphasizing the shine of her recently blow-dried hair.

"Oh, perfect timing. It should stay plugged in, but it's working." I hand her the cellphone. "I'm going to take a shower and get some rest. Will you be okay?"

"We will be. I'll call his uncle right now," she says.

I quickly double-check to make sure I haven't forgotten anything and that the air mattress is still intact. The thing is old so I hadn't been sure it would stay inflated.

Satisfied everything looks good for now, I step away.

It doesn't take long before I'm jumping into the shower. The hot water feels amazing on my aching muscles. I guess running for one's life really does a number on you. My mind rebels at the thought of how sore my body will be tomorrow. I can't even remember having to exert myself this hard in the plethora of dance classes I took growing up.

I wait to soap off until the water on the tile runs clear instead of a nasty burnt color. I wash my body twice and my hair three times before I feel marginally better. I can't help but still feel dirty after everything, no matter how much I scrub. I have always been good at disconnecting or disassociating myself, but now that I'm alone with my thoughts, the mental images from today threaten to overwhelm me—images of the woman next to me on the plane, especially.

Oh god. I clutch my chest as if it can take the ache away. I let her die. *I did that.*

So much death. So much useless death. It's too painful to think about. Everyone who couldn't run away in time. Or the people who were run over only so all those in the cars had a chance to flee. *So we could flee.*

My throat constricts, and my breathing becomes labored.

Breathe. Just breathe. I keep reminding myself, but it doesn't work.

I sit on the shower floor with my back resting against the cold tile. Bringing my knees up, I wrap my arms around myself. My heart is beating erratically, and I'm beginning to feel lightheaded. No matter how hard I try, my mind keeps going back to the airport.

We were so close to dying. *So close.* I wouldn't have made it if I'd had to wait for luggage. I don't even know if most people who were further inside the airport were able to get out. Whatever caused those people to turn into something *other* started inside.

Tears blend with the droplets of water raining down on my face. My sobs aren't controllable, but I try to take deep breaths anyway.

My vision is a cascade of images of the woman from the plane to the man with his throat being ripped apart.

I rock back and forth, inhale for a long moment, and exhale after five seconds. When my breathing doesn't work, I use a grounding method my therapist taught me instead. It's been years since I've had an anxiety attack, but tonight was too much. It's all *too much.*

Glancing around, I try to spot five things I can visibly see, then what I can touch—trying to become aware of my senses and ground my mind instead of spiraling.

It takes time, but my rapid pulse starts to slow. I must have been in the shower for a long time because the water is becoming lukewarm instead of the scolding hot it had been.

When I stand, my mind tries to steer its way to my dad and then to Meg. *God, I don't want to be alone in this.*

Before long, my thoughts wander back to the woman on the plane.

Stop, Dahlia. Don't think about it.

I try my hardest to steer away from the memories. I can't think about the guilt threatening to pull me down. It's too much.

Instead, I hurry to finish and turn the shower off.

I quickly dress in the clothes I was going to wear tomorrow, too afraid to sleep in pajamas in case we need to flee. I pull on a black tank top, faded dark blue jeans, and a flannel. I throw a pair of Vans and a pair of boots by the door. Once I'm satisfied that I have everything ready and put aside, I head for my bed.

I didn't realize how exhausted I was until I lay back on my pillow, instantly falling asleep.

CHAPTER FIVE

Dahlia

Up ahead, light flickers to life. It barely breaks through the darkness, but it's enough to reveal a shape on the floor.

I take a tentative step towards the shadow.

Not a thing but a person huddled on the floor, crouching over two other shapes blurring with the background.

"Hello?" I call softly.

Wait... I stop.

The person's head whips up at the sound. My attention is on her blown-out crimson eyes surrounded by red hair.

Blood streams down her freckled chin and neck, soaking into her tank top.

The other two shapes come into focus, and my eyes catch on white hair. Her dead eyes bleeding crimson, her body twitching.

My heart stops when my eyes fall on the other small figure. His face is concealed behind the woman, but I don't need to see to know who it is. The blue thermal covering the smaller form is enough.

The shriek filling the space is so loud that it feels like it's going to shatter my very being.

The creature is up and running towards me, hands outstretched.

I try to run away, but I'm being grabbed from behind.

No... No...

NO!

Over my shoulder, my own eyes stare back at me.

Teeth are digging into my skin.

Oh god, I'm going to—

I jerk awake, panting, unable to calm my racing heart. "Fuck," I whisper and clutch my chest. "Only a nightmare."

My heart is pounding loudly in my ears while my body trembles. "Just a nightmare, Dahl. It's okay. It isn't real," I continue to whisper to myself, trying to still the panic wracking my body.

I take a second to run my hand through my damp hair. I couldn't have slept long if my hair was still wet. The clock on my nightstand tells me that it's only 2:30 in the morning.

I'm about to lie back down when a loud pounding startles me. I climb out of bed and cautiously walk to the living room.

Sayuri is already by the front door, peering out the peephole. The pounding resumes.

"Dahlia! It's Rick."

Sayuri steps to the side so I can check. The panic lingering from my nightmare only increases. I can't imagine what he's doing here.

Confirming that it's my landlord, I open the door. "What's going on, Rick?"

Behind him, my other neighbors are gathered and casually talking.

"Sorry to wake you, kid, but the police have been broadcasting from patrol cars and helicopters for about an hour. We only have about ten minutes to get our stuff and evacuate the neighborhood."

"Wait, they've been asking people to evacuate? Did they hold a news conference or anything?" I ask since I never double-checked the news before passing out.

"They just did. They mentioned setting up roadblocks and starting to close some streets altogether. Soon, we won't be able to get out even if we wanted to."

Crap, that can't be good. "Thanks for the heads up. Stay safe." I pause with my hand on the door frame. "Hopefully I'll see you soon, yeah?"

"No problem. You too, kid," he replies.

I don't bother shutting the door before running to my room to don my sneakers and grab my boots.

When I head back into the living room, Sayuri and Haruto are already prepared with the last of our bags.

"You have everything?" I ask while grabbing my phone and charger. I do my own mental checklist as I go. *Phone, check. Charger, check. BOB, check. Shotgun, check.*

Shit, I hope I haven't forgotten anything.

"We are ready," Sayuri responds, exhaustion evident in her voice. What I assume are normally soft brown eyes are now shaped with dark circles and worry lines etched between her brows. She stands a little slouched, her petite figure appearing smaller under the weight of our situation.

Hopefully, I can get them to their family safely.

I'm glad Sayuri had time to utilize my washer and dryer. My detergent couldn't rid the clothing of the brownish blood stains, but at least she won't be in something dirty or need to go out in old sweats and the Metallica T-shirt I lent her. The sweats were too large on her small frame. At five feet, I'm not tall by any means, but she is at least two inches shorter than me, and those sweats would only have been a hazard for her.

Poor Ru is exhausted. He also changed back into his clothes, but his raven-colored hair is sticking out in all directions from restless sleep. His eyes are bloodshot and puffy from crying, but he still holds himself up despite the fear he must be feeling.

We rush out of the apartment, and I lock my door, hoping that I'll be able to come back soon. Not because I have any attachment to the place but because getting to come home means this will be over soon.

My neighbors in the hallway don't seem like they plan on leaving at all. One of them catches me and openly rolls his eyes.

"You too? You know, this crap is just that. Crap. If I knew any better, I'd bet this is some political maneuver or some propaganda for some extremist group," he says to me, not hiding his derision.

Staring at him, I wonder if arguing with stupid would make a difference. Resigning to the fact that I don't want more people to die, I speak up.

"We were at the airport." I gesture with my hand, pointing in a vague direction. "I can tell you one hundred percent that this is not a hoax." He rolls his eyes at me again as I continue. "People are dying. People are being slaughtered by their friends and neighbors. I don't know why, but whatever it is, it's real. If you want to die, then stay, but I recommend getting out of here while you can." I leave it at that as we move past the small crowd.

He mumbles something, but I can't hear him as we step outside.

We all stay silent while we walk to the car. I know I need to ask Sayuri if they were able to reach the kid's uncle, but I'm overwhelmed with fear and unending questions.

What the hell is happening? Are they zombies? Are they going to keep multiplying? Why can't the police contain it? If they can't, where am I going to go? I don't have family to run to.

At that thought, I think of Meg. I pull my phone out and try to call her again, but she doesn't answer.

Oh god, I hope she is okay. Please be okay, Megan. Please. I plead to no one, only hoping I can get a hold of her soon.

We make it to my car while I'm shoving my phone back into my pocket. I do my best to force myself away from all the unknowns and worry about what we do know right now.

"Have you guys gotten ahold of his uncle?"

"We did. When we spoke to him, he said he was going to come pick us up in a couple of hours and told me to stay put," she says. "I need to call him to let him know we are leaving."

Just as she finishes, my phone vibrates in my back pocket. I pull it out while throwing all our backpacks and bags into the back, but I don't recognize the number on the screen.

"Here." I hand her the phone. "I think that may be him now."

She takes the call and answers in what I think may be Japanese. As she's talking on the phone, we all get strapped in, and I take a moment to breathe through the paralyzing anxiety. I wish I didn't have anyone else to worry about but myself.

Fuck, what am I doing? I can't do this.

Before I can allow those thoughts to debilitate me, I turn the key to start the ignition. *You have no choice. Just get them to the kid's uncle.*

I'm itching to start driving to distract myself from my rising panic, but I need to know where we're going first.

Sayuri gently nudges my arm and says, "He would like to speak with you."

She reaches over to hand me the cell phone.

The awkward part of me hesitates, but I take it anyway and put it up to my ear. "Hello?"

"Do you have a GPS app on your phone?" a deep, masculine voice asks.

No hello, no introductions. Not that I expect much, but who the heck starts a conversation with a stranger like that?

"Hey," he says gruffly. "I'll give you my address."

"Ugh… Yeah, sorry." I put my phone on speaker before opening my maps app. "Go ahead with the address," I tell him.

He quickly gives me an address in Malibu, and then asks if I can share my location with him. "Yeah… Shit. It might take me some time to get there," I mumble, reading through my route options. On a clear road without issues, that drive would usually take at least forty minutes.

Unfortunately, we have multiple issues. We don't have much time, if any, and normally, the quickest route would put us right past the airport. I'm going to have to go out of the way a bit.

"Just share your location," he barks. "I'll meet you halfway. Put Sayuri back on."

My eyes widen at his demand. *For fuck's sake. Who raised this man? It couldn't have been this sweet woman, that's for sure.*

I share my location before handing my phone back to Sayuri and pull out of my parking spot.

She gives me an apologetic smile before saying something I can't understand in a clipped tone to who I presume is Ru's uncle. Although I don't understand her, I can't help but hope he got a little lecture for his manners. *What an asshole.*

She keeps the phone on speaker, and he responds in the same language, although the way he speaks gives me the impression that he doesn't use it often. Sayuri thankfully turns the screen towards me so I can see the directions, but she keeps the call connected.

Sighing, I flip the radio on and turn the volume on low. Expecting to hear automated system alerts, I'm surprised to hear one of our local news reporters.

"...your homes. Stay tuned momentarily, and we will read off the locations of the emergency evacuation centers. If you are unable to evacuate, we strongly recommend locking all doors, turning off all lights, and staying hidden. Do not leave your residence.

"Again, we strongly recommend that you follow the evacuation notice. We still have not been informed on anything other than the increase in violence that has begun to spread beyond the Los Angeles International Airport as well as the Union Station. I hope all you Angelenos stay safe out there. Here are the locations for—"

"Fuck, nothing they are saying is helpful." My hand slams on the radio's power button a little too harshly. "Crap! Sorry for the language." I cringe. Sayuri doesn't say anything, so I hope she hasn't been paying attention.

It's only a few minutes before we pass the Magic Johnson Recreational Center and Park and drive through the city's more residential area. There are a few cars on the street, all appearing to be evacuating. At least, I think they are, based on the few cars with luggage on their roof racks or what seems to be families crammed into smaller vehicles. It's a little surprising how many people aren't on the road.

A shattering shriek pierces the quiet night. Gunfire follows, eliciting more screams.

Both our heads whip around towards the direction we just came. In the near distance, houses and buildings stand as silhouettes against a blazing fire, the reds and oranges lighting up the night sky in stark contrast. There are people beginning to run on foot in our direction, crossing the main intersection behind us. There are others following them, all frantic and glancing over their shoulders as they run.

My eyes meet Sayuri's, sharing a look of dread. A look that says, *we are going to die, aren't we?*

I speed up, noticing the others ahead have had the same idea. I bet my neighbor is going to learn the hard way that this was no propaganda stunt.

Sayuri is talking so fast and breathlessly that I wonder if the person on the other end of the call understands what she's saying.

Another screech startles us, much closer this time.

Shit.

How are they already so close, and where are the police or military? I don't see them, but I can hear more gunfire coming closer.

"Just keep going straight," Sayuri says, reiterating what the app is telling us before speaking to Ru's uncle. She stops to try to slow down, her own panic palpable.

A car speeds past the stop sign to my left, nearly clipping me as it cuts me off. I slam on my brakes, trying to avoid getting hit. Down the same street, those creatures are sprinting this way. At the sight of them, I slam my foot on the gas harder.

They don't slow for any traffic, showing no concern for their own welfare. They are far enough away that I can't see their features, but even from here, I can make out the blood coating their bodies, the unnatural ash-gray of their skin, and the chunks of flesh missing from parts of their bodies.

"Holy crap," I whisper. There are so many of them. "Shit!"

I barely swerve out of the way. We nearly go up the curb before I can right the car.

One of those things jumps on the Sedan next to us. The driver loses control before crashing into a tree. Sayuri and Haruto scream.

I don't bother to stop the stream of curses from my mouth as I head towards the freeway. My heart feels like it's going to implode in my chest.

Mother fuckity fuck, I can't do this. I can't do this. Fuck!

I take a deep breath, trying to calm myself, but another screech resounds close behind us. Too close.

Drive, Dahlia. You have people depending on you. You need to do this. Get them to safety. Come on, you can do this. You need to do this.

I don't believe it, but I try to convince myself anyway, trying to keep my shit together as I focus on the road.

The streets are now a full frenzy. The right lanes are filling with more cars trying to get to the freeway not too far away. Some people speed up to go around each other, only to crash into someone else on the opposite side of the road. Some cars are consumed in flames, while others are now being swarmed. Bodies are beginning to litter the road while more and more of those things run from the streets to my left.

I don't even realize I'm sobbing until I notice the heat running down my cheeks. The only thing I can do is take deep breaths in an attempt to keep myself from losing it. I can't have a breakdown, no matter how badly I want to.

The only way past it is through it. I remind myself, my dad's words echoing in my mind. Shit is pretty nasty now, Dad.

Ha! That's an understatement.

I swerve left, narrowly avoiding hitting the car that tries to cut me off right before they slam on their brakes to avoid another speeding vehicle.

I slow down as more cars congest the lanes. We pass by one vehicle that has pulled over to the side of the road. What looked to have been an innocent flat tire turned out to be a massacre; the person who was changing the tire is now lying face down with one of those things on their back.

As the traffic comes to a standstill, I glance over at the residential lane to the right, which is separated by a divider. Trees intersperse the space, but there is enough room for a car to go through.

"Fuck it," I say to myself, thankful that my car is a 4x4. Making a sharper turn, I drive up the curb and onto the frontage road. I slam my foot on the gas, and a few other cars follow. A couple of people run in front of us, trying to get to the houses on this road before they get tackled by those zombie-like people.

Passing the bloody scene, I keep my eyes peeled for any more of those things. I breathe a little easier with less traffic in front and no sign of more of those creatures up ahead. All too soon, I need to get back onto the main avenue we were on previously.

My body trembles from the adrenaline coursing through me. Or maybe it's the raw terror.

Holding my breath, I speed up but also make sure not to go too fast, fearing someone will cut me off again. There are still people running, not caring about the cars nearly running them over as they flee.

A loud horn blares as tires squeal. The impact of the person and the car to the left of us is sickening. Their body cracks the windshield before being thrown in the air.

Those things don't waste time targeting the car and the still body now on the road.

"His uncle said he was already on his way, but it's spreading over there, so it may take time before we meet," Sayuri says.

All I can manage is a stiff smile as if that'll make our situation better.

The only thing I can focus on is listening for more of those awful sounds and praying no creature jumps on our car. They appear to have all fallen behind in the cluster of traffic that we narrowly missed.

More screams fill the air. All close.

Crap. I hope the people running away don't lead those things this way.

Something wet splashes my windshield just as that thought passes my mind.

We all shriek in tune with the other screeches rising to the left of us. Despite the risk of other drivers, I speed up, hoping to avoid whatever caused the blood to coat part of my windshield and passenger window.

We pass another crash, a white Prius wrapped around a tree. The passenger in the car is eating the driver, which must have caused the accident.

"Oh, god... why?" Sayuri whispers to herself.

A few drivers are honking rapidly now. The person directly behind me accelerates like they plan to play a game of deadly bumper cars.

"Oh my god, they're going to try to hit us!" I exclaim. "What the hell is wrong with people?!" I try to put more weight on the gas. Frantically searching for where to go, I spot the back alley behind the liquor store just up ahead.

Taking the chance, I hop the curb, driving along the grass before we make it to the alley.

Fuck, I hope we make it.

Glancing for oncoming traffic before I turn, another vehicle comes into view. It's not slowing down as it barrels toward the car that was behind us. I make a sharp turn just in time to avoid the collision as one of the cars spins out, crashing into the building on the corner.

Those creatures are climbing his car now, trying to find a way inside. Beneath my panic, I'm morbidly curious to see how smart they are and if they can purposefully break the window or problem-solve to get to their goal, but I force myself to stay focused.

You need to get them to safety.

We speed past the liquor store, driving all around the building before we make it back onto the original street.

It seems like hours when it only takes us a few minutes to finally clear the neighborhood's traffic and get to the onramp.

As we merge onto the freeway, we collectively exhale. I glance over at Sayuri, meeting her gaze. "Well... shit," I say, at a loss for words. I can't help the awkward chuckle that slips past my lips. "We made it."

I honestly have no idea how we got so lucky up to this point. We didn't hit that many roadblocks, get stuck in dead-stop traffic, or, you know, get mauled.

I wonder if most people assumed the same thing my neighbor did—that it was rioting or some extremist group—since there aren't as many people on the roads as I'd expected. That was what most of the news was saying, right? With no new information, I'm guessing people thought it was either a hoax or they were safer at home.

It shows how lost people can be in their own problems instead of taking the evacuation notices seriously. I'm grateful to have been one of the few to escape because now I know what we face while everyone behind us pays for their ignorance in blood. Well, I'm almost grateful. I don't want people to actually die, and something about how we don't know what's happening is unnerving to me. It's as if we were all purposefully left in the dark.

I wonder if we'll ever know why.

Somehow, it only makes me more worried about the extent of the situation. My stomach drops. It must be a lot worse than we think...

Will anywhere be safe?

CHAPTER SIX

Ren

"Excuse me?" My brother's voice is eerily calm, but I know better than to believe that he is.

Switching my phone to my other hand, I enter the code to my gun safe in my closet. I pull out my LWRC IC-A5 rifle and my Smith & Wesson MP 2.0, along with an extra 9-mil mag. "I already told you, Reiji, I have it handled," I tell him while shifting my phone to my shoulder so I can zip my duffle.

I know I fucked up. Not only because I waited to call him, but having thought I could surprise him in the first place. My brother hates surprises and yet I followed along with Haru's wild idea that they should come out to visit. Emi, Haru's mom, gave us the approval, thinking it would be fun for Haruto.

"What the hell do you mean you have it handled, Ren? My son is not only with strangers, but from what the news reports are saying, riots are gaining traction, possibly spreading further out past LAX," he seethes.

I don't even know what to tell him, but Haru is safe for now, from what Sayuri has told me. I wanted to get the house ready and make sure Hana was secure here alone before I left. I couldn't leave her unprotected.

My house is secluded from my neighbors in the hills, and the whole property is fenced off. I also have state-of-the-art security cameras and other hidden gems in place in case of a trespasser; not all of it legal, but I value my privacy. Especially with who my brother is, I can never be too careful not to get stuck in the crossfire, so to speak.

Even with the house secure, I can't be sure any of my brother's enemies will take advantage of the chaos we've been hearing about and try to come after us, or maybe just people seeking shelter and wanting a secluded home to flee to.

"Look, Rei, I'm on my way to go get them right now." I take my duffle and head to my garage before shoving the bag in the front seat of the truck. "It'll be about an hour or so to get to their location."

My brother's silence isn't lost on me. I'm just glad I'm having this conversation on the phone and not in person. It's been years since I've been on the receiving end of his anger. It'll be a shit time when he finally gets here, but thankfully, I have some time before I need to deal with that.

"You better be back by the time I get there. I'm having Don and a few people meet at your house. I don't know much of what's happening, but I lost contact with some guys who live closer to the airport. It doesn't look good. We'll regroup there." He hangs up without saying anything else.

Fuck. I inwardly groan. Great, more people to invade my space.

As if she knows she's the other one invading my space, my sister walks into the garage. *Not that she gives a shit, she loves to meddle.*

"You going to be okay? I can come, you know. I get that you think you need to do this all on your own, brother, but our safety isn't only on you," Hana says from the doorway. "Plus, it's been a while since I've gotten to play."

I snort at that. "Hana, Reiji would have my balls if you came along. He lets me get away with a lot since I'm *technically* not a part of the clan, but that wouldn't stop him this time."

Her typical positivity morphs into a rebellious laugh. "Just because he's an *Oyabun* doesn't mean he's *mine*. You damn well know I'm also not a part of his organization. I'm just the little daughter of a once powerful man. You know that even after all the changes our father implemented, I could still never be a true member. I only work for him sometimes when he needs a nurse or a doctor. And I know how to take—"

I cut her off with my hand. If I let her continue, I'll never get out of here. My sister knows how to talk. "Look, Hana, I need to go. Stay put."

Annoyance replaces her humor as she puts her hands on her hips. "Ren, you can pretend all is well with you, pretend you haven't woken me up the past two nights because you can't admit you need help, but can't you fucking admit you need help with this?"

I try to cut her off again, but she only gets more upset. "No! Do not try to cut me off. That is my family out there, too. I can help. Why can't you see that?" She throws her hands up in frustration. "I am thirty-one, Ren. I'm older than you by two years. When will you finally see that I don't need to be protected anymore?"

I let out a deep sigh and rub my hands over my face. I'm exhausted from little sleep; our nephew and Sayuri are god knows where, and of all the times, my sister wants to put her foot down and argue. Before I can respond, my phone vibrates in my pocket. I half expect it to be Rei again, but I'm surprised when it's an old military buddy of mine. I hadn't thought he would get back to me so fast.

As soon as Sayuri called me about what happened at the airport and the very vague information the news was alluding to, I reached out to him.

I unlock my phone and open his text.

Ryan

> I can't tell you much, man. Shit's happening, though. If you can, bug out.

Me

> What do you mean?

Ryan

> It's been confirmed that the attacks throughout the country were all planned. They're all connected, including the ones in other countries.

"You can't ignore me, Ren. Wait…" Hana pauses. "What's that serious look on your face for? Is it Haru and Sayuri-san? Did something happen?" she asks with panic clear in her voice.

"Not sure what's going on, Hana, just more reason for you to stay put. I need to go." I don't bother responding to her outburst about helping.

Instead of texting my buddy back, I hit the call button and climb into the truck. Hana sighs dramatically, throwing her hands up in the air again as she walks back into the house.

I'm pulling out of the garage when Ryan answers. "Hey, Ren."

"So, they aren't riots like we thought?" Using one hand, I connect my phone to the truck's Bluetooth and pull up the address Sayuri sent me on my maps.

Ryan's response is loud in my truck's speaker. "Nope. Possible chemical warfare, most likely terrorist attacks, but unsure by who. All they told us was that it's causing people to act violently, and it's contagious."

Fuck. Shit is a lot worse than I thought. "It's spreading then?"

Shuffling sounds through the call, and it takes him a moment to respond. "All hits were on places of travel. Mostly international airports but some smaller domestic airports and train stations. Made it possible for it to spread and spread quickly."

The roads are dark, and no other cars are driving through the hills. The city lights glimmer in the distance, but as I turn down a bend, the night sky is lit up with reds and oranges. A fire is spreading far off in the city across the water where the airport is. *Shit.*

Ryan lowers his voice to a whisper. "Look, man, it's not good. Uncle Sam is keeping this shit close to their chest. They're not telling us much despite sending us to one of the hot spots that was hit. My advice? Get out and head somewhere you can stay safe while it passes."

"Thanks, man," I say. He doesn't stick around to chat and hangs up.

As I clear the more secluded roads and reach residential areas, more people are crowding the streets.

Gunfire sounds somewhere close, followed by screams. It feels as if my heart stops before erupting in my chest. *What the hell?*

I'm well acquainted with the sounds. In some ways, they are more comforting than the quiet, but not when accompanied by civilian screams and the disarray unfolding as I drive.

My ringtone blares through the speakers of the truck, startling me. I answer it while keeping my eyes focused on the shit show outside.

"Yo, dude. Have you seen what's happening?" James asks me over the call.

He must be talking about what's beginning to look like a war zone around here. "Yeah man, fuck, I'm on my way to go get my nephew in Willowbrook. I just passed the Civic Center, and it's a mess." I run my hand through my hair out of habit.

There's gunfire, but I can't tell where it's originating from. It's only people running in fear, but from what, I can't figure out either.

"Bro, you won't get there easily. The county has evacuation notices for the surrounding areas and has started blocking off the freeways near LAX." He pauses for a moment, mumbling to someone in the background. "Why is the kid in Willowbrook?" he probes.

"Shit!" I slam on the brakes just in time, barely missing the person running in the middle of the road. They came out of nowhere, not sparing me a glance. They're sprinting with such focus on a transient sitting at the bus stop that they don't seem to notice almost getting hit.

In a snap decision, I change my plans and make a left turn towards the office. I may not know exactly what is happening behind me, but it isn't long before I find out.

Chaos. Utter fucking chaos.

People are running everywhere while others are attacking. They're biting and clawing at anything living.

"Ren! You good?" he shouts into the phone.

"Can you rally the guys and meet me at the office?" I ignore his question and counter with my own instead. "I'm five minutes out."

Another person jumps out in front of me.

Fuck! I swerve, nearly hitting them.

"We're here already; Juan gave us keys earlier today," James responds. "I thought you'd be here."

Habits die hard, I guess. "Alright, I'll be there." I hang up and try to avoid the cars and people on the roads.

I shouldn't be surprised they'd try to meet up. James and the others were among the few who managed to stay alive long enough to become close to me and stick around after we were all discharged from the service. That's what led me to hire them for my upcoming security company.

I originally wanted my military career to be a life-long thing. At eighteen, it was a way to escape my past, a way to focus my anger on something useful, so I took the first opportunity to enlist. But, after eleven years of nothing but death and filling greedy bastards' pockets, there was no real tangible reward to make it worth anything. Even after finishing officers' school early on and busting my ass to rank up, it wasn't worth it anymore. No matter how hard I tried, I couldn't care about the most recent promotion, or anything. So, although it wasn't the easiest choice, I decided to step away and create my own business.

As if you weren't getting close to not having a choice anyway.

I push those thoughts aside. I left of my own accord; that's all that matters. Unfortunately, with me out of the service, my brother wanted me to work with him if I wouldn't formally initiate into the clan.

I never wanted anything to do with what my family was involved in since my parents died, and I still don't, but I couldn't say no to him. He wouldn't let me.

More gunfire sounds as a few men in ACUs, Army Combat Uniforms, finally make an appearance. They are trying in vain to push back the attackers.

There aren't enough service members in the area to contain it, and no law enforcement around to help. Were they unable to get more National Guard or other reservists out fast enough?

Is it becoming impossible to contain?

A high-pitched screech blankets the screams of those on the streets. The noise is utterly alien, vaguely resembling a squealing pig. I don't think it's possible for humans to get their vocal cords to work that way without hurting themselves.

Chills break out across my body. The ones getting hit aren't going down. They keep taking shot after shot. Some have bullet wounds throughout their chests. One has a shotgun wound in their gut. Yet they're still running, sprinting towards anyone alive.

I push my foot on the pedal and turn again, finally coming up to my office building. I don't bother with the parking spots. Instead, I park halfway up the curb right next to the entrance. I grab the Smith & Wesson and get out.

"James!" I shout as I reach the entrance, knocking only once before they open the door, and I'm roughly pulled inside. The door slams behind me.

"You weren't bit or anything, right? I don't see blood, but just making sure." James gives me a once over, looking for any wounds.

"Bit?" I ask in confusion. If I were bit, I'd probably be dead based on the fucking disaster that's happening outside.

"We got a hold of Juan. He seemed to know something we don't but wouldn't talk about it." He pauses, most likely for dramatic effect. "He did tell us, though, that if you get bit, it spreads. We are now living in a damn horror movie. Best to find a place to hunker down, not take in strays, and stay away from busty blondes."

I chuckle despite the horrible situation. James and his morbid humor. This isn't the time for shits and giggles, but how else can we stay sane? Unfortunately, some of the things we've seen have only desensitized us. *Slightly.*

"You guys good?" I glance at each of them, taking them all in.

I may have just hired them, but I haven't seen them in a few months. I was the last to discharge only a couple of months ago, and we hadn't planned on meeting until tomorrow.

James' appearance is the same as always. Shaved blonde hair, blue eyes, and a scruffy-ass beard he refuses to shave now that he's free to grow it.

Mateo, on the other hand, is surprising. He grew his dark hair long and tied it up. He's sporting a Misfits shirt and black faded jeans, topping it off with a pair of steel-toed boots. When we served together, he kept himself within regulations—clean-shaven, short hair, and never advertised a select lifestyle in his wardrobe other than military pristine.

Dirk gives me his signature manic smile and says, "We good, man. Ready to go back out there and see what all the fuss is about." He also looks more or less the same—with his slicked-back brown hair, gray eyes, average height, stocky build, and a 'ready to fuck shit up' look on his face. Sometimes, I question his sanity. I swear he gets off on violence, but I remember hearing a chick he dated talk about how he's the biggest teddy bear she had ever met. Truthfully, I don't believe it, but whatever. Doesn't matter one way or the other to me. All I know is that these men will have my back out there.

"Juan didn't disclose anything else?" I ask them.

Matt shakes his head while James speaks up. "Nah, but he texted me sayin' he'll meet up at your house. You got anything? We ran into a little trouble, but not as bad as it sounds now."

I fill them in quickly on what Ryan told me and what I came across on my way here.

"Whoa. So, they're really like fucking zombies then?" Matt asks.

Thinking back, that's a good way to describe it, but that's impossible. "Save that for fiction. This is real. Whatever it is, it's spreading through bodily fluids or bites or whatever. I don't know, but I need to get back out there and get to my nephew. I'm going to grab some supplies here and then head out," I say as I walk past them into the only room finished with construction. The office has a decent-sized gun safe, partially filled, and office furniture littering the space.

The building is still being renovated. We didn't plan to open officially for a few more weeks, but we wanted to get a head start on securing contracts other than the one my brother already signed and start getting what we could set up.

"We can come with you. Planned to find you anyway since we have no other plans or anyone to find." Matt tightens his hair tie and grabs a bag near the small desk in the corner.

I hesitate in answering, unsure if I want to have the help. I know I came up with the idea of them following, but I still can't help but pause when it comes to my family's safety. Before I can respond, James answers for me. "Bet your ass. Let's get a move on."

Resigned to them tagging along, I step aside to call Sayuri and update her on my whereabouts and hopefully find that she hasn't had to leave. To my disappointment, when I reach her, she tells me they are having to do just that.

"Fuck. Sayuri-san, can you put the girl on the phone?" I don't bother asking for her name. I only want to get the kid and Sayuri home.

Sayuri may not be blood, but she's like a second mother to me, and I'd be damned pissed if something happens to her as well as my nephew.

"Hello?" A tentative voice asks.

Straight to the point, I ask her if she has a GPS app, but she hesitates. It only irritates me further. This isn't the time to be hesitating.

Fucking great. My nephew and Sayuri are with a walking liability. "Hey. I'll give you my address." This manages to get her response.

Once I give her my address and get her location shared on my own phone, I tell her to put Sayuri back on.

"Don't be so rude next time. You know better," Sayuri chastises. "Your mother would be ashamed." At the mention of my mom, I flinch but brush off her statement.

"I'm sorry, Sayuri-san," I grumble.

We're on the phone for only a few more minutes when hell seems to break loose. Before I know it, Sayuri is going off, explaining their situation. It takes me a second to understand her. Not only have I become rusty in speaking Japanese while living in the States since I was a kid, but she's talking so fast I don't think anyone could understand her.

The blood in my veins is like ice as she keeps talking, but I can't catch all of what she's saying. "Sayuri-san, slow down; I can't hear you."

Instead of a response, both she and Haru scream. In the background, the chick surprises me by losing her tentativeness and letting loose a few very colorful vocabulary choices that would put a sailor to shame.

Sayuri relays to me what's happening between her sobs. As she talks, the gnawing anxiety catches in my throat and puts a flame on my heels. We need to leave now. Any wasted time is putting them at risk.

"I'll find you. Things have gotten bad here, too. It may take me longer, but nothing will keep me from getting to you, you understand?"

"Yes, Ren-kun. We love you," she says, crying, before hanging up.

Her last words hit me like a ten-ton truck. If she hadn't already told me what was happening, those three words have told me enough.

She's been with us since we were children and loves us like we're her own, but she's not the type of person to say the words. She has always told me that actions speak louder than measly words and expresses her affection through her actions. For her to feel the need to tell me is causing my anxiety to morph into borderline panic.

I turn to the guys. "You ready then?" We need to leave. Now. My chest tightens at the possibility I won't make it in time.

They all answer in the affirmative, nodding and grabbing any gear they have and readying themselves by the door.

"Wait. So… we're supposed to actually shoot these people?" Matt asks. "I mean, I know what Juan mentioned, but are we sure this is right?"

I can't blame him for asking, but I also can't help the irritation. Sometimes, I forget that our moral compasses don't point to the same north.

"Look, if you get attacked, you protect yourself," I explain. Hopefully once they see what it's like, they won't be questioning this anymore.

"Oohrah, motherfuckers!" James exclaims, trying to amp us up for what we're about to face. "We might be in civvies now, but Raiders for life!"

Fucking James. I shake my head, unable to control the smirk.

All in tandem, we say, "Oorah!" We snap into motion, filing outside with arms at the ready.

Stepping outside is like walking through complete mayhem. All I manage to think is that my nephew better be safe. I've lost enough people throughout my life and time served; I won't lose anyone else if I can help it.

Chapter Seven

Dahlia

"Exactly. You want to ease your foot on the break; otherwise, you'll jolt to an abrupt stop," I say to Ru.

He mentioned that he likes to drive go-carts with his friends sometimes. In an attempt to distract myself from my overwhelming thoughts, I decided to take a page out of my dad's book—the always-be-prepared-for-anything book. I learned how to drive at a young age only because my father had a tendency to overprepare for things. So, instead of sitting in silence, I started going over how to drive in case of an emergency.

He bombarded me with questions, and thankfully, the conversation distracted all of us, if only briefly. Before we started talking about go-carting, he asked me all kinds of questions about my life, which led to my tattoos covering my right arm. He mentioned that they reminded him of his family since they all had them.

The kid knows how to talk when we aren't under duress.

"So, it is similar to the go-carts I've driven. So cool!" he responds, his face lighting up like we didn't just go through hell on earth.

Sayuri chuckles lightly at his response. I can't even imagine what it's like for her. Having to endure all of this as well as having to worry about him too. The fear and responsibility of having to keep him alive. This has me curious about how they are related. She seems to care for him, but I don't think she's his mother.

I push past my initial awkwardness, the part of me that wants to stay quiet, if only to fill the growing silence or to distract us further. "So, you both were on your way to his uncles. Were you just visiting?" I ask.

Sayuri gives me a hum of agreement. "Haruto wanted to come surprise his father. He employed his uncle in his plan, and with his mother's approval, we got the tickets."

"Oh, that sounds fun," I respond, a little unsure of what else I can say. I'm more curious about them and who Sayuri is to the kid, but I'm too afraid to ask.

"Ren-oji, my uncle, just got home a few months ago. We actually came to see him," Ru tells me from the back seat. I find him staring back at me when I glance in the mirror. He still has my jacket, having put it back on after we left the apartment. Although he appears just as exhausted as us, he still seems to have a little reserve of energy to burn if his heightening mood is an indicator.

"Back home?" I ask while I focus on the road ahead.

So far, the freeway has been mostly clear. What would have been typical early Monday morning traffic hadn't started to crowd the highways yet.

"Ren recently was discharged from the military, and Reiji came out to..." She drifts off for a second as if she needs to think of the right words to say. Almost like she's trying not to say too much. "He had some business meetings that he wanted his brother there for."

Well, that isn't vague at all. And lovely—more cocky servicemen.

No wonder he was so demanding. He's probably used to getting his way in all things. Probably also overly sure of himself. I can't help but roll my eyes but catch myself before Sayuri can see my annoyance.

"Oh. My dad was also in the military. Not always easy for the family, huh?" I glance back at her.

A Tesla speeds by us, swerving in and out of the lanes in a hurry. I roll my eyes. *Things never change with these drivers.* At least that in itself feels familiar, instead of the other type of rush we had to experience last night—or tonight, if you count almost three in the morning to be the same night.

"It isn't easy. I have known Ren and his family since they were little children. I was close friends with their mother before she passed." She stares out the window as if being transported back into a memory. "When she died, I was ready for something different, and I was already leaving my teaching job. I offered to nanny them when they were still young."

So, she has been with them for a long time then. They must care about her if she continued to stay with them not only once they grew up but also eventually with Ru.

She stays quiet for a long time, and I think she's going to leave it at that, but she surprises me when she keeps talking.

"I did it more for myself than for them. I knew they would be grieving and needed support, but for me, they were what was left of their mother, and I couldn't let go. I love them like they are my own niece and nephews. Haruto is like my own grandchild. I never had kids of my own and lost most of my family young."

I can understand what she means. Sometimes, grief brings us closer to people. For me, I wanted to get closer to others but always felt I couldn't. It wasn't as if people were always unkind or I hadn't tried; I just never found anyone other than Meg where I felt like I belonged. So, I allowed my grief to do the opposite.

I still haven't gotten ahold of Meg and it's starting to plant the seed of doubt that she didn't make it. *Don't go there, Dahlia. She'll call you back soon.*

"I'm glad you have them, then. It's hard to lose someone you love. Having them and getting to watch them grow must have been a bitter-sweet way of holding on but also getting a sense of closure."

Did that even make sense?

Seemingly, it did since she dips her chin in understanding. Or maybe she just doesn't want to be rude. She looks over her shoulder to Haruto, who finally seems to be crashing a little. My heart aches for her. My thoughts go back to how burdened she must be. Not that having Ru is a burden to her, but the burden of having to stay alive long enough to get him to safety.

I can't wait to get them to their family so I can figure out what I'm going to do. Then I'll only need to worry about myself.

Hopefully, I will get through to Meg soon. Maybe I can survive long enough to make it to where she is. Maybe we can survive this together.

If she is alive.

My eyes brim with tears. Shit, I can't think about that. I can't lose Megan. She's all I have.

Another two cars speed past us, both weaving through traffic. Then, another zooms past.

Damn, where are they going in such a hurry?

That thought brings me back to my own plan. I wonder where I could go if I can't get to Meg. Maybe the mountains.

What if I'm likely to be in this alone?

That thought fills me with such dread and loneliness that it takes me a moment to realize I'm crying again.

"Are you okay, dear?" Sayuri asks softly. She's looking at me now with such kindness that it causes me to sob harder. We are both in this horrible situation and here she is, concerned for me.

I'm terrified of what the future holds. "Yeah, it's just been a long day," I say instead. Wiping my face off, I continue to focus on the road. Although it's still late or early, depending on how you look at it, it's odd that the freeway is still this clear of traffic.

I do a double take of the time when I notice a light in the distance. It's not the sunrise. It's harsh and all wrong. After a few seconds, the orange glow on the horizon grows brighter and brighter.

More fires.

"Has it spread already? But how?" I ask myself.

"Maybe it is only a fire?" Sayuri responds, sounding as if she doesn't quite believe it.

I must have jinxed it. Up ahead, the traffic is starting to slow down to a stop—not a slow roll but stopping altogether. The onramp looks to be the same. Fortunately, there is an exit just up ahead. Taking the streets the rest of the way to PCH, the Pacific Coast Highway will take longer, but we'll get nowhere on this.

"Fuck it," I mumble. I'll risk a ticket. *As if that would even matter at this point.* I jerk the steering wheel to the right and drive on the shoulder towards the exit. A few others behind us follow suit.

In the line of traffic, some are honking, others trying to pass on the shoulder, only to be stopped by cars trying to cut in front.

Once I pass the initial cluster of cars, the exit ramp is completely clear, other than the few behind me. Everyone is trying to get onto the freeway, not off. That can't be good.

The offramp merges with a small highway before I can turn right down a main street.

For the late hour, seeing so many people outside is jarring, especially in this industrial area of whatever city I'm in. I'm not sure exactly where we exited but my maps is lagging which only has my nerves skyrocketing.

A woman in green scrubs rushes inside the Shell Gas Station to my left while others frantically run to the other side of the street to another gas station.

The GPS updates and leads us further down before I need to make a few turns. The further I drive, the more frenzied the people look outside. Apartment buildings are bustling with people shoving stuff into their cars in the parking lots, and some are trying to board up their windows.

So far, I can't hear any of those creature-like things, but seeing how people are also running or driving in the direction we just came from, I know we aren't heading into a clear zone.

I flip the radio on, curious if there is any new information and partially to distract myself from my growing nerves. Unfortunately, I don't think there is. Instead of a typical news report, it's a discussion between callers.

"No. No. It's just another rendition of the last riot we had. Every generation is bound to have one. The only thing I can't figure out is what the cause is. Maybe it's because of—"

Another voice interrupts. *"It isn't. We were there. I barely managed to get out of LAX. I don't understand why no one is talking about what's actually happening!"*

Glass shattering startles me. I whip my head to find a small group, all dressed in darker clothing, climbing through the window of a jeweler. People must actually believe it's a riot. These guys seem to be taking advantage of it from the look of what they're wearing and the large empty backpacks they're holding.

"I don't believe it. People biting each other? Are you high? That's impos—"

"I swear to God, you people are ridiculous. This isn't some mass hysteria or a group of rogue extremists. This is something straight out of a horror mov—"

He interrupts her now and says, *"You're delusional, woman. Then why isn't there any footage? Where is the evidence?"*

I glance in my mirrors, keeping my eyes peeled. The car is quiet as we listen to their argument. It's bizarre, to say the least.

She basically growls with her response. *"I don't know! But I'm telling you. I saw people recording. The government is probably involved. They must have been keeping it a secret or something. Taking down people's social posts. I don't know, but I do know what I saw!"*

His responding chuckle grates on my nerves. Irritated, I flip the radio off when they only continue to argue.

I saw people recording with their phones at the airport, too. Even if most didn't survive, there has to have been some footage somewhere. It is odd that none of that is making it to social media or the news.

I hate that people aren't getting the truth from where it matters, but on the other hand, I picture what things would have looked like had we all been warned.

The freeways would have all looked like what we came across. There would have been an immediate panic outside of the areas being attacked. We probably never would have gotten this far.

Although now that it seems to be spreading quickly, it's only a matter of time before nowhere is safe.

My eyes are as wide as saucers as I drive, taking in the rising panic. More cars are flooding the roads, speeding off towards the freeway entrance. My GPS has taken me close to a road running parallel to the freeway, and from here, I can make out the stationary red and white lights.

"I thought it would be safe this way," I whisper, more focused on our surroundings. I'm not naïve enough to think it will always be safe, but I had hoped we would have more time before the entire state went up in flames. The fact that we got out of the airport and were met at first with clear freeways and zombieless cities had implanted that small hope that we could get away.

"Crap," I exclaim as we come up to two crashed cars. Neither of the drivers are still here, as if they have fled the scene. Good for them that they are alive, bad for us that their cars now block the road. I make sure no one is behind us before I back up enough to turn down the street to our right.

My GPS tries to reroute us due to a collision, but it doesn't take long to realize it won't help. An abandoned United States Postal Service truck sits in the middle of the smaller road. *Shit.*

To my left, I spot a small Urgent Care and two other closed businesses in a mini-mall-like center. The two smaller buildings take up most of the tiny lot.

Before I can back out again, a car blares its horn at me, followed by screams. A couple of people come out of nowhere, running between me and the other angry driver behind us.

I give up and drive up the sidewalk into the center parking lot instead. I may have taken advantage of other people's lack of concern for pedestrians, but I don't want to be the one to hit them first.

Hopefully, I can find a way around the cars through the other end of the parking lot to get to the right road. My GPS keeps trying to reroute me as I drive. Its confusion about the situation only mirrors my own panic.

There! I find the back exit from the parking lot leading to the other side of the blocked intersection. A few cars obstruct the small exit, but when I drive closer, we notice that one car's lights are still on with the driver's door left wide open.

Scanning the area, I can see that the sidewalks are all obstructed from one thing or another, so going around isn't an option. I don't want to get out, but with a quick look around, there is nothing but cars trying to avoid the new obstacles or a few people running away. The car behind us must have followed because it's there. Except now it's parked, and the doors are left ajar.

The driver is gone. *Shit. That really, really can't be good.*

There are no sounds to indicate anything *other,* but clearly, something is up if the car has been abandoned. If I hadn't already seen what was lurking behind them somewhere, I would have thought the people in this town were off their rockers. If we could see them from above, they all probably look like cockroaches fleeing a disturbed hiding place.

Stopping my senseless train of thought, I make my decision. "Sayuri," I say as I park the car. "Just wait here. I parked a little further away to give you time should you need to leave quickly." Not that it would be easy to get away without the other car moved, but it's better than nothing.

"Sure," she responds and unlatches her seatbelt.

I slowly get out and make my way over to the other car, a beat-up Honda Civic. I ease my way into the driver seat, and I'm thankful I don't need to adjust it.

A car door shuts, causing me to whip my head around. My nerves are so on edge that I'm surprised I'm not falling apart anymore. Sayuri is walking towards me, concern etched on her face.

"Ren texted your phone, but I can't open it. The phone has a passcode," she whispers. She doesn't look at me, though. Her eyes are anxiously taking in the parking lot.

I'm such an idiot. I should have given her my PIN. I type it into the phone and repeat it to her, so she has it for later.

"Thank you, I'll wait in the car for—" She's abruptly cut off by a screech.

In the distance, more inhuman, shrill screams arise.

It looks like our luck has run short. Coming into view, they are all running at anyone still outside on the street.

They are so fast! Who knew I would wish they could be like the zombies with an abnormal gait like they do in horror films or books? Granted, I wish they weren't real to begin with.

"Shit." I quickly put the car in reverse, and Sayuri hops out of the way of the open door. I back out, hoping I gave myself enough room to drive past.

"Dahlia-san!" Sayuri yells.

I'm climbing out of the Honda as multiple zombies run towards us. *Where the hell did these ones come from?* They're closing the distance quickly.

Too quickly.

They are too fast for us to get back to the car, and this vehicle is too small; they would manage to break the windows. Shit, why didn't I park closer?

Ru! He's still in the backseat. *Fuck.*

Before I can second-guess my half-assed plan, I grab Sayuri's hand and pull her toward the buildings. My heart feels like it's going to beat out of my chest. Terror is clutching its talons into me yet again.

I don't look back, but I yell to Ru over my shoulder. "Lay in the back seat on the floor. Don't make noise or show yourself!" A screech is the only response I get.

I hope I didn't get the kid killed, but there is no way I can fight these things head-on in the open like this, especially without a weapon.

The shotgun.

"Fuck," I say aloud.

I forgot I brought it with me!

See? You can't do this.

I push my thoughts aside, focusing on what I can control right now—running away.

The sound of their feet pounding against the pavement as they gain on us spikes my terror further. We reach the building and run straight for a door flanked by windows that are lined with black curtains. The door is slightly ajar, and I pray I'm not running away from one viper directly into a nest.

We all but hurl ourselves inside the building and are met with a dimly lit reception area. Straight ahead is a long hallway with a neon green sign on the ceiling directing to another exit. I make an even more idiotic decision.

"Leave it open," I say breathlessly.

If we can get out via the back entrance, we can close the door and make it back to the car before they can reach us. I pull on Sayuri's hand to run faster. Hopefully, they aren't smart enough to turn around and go back out the way they came. Or, hopefully, the door is unlocked to begin with. *Fuck. Don't be locked. Don't be locked.*

I don't stop, not even when I notice two men are going through a few cupboards in the back of the room. Startled, they both pull their guns up before recognizing that we aren't a threat. They hesitate, not pointing the guns directly at us, but they look over our shoulders and curse in another language. The gunfire that follows causes my ears to ring, and I instinctively throw my hands up to shield myself.

We keep running down the hallway, somehow holding onto that sliver of luck again, when we find the back door unlocked.

Rushing outside, I quickly shut the door behind us. A loud bang on the other side sounds right as the latch catches. More gunshots permeate the air, followed by gargled cries behind the door I'm still clutching.

Not allowing myself to think about how I got those two men killed, I turn on my heel and keep running. I'll analyze that later if we get out of here alive. I check to ensure Sayuri is behind me and nothing else is following.

Rounding back to the front of the small building, I find my car still there, but I can't spot Ru in the back seat or any zombies. Hopefully, he's only following directions and hiding. I slow down, scoping the lot and straining to hear any sounds. "I think we lost them for now. Although unfortunate for those guys, they are distracted," I whisper. I glance back to the building and notice the door is closed.

Odd. A little confused, I brush it off and continue forward, but as we reach the car, the silent engine makes me falter.

Peeking inside, I find the ignition empty. "What the—"

"Looking for these?" a slightly accented voice asks quietly behind me.

Startled, I jump and inhale sharply at the unexpected presence.

It's a man. His straight, dark hair touches his brows and casts a slight shadow over his face from the dim lights in the parking lot. He's well-built, sporting a full-sleeve tattoo on his left arm. It's a blend of colors, and what may be Chinese characters peeking out of his rolled-up sleeves. In another time, I may have found him attractive, but now, I'm only scared. He's holding my keys in one hand and clutching Ru by the shoulder with the other. The man is not much taller than me, but it doesn't take away from the dangerous vibes he gives off.

The Civic had to have been his. He was hoping for a fast getaway, maybe.

Sayuri gasps at the sight of Ru being held by a stranger. The man looks over us closely, lingering on me for a moment too long for comfort. He directs his attention back to Sayuri. When he glances down at Ru, his brows go up.

"You two look familiar. Where have I seen you before?" he asks. They don't answer him, but two other men jog over from the Urgent Care.

"Looks like the others got trapped in with those flesh-eaters," one of them says as they reach us. His hair is pulled up with a shaved undercut, and he has a gnarly scar running from the back of his right ear along his cheek to meet the corner of his lips.

"I saw that; I closed the door to keep the others in before they got to us, too. This bitch led them inside," the one holding Ru replies with his deep brown eyes trained on me.

Well, crap...

They were friends... and he saw us run inside before his buddies inevitably became an all-you-can-eat buffet.

He shoves Ru back towards us. The kid stumbles but manages to grab onto my hand. Instead of hiding, he stands tall, chin up defiantly. I would have been fooled if I couldn't feel his hand trembling.

"Why do you look so familiar?" The third man mumbles to himself. "You look like that Ryūko brat." He stares down at the kid, but finally brushes it off when Ru doesn't respond.

The third guy is taller, both arms covered in tattoos, and he has aviators on. *Who the hell wears sunglasses at night?* Even without the glasses, I can tell he's staring at the boy, then Sayuri. "Hmm." He snaps his fingers in recognition. "That's right," he says but doesn't disclose what he's thinking.

He peers at me for a moment as if he's coming up with a plan. "Might as well take them. A little collateral wouldn't hurt," he says.

He barks something to the others I can't understand and disappears through the door of the Urgent Care. The man with the undercut takes out a gun, and the one who took my keys tosses them to the ground and unholsters a knife.

Before pulling the gun on us, Undercut curses.

My stomach drops when I follow his gaze. Four of them.

These seem slower than the others, but it's only a matter of time before they reach us. They aren't screeching. Instead, they make a low rumbling sound, almost a growl. I can't help the shiver that wracks my body in response. The stranger with the gun shifts slightly to get a better shot while the first tattooed man who stole my keys inches closer to me.

I may not understand what they want with us but it's definitely a nefarious reason. I go through my options. Go with them quietly... or try to fight back.

The growl-like rumble coming closer has me finding my resolve.

The kid needs to get out. Whoever these guys are, they're trouble.

Before I can conjure a plan, the tattooed man clasps my arm and drags me, his hold painful. Fear grips my heart, and I can't seem to do much but follow along.

Roughly dragging me, he points the knife in Sayuri's direction. "Come on, bitch, grab the kid and follow, or she dies," he tells her.

I must look as afraid as I am because she gulps and takes Haruto's hand.

I can't let them take the kid. I think back to some of the self-defense moves my father taught me and the few tricks I came up with on my own as we practiced.

Not allowing myself to think through the consequences, I throw my head back while simultaneously shoving with my hips, throwing the man off center when my head connects with his nose. Ignoring the new blossoming pain in my skull, I take a step and kick the keys towards Sayuri as the man seizes me by the hair. "Get him home. Take the keys!"

A scream escapes my throat while he wrenches down hard with his fingers in my hair, causing me to stumble back. My own is drowned out by the new screams from across the road as people are still trying in vain to flee or fight. The mixture of cries edge closer, and I soon realize there are more zombies coming.

Sayuri hesitates but lowers her chin once while tears fill her warm eyes. She understands. She must feel the same way. We've had our chance at life; the kid hasn't.

The man yanks me harder. He has already dragged me quite a way, tearing my jeans on the asphalt with my struggle.

I plant my feet the best I can and grip my hair under his hand.

Using my weight, I pull. He's not expecting it, and his hand slips.

I land hard, unable to help the groan that escapes me as I roll onto my stomach.

The sound of gunshots erupts behind me. It's followed by a pained shout, but I can't see who Undercut is shooting at. Two other men join in, providing cover from the zombies coming closer.

"Fucking bitch, if you want to die, then fine," he says. "Let me help you." He flips me over and brings the knife to my chest.

My hands barely grab his in time to stop the descent of his blade.

I don't know if I have ever been as afraid as I am now. Death is sprinting towards me in the guise of a human while the threat of it is straddling me with steel at my collar. I'm caged and at the complete mercy of my own mortality. I don't want to fight. I want to hide or run away. *To let it be over.*

"Things don't stay nasty forever, my little butterfly. Stop quitting on yourself." My father's voice floods my thoughts. It's a reminder of one of our last conversations.

God... I only want to make you proud, Dad.

Tears are streaming down my face as I struggle. Wrestling against his strength, I manage to shift his hand down further toward my stomach.

The man looks up briefly, cursing before putting his other hand on my throat.

The zombies are getting closer. The gunfire is causing a warlike scene to resound around me. Then, the sound of my car peeling out of the lot follows.

Relief floods me knowing that they made it out. They had to have made it. I only hope they find the kid's family soon.

Blood is starting to rush to my head, and the pounding in my ears intensifies as I fight to breathe. White and black spots obstruct my vision, fluttering like insects. Hot tears continue to roll down my face as I try to grasp some kind of escape.

I can do it. You can do it. Make him proud, Dahlia.

I fixate on those words, but my arms are starting to weaken despite my efforts.

The man's focus is now solely on choking me, and the pressure in his knife hand lessens.

Using my last remaining strength, I shove my thumbnail into his eye. I push as hard as I can, and he lets out a glass-shattering cry. Ignoring the sickening, squelching feeling under my finger and beneath my nail, I push harder.

He falls back on his ass, shuffling while gripping his face. I take a second to cough, gasping for air when I remember the need to get the fuck out of here before I turn into a ready-to-eat meal.

Regardless of the hot pain in my side, I jump into action. Slipping a few times before gaining traction, I finally manage some stability.

Arms wrap around my waist and hoist me up. "No!" I scream desperately.

An involuntary cry leaves my mouth as pain in my side flares and leaves me breathless.

Ignoring my protests, he pulls me into the building behind the others. The door slams, and only a few seconds pass before we hear the thump of zombies ramming into it. Once placed on my trembling feet, all I can do is stare at the door in a daze, not realizing how close the zombies had gotten.

"Why didn't you let the *sohai* die? Look what she did!" someone snaps behind me.

Turning, I find the man who choked me with a scowl etched across his face. His right eye is swollen shut, with blood dripping down his cheek, and the bridge of his nose is beginning to swell. He's sitting on the floor leaning against the wall, breathing heavily while someone fusses with a cloth near his eye.

While he glowers at me, his disgust has me involuntarily stepping back until I hit the door. Another loud thump makes me jump. I must look like a small rabbit amid wolves because that's exactly how I feel.

A chuckle across the room brings my attention to the other man, only partially forgetting the threat behind my back. It's the same man who wanted to take us. He must be the one in charge. "Were you able to get the other two?" he asks his men.

The one who carried me in, responds, "No but I managed to clip one of them. They were able to reach the car."

The boss rubs his chin, annoyances marring his face. "We can try to find the other two later then. They can't get far out there, but she was with them." He jerks his head at me. "She must have some importance. I am not one to stare a gift horse in the mouth." He directs his attention to me then. "Name's Leon."

His glasses are off this time, showcasing rich brown eyes. His intense gaze slowly roams down my body before landing on my abdomen. My skin crawls when I think he's checking me out, but then the pain in my side flickers to life, reminding me that I was hurt.

"Was she bit?" he questions the other men.

"Knife," One-eye manages between heavy breaths and a mirthless grin.

My shirt is soaked red. He must have managed to cut or stab me in the scuffle. My adrenaline is starting to fade, and the pain is more prominent. I whimper slightly, clutching my side.

Leon gives them an order I can't catch when suddenly I'm being grabbed by the arm and taken roughly to what looks like a break room.

The lights are bright compared to the softly lit waiting room, and there are a few other people inside. Four other men and two women sit around a table, playing cards. One is lighting a cigarette as they all look up at us. The boss tells the women to clean me up, and I'm shoved inside.

The two women look like they could be sisters or even twins, sharing the same dark hair, brown eyes, and long jawline. The only difference is that one has a small beauty mark on the left side of her chin. They are both beautiful, but the frowns only spoil their beauty. They are both thin and dressed in expensive, high-end clothing. Although they are only in jeans and colorful blouses, I can tell just by the huge Chanel bag one of them is clutching.

Neither speaks to me, but one walks towards a counter on the other side of the room and opens a drawer. She pulls out a small first aid box.

I'm pulled to an empty chair on the other side of the table. I'm unable to reposition myself before she starts cutting my shirt up the middle. I try to protest, scooting back, but she slaps me across the face. As I stare dumbstruck at the woman, my eyes water with the residual sting.

Her face is utter indifference now as I try to process what's happening. Knowing there isn't much I can do, I ignore them as best as I can through the pain and take in the room around me.

It's a typical break room with a fridge, chairs, and tables. A flat-screen TV mounted on the wall takes up much of the space on the left side of the room. Although on mute, it appears to be turned onto one of the news stations. I can't read the subtitles from the angle I'm sitting, but I can see the emergency broadcast flashing at the bottom of the page. I try squinting to see if I can read it, but I give up fairly quickly when one of the women pushes hard on my side.

I gasp from the pain, clenching my eyes shut.

It was worth it, Dahlia. You allowed the kid to get away. Even if you die, they didn't.

Yet.

Biting the inside of my cheek, I try to remind myself not to allow my thoughts to drift to such dark places. They got away, and clearly, these people aren't going to kill me.

Yet.

Fuck! Stop, Dahlia.

They didn't let me die. They need me for some sick reason. I hope they only keep me locked up and not take advantage of the fact that I am now partially shirtless in a room full of leering men.

While the adrenaline depletes, it allows the fear to slowly trickle in tenfold. My eyes are tearing up, and I just stare at my hands. Where is the brave shithead who grabs a kid with zombies on their tail or helps fight against the bad guys when the kid is in danger? Where'd that woman go?

It's a wonder I had managed to muster that courage at all.

One of the men, the one with the cigarette, gets up and walks over to us. He grabs me by the arm and starts shoving me towards another door across the hall. At that moment, dread so heavy roots my feet into place that he needs to physically drag me. He pushes me into a closet and slams the door in my face.

"Did you strip-check her?" asks a muffled voice on the other side of the door.

The reply only fills my belly with dread. "No, but I will."

Somehow, I wish those zombies had got me before they did.

CHAPTER EIGHT

Ren

I'm losing my fucking mind. I've tried calling Sayuri multiple times and haven't been able to get through. The phone continues to ring through my truck's Bluetooth until it abruptly stops. I almost hope someone finally answers until the same response sounds over the speakers.

"Sorry, I can't reach my phone. Please leave a message," the woman's voicemail repeats.

It's the same one I've heard about ten times now. A stark difference from how tentative she sounded when we spoke. At first, her voice was a relief. That was until I'd heard the same message repeatedly telling me the same thing—that I have no idea what's happening to Haru or Sayuri. No idea if they are still alive.

We've been driving down the coast for a while now. We were able to get out of our town without having to stop, bypassing all the madness spreading at an alarming rate. Unfortunately, we aren't the only ones trying to head in this direction. The traffic is still moving, but more and more cars are filling the three lanes heading south. I have no idea where most people are going to go. How the fires are spreading in the distance, we're screwed and sandwiched in.

I glance at my phone to check Sayuri's location but notice they're no longer on the freeway. Instead, they got off and stopped. I turn my blinker on to merge into the turn lane as we approach an exit, changing my original route.

A loud honk drags. Tires squeal before the sound of crunching metal reverberates through the air.

"What the..." *Shit.*

Many of those *things* surround a silver Sedan in the middle of the intersection that swerved into an SUV. Another one is pinned under the car. It's partially under the tire, clawing at the cement with wild abandon.

I make my turn and am about to keep driving past when James speeds up in front and pulls over, partially blocking one of the lanes. "What the hell is he doing?" I say to myself.

Matt and Dirk, who carpooled, pull over behind James.

What the hell, guys? Inwardly groaning, I also pull over and hop out.

The guys don't waste any time before they converge on the vehicles. I grab my S&W and join them.

"What the fuck. I need to get to Haru!" I exclaim as I pull up my firearm and scope the surrounding area. Cars continue to speed and swerve around us. No one else stops to help like the guys did.

Dirk fires first, clipping one of those people surrounding the vehicle in the shoulder, but it keeps trying to get to the driver inside the Sedan. The person inside is screaming, frantically trying to get into the backseat from the front. He fires a second time in the center of their back.

It's still moving as if it wasn't shot in the spine.

"Why aren't they going down?" Matt shouts as he shoots another in the leg.

"Maybe go for the—" James is cut off as one breaks off from the small crowd and charges him.

I bring my hand up and pull the trigger.

"...head," he finishes, staring at the body on the cement and the blood seeping from between its eyes. It lies unmoving. Its eyes stare lifeless at the night sky.

James glances up at me. "Thanks, man. What the hell is happening? These things are like goddamn zombies." He appears shocked. Like it's finally hitting him what we are up against.

We make quick work, aiming to kill and clear the small crowd of those things. Screams reach us from further down the street, followed by more screeching. It's like they are attracted to noises, following the screams and gunfire.

Matt and James speak with the drivers of the two vehicles, checking on them, but neither waits around. Although their cars are messed up, they manage to start them and speed off.

"We need to go. I can't stop to help everyone. My nephew is stuck out there," I say to the guys while I gesture in the direction we need to go. The screeches are getting closer. It's only increasing our urgency to leave.

We waste no time running back to our vehicles and taking off.

My anxiety is only rising every time we need to get out to kill more of these things. Thankfully, the guys haven't pulled over to be heroes again, but we needed to stop to clear the road from debris or abandoned cars. Once we realized that sound is like ringing a huge dinner bell for them, we have only used our firearms in absolutely necessary circumstances. I used one of my knives to terminate a few while the guys either used a knife or tire iron from their car.

Although having the guys here with me is a huge help, it's also fueling my fear of more people I care about dying. My thoughts stray to Haru. Their location has started to move again, but they haven't traveled far. I can't lose him either. Fuck, I don't know what I'd do. I have lost enough people throughout my life; I can't lose anyone else. I refuse to.

My phone buzzes, getting my hopes up until I read Reiji's name flash across the screen. He's been texting and calling nonstop since he got to my house. His last text was to inform me that he had lost contact with the last remaining family we have in Mexico—our mother's side of the family. Whatever this is, it's spreading everywhere.

Up ahead, with the truck lights and streetlamps illuminating our path, we can make out about ten zombies running in the same direction we are heading. A few screeches reach my ears.

What has their attention? I glance at my phone, and my stomach drops. Their location stopped again.

As I drive closer, a crowd of those things comes into view. They are all trying to reach for a small figure on top of a car.

Dread fills me as we drive closer, and when my eyes make out a child fending off the zombies, my heart all but stops.

Haru.

"Fuck!"

He's using what looks to be a rusty tire iron, trying to bat their persistent hands away.

I waste no time putting the truck in park and jumping out. The others follow suit, firing at the zombies converging on the old vehicle. He appears utterly petrified but doesn't shy away with each swing. I don't see Sayuri, but we work quickly on clearing the area, not bothering to try to be silent this time.

"They are going to start coming in hot now that we've made this much noise. Grab the kid and nanny, and let's get the hell out of here," James yells behind me.

"That's the plan. Spread out and cover me until I get them out," I shout back.

The guys fan out, watching to ensure none of the zombies sneak up on us while my focus is solely on Haruto. I help him down and hold him tight to my chest, needing to feel that he's there, that he is okay.

"Ren-oji!" he cries into my neck. The poor kid is sobbing so hard I can barely recognize that he's trying to tell me something. I reluctantly put him down and step back to cup his face in my hands.

"Were you hurt?" I ask him while checking his body for any bites or wounds.

"No, but we need to hurry!" He points to the passenger seat, and I bring my attention back to the car. It takes a moment to register that Sayuri is inside, hunched against the door.

She's not moving.

All thoughts of what's happening around us vanish as my focus zeros in on her.

I rush to the door and throw it open. She sags sideways, and I catch her before she falls out of the seat. I gently pick her up and place her down on the ground to check her pulse. Finding it faint and irregular, I stare at her in horror.

Oh god.

Immediately, I start searching for the cause of her skittering pulse and discover a bullet wound in her chest. Confused, I look back at her pale face. *No...*

No. No. "No."

Not Sayuri. I can't lose her too.

She was the only one who cared, the only one who truly saw me but never judged. She always took care of us, loving us unconditionally.

My mom's friend.

Our caretaker.

Family.

As if she feels my gaze, her eyes flutter open. She tries to smile but only manages a grimace while tears fall down her cheeks. It seems to take all her energy to speak the next few words.

"Made... it. What a... miracle." She coughs. "She needs... help. Save—" Her eyes close, and her breathing grows shallow.

"—her." Sayuri's last whisper is so faint I almost don't hear her.

Within a matter of seconds, her chest descends for the last time but never rises.

All I can do is stare at her in disbelief and utter shock.

"Oh god," I choke.

Gently placing her down, I try to administer CPR. "You can't fucking do this, Sayuri-san. You can't!" I'm breathing heavily as I push down on her sternum, unwilling to give up. I keep pushing my hands down rapidly. "You can't leave me too."

A hand gently grabs my shoulder, but I shake it off, not stopping.

"Ren," James says, barely above a whisper.

Heaving breaths, I still. My hands are coated in her blood, and my eyes stare blankly at her unmoving form.

I stand up but can't take my eyes off the woman who refused to leave us.

But now she has.

She was taken from us.

It takes everything I have at this moment to step away. All I can think of is how this happened or who shot her. Who shoots a defenseless woman?

I walk back to the truck and slam my hand against the metal, ignoring the pain in my palm and the absurdity of the action. "Fuck!" I shout into the air.

I failed.

Again.

I failed her.

What if I had brought my sister? Could she have saved her?

This is my fault...

If I had left earlier. If I had brought Hana with me. If we didn't stop so many times. Fuck, we could have saved her. I should never have bought those fucking tickets. Haru and Sayuri would be back home. Safe. Away from this hellhole.

My chest aches, and my whole being feels like I was thrown in a meat blender. Breathing deeply, I push all this pain, this hate, this rage and lock it away to deal with later. I still need to get this kid home. We aren't safe yet.

Wiping my suspiciously damp face, I walk back over to Haru.

"We need to get out of here, kid. Your dad is waiting at the house."

I grab his hand gently, but he pulls away, shaking his head. "No, we need to go back. They took her. They were going to hurt her. We can't leave!"

My brows scrunch in confusion. "What do you mean? Sayuri is right here."

His cheeks redden as he becomes more flustered. "No. Dahlia-neesan! She fought the bad men. She fought them to save us. We can't leave her, too," he exclaims.

That's right, the girl that they were with. I realize that the car is most likely hers. My eyes widen in shock when I realize what he said. *Neesan?* How in the hell had he grown so attached in such a short time? *Shit.*

"I'm sorry, but she's on her own. I can't risk your life. If she risked herself for you, then she probably wouldn't want you going back either," I say as I grab his hand again, but he doesn't pull away. He follows me to the truck with his head down.

Once I get him strapped in, I step over to Matt. "Take the Plymouth. We could use it; if not, we can siphon gas from it later."

"Sure thing," he responds.

When he hops in, he leans over the passenger seat, focused on something on the floor. "Whoever owned this car must have been the shit, they had a fucking shotgun in here."

He messes with something on the dash before his smirk turns into an amused chuckle.

Ignoring him, I hesitantly walk back over to Sayuri. Taking a deep breath, I pick up her still body and bring her to the bed of my truck. We have little time before more zombies come, but I can't bear to think about those things eating her. I have some room on my property where we can bury her.

Once we're all in our vehicles, we begin the drive back to my house. Hopefully, the roads aren't starting to congest to the point of full closures. The last thing we need right now is to get stuck or take the longer way around.

Soft sniffles reach my ears from the back seat. I hadn't noticed before, but Haru clutches a black denim jacket to his chest like a lifeline while staring out the window.

Closing my eyes briefly, I take a slow, deep breath. I hate seeing him in pain. I don't know what happened in the short time he was with this girl, but he seems to have formed an attachment. It doesn't help that Sayuri is gone.

Dead.

Killed.

Memories of my parents trickle through the walls I have been trying to keep erect. The familiar feeling of anger boils to the surface.

What if I go back...? Do to them what they did to Sayuri?

I shake my head at the thought. I should know better. The last time I allowed those feelings to lead me, it took me down a path I barely came back from. It would only be another gaping wound on my conscience.

Fuck, I can't handle this shit right now.

I try to focus on the roads instead of allowing my memories and guilt to gut me. The roads are no better than they were previously. People are still driving and running, and more creatures continue chasing after anyone on foot. The roads are total chaos, but thankfully, they are not blocked off.

Haru's soft cries bring me back to my dark thoughts, and Sayuri's last words hit me like a ton of bricks.

Save her...

Her... Dahlia?

Of course, Sayuri asked the same as Haruto now is. Even in her last fucking moments, she cared about someone else over her own welfare. Breathing in to try to calm my nerves, I peer back at my nephew in the mirror.

The jacket. My guess is it's Dahlia's.

I slam my hand into the steering wheel, cursing before speaking up. I hate this idea. I hate it with my very being. Not because I don't relish getting the revenge my anger is calling for but because I can't afford to lose my nephew. If something happens to Haru or the rest of my family while I go play hero, I'll kill the woman myself.

"I'm going to get you home. Once I know you're safe, I'll go back, but I'm not leaving you until then." Our eyes meet in the mirror, and despite his age, his stare is unyielding.

A part of me hopes that I don't regret this. Another part of me is ready to direct the anger and guilt and all the murky feelings simmering below the surface towards the men who made the mistake of fucking with us.

In fact, I'm anticipating it.

CHAPTER NINE

Ren

The drive home went a lot smoother than I thought it would. Pulling up into the driveway, I don't wait for Reiji or anyone to notice we're back. I don't need him talking me out of this. Admittedly, I'm also not ready for that lecture I know he has for me when I see him.

I get out and walk around to my nephew's side of the car. His wide eyes find me through the window before he opens his door. "So she knows I didn't leave her," he says as he hands me the jacket.

Shit. Why did my brother have to raise such an honorable pain in my ass? I should be surprised, considering his occupation, but Reiji took a lot after our father. Or who our father was once he met our mother.

"Can you tell me who took her and where, if you remember?" I reach for the jacket and throw it over my shoulder. The floral scent of the material surrounds my senses for a second. The smell triggers a memory, but I shove it back, not wanting to dive deeper into my darker thoughts.

His breath hiccups before he tells me what led them to the men who shot Sayuri.

"We needed to get off the highway. Dahlia-neesan drove for a little while. People were screaming and leaving their cars." He pauses to look down at his now fidgeting hands. "She had to get out to move a car that was in the way."

I interrupt, "Do you remember where you guys ended up?"

"I think it was a doctor's office… Oh, and there was a building with curtains and a picture of a lady with stones on her back," he tells me.

Thinking back to where we found him, I also try to remember where their location stopped on my phone. I think I have a general idea.

"They ran away from some of those things. I hid in the backseat, and before they came back, a man grabbed me from the car. They knew who I was."

My brows shoot up. "What do you mean?"

"They knew our family's name," he says, tears slipping down his cheeks. "I'm sorry, Ren-Oji. Dahlia-neesan tried to hold them back, but one of the men shot at the monsters, and it hit Sayuri..."

I crouch in front of him and place my hand on his shoulder. "You have nothing to be sorry for, kid. You didn't do anything wrong. There was nothing you could have done." I think back to when my parents were killed. So many times, people told me there was nothing I could have done, but I still couldn't convince myself to believe it.

I hope he doesn't feel the same way. He doesn't deserve to live with that type of remorse.

"We were able to get into the car, but Sayuri had to stop. Those monsters started to get too close, so she helped me onto the top of the car and closed herself in. Then you found us." He sniffles and wipes his eyes with the back of his hand.

"Can you tell me what these men looked like?" I ask him. I'm curious as to who they are. If they knew him, then it would have to be someone we'd met before.

As he gives me the description of the men who took her, my body slowly grows cold. He describes a lion-like tattoo that seems familiar to him but can't remember where he has seen it before. Unfortunately, or maybe rather fortunate in this situation, I do.

If the world ending doesn't end their petty shit, what would?

I know who took Dahlia. Who killed Sayuri. Who almost kidnapped Haru.

If I hadn't wanted to let my anger reign before, I certainly do now.

"James." I motion to the truck bed. "Can you help my brother..."

...bury Sayuri.

I can't say the words. I can't imagine having to dig a grave in my yard for someone as special as she is. Burying her as if I were hiding a body and not respecting the woman she was. I can't even imagine saying the words aloud.

In understanding, he dips his chin before walking to the back of the truck. Dirk follows him to help. I take a second to grab my duffle from the passenger seat and the S&W in my center console.

Matt pulls into the driveway after falling a little behind, and I run up to him before he can even put it in park. A sliver of guilt gnaws at my chest. My thoughts were so caught up on Sayuri and Haru that I didn't even think about what was taking him so long. His brows furrow in confusion when I open the door.

"The chick." I motion back towards the road as I climb in. I half debated bringing a few other men, especially with what we face, but I can't think about removing the added protection they provide my family here.

When he understands what we're doing, he lifts his chin. "Rah," he says in acknowledgment, putting the car in reverse.

Pulling out my phone, I do a quick search for any doctor's offices near the location we found my nephew. I give Matt a quick rundown of what Haru told me, thankful he'll see these men as only insurgents who killed and kidnapped someone.

If that hadn't been the case, I'm not sure how else I could explain the situation and why I am willing to do what I need to. He doesn't need to know that it's personal for me. Or how I know who these men are to begin with. I'm a little surprised he doesn't bother asking me the latter.

The Yeun family just opened a few 'massage parlors' in the surrounding neighborhoods to launder their money and most likely where some of the unfortunate girls they traffic end up.

"Man, things are starting to look really bad," Matt mumbles as we pass a group of people fighting off those things. "They're like zombies for real. What a trip."

He's right. The only difference is their speed and how normal they would look if not for the color of their skin or their eyes.

Screams are becoming background noise now as we continue to bypass cars stopping in the middle of the road or people sprinting across the street. The fires must be spreading closer because the air is beginning to smell strongly of smoke, and the thick gloom is blending with the clouds in the lightening sky.

With everything happening outside, knowing the Yeun brothers are starting problems is slightly jarring.

From what my brother has told me, they have been causing a lot of issues for him since the opening of his hotel and casino, but you'd think that when the world goes to shit, they would care more about their survival.

My brother met with them a few times before they lived in this area but recently, they came in unannounced and have been trying to lay claim to territory as if they are a petty street gang instead of what they actually are. Triad.

They don't care if they shit on any prior feeble truce or respect they may have had in place with my brother.

They deal in some unsavory business, which heightens the risk of exposure to the law, which my brother doesn't want. They've been a thorn in my brother's side, especially since this isn't something he often needed to deal with back home.

"You good, man?" Matt asks, side-eyeing me as he swerves to avoid being hit by another car weaving through traffic.

"Yeah. Just thinking," I say. It's not as if I can tell Matt what's going on or what my family is involved in.

My brother may be heavily involved in illegal business, but my father led the clan away from drugs and trafficking, sticking with weapons and money—in other words, gambling. That alone is why my brother never did any business with the Yeun family. He only wanted things to stay amicable to keep the violence to a minimum.

Seething wouldn't be a bad description of how I feel right now. Everything they've done... What would be the purpose anyway? Nothing from our previous lives matters anymore. We are surrounded by death and a changing reality.

Then why are you chasing after revenge? I push that thought aside. I'm doing this for Haru. For Sayuri.

I snort to myself. *Sure. Keep telling yourself that.*

Matt side-eyes me again but doesn't say anything.

As we get closer, we come up with a quick plan. Both of us are familiar with the area, so it doesn't take long. I have him drop me off in the front, and he parks behind the building near the small side street, trying to quietly kill any zombies we come across. It's a walkable distance but not noticeable if they look outside. We both have our weapons on hand—a blade and firearm each as we set off.

Matt's whistle reaches me, signaling that we are good to go. I jolt into action without any hesitation, slowly opening the door and allowing my years of training to guide my movements.

All is silent as I move towards the hallway beyond the general waiting room. Listening for any signs of threats, I approach the first door, but before I go through, a high-pitched scream can be heard from farther inside the building. My first instinct is to move towards the scream, but the logical part of my brain keeps my movements steady as I continue with our initial plan. Acting rashly can cause mistakes and bite me in the ass in the end.

Advancing through the hallway, I continue to stay alert and clear each room as fast as I'm able. The urgent care facility is small, and I reach the end of the hallway quickly. The layout in all these buildings is the same, just one long hallway with multiple rooms flanking each side.

Meeting Matt by the last two rooms, he signals to me how many people he's run into. He's terminated two so far. I haven't come across any, so chances are they are behind these last two doors. The screams are coming from the room to my left. I can hear laughing and muffled conversation in the room to the right.

We share a look, both understanding there may be too many to stay quiet. I motion him to the room where the screams are coming from, and I position myself in front of the other door.

Counting silently to three, I open the door and scan the room. Based on Haru's description, the woman doesn't appear to be inside. As soon as I come to that conclusion, somebody screams again, just as Matt fires on someone.

The men pulling guns on me grabs my attention.

Well, shit.

I act fast, targeting the armed men first. Before I know it, only two are standing there without a weapon, beginning to kneel with their hands up in surrender.

I don't hesitate.

It takes less than a full breath before they fall.

Normally, I wouldn't fire on an unarmed man or woman, but they killed Sayuri. They took someone from me, and I couldn't care less about who they are. I relish in knowing they got what they deserved.

I shift to the side so I can view the hallway and the room in front of me in case anyone has managed to hide. Matt kneels down on the other side of the hall, but I can't see much farther in the room because his broad shoulders block the doorway.

"It's okay. We're with Ru," he says softly before leaning forward and standing up again with a small woman in his arms. I recognize her by her description. Her dark red hair is messy and covering her face, but the quiet sobs and the way her shoulders tremble, tell me she's crying. Even as distraught as she is, she appears stiff in his arms, like she doesn't want to be touched.

Matt tells her again that it's okay while he carries her towards the exit. I close the door before I follow, focusing on our surroundings as we step out of the building. I glance briefly at the head of red hair when, suddenly, bright blue-green eyes clash with mine over Matt's shoulder. They're puffy and bloodshot, only causing the crystalline color to stand out starkly amongst the red covering a portion of her face.

Her intense gaze forces me to look away. A small twinge of guilt guts me when I remember how I was ready to leave her. I might be a dick, but I don't want women to be harmed.

The gunfire attracted some attention. The zombies approaching are slower, so we have enough time to run to the car. My eyes are peeled for the ones that pose the larger threat, but thankfully, none of the faster ones are nearby.

I clip off a few in our path as Matt helps Dahlia climb into the back before he hops into the driver's seat. A screech sounds somewhere close.

"Shit," Matt mutters.

I climb into the back to help cover Dahlia with her jacket, but before I can grab it, Matt starts driving like bats out of Hell, and the door slams behind me. I'm thrown further onto the bench seat while she barrels into me with an audible whimper. I tentatively reach for her, trying to keep her from hurting herself further.

"Shit. I'm sorry," she says. Her voice is so soft that I need to strain to hear her. She struggles to sit up straight, holding onto her side. She doesn't look me in the eyes. Instead, she stares at her legs as she tries to shy away.

As I reach over to grab the jacket, she scoots back nervously, raising her arms to try to cover herself.

"I won't hurt you. I only want to help you with your jacket." I hold my hands up, hoping to show her I won't do anything to harm her. "I'm Ren. Haruto's uncle."

Her head lifts quickly, and she squints a little—no doubt looking for the resemblance, but she won't find much. I took after my mother's family, and my nephew is a spitting image of his mom. His eyes are like onyx compared to my chestnut brown, and his skin is paler than my tawny-beige complexion. He's a lot slimmer than I was at his age as well.

I lean down to retrieve the jacket from the floor and drape it over her shoulders. While I button it, she shudders violently.

Shit, I have no idea what to do in this situation. "Sorry," I mumble.

I catch Matt giving me an incredulous look through the mirror.

"I'm sorry they hurt you," I try again.

She looks up at me again. Her piercing eyes penetrate my own to the point that I swear she can see straight into my soul. I shake off the uncomfortable feeling it gives me and focus on fastening the buttons.

"They didn't... I mean. They did, but I'll be fine." She falls silent momentarily, trying to pull the jacket down to cover her bare legs. "You guys came in time before things could get worse," she tells me.

My eyes narrow as I peer at the fresh bruising on her throat and her face. My jaw ticks at the thought of what they did to her. As I fasten the last button, my hand brushes something wet on her skin.

When I pull my hand away, there's red coating my fingers.

She's covered. Too much blood. "Where are you hurt?" I ask her, reopening the jacket. I only open it enough to find the source of blood, but she grimaces.

"When I fought back, one of them managed to stab me. I don't think it's that deep, but I can't tell. The women there put gauze on it, but that was it."

She drops her gaze again, moving her hand where I can see a small patch of bloody gauze. I search for anything I can use and find a backpack on the floor by her feet.

I point to the pack. "Do you have anything in there I can use to put pressure on it? My sister is a nurse; she'll be able to help you when we get back."

"There should be clothing in that one." She points to a second backpack.

Ignoring her tentativeness, I bend down and open the bag, pulling out the first soft thing: a black shirt. Leaning forward, I push it against her wound. She flinches.

"I know it hurts." I press harder on her abdomen. "Talking may help distract you." I'm not great at small talk, but it might work for her.

"Did Ru make it home? Are they okay?" she asks softly.

The pain is instantaneous. Her harmless question is the same as if she shot me point blank in the chest. She might as well have.

Tears begin brimming her eyes again when I don't respond right away.

Schooling my features, I tell her what happened. "Sayuri was shot when they fled." I pause and try to shake off the swirl of rage and torment threatening to break free. "They stopped not far from where you were." I look away, her broken expression causing my own to slowly slip.

"I am so sorry, Ren." Her breath hiccups. "I tried. I tried so fucking hard to get them both out."

She's fighting back her tears as she glances away and blinks rapidly.

I wonder if I should blame her for Sayuri's death. A part of me wants to. If only to find someone else to blame other than myself.

My anger is simmering beneath the surface, ready to lash out regardless of who's at fault. Shit. I want to blame her, but I know it wasn't her. She's not the one who fucked up.

It's *my* fault. I'm to blame for this. She's only some random woman who helped them. If anything, her doing all she did says a lot about the type of person she is.

Me? I saved her, yeah, but it was easy. People would expect that from me, given my experience in the military. It doesn't make me a hero anymore. It's a job. I'm no brave little soldier who fought for what he believed in. Or the man seeking atonement.

Not anymore. That ship sailed a long time ago and at the cost of many lives.

I did it for Haru. He was so crushed that I couldn't handle it. I don't want him to feel any more loss than he's already feeling after knowing he lost Sayuri. I don't want the pain I experienced as a kid to be his reality, either.

But I also did it for Sayuri...

You did it in retaliation.

I shake that thought away and turn back to meet Dahlia's gaze. But her? She's just a woman, getting off a flight who decided to risk her own life to help strangers. It may have benefited us, but it was stupid of her to want to help.

Her compassion will be a liability. A weakness.

I won't stop to help every stranger we come across. I may not be a hero, but not being one will keep my family alive.

Look what being a hero did for her. It'll only get her or someone else killed.

I don't realize I'm staring until Matt clears his throat.

"We are making better time than before. Anyone on foot is giving us the distraction we need."

Her turquoise stare has me transfixed. I'm reluctant to look away, and I'm not sure why, but when I finally manage to, Matt's giving me a quizzical look. Shying away from his glare, I scope out the surrounding areas and hope we can get home soon. I could use a stiff drink and a day-long nap.

Chapter Ten

Dahlia

The pain flares back to life, and a small whimper escapes my lips. I dozed off despite my situation, but the jolt of the car braking must have woken me. Or maybe it was the combination of pain burning hot in my side and the ache in my burnt-out muscles. I wonder how long we have been driving.

There are sounds of gunfire in the background, but my brain is too foggy to understand why. A warm hand gently brushes my hair out of my face in a soothing motion as someone shushes me, telling me to go back to sleep. Still half-conscious, I doze back to a semi-painless state and ignore the world and its troubles for a little bit longer.

When I wake again, it takes longer for me to make out where I am. This time, I realize I'm not only lying down, but I'm lying on someone's lap. Embarrassment and fear causes me to jolt up only to gasp at the now severe, hot pain in my whole abdomen.

"Hey, it's okay; you need to take it slow," a soft voice says above me. "Matt, can you grab Hana?" I hear them saying, followed by the slamming of a car door. I'm fading back out of consciousness, allowing the exhaustion to take me under again.

I no longer feel the movement of the car, only the warmth of something soft beneath me. Fluttering my eyes open, I'm blinded by bright sunlight and a headache strong enough to knock out a professional fighter. Grumbling, I shield my eyes with my hand but try to keep them open.

Once my vision adjusts, I take in the unfamiliar room around me. The natural light streaming from the large window reflects off the smokey taupe-painted walls and illuminates the whole space.

There are no personal effects littering the room besides the matching natural wood furniture. No personal photos, only a scenic copy of the painting, *The Red Road* filling an empty space on the wall similar to the galleries I used to enjoy browsing.

A guest bedroom, I bet.

Trying to sit up, I'm immediately reminded why I'm in bed to begin with. My whole body is sore, and my abdomen is on fire. Groaning, I pull myself up and lean against the headboard.

A soft knock sounds before the door across the room opens. A beautiful woman walks in carrying a stethoscope and what might be a blood pressure monitor. She's wearing a beige long-sleeve sweater tucked into a pleated skirt, accentuating her long legs. Her wavy, dark brown hair cascades over her shoulders, curtaining russet-brown eyes and delicate features. She smiles softly as she strides up to the bed and sits at the end.

"How are you feeling?" She adjusts the blankets around my ankles that had twisted up. "I did the best I could in cleaning and stitching that wound of yours, but unfortunately, I don't have much for bruises. I put a salve on them to help with the discomfort, but it may be a while before they fade completely. The good news is that the wound wasn't as bad as it looked. It will heal in no time."

I hesitate for a moment before telling her the truth. "Honestly, everything hurts like a bitch," I croak. My voice is hoarse, and my throat hurts even more now that I'm speaking. *Those jerks did a number on me.* My stomach churns at the reminder.

She chuckles in response and stands. Her hand gestures to the stethoscope, and when I tell her it's okay, she begins listening to my heart. "It's been a while since I've given you some pain meds; I don't doubt you're feeling it."

She helps me shift forward so she can listen to my lungs. The cool metal seeps through my shirt, causing goosebumps to break out on my arms. "Take a few deep breaths for me," she says and takes dramatic inhales and exhales as an example. "I don't have any supplies here to give an IV drip, so I needed to wait for you to wake up to administer more. My name is Hana, by the way. I am Reiji and Ren's sister. It's a pleasure to meet you."

Her smile is blinding, and she extends her hand for me to shake. I can't help but smile awkwardly in return. She's so energetic, exuding joy. Considering the nightmare I ended up starring in, a little positive energy feels good.

"Dahlia," I say quietly, ignoring the throbbing in my throat. "I can't express how thankful I am for your help. I won't lie, though. I could definitely go for something to take the edge off."

She wastes no time putting the blood pressure cuff on my left arm and turning it on. "I don't blame you. You've been out for over twenty-four hours now. I didn't want to disturb you, but I think you were having some bad dreams." Her eyes track the monitor as she talks. The cuff tightens and holds for a brief second until it slowly releases pressure. "I almost woke you, but Ren told me to let you sleep. We figured all the stuff you saw was finding its way into your dreams, but any rest is good right now.

"I am so sorry you had to go through all this. Especially those men hurting you. When I first saw you in the car, my heart broke to see that someone could do that to another person. Ren was reluctant to let you go; he was afraid you'd hurt yourself even more if we moved you. I was actually surprised he care—" She abruptly stops as she meets my eyes. She takes the cuff off, appearing satisfied with my vitals. "Oh! I am so sorry. I never know when to shut up. Usually, someone tells me by now. Don't be so nice; otherwise, I will never leave your ear alone. I'll go get those meds before I forget."

She rushes out, leaving me to stare after her in utter bewilderment.

I chuckle a little but grimace at the pain. I think about what she said about Ru's uncle, Ren. My cheeks warm as I recall the car ride. Feeling slightly embarrassed, I slowly move myself to lie down on my back.

I was out for a day. *Damn.* It's a testament to how exhausted I was by falling asleep so quickly amongst strangers. I don't remember too much, but I do remember someone having me swallow something at some point. There's also a vague memory of someone gently stroking my hair and whispering to me to sleep.

My cheeks are so flushed now from the flashes of memory that when Hana walks back in, her face morphs into concern.

She places a bottle of water and a pill on the nightstand and puts the back of her hand against my forehead. "Hmm. Are you okay? You look like you just ate the world's spiciest chili pepper."

Logically, I understand that she can't read my thoughts, but that doesn't stop the embarrassment that blossoms from the memory. "No, I'm fine, other than the pain."

Hana grabs the pill and water, handing them to me in response. "Hopefully, that will help. I wanted to check that you don't have any allergies to medications, correct?" she asks me. "I asked when you got here, but you were barely lucid. I just want to be sure."

With a shake of my head, she smiles and gives me a pleased hum. I take the medication and down half the water bottle, not realizing how thirsty I am, and relish the coolness against my raw throat. I set the water bottle back onto the nightstand and think about what I should ask first, like where I was or when I would be in better shape to leave. I wonder if whatever had been spreading was contained.

I need to try to call Meg again. *Shit.* I hope she's okay.

I'm about to ask if my stuff is still in the car, but Hana speaks up first. "If you are feeling up to it, I can help you shower. I did the best I could to clean you up, but you're still covered in dried blood. I wrapped your wound and can tape some cellophane over it to keep it dry while you bathe." She doesn't wait for me to respond. Instead, she disappears behind the bathroom door and turns the shower faucet on.

I guess it really wasn't a question. Although I need to call Meg and start figuring out my plan, I could use a shower… and brush my teeth. My hair feels gross, and my body itches from the dried blood flaking off my skin as I move. Even without a mirror, I can tell my normally curly, long hair looks more like a bird's nest. I shudder, thinking how nasty I must look as I ease my way up to a sitting position.

Hana comes back inside the room and helps me out of bed. She's gentle when she wraps one arm around my waist and under my arm to support me while we walk to the bathroom. As we step inside, I notice that all I'm wearing is a man's t-shirt. "Did you change me? Wait. Never mind. That's a dumb question," I mumble. I was clad in only my undergarments when they found me back at the Urgent Care facility, and I don't want to be reminded that everyone here most likely saw me that way.

Her gaze is thoughtful when she regards me. "You don't need to tell me anything but… if you need, I can see about getting a Plan B pill if it's needed." She directs me to the closed toilet seat lid and helps me sit down.

My body involuntarily shutters at her words. "I was stripped and searched for any weapons and…" I trail off, thinking about what happened. What *could* have happened. I'd already lost my flannel and shirt when they cut it off, but they returned to strip me of my jeans and sneakers as well. The man who had the honors groped me while 'searching' but then left me alone.

Hana's mouth opens as if she'll say something, but I continue. I'm not sure why. Maybe because her presence is comforting or maybe because I just need to say it out loud to validate the situation… or maybe it's both. "I overheard the man who had strip-searched me arguing with a man who called himself Leon."

Her shoulders stiffen at the mention of Leon's name, but she quickly leans against the bathroom sink to cover her reaction. *Does she know him?*

Shoving that thought aside for now, I continue. "I think he was the boss. He told the man that he was going to take someone home before he'd be back." I cringe when I notice the dried blood underneath my thumbnail. Nausea churns in my belly at the thought of what I had to do.

Hana's hand finds my shoulder. "You don't need to continue if it makes you uncomfortable. It's okay, really."

I stop picking at my bloody nails and drop my hands in my lap, but I don't look up. "No. It's fine. I just—" My breath hitches. "I just need to get it out, I think."

She removes her hand from my shoulder and leans back against the counter. I feel her gaze on me, patiently waiting, but she doesn't push or demand answers. Her silence is reassuring and gives me the confidence to keep talking.

"Leon told the other man to leave me alone. He just wanted to be sure I didn't escape or bleed out. When he left, and no one came back in, I thought they were going to listen." My vision blurs, and I squeeze my eyes shut to stop the tears from falling. "But after a while, the man who searched me came back..." A tear manages to slip past my defenses. His intent had been clear, silently announced by the erection that grew in his jeans.

"He smacked me hard before he groped me and—" I try to get more words out, but they lodge in my throat. How do I admit that I hadn't been able to do anything? I screamed and fought as best I could, but my fight had been laughable. My body had been completely spent and bruised.

"It's the end of the world; what the fuck do I care about what Leon tells me anymore?" he had told me. When he had been done toying with me, he unzipped his jeans and fondled himself.

I run my hands through my matted hair. It had felt like a bad memory. Another reminder of the past.

No. Not just a reminder but a fucking sick joke. To have to go through something so horrific for a second time?

Despite swallowing to fight back the persistent nausea, it doesn't abate. I take in another deep breath, desperate to just get this out so I can move on. "After he told me he didn't care what his boss said anymore, he had told me, 'We are all going to die anyway. Either from the bite of a zombie or the bite of a bullet.'" I snort. "Thank fuck he hit that one on the mark."

We had both been taken by surprise when the door opened. At first, I thought his friends were coming to join, but thankfully, I was wrong. He was too slow to react before he was shot in the head.

Bit by a bullet.

I already knew there were sick people in the world, but with what's happening outside, I'm more and more afraid of people showing their true colors. I honestly have no idea how I will navigate this on my own if it worsens.

I don't have much of a choice, though.

Hana speaks up, tearing me from my thoughts. "You know nothing about what happened is your doing right?"

Her question hits a raw nerve. "I know," I whisper and look up into her eyes for the first time since we came into the bathroom. I know this time wasn't my fault, but that can't be said for the last time I found myself in a similar situation. At least this time I was successful in protecting someone. I have no regrets for throwing myself to the wolves to protect the kid.

"Thank you for listening." My cheeks heat, but I continue, ready to change the subject. "Anyway, I think I'm ready to shower." I offer a weak, tired smile.

She returns my smile but only brighter, understanding I wish to move on. "The shower is a walk-in, thankfully. Would you like me to help, or would you like some privacy?"

I do a quick mental check of my body and move a bit. I'm incredibly sore, but I think I can manage most of it. "I may need help with my hair, but I can wash everything else, I think."

She helps wrap my bandage in plastic and waits for me to step under the spray in the shower. When I'm ready, she helps rinse my hair with the detachable head and lathers my scalp with shampoo. After she rinses, she washes a second time to get all the blood and grime out before grabbing the conditioner and working it through the ends of my hair.

Once she's done helping me rinse my hair, she gives me a few moments alone to wash and announces she's going to change the sheets.

The warm water feels heavenly, but I don't want to dwell on the memories of the past few days. So, I wash as quickly as my stiff body allows while trying not to think too hard. Once I'm done, I step out and wrap the towel around myself.

Walking into the bedroom, I stop short. There by the door is Ren, leaning his back against the frame. He doesn't seem to notice me right away as he types something into his phone, but as soon as I take a step, I stub my toe on the nightstand. "Ouch!"

He straightens quickly as if there's a threat, but when he sees me, he stops from coming into the room.

If I had to guess his expression, he seems slightly annoyed. He's not too broad and bulky, but as he stands there, he seems to be taking up the whole doorway. It's a little intimidating. I wouldn't be surprised if people are a little afraid of him. It's not so much his size but how he carries himself. Like danger on a stick.

He's much taller than I am, at least a foot taller, and through his gray t-shirt, I can see that it's not just his arms that are muscular. The outline of his pecs peek through the shirt, and his arms are straining slightly on the sleeves. Both arms are covered in tattoos and devoid of his warm skin tone; both sleeves are cut off at his wrists. He must have paid big bucks for those. They are stunning from what I can tell at a distance. On his left arm, there are deep reds and other dark colors that blend with black to create a multitude of designs; a large portion of it appears to be scales, among other things. In contrast, his right arm is covered in black and grey designs.

He clears his throat, and in horror, embarrassment, or maybe both, I realize I am staring at him.

More like ogling.

Oh lord, help me, but he's gorgeous. He may just be another cocky veteran, but he's something to look at, that's for sure. I pull my eyes away from his tattoo-clad arms and up at his face.

His dark hair is cut close to his head at the sides, while the top is a little longer and slicked back. There's about a day's worth of scruff on his jawline. Combined with his expression, it only causes him to appear more intimidating.

"Just wanted to check on how you're feeling," he says. His voice is low and rough but still manages to sound like whiskey and honey all at the same time. Shit, even his voice is sexy. I wonder if he can tell my face is three shades of red right now.

His eyes drift down my frame, landing on where the towel covers my wound. His expression is still unreadable. The irritation I thought I saw earlier is no longer there, but I have no idea what he's thinking. My heart picks up its pace the longer his eyes linger.

Is he taking my measure, or is he checking me out? Normally, my lack of clothing would make it obvious, but with him, I can't tell. I know I shouldn't care, but I want to know. His gaze is like fire dancing across my skin, yet a chill rakes down my spine from his attention.

Before I can say anything, Hana walks in and looks at us both before shoving her brother, breaking his attention from me. "Ren. What the hell! You couldn't wait until I told you she was decent?"

He briefly looks over at her before he glances back at me with the same neutral expression. He walks out without saying anything or sparing another glance, leaving me with unanswered questions and an awkwardness replacing the heat from moments before.

Man of few words, I see.

Get a grip. Of course, he's a man of few words. From my experience around my father's friends, many of them were like that. The surety of themselves. The inability to express real feelings. Barking commands and expecting everyone to fall in line.

I can't help the eye roll when I finally get my racing pulse under control.

Hana approaches, carrying my backpack and a set of sheets into the room.

"I'm sorry. I told him you were showering. I didn't expect the idiot to come in while you were still getting cleaned up." She places the backpack on the nightstand. "Hopefully, you have clothes in here. And oh! I found this, too." My phone slips out of her palm and onto the nightstand.

It's a relief to know my phone made it. I slowly stand up before grabbing underwear, a bra, a pair of dark gray sweats, and a black V-neck t-shirt. I find a pair of socks, too, since the room's a little chilly. Hana ends up helping me put on my clothing before quickly changing the sheets on the bed, revealing nasty blood stains. I can't help but feel guilty. "Thank you, Hana," I say as I sit on the edge of the bed once she finishes.

"Of course. You not only saved my nephew twice, I might add, but you also kept him alive and brought him home to us. I don't know what we would have done if we had never found him or if he hadn't made it." Her smile falters, and her eyes mist slightly.

Sayuri.

Guilt pierces my heart. There must have been more I could have done to prevent what happened.

"I am so sorry about Sayuri. I wish I could have gotten her home."

"Yeah." She sighs. "I wish my brother would have taken his head out of his ass and brought me. Maybe I could have helped…" She pauses, a hint of anger slipping into her tone. "Well, you did your best to keep them both safe."

Her hand comes up, brushing hair behind her ear as she stares out the window. She's trying not to cry. The urge to hug her is strong, to offer her comfort, but I don't move. I don't know how well it would be received.

"You think you're up for a little grub?" she asks, her smile returning.

As she mentions it, it's like my body remembers how hungry I actually am. I'm not even sure when the last time I ate was. "I could probably eat an entire house at this point." I laugh. "But I should try to call my friend first."

There is understanding in her gaze, but she doesn't relent. "Let's get you something to eat, and then you can call them, yeah? You need to eat and get some rest, too. I promise it'll be a quick early dinner."

Dinner? What the hell time is it? I glance over to the window that was so bright before to find that the sun is starting to set.

Hana doesn't wait around for me. Instead, she starts walking out of the room and down the hall, and I follow.

The décor, similar to the room we vacated, is all very simple with natural wood or earth tones. The house reminds me of a craftsman-style home. More art is scattered throughout the space. All copies of well-known artists—at least, I think, they are copies since most of these are supposed to be in museums. Some look like the real thing at closer inspection, which must have cost a pretty penny even for copies. I can't help but be impressed. I rarely get to go to museums or galleries anymore, but I have always enjoyed art. One piece stands out to me as we pass by, but I'm too nervous to stop and stare.

We walk into a huge chef's kitchen, and I'm completely stunned at how beautiful this room is. Before I can truly admire the space, multiple voices behind us make me glance over my shoulder.

The kitchen has an open floor plan with a family room where a large group of people are conversing. A few are also standing around in the kitchen.

"Got any preferences for sandwiches?" Hana asks me, pulling my attention back to her.

"Anything is fine, thank you." My stomach growls loudly at the mention of food.

She points to the kitchen island and barstool, so I sit down while she makes our dinner.

Resting my elbow on the granite and my face in my palm, I listen to the conversation.

"—that crazy? I mean, that is a long trip. Where will we find somewhere safe to board a plane?" a man asks. He's standing in between Ren and a man who looks like he may be his brother.

"It may be, Don. But we don't have much of a choice. Don't forget my wife is still back home," says the one I presume to be Ren's brother.

"You're right. Apologies, Reiji-sama."

Hana places a plate in front of me and sits beside me. Leaning close to my ear, she whispers, "That is my brother Reiji. The other one is Don. He works for my brother but just moved here. I forgot they were going to have a meeting."

"Oh," I say before I take a bite of the sandwich. The taste barely registers while I focus on their conversation.

"I've been in contact with Emi and our uncle. They were able to block off the Seikan Tunnel before things spread to the island. For now, it's safe," Reiji says to the group.

Seikan tunnel? My brows wrinkle at that.

I glance around at all the faces to see if any of them are following. A few women and children are lounging about, listening intently. If I had to guess, they all look scared. The men, on the other hand, are taking this in stride.

"You guys know someone who can fly here?" a blonde man in the corner asks.

My eyes travel back to Reiji, but they stop on Ren. He's looking down at the floor, and his body seems tense.

"Yes, we have a… family member who's a pilot," Reiji says. "I'll need your help getting our group organized," he tells his brother. "We'll need to work together for this to work. I will look into some locations in the meantime, but for now, I want to have the rest of our plan solid."

Ren's head comes up. His eyes briefly catch mine before he clenches his jaw and refocuses on his brother. "Sure."

"Last thing," Reiji calls to the group.

As he tells us what he knows about the attacks, the weight on my chest only gets heavier.

He mentions that Japan was slower to be hit, but no country is clear from what he's heard. "Just before we lost the news coverage, some government officials spoke up, admitting that we are all under attack, but it's unknown as to what and who is attacking us," he says.

I can't help but wring my hands as I take it all in.

From what it sounds like, some countries feared another epidemic after the last pandemic and, after limiting and cutting all travel off as soon as word got out, are faring better than others. All initial attacks started at airports or other places of travel. Although the US hasn't been forthcoming about what is happening, other countries appear to have been more informed.

"This shit is so crazy," Hana whispers to me as Reiji keeps talking.

I hum in agreement as I chew my food. "It's surreal, that's for sure."

Surreal doesn't feel like the right word. It's all impossible… Yet here we are in the middle of it.

"They are straight-up zombies. They bite, eat you, and spread. That sounds like a zombie to me," the man with a low bun says. His warm, bronze skin appears soft gold in the dim living room lights. He was the one who carried me out of the building where they found me, but I haven't spoken to him yet.

The blonde laughs. "You just described my last date." A few of the other guys laugh.

I roll my eyes while Hana snorts.

Once his laughter calms, the blonde speaks up again. "But I told you that already. We've all been either thinking it or mentioned it at one point. It's a fucking horror movie."

Instead of laughing with the others, Ren firmly speaks up. "That may be the case, but they're different than you'd expect. Some are fast and loud, while the others are slow but just as dangerous." His voice is how I remember it being over the phone, but even more stern as he addresses everyone.

One of the guys snickers and mumbles something I can't catch, but Ren's cold glare wipes their smiles off their faces.

"Ren, I want the groups settled. Now would be best while we are all together," Reiji says to his brother. Or more like commands.

I don't know how I can tell, but Ren doesn't want to. It seems like he doesn't even want to be here in this room because his body posture is all stiff, and his jaw has been clenched the whole meeting.

"Sure. I need you all to line up," he demands. His own command should be off-putting. Unattractive. But something about the power behind his voice only makes him more attractive.

Damn. I'm going to ignore the way that had a shiver run through me. *Nope.* That wasn't hot. Men who take charge are assholes.

Drop it, Dahl.

"I'll ask you all questions and place everyone in groups. They will rotate based on when we need to follow through with a task. Anyone not willing or unable will be with the children," Ren says with the same commanding tone. He doesn't even have to raise his voice. There's just something in his tone that calls to follow.

Damn. Definitely power.

Yet, his brother is in charge. I wonder why.

"We will start with the acting CO and XO, which is Reiji." Ren points to his brother. "Then myself."

"The fuck is an XO?" one of the men asks.

Ren's features harden, almost menacing, when he focuses on the guy who spoke. "What's your name?" he asks.

"Tyler," the man responds. His shoulders slouch a little at the intensity of Ren's glare, and I swear Ren's eyes darken.

"Ask your questions when I'm done. But to answer you in simple terms, my brother will be in charge as you'd expect, while I will be his second." He directs his attention back to everyone else. "Recon and runners will help scout or deliver messages should we need them to."

Tyler looks like he's about to ask another question when Don catches his eye and peers at him.

"Fire-watch will be guard duty. Then we have supply runners and child duty." Ren describes each group in detail and how they may need to help out in different areas if told. He then starts sorting everyone by their response to his questions.

Since I don't need to be here for this, I finish my sandwich and prepare to excuse myself. I need to try to get a hold of Meg and figure out what the hell I'm going to do. Although, as my eyes continue to find Ren, I wonder what it would be like to stay with them. It *would* be safer in numbers. There's also something about Ren that gives me the feeling he would be safe to be with.

But then I'd never get my chance to see Meg. And by the sounds of the duties these guys expect from everyone, I don't think I can handle that. I wouldn't be a help to them. Shit, I'd probably get them killed. What the hell can I offer them?

These guys are ex-military. At least some of them are. The ones that aren't, or at least I don't think are, don't seem incapable. I don't know what it is about the group that I find unusual, but something about them hints at some experience in violence. Maybe the way they are all taking this in a calm, collected manner. Or maybe it's the weapons they have holstered beneath their belts or shirts like it's normal to be open-carrying in California.

I know I can handle myself sometimes, but not like this.

"You know, if you took a picture, you could continue to stare without it being so obvious." Hana's chuckle startles me.

She has a cheeky grin while wagging her eyebrows. I'm confused until I turn around and find Ren staring back at me.

Holy shit. I was staring, wasn't I?

With cheeks reddening, I turn back to Hana. "Excuse me. I think I'm going to rest and try to call my friend. Thank you again." I go to pick up the plate, but Hana waves me off.

"A-huh." She smirks. "I see the way you're looking at him," she whispers.

I choke on air as I try to figure out what to say, but she interrupts me before I begin. "It's okay. I mean, it just gives me hope for my sad little brother." She chuckles. "Now, go get some sleep." She winks at me, her smile grows, and a mischievous glint appears in her eyes. "Goodnight, Dahl!"

I turn around and retreat as quickly as my battered body allows, my face feeling as red as my hair. Somehow, Hana, being as observant as she is, feels dangerous. Dangerous that she'll read me like an open book.

Thankfully, I'll be leaving soon. Even if that causes a pang of longing and loss with the thought, it's the best thing I can do.

Right?

<u>COA</u>

<u>ADULTS:</u>

HANA, REIJI, MYSELF, DAHLIA?? MATT, DIRK, James, Juan, CHRIS, MARIA, DON, KEI, JAKE, ANN, JEN, SUSAN, MICHAEL, TOBI, YUNA, BEN, IAN, KEN, TYLER

<u>CHILDREN:</u>

HARUTO, LIZZY, RACHEL, TOMMY, LUIS, LAYLA, LINA

<u>*GROUP LEADERS:*</u>   (REIJI) ↘
(1ST/ACTING CO)

MYSELF ⇒ (2ND/ACTING XO)
HANA, JUAN

<u>RECON/RUNNERS:</u>

*JUAN, MATT, JAMES, DIRK

<u>FIRE-WATCH:</u>

*MYSELF, *JUAN, MATT, JAMES, DIRK, JAKE, TOBI, CHRIS, KEN, DON

<u>SUPPLY RUNNERS:</u>

*MYSELF, *JUAN, MATT, JAMES, DIRK, JAKE, SUSAN, IAN, TYLER, KEI, CHRIS, KEN, MICHAEL, TOBI, DAHLIA??

<u>KID WATCH</u>

*HANA, *JUAN, DON, JEN, MARIA, YUNA, ANN, MATT, DAHLIA??

-GROUP LEADERS WILL BE ON ROTATION.
-GROUP MEMBERS WILL BE MOVED WHERE NEEDED.

**KEEP HANA ON HARU.

<u>F/U W/ REI.</u> → DAHLIA TO STAY??? UNKNOWN

CHAPTER ELEVEN

I've been trying to fall asleep for over an hour. It's all I want to do right now, but it keeps eluding me.

My mind won't calm down enough to allow me to fall asleep. So, instead of fighting it for another hour, I grab my sketchbook and prop myself up in bed. Nothing specific comes to mind, so I start drawing a set of eyes. The meeting of graphite and paper allows my mind to slip into complete silence.

Unfortunately, it doesn't last. Although it's calming my nerves, it's doing nothing for the whirlwind of thoughts.

After the meeting, I wrote out a physical list categorizing everyone into the groups I came up with. Knowing everyone would work together should have helped calm some of our worries. Instead, it's made me even more stressed because I need to help my brother keep thirty people in line, including the seven children.

To make matters worse, my thoughts keep circling back to Dahlia. They're a conflicted mess.

My brother and I can't afford to take on even one more person, but I can't help but feel obligated to keep her with us. To keep her safe.

She helped Haru, and I don't know if we can ever repay her for that. Regardless of my thoughts on her kindness, she sacrificed her safety and life to ensure he had a chance. Then, there was something about the vulnerability she exhibited when we found her. She was injured and helpless, but once she knew who I was, she gave me her full trust, even if she didn't realize it. She didn't shy away from me, even leaned on me when she fell asleep, and that type of trust is rare for me. Mixed with the knowledge of what she's done for Haru, it's affected a part of me I didn't know existed.

I rub the back of my neck before returning to the small details in the right eye on the paper. There are no blending sticks near the bed, so I use my finger to blend in where I focus on shading the eyelid.

It's like a never-ending storm of unknowns and uncertainties as I try to push Dahlia from my thoughts and focus on the more important issues.

My brother hadn't disclosed any good news. In the past twenty-four hours since getting back, whatever is causing people to become violent has spread indefinitely. Nowhere is safe here in California. The news channels are stuck on emergency broadcasting.

As I start filling in the bridge of the nose, my mind calms again. The sound of the pencil against the textured paper itself is like a comforting balm. I pull my hand back to take in the whole piece so far, but something about it only irritates me further.

Giving up, I put my sketchbook on my lap and lean over to grab my cellphone on the nightstand. Unplugging it, I swipe to unlock the screen, but there are no new notifications. I place the phone on the bed and move over to the closet, where I pull out some clothes and a backpack.

I haven't heard back from anyone I've tried to reach out to for more information, and Ryan never responded when I tried calling again.

A firm knock sounds before my brother strides into the room. Since I've been back, I've been able to avoid his lecture, partially because he is relieved his son is home and partially because the ever-mounting tasks piling up with the arrival of his men and their families.

He scowls at me without saying a word. Instead, he crosses his arms and leans against the wall.

Sighing, I walk past him to my closet and grab another couple of shirts to fold. "Might as well get it over with," I tell him. I place my clothing on the bed before I turn to him.

His face doesn't give anything away as he watches me. It takes him a moment before he finally says, "I'm still trying to understand what the hell you were thinking, Ren."

My brows go up. I don't know why I'm surprised he's still pissed. I was expecting it, after all.

"No, I haven't forgotten," he says in response to my expression.

I run my hand through my hair and sit on the edge of the bed. "Look, Reiji, I know I fucked up. I know I should have called immediately. I underestimated the situation, but I also needed to make sure Hana was safe here alone."

"That's not an excuse. That's my son. Sayuri-san is dead, Ren, while my *son* was almost kidnapped. It's only thanks to a stranger that he wasn't. You should have contacted me as soon as Sayuri-san called you. I would have left to go get them right then and there."

Rei is normally cool and collected, but his tone is pure ice. If it were anyone else, they wouldn't notice his jaw clenching or the menace behind his glare. But I'm not anyone else. Even after living apart for so many years, I know my brother better than anyone.

"I know," I tell him. There isn't much else to say. I know I fucked up. I know it's my fault, but I'm sure my own guilt will be punishment enough. I already relive our mother's death over and over in my sleep; this will only add to the growing list of things that haunt me.

"You know? That's it?" he seethes, uncrossing his arms and stepping up to me.

"What do you expect me to say, Rei? I'm sorry? You don't think I already know how badly I fucked up? I care about that kid, too. I cared about Sayuri-san. I made a choice. There isn't anything I can do about it now."

He goes to say something else but is interrupted by a knock. We both turn toward Hana as she walks in. She has a huge smile on her face, and I can't help but wonder what has her in such a good mood. Whatever it is, I wish I had it. Sometimes, I'm curious as to how she smiles so brightly when I know for a fact she's hurting inside.

When she takes us in, though, her smile falters. "Whoa, now. What I miss?"

"It's nothing, Hana. What's up?" I say, ignoring the glare my brother directs at me. Knowing him, he'll find me later to finish our conversation.

She glances between us before her face transforms into a look that tells me she's planning something I may not like. If I do or not, she'll follow through regardless.

"I was wondering if we could talk about Dahlia," she says.

"Sure. What about her?" I ask.

Rei now directs his attention to Hana, one brow raised in interest as if he wasn't ready to throttle his only brother.

Her eyes catch onto something on the bed, and her smile grows even larger. "Well, I wanted you to ask her to stay with us." She raises her hand as if to stop me from speaking up. "I know we were going to let her anyway until she's healed, but I think it would be good to have the extra hands. Plus, she has the vehicle to fit more of our rag-tag group in."

I go to interrupt her, but she keeps talking.

"Lastly! Our little nephew has been trying to sneak in there to sit in her room all day when she's resting. It's taking a lot of ice cream to keep him out. He really took to the poor girl. And I think she would be…" Her brows furrow. "I mean you…" She trails off as if she's unsure if she should say something or not, which is odd. She usually has no problem speaking what's on her mind. I peer at her curiously, waiting for her to continue, but she waves her hand as if brushing the thought away.

"Never mind. Anyway, I like her, and I think it would be a benefit to have someone else around who can help us keep this group in order. We don't know a ton about her, but from what Haru has divulged, she seems like she may be a great addition to the family—I mean, group," she chuckles.

Our brother waits for Hana to finish, interested in the conversation.

I turn back to my clothes and start folding them while my sister keeps talking.

"Plus… I may or may not have snooped in her bag and her phone…"

That got my attention. My brows practically fly off my face.

"Don't give me that look."

I can't help but scoff.

"Why would you do that?" Rei asks her.

She startles, almost as if she forgot he was standing there. "I was curious." She shrugs. "Haru mentioned her dad having been in the military. But before her phone died, I found a text to her boss. It wasn't hard to find out where she works. After going back through her texts aways, I found some juicy stuff. She was planning to apply at the LAPD. There were also some photos of her target practicing with who I think was her dad," she says while giving me a sly look.

Jesus. I pinch the bridge of my nose, taking a deep breath. Why am I not surprised my sister would fucking snoop?

"Please tell me how it's a good idea then?" I turn to Rei. "Do you believe this?"

He rubs his chin in contemplation. "I don't have an issue with it. I think she'll be a good addition. Not to mention, we're in her debt for Haruto." Of course, he agrees.

"Seriously?" I scoff. "She's a liability."

Rei snorts at that. "And what makes you think that?"

"How the hell is she a liability? Because she's injured? It wasn't that bad," Hana interjects.

They can't be serious. "Her kindness. Her playing hero is going to get one of us killed. It could get Haru killed!" I exclaim.

"That's enough, Ren," Reiji says firmly.

I respond with a glare of my own.

"Look, we need people who won't be terrified in this situation. People with a clear head. She's survived this long already. I know it's kind of a bold assumption that she is all these things, but still." Hana throws her hands up as if to make her point and plops herself down in the chair in the corner.

"You know I'm right. Or think of it like this—you'll need someone else you can depend on when I can't be your extra pair of hands. As much as I want to help you guys with what comes next, I have a feeling I'm going to be the only medically experienced person we may come across for a while. Meaning I'm valuable right now. You'll need someone else to help. I'll most likely be the furthest away from trouble," she says as if she has no doubt I would agree, a little humor mixed with her seriousness implying she's probably full of shit.

Yeah, Dahlia survived this long, but look where we found her. I get up and start pacing, running my fingers through my hair.

"Would you actually leave her behind? After everything?" Hana says softly, all humor gone.

If I'm going to be honest with myself, whether I like it or not, I don't want to leave her on her own, either. I just can't figure out for the life of me why. That's what's pissing me off.

I owe her one, yeah, but there's something else I can't put my finger on. Maybe it was because of those unexpected feelings that reared their head earlier. Or maybe it is that I feel indebted to her. Who knows? I certainly fucking don't.

All I know is that she's a complication I don't want or need. When I get down to the grit of it, I don't want to be responsible for anyone other than my family. How can I keep them safe if my focus is split?

Sighing and running my hands over my face, I give in. "Whatever, it's Rei's call anyway. I don't know if she's willing to stay with us either. We don't know if she has anyone waiting for her somewhere." I frown at the idea. "Have you asked if she has any family or anyone she was trying to get back to?"

Her brows wrinkle in thought. "Mm-hmm. I don't know. She mentioned calling a friend, but that's it. Maybe you can talk to her."

Why the hell would I need to talk to her? I already have a lot I need to worry about, and we also need to have another group meeting on top of everything else.

"Hana, you already know we're going to have a list of shit to take care of. We have a couple of days tops before the grids go down, but even before that happens, we need to prepare for those things showing up here. We can't stay here long. My house isn't prepared for this type of emergency. I planned for a blackout, not Armageddon." I chuckle despite it lacking humor.

She snorts, rolling her eyes as if she doesn't believe me.

"I don't have solar panels that can light the house, just a tiny generator that wouldn't last more than a day, and I don't have a well or anything that could sustain us long enough with water. I need to start getting us ready to leave." I raise my hand to stop her when she goes to argue.

"He's right, Hana. I need his help. Talk with her, ask her if she'd want to travel with us," Rei steps in.

She noticeably deflates and lets out a harsh sigh. "Fine, I'll talk to her," she says.

Good. The woman isn't my responsibility, no matter how conflicted she makes me feel. If Hana wants a new friend or genuinely believes she can be of help, she can deal with it.

With that, Hana goes to leave, but Reiji stays firmly in his spot.

Great. He wants to finish hashing this out now.

"You know what, Rei, I forgot to mention Haru was looking for you," our sister says.

Rei's jaw noticeably ticks as he walks out.

"You're welcome," Hana whispers before also leaving.

Once they are both gone, I lie down and abandon my backpack and sketchbook.

I hope sleep finally finds me.

'Ren! Wake up, sweetie. Ren, we need to go, hurry, wake up!'

My eyes flutter open to see my mother standing over me in her cherry blossom pink nightgown. It was a gift I got her for her birthday a few days ago.

'Ren. Hurry!'

Why is she telling me to get up? Is it time for school already? A loud crash in the other room has me looking towards the door. Another crash and then the door is thrown open. My mother shoves me behind her.

'Ren, you need to leave. Go out the other door. Now!'

A flash, and then my mother is on the floor. Blood covers the room. So much blood. Another flash, and there's a man above me, grabbing me by the throat.

'Ren.... It's okay... Ren... Wake up... Ren!'

It's a different voice this time. It's faintly familiar.

'You need to stop Ren. Ren!' A third voice screams.

It takes me a moment to recognize my surroundings as my mind clears and a second longer to register that I'm being held in a headlock. My right arm is being restrained tightly against someone's chest. My breathing is harsh while sweat beads my brows as if I have finished running rather than falling asleep.

Residual fogginess clears, and I finally recognize why I'm being detained. In the hand being held is my P226, the SIG-Sauer I normally keep near the bed.

Across the room, Hana is crouched down, partially obscured with the bed between us. She's talking to someone, but I can't see who it is while her body blocks them from view. Her eyes meet mine over her shoulder, and the realization of what happened hits me. And I had been sleeping through the whole thing.

Fuck.

Hopefully, Haruto hadn't come in here. Everyone knows to leave me alone if they hear I'm having a nightmare. I never intentionally hurt someone in my sleep, but if I'm beginning to have a night terror and someone tries to touch me, my body reacts as if I'm fighting my dream itself.

I remember the forced therapy session I needed to take. The therapist talked about post-traumatic stress disorder and some of the symptoms. The skills I have learned to react first and question later have carried their way into my subconscious, mixing with my horrid thoughts, creating a nasty cocktail of reflexes. It's like I'm locked in my head with immersive memories while my body responds to its perceived threat.

Night terrors and severe flashbacks are nasty for anyone, but it's dangerous when you have the experience and training that I have. Not only that, but there is a slew of other longer-lasting effects I try not to acknowledge.

If I hadn't decided to leave the service, they would have eventually sent me home without a choice. As soon as it started to interfere with my work, I would've been discharged. With how it progressed, it may have happened a lot sooner than I would have thought.

"Fuck, Ren." Rei lets go of my neck. "Why the hell are you sleeping with goddamn guns near your bed? You could have killed someone. What if Haruto came in here."

He's right. I don't lock all my weapons up since I live alone, and Haru knows to stay away from them and my room, but it shouldn't matter. Reiji always has weapons on him. He even has them near his own bed at night, but he and Hana both know what I've been going through despite my stance on not talking about it.

Not to mention my negligence when it comes to gun safety, but I can't think about that right now.

"Fuck," I mumble. I'm a fucking idiot. I move to step forward but stop short; the tell of her bright red hair peeks into view from behind my sister.

A part of me wants to ask if she's okay; another part wants to ask why the hell she was in my room. But mostly, I'm confused at the feelings of guilt and something else I can't name.

Shit. Well, if she wasn't afraid of me before, she certainly is now. Her head is down, so I can't tell what she's feeling.

Still unsure of what to do, I force myself to walk over and crouch in front of her. Hana gets up but pauses before deciding to leave. The others follow, but they linger outside the open door. I'm sure preparing to rip me a new asshole for my idiocy.

She keeps her head down as she stands up. Her hair slightly covers her face, but I can make out the damp sheen covering her cheeks.

Of course I made her cry. God, I wonder how scared she is. Since knowing her, she's been nothing but an emotional mess. Granted, I can't quite say I blame her, but I still can't help but wonder if Haru was bullshitting me about their time out there. Or is that the guilt trying to find validation when I know I'm just a fucking dick. Wasn't it the vulnerability she displayed that nearly gutted me?

For fuck's sake. I take a step back to give her room, but before I can say anything, she speaks up.

"I'm so sorry," she whispers and raises her gaze to me. There's no fear in her watery eyes. If anything, there's only... sadness and... pity.

On some level, I'm relieved, but on another, I'm even more confused. I have no idea how to handle this situation. I can't even handle my own sister when she cries, let alone a stranger.

She stares at me for a moment longer and then walks around me. Without thinking, I reach out to grab her arm and stop her. She stiffens slightly from my touch. Surprised, I let go as if her skin has singed my own.

There's an unspoken question written on her face, but I don't have any answers. Guilt, annoyance, and a plethora of other emotions weigh on me as I stare into her eyes. The way she sees through me is going to be my undoing. There's no judgment there, no fear. The urge to brush the strand of hair covering her eye is strong, but instead, I step back and break whatever moment this is morphing into.

There's something on the tip of her tongue, but she seems to think better of it and walks out of the room without looking back. My eyes follow her out until I focus on my hand instead. It must have a mind of its own to grab her.

Did I want to comfort her or apologize? Fuck, I have no idea. It doesn't help that she's already been beaten once this week. Then, to top it off, she needed to deal with my unstable ass.

"Jesus, bro. That could have been bad," Matt says as he stands crossed-armed against the door frame. "Maybe you should have warned everyone you sleep as if you're starring in a Freddy Krueger movie." He steps into the room.

I rub both hands over my face and sit on the bed.

"What was she doing in my room, Matt?" I can't quite read his expression. He's gotten pretty good at locking his emotions as tight as mine.

"Hana mentioned Dahlia was walking by to grab some water in the kitchen when she heard you. Apparently, her old man used to have nightmares a lot after deployments, and she was used to being able to calm him down. I guess she thought she could help you, but damn, if she knew what to expect, maybe she should have let you deal with it. Not that it's her fault." He raises both hands in defense.

"Anyway, we heard her calling your name, and when we rushed in, you had her by the throat with the gun in her face. It's fucking lucky you weren't actually gripping the trigger, but I managed to pull your arm away so Hana could grab her, and Rei could detain you." He shifts uncomfortably, his face slipping slightly. He's worried. Either for me or Dahlia, I'm not sure.

"What a fucking shit show, bro. I felt like we were a part of some damn novella my mom used to love or some shit. You good, though? I didn't know it had gotten worse."

Staring back down at my hands, the numbness slowly weaves its way in, attempting to cut me off from the swarm of emotions. To disassociate. So far, all I have done is fail to protect those closest to me. Now, I need to worry about protecting them from myself. How the fuck am I going to keep these people safe if I'm going off my fucking rocker? And what the hell am I going to say to Dahlia now? I'm not sure how I feel about her wanting to help. She doesn't know me. She should stay clear and keep to herself. Again, her kindness almost got *her* killed.

That's not fair though, is it? This is your fault. Your failure.

"Yeah," I say, ending the conversation. I don't need to explain to him that these nightmares have been slowly eating away at me, and the added stress of what has been happening has made it worse. Nobody needs to know the extent of how fucked I'm beginning to feel.

Matt lingers for a moment. "If you're going to sleep with a gun, maybe have one with a pivot safety or something. That could have been bad, man," he grumbles, disapproval written all over his face when he walks out.

What the fuck am I going to do? I walk to the closet, take out the small case, and lock the SIG inside.

They're right. I used to talk a lot of shit about arrogant gun owners, and I just made the worst possible mistake, forgetting I'm not home alone anymore. Worse, there are kids here.

Those thoughts are like a key unlocking a padlock, letting unwanted thoughts spill in.

My head aches, and my body won't stop its relentless shaking. I try to breathe through it, but when it doesn't help, I walk into my bathroom and turn the shower faucet on to hot.

I quickly strip and let the water rain down on me. The water is just hot enough to bring my mind to the twinge of physical discomfort instead of the darkening thoughts.

When my pulse slows and the tremors in my hands still, I wash off quickly. I try to shove the relentless anxiety away and allow the numbness to replace it.

I throw on another pair of sweats and brush my teeth. I'm thinking about maybe doing a run to scout out a path we can take with such a large group or maybe a supply run. My biggest task is steering clear of Dahlia from now on. It's an asshole move, but I never said I was a good person. I have no idea what to say to her. If she thinks I don't give a shit, maybe she will leave me alone.

I can apologize to her eventually.

Maybe when the guilt stops pushing back the walls I've erected. *As if it will.*

As I walk down the hall towards my garage, the sound of crying becomes clear. Passing by Dahlia's room, I hesitate by her door.

I'm about to just say fuck it to my stupidity and cowardice when I realize she's talking on the phone. Although I cannot hear much, I can make out bits and pieces.

"I love you so... What... I'm coming."

"You know, it's incredibly rude to eavesdrop," Hana says behind me. She pushes me on my way and follows, waiting until we reach the garage before saying anything else.

"Were you going to apologize?"

Sighing, I meet her eyes. "I don't know. She's leaving anyway. I might as well continue to be the ass and ignore her. It doesn't matter to me one way or the other," I say, trying to convince myself.

She gives me one of those 'you are an idiot' looks and rolls her eyes. "You should apologize. You did a number on the poor woman. As if the last few days weren't hard enough, you think?"

She walks off, not bothering to listen to my pointless argument, and walks back into the house.

Whatever. I need to start getting everything ready. I go through the stored supplies and grab anything else left in my gun safes. I spend a considerable amount of time getting everything I may need loaded in the bed of the truck. I'm about to head back inside the house, but before I can make an excuse, I walk to the other door instead.

Stepping outside, I walk down the slight incline in the grass off to the side of the property. There's a small, leveled section recently covered in fresh soil. The mound smells of wet earth, masking the truth that lies beneath. Although it's still dark, I can make out the makeshift grave.

My breath catches when I remember Sayuri's gentle smile. Staring at where she lies, the feeling of failure clutches my heart as it did so many years ago.

The regret is so suffocating that I sway as I crouch to place a hand on her final resting place. She was like a second mother in my life. The one woman who helped keep me sane when I lost my parents. She stuck to me like glue as I grew up, recognizing how close I was to shattering. She sacrificed a lot to move to the States to stay with me. She even came before my sister decided to move here and would only travel back every other month to help or spend time with my older brother. She supported my sister and I, assisting my grandparents in raising us.

She provided the nurturing and care I couldn't find anywhere besides my mother. Although my grandparents loved me, they didn't know me well enough and struggled to handle me at times. For a long time, the cultural difference between being raised in a Japanese home and being raised in a Mexican household was a challenge for me and my grandparents.

My sister didn't have as hard of a time adjusting—her loud and outgoing personality fit right in with our mother's family. I, on the other hand, struggled. I took the stoic attitude from our father, and when they died, I all but retreated into myself.

There were some similarities. There were also some things I came to expect, mainly because before her death, our mother acted as a bridge between the families, but the differences between the two households were a lot for me to handle for a long time. *Especially* the way my grandparents showed physical affection to an extreme. Some may call it warm and welcoming, but as a traumatized child, it was hell for me. Big hugs and large smiles weren't normal for me. The only one who ever showed that type of affection to me was our mom.

I fall to my knees slowly and dig my fingers into the fresh soil, taking a deep breath before I sit on my heels. I refuse to look away from the mound in the earth. My mind is lost to the past as her loss eats away at me. The emptiness is trying to dominate the already gray mass, further corrupting who I am. It's fighting to let loose the worst in me, to let it all go, to stay lost.

The memory of Sayuri's smile is the only thing holding me together.

She did *everything* for me growing up.

I rub my dirty hand through my hair as I think back to her sacrifice to stay with us.

Her patience.

It took a long time and a lot of patience from my grandparents, but it also took a lot of patience from Sayuri. She was a rock for me, and eventually, being in an American school and having her there helped create the balance that my mother's parents struggled with.

To top off all their problems, I was suffering and was an incredibly angry child. Sayuri was the one who kept me calm enough to survive. She loved us all as if we were her own. She took care of me most of my life, and I repaid her with failure. I led her to her death.

The forsaken apology never leaves my mouth as I stand. She doesn't *need* an apology. I don't deserve to give one. *She* deserved for me to get her home alive. I should have gotten myself out the door faster. Should have accepted Hana's help. I should have done a lot of things differently. Even in death, she *deserved* respect and honor. She should have been cremated and placed with her family like she always expected. Not buried as if she was a body to be hidden and forgotten in some yard.

Closing my eyes to fight the whirlwind of pain, I take a deep breath before standing up and making my way back into the house.

On my way past Dahlia's room, I stop with Sayuri's last words on my mind, her very nature causing me to stumble in my decision. She would've been ashamed of me. She clearly cared about this woman even after only knowing her for a very short time. This time, her last words hit me harder. *Save her.*

Sayuri wouldn't have wanted me to turn my back on this woman. Even after I saved her once.

Swallowing back my pride, I decide that maybe I can offer her safety.

Chapter Twelve

Dahlia

I lean over the bed to check my phone for what feels like the hundredth time. I'm waiting for the thing to charge so I can call Meg again, but it still won't turn on.

Great. Just great. I knew I should have traded the thing in. I just didn't have the heart to spend the money since it was only the battery that sucked. Everything else was working fine.

Waiting longer to get ahold of Meg isn't helping my increasing panic. Hopefully, she's alive and safe.

"Don't think about that. Not unless you want the floodgates to reopen," I remind myself.

Since finding these people, all I have managed to do is cry, and I can't say I'm enjoying it. I've never minded crying in front of people, but not this much. It's making me feel more and more defeated.

Razing emotions are swarming me like a sandstorm. My heart fucking hurts. Not for myself but for not knowing if my best friend is alive. Not knowing if I'll survive this. And... also for Ren.

I don't know him, and I shouldn't care. I'll be leaving soon anyways, but no matter how hard I try, tonight's events continue to play back in my mind over and over. When his hand found its way around my already tender throat, at first, I was terrified. Memories flooded me of another time, but before I allowed them to paralyze me, the memory of Ren appearing so pained and crying out brought me back to the present.

I cast another futile glance at my phone, but it's still off. I only want to talk to Meg, figure out what the hell I'm going to do, and live happily ever after away from flesh-eating monsters. At this point, I'll go back to being miserable at a job I didn't enjoy and stay feeling lost in my life just to get away from all this chaos. *Is that too much to ask for?*

To add to it, Ren's episode also reminded me about how tortured my father was in the later years of his life. He never hurt me, but I know that was a real fear of his, with his night terrors and flashbacks getting worse. As I got older, I realized that it dictated how he lived his life. His past haunted him. More so in his sleep. I've heard of post-traumatic stress disorder and that everyone may experience it differently, but I didn't think it could affect his sleep in that way.

I cross my legs on the bed and pick at a loose thread on the hem of my shirt. It takes everything I have not to grab my phone again. Instead, I grab the old romance novel I had in my backpack and flip to the dog-eared page. Barely a few lines in, I need to go back and reread.... and then reread a third time. "Ugh." I throw the book down. It's pointless. My thoughts won't stop running.

When my dad passed away, his later years broke my heart. He didn't get to truly live his life. My father was an incredibly brave and selfless man. He was also an incredibly sensitive man. Not in the way as to be offended or hurt easily but just the way he felt in general. He felt things hard—love, pain, happiness, or sadness.

When I cast his brave and fearless nature aside, I would wonder why someone like him joined the service. He felt things too deep to have to bear that kind of trauma. I think deep down, I fear I'm the same way. I already deal with anxiety and have had depression from my own trauma, but I'm terrified to experience the type of pain he had. It was something on my mind more frequently the closer I got to finally applying at the police department.

I look back at my phone for what is probably the tenth time but still meet with the same disappointment. My head is throbbing and no amount of rubbing my forehead or temples seems to give me relief. Seeing this other man suffer in the same way my father had tore into me like lethal claws. It reminded me that even the sturdiest of boulders can fall in a landslide.

Like my father, Ren appears strong, confident, and fearless on the outside but is being torn apart by something none of us can see on the inside.

Is he feeling alone? Does it cause him to be distant with everyone around him as well? Is he afraid?

Groaning, I lay back, close my eyes, and throw my arm over my head. Maybe I'm just projecting. I'm only seeing what I want to see. Maybe I'm trying to find something I lost years ago. A second chance. The ability to change things—for them to end on a happier note. You should never have to fix someone. Isn't that what they say?

Sure. But sometimes, they just don't know how to ask for help.

Fuck, I'm pathetic. The fact I'm overlooking how incredibly dangerous this man is… It's plain stupid. It would do me good to remember the last time I overlooked that danger in someone. The enormous hassle it took to be rid of him finally.

A chiming sound interrupts the dark precipice my mind was edging closer to. The lit-up screen has me getting up so fast that I almost fall off the bed, but I ignore the ache accompanying the movement. I type in my PIN and see missed calls and text notifications.

Meg.

A sob escapes my throat. She's still alive.

I would seriously love to stop crying now; I'm like a damn waterworks attraction.

The last text was only from a few hours ago. Without thinking twice, I hit the call button and put the phone to my ear.

After only one ring, she answers. "Dahl? Oh my god, Dahl!" She's crying so hard that I can barely hear what she's saying.

"Meg. Are you okay? I was so worried."

"I'm fine, DD."

I laugh before telling her, "Even at the end of the world, I hate that nickname." Although I am crying, I can't stop the smile from taking over my face. "Why the fuck didn't you answer when I tried you so many times?"

"I'm so sorry. A lot has been going on. Once they started to find out more about what was happening, anyone from the airport needed to come back to answer questions." She sniffles into the phone. "They wouldn't tell us much, but they did disclose that someone had been attacked on the flight. That's why they landed. This wasn't where I was supposed to stop for my layover."

My breath hitches. How in the hell did they contain it on the flight?

As if she can read my mind, she says, "They wouldn't tell us much about it. Just that someone was attacked, and a marshal was luckily there to restrain them before they hurt the person."

Holy shit. "What?" My eyes are bugging out of my head as I try to picture that. "You guys are lucky as hell. What did they do with the thing?"

There is a muffled sound behind her as if she's shifting in her seat. "Once I saw some of the news before it cut to the emergency broadcast, I figured as much. I'm not sure. They said they detained it."

That doesn't calm my nerves. If anything, it only heightens them. If the authorities had gotten word of what's been happening, though, they must have already killed it. I can't imagine them being stupid enough to leave it handcuffed in a room or something. Hopefully...

Meg tries to hide that she's still crying, but it's obvious. "Dahl. I can't even express how relieved I am to hear your voice. I heard that one of the outbreaks happened at LAX. I freaked out. I was scared you didn't make it out of the airport," she says.

A twinge of guilt hits me, but it wasn't either of our faults that we couldn't reach each other. "I'm sorry I had you worrying. I was worried about you too," I tell her.

"I left my phone in the hotel room when they wanted me to go back, and with all the unknowns, I lost it. I probably scared most of the people around me because I was so freaked," she tells me, her voice breaking into a half sob, half laugh.

I can't help the small chuckle myself when I picture her freaking out. The in-control-always-has-a-plan woman losing it would have been hilarious to see, well, if not for the shit circumstances. "I'm glad you're somewhere relatively safe. Were you able to get ahold of Jax?"

When I originally spoke to her, she thought they weren't answering due to their shift at the hospital. But now... I fear it was from everything else happening.

Her voice cracks again when she says, "It is so far, and yeah when we talked, they were trying to get out of the city. Jax told me they were coming, but I haven't heard from them since. I'm worried, Dahl. Chicago got hit hard. The airport over there basically went up in flames from planes crashing, and the fire started to spread." She sobs and needs to take a second before she can speak again. "How is it where you are?"

I take a moment to respond. I don't want to push her worry for her partner off, but I also know she wants to know both to distract herself and because she does care about me. Sighing, I decide to tell the truth.

"It's pretty bad, Meg. Thankfully, no planes crashed, well, at least while I was still there, but I barely got out myself. I ended up helping a kid and got him to his family, so I'm alright for now. I'm trying to figure out what to do, though. How am I supposed to get to you, especially when the lines all go down?"

It's not even just the thought of getting disconnected. It's the fact that I am going to be alone. I can't ask anyone to come with me. Even if I wanted to, they all have their own plans. I'm a stranger to them. They have already done so much for me. I can't expect more.

Meg sniffles, but she doesn't say anything. I think we're both in shock. Or maybe it's only dread for our situation.

Taking a deep breath, I break the silence. "I miss you so much. I don't know what to do. Do you think you will stay put for a while? I have no idea how long it would take me to get there. Not to mention what I'll have to do to get there or the people I could come across. I'm more afraid of humans right now, and I'm scared. I love you so much, and I... What if—"

I break down again, reality hitting me hard. I probably can't get to her at all. It would be suicide to travel alone in this shit storm. I'll most likely never see her again.

"I love you too, Baby Dahl," she says softly, her voice slightly hiccuping, "I'm going to stay here for as long as I can. All I can do is hope Jax makes it to me. I don't know what I am going to do if they don't."

Although this is probably the stupidest decision I can make right now, I make it regardless. I'd rather die trying to get to the only family I have left instead of hiding alone and still dying anyways. This way, maybe we can find shelter together. Somewhere safe. What other choice do I have?

"I'm coming to you then. Can you give me all the details? I'm going to try and get as many directions written out and different routes before the grids go down." I take a shuddering breath as I steel my resolve. *This is the right thing to do.* "I'll keep you updated as long as I can, but when things shut off, please know I am coming, okay? I still have Dad's old car and his lucky shotgun to boot. I can make it work," I say with a confidence I don't feel in the least.

"I will be here. Please be careful. I will send you everything via text. I am going to try to call Jax again. I love you, Dahl. Please, be careful."

A few moments later, I get her text with what I need, and I take the time to map out my route and a few others. I decide to spend the rest of the night planning. Tomorrow, maybe I can go on a supply run of sorts and find weapons and provisions. I just hope I can get there.

Time to get to work.

Not having anything to write on, I needed to venture to the kitchen earlier, thankfully running into Hana. It was late or early, however you wanted to look at it, so I thought I'd have to wait before finding what I needed. She gave me some paper and pens and went on her way. She didn't ask me why I needed it, for which I was grateful. I plan on letting them know later today when I have my directions written and my careful plan on paper.

I am just finishing up, stuffing all my papers into my bag and making sure my phone is still charging when there's a soft knock.

The man-bun guy is there, taking up the whole space with his broad shoulders. His thick hair is tied up behind his head, although a little untamed-looking now, and his shirt sleeves are straining against his arms. So far, the few glimpses I've got of him, he's been rocking some sort of metal or punk band paraphernalia. He's an attractive man. Kind of rough around the edges but not in the way I tend to like. He has a more careless, wild look that I can't help but glance over.

"Sorry to interrupt. I wanted to make sure you were feeling alright."

What? I stare at him for a second, confused, before remembering what happened. I'm surprised I already forgot. I guess this plan to find Meg has already taken center stage inside my head. Or maybe I need to reevaluate myself if I can overlook what happened so easily.

"Thanks. I appreciate that, you know... You checking in, I mean. I'm fine. Used to it." I chuckle dryly.

He steps into the room now, coming over and placing his hand on mine. It takes a lot out of me not to recoil. I know it's meant to be a comforting gesture, but I tend not to like men touching me. If they're not someone I'm comfortable with, which is very few people, or someone I trust, I'll tend to stay away from their physical touch. Ignoring my initial reaction, I bite the inside of my cheek.

"It's okay not to be okay, you know. I can't imagine what the last few days have been like for you and then for that to happen. If you need anything or need an ear, I'm here, alright?"

Although a little guilty for feeling so, I can't help but be uncomfortable with the implication of the offer. It seems as if it's meant as more if the way he is looking at me is any indication.

"Thank you... uhh..." I stop, unsure as to what his name was. Had he mentioned it?

"Shit, sorry. I'm such an idiot. I'm Matt," he says, but he doesn't move his hand as if he's waiting for me to say something else. He shifts awkwardly when a light knock sounds, and someone clears their throat behind him.

Matt finally lets my hand go. "Anything you need, okay?" he says before facing whoever is at the door.

Ren's standing there, leaning against the doorframe. He glances between us before settling his eyes on me. He's only wearing a pair of low-cut sweats, similar to the ones he had on earlier, showing off his completely tattooed arms and torso.

Holy crap. I glance back up at him before he realizes I am ogling again. Apparently, even as emotionally wrecked as I am, my libido works just fine. I try to ignore the vastly different reaction I have to the man who had his hand around my throat not long ago to the one who's trying to offer comfort.

"Were you looking for me, man?" Matt asks him.

Ren shakes his head in response. Only needing a wordless gesture from his friend, Matt leaves, squeezing his large frame around Ren.

I quickly text Meg, taking advantage of the phone service while it lasts. Smiling softly, I glance up to notice him giving me his most intense stare yet. I can't tell what he's thinking or why he's glaring like he wants to murder me. He almost appears reluctant to be here.

He's silent as he stands there, but his expression finally softens.

"I wanted to apologize," he murmurs.

I gape a little, a tad dumbfounded. I get the feeling this man doesn't even know what an apology is, let alone how to give one.

My smile this time is genuine. His eyes fall to my lips, and then he's walking away.

Before I can stop myself, I call out, "Wait!"

He stops at the edge of the threshold but doesn't turn back.

"I'm sorry, too. You guys saved my life, and I haven't been much help since being here. I wanted to tell you... Uhm, I'm going to be leaving. I think maybe tonight."

He tilts his head slightly while his brows furrow in confusion. This is probably the most emotion I've seen on his face other than the pained expression he let slip from his night terror.

"I got a hold of my best friend, Megan."

He seems to relax a bit at that, if that's even possible for him.

"We were on a trip together but left on different flights. She had an emergency landing in Utah, close to the Nevada border. It's an incredibly small town. Most likely a safe place to lay low for a while since the population is small. She said her spouse is on their way from Chicago."

I fail to mention that Jax may not even be alive. She still hasn't heard back from them.

"I know it's most likely a stupid decision, but I don't have anyone else, and honestly, if I die, I guess it would be better to die trying than die hiding." I sigh, brushing my hair out of my face. He still doesn't say anything, so I continue. "Anyways, I plan on leaving as soon as I can to find more provisions and such. I wanted to let you know I will be out of your way soon."

His eyes track my face before glancing blankly over my shoulder as if contemplating something. He asks, "What city did she land in?"

His question takes me back. What does it matter?

"Parowan." I also fail to mention that driving to Parowan would roughly take eight hours on a normal day. During the apocalypse? Who knows.

He stays silent, shifting his attention to the lightening window. The sky is now a light gray; birds are starting to wake regardless of the death surrounding us, disguising itself as an average day. It's a bit unnerving. Natural life is still going on even though it's the end of the world for humanity. It's like a sick joke.

"Don't leave yet. Give me a day, and we'll fill you in." His features have softened again, but I still can't read into it.

Damn, this guy probably wins at poker every time. *Someone should take this man to Vegas.* I bristle at the slight command he weaved into his statement. It may have been hot when he took charge of the room in their meeting, but one-on-one with me is only annoying.

"That should be fine. I was planning on still trying to go out, though. I'd rather get what I can before it becomes harder to go out alone," I say.

"Whatever you need, we can give you. If you make a list, just give it to me. I'll find it for you."

Not understanding why he's stalling my departure, I tell him it's okay and thank him. He rakes his hand through his hair, causing his body to flex with the motion. I reluctantly pull my gaze away to text Meg my updated plan.

He lingers for a moment. I'm starting to believe he's done talking, but he finally says, "Just have your list ready. I plan on going out on a run soon." And then he's gone.

Hopefully, he doesn't get himself killed. Only for the sake that my time is going to be wasted and not because I care.

Yeah, keep telling yourself that, Dahl.

CHAPTER THIRTEEN

As I walk towards the garage to meet Matt and Juan, Hana steps in my path.

"Here: a list of a few medications to be on the lookout for. Hopefully, we never need them, but some antibiotics or pain medication can go a long way when we no longer have readily available hospitals. Oh, and basically any first aid supplies you can nab, too!" She shoves a long, handwritten note in my hand.

"Hana, this is more like a CVS receipt than a realistic list of things to find." I can't help but chuckle. Sure enough, she gives me the longest damn list out of everyone in our group. To be fair, her request is probably one of the more important ones besides water and food.

"When your dumbass gets an infection, you will be thanking me, you jerk!" She swats me playfully, clearly in good spirits. She goes to leave when she spots Dahlia, who gives Hana a small, tentative smile.

She reaches out, handing me a small list. "Sorry. If you can't find any of this, it's fine. I should be able to find some outdoor stores or whatever."

Skimming through it, I note that most items are nonperishables and first aid supplies. Pausing on one thing, in particular, my brows raise.

"Some shells and an M9 bayonet?" I ask. A bayonet... seriously?

I'm not sure if I can honestly hide the surprise from my face. My eyebrows feel like they are going to fly off my face. She drops her gaze briefly, fidgeting with her hands.

"I used to have one; well, I mean, my dad did. The Mossberg has a lug mount, but he dismounted the bayonet at some point. I figure it could be a good weapon to use. Otherwise, I'd have to bludgeon the zombies with something, and I don't know if I have the strength for that. I mean... unless you think that's not a good idea?" she asks tentatively with furrowed brows.

"Yeah. No. I mean—" I clear my throat. "Actually, it's a really good idea. I'll see what I can find."

I pocket the list and stand there for a second, transfixed on the redness spreading across her cheeks, before I need to remind myself what I'm supposed to be doing. I abruptly turn and walk away.

I knew she had a shotgun, but truthfully, I didn't believe she knew shit about it. I genuinely thought it was something she may have bought for home defense or something, that it sat in the closet and was never touched. I wasn't even sure what kind of shotgun it was.

Taking a second, I slip out the side door leading to the driveway from the garage. We all agreed to leave our keys in the cars outside and keep them unlocked. We know it's a risk, but we don't want to chance any of us getting stuck in an emergency.

I approach her car, finally taking a moment to appreciate it. She drives a 4x4, and it's well taken care of. It's older, but you wouldn't know how old by the obvious love that went into it. The only thing marring the poor car seems to be the fresher paint nicks and dings from the drive out here. I can appreciate someone who knows how to take care of their belongings.

Opening the driver's side door, I immediately find what I was looking for on the back bench seat. Shit, a Mossberg 590A1.

Damn, now Matt's fascination makes sense. If she knows how to shoot this thing, I haven't given her enough credit. This woman isn't messing around. I grab the 12-gauge shotgun from the seat and take a quick look at it. It's been used and is not just a trinket on a closet shelf, after all. It's a little worn down, but like the car, it's well taken care of and freshly cleaned.

Interesting. I make a mental note of the shell size she'd need and other things I can grab now that I know what she has. I put the shotgun back and close the door. Turning, I find Matt waiting by the house.

"That chick is not someone to mess with, bro. I mean, she seems quiet, but fuck. The quiet ones always are the wildest, you know?" He chuckles. "Anyway, we are ready, man. Where do you plan to head first?"

"It'll probably take a lot longer than usual, but there are some shops out in Thousand Oaks. I think getting some weapons should be a priority. We need ammo, and some more practical weapons anyone can use that are silent. Then maybe hit up a market or something after," I say as I walk over to the truck parked in front of the garage.

"You *pendejos* ready, or no?" Juan's voice sounds behind me as he steps out of the house. I met up with him before everything hit the fan, but it's still shocking to see him out in civilian life. He no longer has the buzz-cut but let the top grow out, his curls barely contained with whatever styling product he uses.

I've known Juan the longest from my team here. We met when I was going through ECP, Enlisted Commissioning Program, and later joined the same Battalion in the Marine Raider Regiment. Somehow, we managed to stick together. The others came later. He is also the only one that knows who my family is. He used to laugh at the irony of what my family is involved in and me being a decorated Marine.

"Let's get on with it, then." I get into the driver's seat and wait for them to all load up. Once they are in, we make our way out into the new world.

All is quiet as we drive through the hills. The stillness isn't unusual where I live, but as we get closer to town, the silence is unnerving, to say the least. I'm slightly regretting taking the truck. The sound alone may attract more attention from our unwanted zombie friends than if we had taken one of the eco-friendlier cars shamelessly parked in front of my house. I slow down when the devastation of the town becomes visible.

"Holy shit," I say, dragging out the words.

Some buildings are entirely burnt down, cars abandoned with doors hanging on the hinges, and bodies littering the ground. Or, more accurately, parts of bodies.

"Where are the dead things?" Juan whispers next to me.

Good question.

We are all stunned silent as we take in the utter devastation that has become of our town.

It has only been a few days since this began. Only a matter of days for our small world to implode and crumble to nothing but what we see in front of us.

We drive on for a while and get off the freeway near our first stop before we come across our first block in the road. A minivan T-boned another vehicle and spun out. The van is blocking the intersection and the current path we need to take.

Coming to a stop, we all take our time observing the road around us before getting out. I leave the keys in the ignition with the truck still running. We don't talk as we slowly walk toward the van, trying not to make any noise for fear of attracting unwanted attention.

We make it about halfway towards the van when we hear a loud thump in the backseat. We stop for a second before I use my hand to signal which direction to take. Converging on the van, Matt and Juan follow a flanking maneuver while I stay center.

The thumping becomes more erratic as we get closer. Shit, whatever this is, it's going to bring more trouble upon us.

On closer inspection, I noticed the sticker on the back of the car window—those stupid little family stickers that I could never understand the purpose of. The thumping sound makes much more sense when I notice the two smallest little stick figures. One holding a soccer ball, the other in little pigtails standing next to a small dog.

"Fuck," I unintentionally whisper. I lift my head at the sky as if it could change the reality in front of me.

Of all the fucked-up shit we knew we would run into, this was something I hoped we wouldn't have to deal with. When people think of the apocalypse, most brush off the reality of who the real victims would be.

Seeing the doors shut, I wonder if the parents realized their children were infected and left or if they abandoned them. Or maybe the parents were sick and tried to save them by shutting the doors. Looking closely, there's only one figure inside. Maybe they took the other child and left. I hope they survived only for the other child's sake.

I signal to the guys. Understanding what needs to be done, Matt walks at a steady pace to the trunk and hits the glass softly. It's enough to distract whatever is inside while Juan stays near the front of the vehicle. I am half praying that it will be a live person. Not a zombie. Not death.

Taking a deep breath, I open the sliding door to the back seat. My hope is killed immediately when I find the small figure clawing at the glass, making inhuman noises. I close my eyes for a second, breathing in and out deeply.

If this had been Haru, would I have been able to do this? There could be a cure, an explanation, a viable solution to save these people.

I already know what I need to do, even if it makes my gut wrench.

Slowly, I crawl into the van. Before the zombie notices, I draw my knife and stab it through the base of its skull upward, where the spinal cord and skull meet.

It takes a second—a second to end a life so meaninglessly. I may not be a good person, but I'm not heartless. I have lines I won't cross, and this feels to be a very fine line. I'm smart enough to recognize these things are no longer alive, not really. Even so, I can't help but feel like I wasted someone's opportunity at a life. The only grateful thing is that I didn't have to see their face, their dead, accusing eyes.

Before I can allow myself to drown in these disgusting emotions, I crawl back out and walk around to the driver's seat. Without saying anything, I open the door, put the van in neutral, and step out. Matt and Juan both look sorrowful as we push the van. I grab the steering wheel and turn it so we can steer it out of the way.

Once we push the van enough to clear a path, we silently make our way back to the truck. As we climb in, we hear a screeching sound in the distance. Unable to tell where the sound is coming from, I start driving slowly, ignoring every instinct telling me to hit the gas and drive as fast as I can. That would likely make things worse.

I can admit to myself right now my nerves are shot. I don't want to see anyone else die, and if it were up to me, I would have come on my own. Not being a total idiot, I know I need the help. Anything can happen, and having someone by your side can save your life.

Out of nowhere, a man comes into our line of sight, running straight for us. Before he can jump in front of the car and get hit, I stop. The man looks to be in his fifties, with graying brown hair, a beer belly, and a stained gray jumpsuit like a mechanic would wear.

Juan stars to roll the window down but stops. "Keep going, Ren," he says.

I don't question him and push the gas again, not caring if the man jumps in front of us. He falls to his knees, panting. Driving past, his head comes up, exposing his eyes, veins erupting into a startling red as if they burst in their sockets. He gets up then and starts sprinting towards us. The noise from his throat sounds like he's yelling so loud that his vocal cords give out before morphing into the familiar sound.

"Oh, shit," Matt says as he rolls his window down.

Before I can stop him, he shoots the freshly turned zombie in the head without blinking an eye.

"Fuck, Matt! We're trying to be quiet. What the hell!" I yell back at him. What the hell is he thinking? Shoving caution aside, I push the gas harder, trying to get out of the area before all hell breaks loose.

All around us, screams break the silence, echoing off the abandoned buildings. I push the gas as hard as I can, hoping we don't get blocked in by another car. Otherwise, we might as well be dead.

I'm trying to think of the safest way out and where to go before Juan shoves his arm in front of my face, pointing over at the road leading in the opposite direction to where we planned to go.

"Why the hell would we go that way?" I ask. I trust Juan when it comes down to scraping us out of crappy situations. He can typically be a quiet, reserved man, but he is always two things. Loyal as shit and smart as hell. Ever the strategist. He doesn't answer my question, meaning it will become obvious soon.

Sure enough, up ahead is a fire station—one still under construction. The only thing I notice is the perfectly erected walls that have been freshly painted. The main building looks complete. The second building off to the back is still being built, but who knows what they were planning to use it for.

Without thinking, I pull into the lot through an open gate and drive all the way to the back. Juan hops out, removes his firearm, and runs to the backdoor to find it open. He motions to us while keeping his eyes on our surroundings. After debating for half a second, I switch off the engine, take the keys out, and shove them up in the visor.

I grab my weapon while Matt is already out the door. In a matter of seconds, zombies come into view from the street.

Crap. There are at least twenty. We pick up the pace, run into the building, and slam the door shut. I hold the door closed and hear the telling sign of the bodies ramming into it. I stand there for a moment, wanting to ignore how close we could have been to being dinner. I wonder if I will ever get used to that sound.

Taking a deep breath, I let the door go, ensuring it's closed fully. When I'm satisfied it won't open, I look around for anything to use as a makeshift barricade. When I don't find much, I can only hope they don't figure out how to open doors or that there aren't enough of them to break it down.

At the end of the hall, there are stairs leading up, and I gesture to Juan to go left and Matt to go right before I continue forward. The back door opens into a small room with three other points of entry. I wonder if this building was vacant when everything happened. So far, it looks to be operable other than the building under construction. The electricity is still up and running, illuminating the halls.

Instead of raising my gun, I pull out one of my knives. I know we've already attracted enough attention outside, but I don't want to attract any in close quarters. Up ahead, a few doors are scattered on both ends of the hallway before ending with a larger door. Assuming the last door is the way to the garage, I can't determine where the others lead. I would think maybe sleeping quarters. I'm not familiar with anything related to the fire department, but this building seems larger than the ones I have seen. Maybe this is a new training center. That would make more sense.

I stop at the first door to my right and slowly open it. The lights are on, but the room is empty except for a few boxes and bolted bunks against the walls. There are no other doors inside, so I move on to the other rooms in the hallway, shutting each door behind me as I go. I make a mental note as to which rooms I've cleared as I move forward. Only a few rooms have anything inside, but most are empty. It seems this building wasn't fully functional after all.

A soft shuffling sound makes me pause at the last two doors. It's loud enough to hear, but not easy to determine where it came from.

Slowly, I open the door on the left, finding it exactly as the others—empty except for bunks. The only difference is that this one has rumpled bedding on a few of the bunks, like someone had to leave in a rush. After shutting the door, I turn to the last one at the end of the hall. The sound must have come from this room.

No other sounds break the silence. I open this one even slower and tap the door frame as I wait. I hope that if anything is inside, it will make itself known.

Nothing jumps out at me, but I can't help but hesitate. I brush my palm against the inner walls, searching for the light switch, but I find none close enough to reach.

The room ahead of me is so dark that I squint to make out the vague shape of all the equipment lining the walls and the firetruck further into the garage. There are no lights except the muffled light from the windows, slightly blocked by the truck and the dimming sunlight outside. It's not bright enough to pierce the blanketing shadows but enough to reveal the discoloration on the ground and walls.

Maybe a curtain or something is blocking the other windows.

Bringing my left hand to my pocket, I search for the small flashlight I thought I had packed. Coming up empty, I reach awkwardly around my torso to check my other pocket.

Shit.

I must have left it in the truck. I stifle my groan, unable to control the slight annoyance at myself. Small mistakes like this could be detrimental, and I know better than to make them.

My ears strain to pick up any sound that might indicate I'm not alone, but my racing pulse is drowning out everything else. My breaths pick up with the adrenaline etching through my veins.

The metallic scent hits me first. My foot slips on something wet and skids forward.

Before I can brace myself, my back connects with the floor.

A low groan in my throat leaves me as I sit up. It takes me a moment to reorient myself.

Fuck, my head. I try to ignore the ache as I take stock of my body.

My hands, back, and legs are covered in a dark, thick substance. It's beginning to seep through the fabric of my clothes. The coolness of the sticky wetness sends chills up my spine.

Congealed blood.

That must be the discoloration I noticed before. It's clearer now as my eyes adjust to the low light.

There's so much of it. In the dark, it looks like splattered ink across gray walls. The closest window is fully tinted red, blocking most of the light from outside.

So, not a curtain, then.

A pit lodges in my throat.

The door had been closed.

My back slams into the floor.

Pain lances up my spine. The air is torn from my lungs.

The clatter of my weapons is loud as they slip from my grasp and skid away from me.

A mistake that most likely cost my life.

I raise my hands instinctively, narrowly missing the mouth aiming for my now outstretched digits.

"Fuck!" I try to shove the zombie off me.

It happens so fast, yet time seems to slow. My surroundings become a lost thought as I try and fail to dislodge their body from mine.

It was once a strong-built person from the feel and look of it: broad, muscular, and tall. Even if it was human and had a restraint on its own strength, it could easily take me. But it isn't *human* anymore. There is no subconscious restraint on its strength.

My feet slip on the blood-coated floor. I can't gain enough purchase to shove it off.

Even in the dark, I can see its piercing and hungry eyes.

Too close. He is too close.

Its teeth chatter and snap, desperate for flesh like a starved, rabid animal.

I push at it with my forearm, but it doesn't budge.

Shit.

Its mouth is only getting closer. My eyes have adjusted enough to make out the pieces of flesh in its teeth. Its graying mouth is covered in dried blood.

Rancid heat hits my face. The vile smell is something I wish I never had to experience. Bile rises in the back of my throat.

I pull my knees up to its chest. They barely reach its stomach, but it's enough to hold the thing back.

My left hand frantically searches for something to bash its head in.

Finding nothing, I switch arms but lose some of my leverage. It slips closer to my face.

A breath away. *A single breath.*

The weight bearing down on my upper body is increasing. It's so desperate. So strong.

Ravenous.

My heart feels like it is going to implode in my chest.

The stench of copper and death fills my nostrils. It's suffocating.

Shit. Shit. I reach farther, dangerously letting him inch closer.

Thank fuck!

My hand finally wraps around the hilt of my knife. The blade glints in the darkness. It pierces the temple of the monster centimeters away from biting me.

Blood pools onto my face. Some drips into my mouth. The taste is like acid as it hits my tongue.

This time, I gag and turn my head. I can't stop from throwing up as I frantically push it off.

"Oh god," I gasp, continuing to chuck my breakfast from earlier today.

My first clear thought is whether the blood will cause me to turn.

Holy shit.

Is it only the bites that cause you to change, or will their blood or scratches also cause you to turn?

I pat myself down, checking my arms and body, and discover a few scratches. Nothing life-threatening unless they can cause me to turn.

The question of blood contact and scratches stops all other trains of thought. What the hell am I going to do? I can't go home until we know. I try to recall how long it usually takes before someone turns. The last time we were out, my mind was too clouded with getting Haru and the girl, so I didn't pay attention. I think it happened quickly… Shit.

Before I fully come to terms with my situation, I stand. With my weapons ready, I slowly walk around, searching for any other potential threats. My mind is split between knowing I need to clear this space properly and the realization that my family could end up alone if I turn… or *worse.*

That thought, and the stickiness of the blood covering me is like a trigger. My mother's lifeless body. The blood splattered across my dinosaur blanket. The warmth of it on my skin. The heavy scent of metal. So much blood. A wave of dizziness hits me while those images morph into ones that I fear the most. Reiji… Hana… *Haru.* It causes a physical ache in my chest, and the dizziness worsens.

The familiar numbness threatens me. To detach. To let go. I shake my head in an attempt to calm the swarm of chaos clawing inside me. Surroundings forgotten, I walk to the other side of the room and sit. My head rests against the cool metal as I close my eyes. There's a small tremor in my hand when I bring it to my sternum.

My back and head hurt like a bitch right now, but the panic clutching my chest will not relent. If I turn, no one else will be able to protect my family. Even if the guys manage to get home alive, they aren't me. They have their own lives to worry about. Who says they will put my family first above anyone else, including themselves?

I know Rei can manage, but who will protect *him*? He can't do this alone. Even with his profession, there's something about this type of violence that almost makes it impossible. Even with his men by his side, it isn't me. Who's to say they won't abandon him or turn on him like someone turned on my father? He needs me. *They* need me.

It's a battle to push back the realistic images of my slain family. I rub circles on my chest and keep taking deep breaths.

Time ticks by slowly. I have no clue how long I sit there trying to control my breathing and erratic heart rate before someone murmurs a curse.

"Ren?"

Slow and unsure footsteps grow louder as Matt enters the room. "Ren," he says again.

Light flickers on behind my eyelids.

I open my eyes and look up at him as he stands near a light switch far off from the door. He's also covered in blood, only it doesn't look like any got near his face, only his torso and arms.

"Where's Juan?" I ask as I try and fail to get up on unsteady limbs. Adrenaline is still pumping through me, causing me to shake uncontrollably. Instead, I stay seated a little longer to get myself together.

Matt scrutinizes me for a dragged-out moment before glancing over his shoulder. Juan steps into view, also bathed in blood like Matt but unharmed. "We ran into a few ourselves," Juan says, pointing his now-useless flashlight at the corpse.

"Were you hurt or bitten?" Matt asks, unable to hide the concern bleeding into his voice.

"No, but blood got into my mouth. I vomited, but I'm not sure if that matters or not. I think I need to hole up and wait it out."

Matt walks closer and crouches in front of me. He looks me over before nodding, a solemn expression crossing his face before he closes off. His eyes betray him, though. He knows I'm far from okay. But he doesn't say anything.

I slip again in my wet boots, but Matt catches me as I stand. "Fucking blood," I grumble. "Thanks, man." I walk over and pick up the gun that I carelessly dropped. Now, with the light on, the room's interior is fully visible.

"Holy shit," I whisper as I take in the gruesome scene. The zombie who was infected didn't spare anyone here. Body parts litter the floor throughout the space. Blood lines the windows and walls. The motion-sensor light switch is also covered, which is probably why the lights weren't triggered to go on. I can't determine how many people were in here, but it looks like a handful. The garage door is closed, so they must have got trapped inside.

The ones we've seen outside would try to eat and then move on if there was a lot of chaos around them, but now we know what happens if they have an uninterrupted dinner. They won't just bite and move on. No. They eat their fill.

I've seen some fucked up shit before, but damn, this is some next-level, fucked up shit.

"We can wait a while if you need," Juan says as he walks farther into the room. "I don't think you'll turn if you haven't already, man. From what I've seen, it's pretty fast. Maybe a small delay, but minutes, not hours." His eyes darken as he recalls what he's seen. "Once we clear this last space..." he gestures to the closed door off to the side of the room. "We can double back to the kitchen. There's some food there we can grub on. We'll wait with you, *hermano*. It's not like we have much to go back to right now anyway."

Clearing my throat, I say what first comes to mind. "If I do happen to turn now or even some time in the future, will you make sure to take—" Changing my mind, I say instead, "Make sure to kill me quickly."

Part of me wants to ask him to look out for my family, but that nagging thought of them not being me keeps coming up. They have no real reason to want to look after anyone but themselves. It's a hard lesson I learned years ago. My family will be safer if I'm there. If I don't turn, I need to stop making rookie mistakes.

I don't wait for a response. Instead, I ignore the horrors we're currently surrounded by and walk out of the room. The smell sticks to me, making me want to gag again.

"Did you guys find a functioning bathroom anywhere?"

Matt's chuckle has me glancing over my shoulder. He says with a smile, "As a matter of fact, we did. I've been thinking of nothing since. This fetid smell is gross as fuck. Did you guys notice their blood smells almost as if they're dead? But there are no signs that they are decomposing. Wouldn't they eventually rot to no return?"

Thinking about it now, he's partly right. "The one in the room with me had disgusting breath, but his blood smelled normal. The other bodies were starting to decay, but him… not so much." I pause contemplatively. "But you stink like ass, man. No offense."

The blood on his clothes smells rancid. Like he was the walking dead himself. Although disgusting, it was also interesting. Wondering what I could learn from this new observation, I pack that thought away to revisit later.

We take a moment before getting ready to clear the last space. Matt positions himself to open the door, with Juan taking point. I allow my mind to clear, ignoring the growing anxiety of what-ifs as I prepare for what could be on the other side of the door.

We move in sync, all ready and focused. Immediately, we hear that grating sound. It vaguely reminds me of a car losing traction and a pig squeal combined. Then we hear more. Somehow grateful for that sound, we enter more prepared than I was before.

The one closest comes rushing towards me, but before it can touch me, my knife is in its temple. I bring my foot up and kick it back before I turn to the next one, which rushes from the side. The first one was on the short side. The second used to be a woman. Before it was a zombie, she was probably a head-turner with her natural curves, but its once-brown hair is matted and covered in dry blood. Its skin is a sickening gray.

It's bizarre to notice the differences between these things. Unlike the one in the other room, it smells as if it has been dead for days. Ignoring the stench, I bring my knife up under its chin. For a split second, all I notice is its once-green eyes looking cloudier, and the red covering most of their eyes is not as vibrant; the veins all blown and brownish. I could have sworn some of the others we've seen had fully blown pupils, masking any original color. Another thought to stash away.

I pull my weapon, shove it off, and move on to find the rest of the room cleared. "Why the hell are some of these things different from the others?" I think aloud to myself. Juan and Matt both shrug with their brows furrowed in thought.

The room is an extension of what we saw in the garage. Red metal lines the walls, with fire suits and helmets filling the individual lockers. We take a moment to look around but find nothing of use except a few axes, which we decide to take with us.

I follow the guys back towards where the kitchen is. We are in for a long wait, but the longer it has been since coming into contact with the blood, the worry lessens. My adrenaline has finally crashed, and I'm suddenly feeling dead on my feet.

"I think we should be good, but maybe we can wait out the night. Barricade inside the kitchen and then move out tomorrow," I mention. "We should still head to the tactical store and get what we originally came for. I know the group will have to wait, but it will be worth it."

I follow them through the building, and once we reach the kitchen, we set up for the night.

Better not be my last.

CHAPTER FOURTEEN

Red eyes.

Their lips are moving.

My mother.

But... she looks like those monsters. Her mouth is moving, but there is no sound. All I see is the flesh and blood dripping from her mouth.

I jerk awake with my hand gripping my firearm. When my mind catches up that there's no threat, I rub my chest to rid the residual ache.

Of course, my normal nightmares weren't enough. Drawing out a long breath, I run my hands through my hair as I take in the stainless-steel kitchen at the fire station. The clock on the far wall above the door indicates I have only dozed for an hour.

Fantastic. We are all going to be tired as hell, but fortunately, we're used to it with our past careers. We've all been out and in civilian life for a few months, give or take. Although we're no longer needing it, the habit of short sleep and the ability to function with less than a few hours a day will most likely linger for a long time. The only thing I can genuinely be grateful for is that I'm alive. Being tired and partly dead on my feet is worth the fact that I am still human.

Just as they said, the kitchens have food. This place was clearly designed for a large team but hadn't been finished. The only functional bathrooms we have found are in the locker rooms. None of us felt comfortable lingering too long while we took turns using one of the shower stalls, so we decided to barricade ourselves in the kitchen and do our best to clean ourselves with some towels we had picked up instead.

With what I experienced... I can't help but think that some of these zombies are slightly smarter than we expected. I'm curious if they will all hide and wait like the other one or if it's only some of them. Of course, I can't quite say he was hiding, but he didn't come guns blazing to make himself known. He *waited*.

Chills trail my spine and arms at the thought of those things being anything other than the brain-dead, hungry monsters Hollywood wanted us to believe.

Getting up, I walk over to the kitchen counter. We stacked anything we could find in one spot. There is a case of water, although if the zombies are still surrounding the building, I'm not sure we can take it with us. In our rush, we left our backpacks in the truck, limiting what we can carry.

I open a bottle of water and grab a protein bar before facing the guys. They look as sleep-deprived as I am. We tried to rotate shifts to allow all of us some rest, but I guess we all failed at that.

Leaning against the counter near the sink, Matt bites into his own bar before saying, "You know what I can't figure out?"

"What?" Juan asks him as I rip open the bar's wrapper.

Matt pushes off the counter, taking a water bottle and small towel with him, and walks over to a small table to sit down. "Why there are some differences with these things." He takes another bite of his bar and chews for a second. "I mean. Some smell like death, while others smell of copper. Some are fast, while others are relatively slow. Some are loud as hell, too. It makes no sense."

Thinking back to the zombie I encountered, I agree. "That one back there waited, which felt unusual," I say after swallowing a bite of the chalky-tasting protein bar. "Its breath was nasty, but his blood smelled like blood. The blood on you, on the other hand..."

"Fuck, man, I know I stink. Haha." Matt rolls his eyes. "Maybe whatever is turning them is doing something to their bodies we can't see. I don't know, but it's weird."

Juan pitches in his thoughts. "Who knows as to why, but you're right. We have the screechers and the slower ones. That one—" He points with his thumb in the direction of the garage. "—is the one we need to consider.

I think, if more are like that, where they have the *thought* to wait... an awareness..., we can have problems."

Done with his food, Matt pours water onto the towel and tries to wipe more of the grime off his arms. "Least we know the blood won't change us," he states.

"We don't know that for certain." I try not to think about how close I could have been to turning. "I threw up immediately. Which, in retrospect, means jack-shit, but I have a feeling I'm just a lucky son of a bitch. I have enough scratches where that at least is ruled out."

Neither of them say anything but by the look on their faces, they are just as unhappy about the lack of information as I am. Unfortunately, we don't have any answers—only more questions.

"Either way you look at it, I'm a lucky SOB. Just refrain from getting blood in your mouth," I say as I stretch my arms above my head, wincing at the soreness throughout my body. I feel like shit. First, the fall and then getting tackled by a damn undead linebacker messed me up. "You guys ready then?"

Juan looks up at me from his phone. "Cell networks are down. Only getting error messages. You sure you don't want to go back?"

Damn. It's tempting but I decide to stay on course. It sucks, but I know my siblings won't go anywhere unless necessary, at least for a few days. I wasn't expecting it to happen but I told my brother that if we took longer than expected, he shouldn't worry—just to wait a few days in case traveling takes more time than planned. We did expect it to be slower with the reality of abandoned cars and intentional roadblocks.

"They should be fine. If all goes well, we can be back later tonight."

I don't wait for a response. I walk to the barricade we placed in front of the door and move the furniture as quietly as I can. The building still seems as quiet as last night, and the hallways are still clear.

As we approach the exit, we brace ourselves for a possible fight. Not wanting to be caught off guard again is an understatement. Juan opens the door and takes a quick glimpse outside. From the look of it, the zombies must have moved on.

We don't speak as we slowly make our way to the truck. The sun barely peeks over the horizon, casting long shadows throughout the lot. My first instinct was to look for a less straight path to the truck before realizing how stupid that would be. We aren't dealing with gunfire. We are dealing with zombies. It hasn't quite wrapped around my head yet that this is real.

This is our life.

We halt our movements as a scream rents the air. "Shit," Juan says. Now we know why the zombies aren't by the door. They haven't moved on.

Something has just pulled their attention.

We all take off at a run. Once we reach the truck, I hop inside and find the keys where I left them—another lucky break. I'm still alive, and nobody stole my truck. Getting off to a good start.

I slowly drive us out of the lot but stop right at the exit.

"*Oh, dios míjo,*" Juan whispers.

Directly across the street, we can see what has drawn the zombie's attention.

I keep my foot on the brake, worried about drawing attention away from the large collision at the corner of the intersection. The group of zombies from yesterday are all surrounding a delivery truck that's on its side. The driver has been thrown out of the vehicle a few feet away while the passenger is being torn apart through the windshield as zombies crowd them.

Without wasting time, I make a left turn heading in the opposite direction of the accident.

"Shouldn't we try to help?" Matt asks.

I grunt in response, and at the same time, Juan says, "There wasn't anyone left to help." He shifts in his seat to get a better look at the accident. "Fuck, slam on the g—"

A screech drowns out his words. At the same time, something hits the side of the truck.

The truck jolts with the force of the zombie's body.

"Mother fucker is hanging onto the bed," Matt shouts, twisting around in his seat.

My eyes find the rearview mirror.

Sure enough, the thing is somehow gripping onto the bed.

"How in the hell..." I whisper to myself.

I speed up, glancing around for another escape.

Nothing.

Nothing but businesses line the boulevard.

"Yo, just stop. It looks like only a few are fast enough to reach us. We can take them and the one on the truck," Juan states while he releases and reinserts the mag of his firearm. "It'll be easier than trying to shoot out the truck while you avoid shit in the roads."

I glance back at the zombie still gripping the truck. It doesn't look like it can climb, but it's somehow hanging on.

Four screechers are giving chase. They're almost on us. But he's right. Ahead, there are cars and other debris abandoned in the street. It's a fucking Mario Kart track with how crowded the road is. We can risk a roadblock while the zombies catch up and surround us, or we can get out and kill these while we have a slight upper hand. I need to decide fast before they get any closer.

"Alright. Count of three, I break, we get out and dispatch them." I tell Matt, "You get the one on the bed. Juan, you on the left. I'll take the two on the right."

They both hum in acknowledgment.

"Three..."

My foot hits the brake.

"Two..."

I shift to park.

"One. Go," I order.

We jump out. With my pistol ready, I inhale.

Exhale.

Fire.

The red-eyed woman jolts back, her head leading her.

Juan and Matt are following suit. Inhale.

Two more shots are fired. Exhale.

Fire.

The thing in a bloody bathrobe hits the floor in seconds as the last two gunshots echo through the streets.

We don't waste time. The three of us run back to the truck.

A screech in the distance sounds, but we don't stop. Within seconds, we are speeding back down the road.

"I don't think I can get used to this," Matt says from the back. His eyes are focused out the window, probably as on edge as I am now.

"Only a few klicks northwest now. It won't be long until we reach where we need to go," I tell them.

We all fall silent as we take in our surroundings.

Once bustling with life, the streets are now devoid of anything but death. I wonder if we will ever have our old lives back. There are no signs of life as we drive—only the screech falling in the distance. Surrounding us are abandoned cars with doors left open and the odd bike or skateboard littering the street. Any houses or businesses we pass are all eerily still.

After a few minutes, we come across a car heading in the opposite direction. The family of four speed past without even glancing over.

Shortly after, we spot a few people creeping along, ducking behind things, trying to stay hidden from any possible threats. There is a man and woman, possibly in their forties and another woman who is maybe a little older. They wave us down as if they want us to stop but I keep driving.

I don't wish death upon anyone, but I don't need the added responsibility of more strangers. No one else is my responsibility right now. All I need to do is stay alive long enough to grab what we need and get back home.

When we finally come across the tactical store, we all breathe with relief.

"Once we grab what we need, we can look for a market," I tell them.

We have the case of water from the fire department and the small number of provisions we found, but it isn't nearly enough for our group. I'm counting on things being too chaotic for people to have scavenged just yet.

It doesn't take long to sweep the store to ensure nothing is hiding, but I quickly realize my initial thought was a poor one.

Most of the store is cleared out; when I say clear, I mean nearly empty. There are a few knives, a couple of measly boxes of ammo and shells, and a few other things we have on the list, but not enough to last very long.

"Well… at least we found a few axes back at the station." Juan chuckles as he tosses an empty package over a display case.

I grunt in response while walking through the aisles carefully, checking under any racks and behind the glass cases circling the space. Although there isn't much, I do manage to find what I need for the Mossberg in the small storage room. Somehow, that makes me feel good. Definitely a lucky SOB today.

Once we pick through everything, we meet outside.

"Well, that was shit. I wonder how fast it took for people to clear this place," Matt grumbles while he climbs into the truck. "I mean, I got what I needed, but this won't last."

He's right about that.

Juan rests his elbow on the center console and looks over his shoulder at Matt and then me. "I'm sure there are other places we can hit up."

"I thought I'd seen an auto store not far from here. Or maybe a sporting goods store—maybe we could get some bats and beat some nails into them like the movies." Matt mimics swinging a bat in the air. "Or wrap them with barbed wire."

My mind races as I try to recall what's around here. "You know…" I pause, mentally mapping out which direction I need to take. "I think there was another tactical store farther up the road, and there are a ton of tire shops and a gas station right there."

With any luck, this run won't be a total bust, but the longer I drive, the more I worry we may have underestimated our situation.

Chapter Fifteen

Dahlia

The error message keeps pinging back. Every time I hit send, I get the same message. That it failed. *You should have left already…*

I can't help the groan as I throw my phone on the bed and rub my forehead with my palm. This was to be expected. I'm not sure why I thought we would've had more time, but I was wrong. The networks are down… Meaning no connection to Meg.

It feels too final without that connection there. It's all more real, which is stupid in the grand scheme of things. After everything I'd seen already, wouldn't that have made this real?

Ren and his friends haven't returned either. When they didn't show up last night, my grim reality became clearer. If they died out there… how the hell am I going to survive?

I wish my dad were here. He was always ready for everything. He would have been able to keep me safe. I snort at that. If he were to see me now, I'm sure he'd be anything but proud. His little butterfly retreating into her cocoon.

If Ren isn't coming back, I need to leave before things get worse.

Yup. I can do this. I can do this… *Do you honestly want to leave… alone?*

I try to ignore the doubt creeping in. I think of my father. He wouldn't cower. "Buckle up those steel-toes, baby Dahl," I whisper to myself, grabbing my backpack and throwing it onto the bed.

"Buckle up what?"

"Shit!" My hand flies to my chest as I whip around.

Hana's smile is almost blinding with humor as she walks into the room. "Sorry. I didn't mean to scare you. You know, you shouldn't be talking to yourself when there are people willing to hang out." She sits on the edge of the bed. "Haven't you noticed the kid?" she asks just as Ru pops his head in the doorframe. "See?"

My laugh comes freely as he pops farther into the room. "You can come in. That's fine," I tell him as I turn back to my backpack. Before I can pack the few belongings I left out, Hana speaks up again.

"What is this?" Her hand waves dramatically as she gestures to the backpack.

I fully unzip the bag and start shoving my stuff back into it. "What's what? I'm getting my stuff ready to go."

Her warm hand clasps my forearm to stop me from putting my phone inside. "No, I mean, why are you packing at all?"

What does she mean why? "I was planning on leaving anyways, but I waited. I need to get going before things get even worse." I gently pull away from her and grab the book from the nightstand.

"Dahlia-neesan," Ru says.

Neesan? Hadn't he referred to me as Dahlia-san before? I wonder what that stands for. He's standing right next to us with tears welling in his dark eyes. "Why not stay with us?" he asks me.

If I had thought the day started off grim, I had been wrong. This is downright miserable. The poor kid has been through the ringer. He not only lost Sayuri, but he's been in the midst of everything from the beginning. To see him cry again makes me feel even worse.

"I'm so sorry, kiddo. I need to find my friend. She's been waiting for me." The smile I try to give him ends up being more like a grimace.

Hana steps up closer to me and grabs my shoulders in both hands. I need to crane my neck with her standing so close. "Nope. You can wait longer. Give my brother a chance to get back. Our older brother Reiji wanted to speak with you anyway. I mean... if you're comfortable with that?" Her smile is still radiant as she holds me firmly within her grip.

Although she has a smile and isn't being hostile or rude, something about it feels more like an order than a suggestion.

Sighing, I say, "Alright then. He wanted to talk right now?"

Ru's expression transforms almost immediately, his smile takes over his small face, making him appear even younger.

Hana, satisfied with my answer, lets go of my shoulders but grabs my hand instead. She pulls me out of the room without an answer to my question.

"What the heck?" I'm unable to stop from laughing at her antics.

She leads me down the hall and towards the kitchen, but I pull back slightly when the painting catches my attention again.

"I'm curious. Is your brother a collector?" I ask Hana.

"Hmm? Oh. Yeah. He's an artist too, believe it or not. Oh! We should paint something. It might keep us busy as we wait for them to get back!" She all but hops up and down in her excitement.

Dang. She's like an apocalypse Barbie. Or maybe a cheerleader? My smile spreads as I try to picture her with pompoms. Somehow, I can't see her as a cheerleader. She may be bubbly, but there's something about this family that feels different. *Dangerous.*

Definitely apocalypse Barbie.

"You know what? Let's go in here, and I'll have Rei meet us," Hana says as she opens the last door in the hall before it expands into the living space.

We walk into the bright room, and my breath stutters. Slack-jawed, I stare at the large art studio. If I were an artist, I would have died and gone to heaven, but even as a huge art enthusiast, I think I still might.

Ru runs into the room and straight to a long ranch-style table surrounded by chairs. It sits right in front of one of the two floor-to-ceiling windows overlooking the hills.

Canvases, easels, paints, and other materials fill the room. An old leather couch sits in the corner with a coffee table, but besides that one space of tidiness, the rest of the room is organized chaos. It isn't dirty or messy but full of art supplies cramming every surface. The hint of turpentine and oil paints permeate the air, clinging to me as we step further inside.

"Rei will be here in a bit," Hana interrupts my perusal as she walks back into the room. I didn't even notice she left. I was so transfixed in this space. "Wow. I didn't expect you to salivate. You need a napkin?" She laughs.

My head is practically on a swivel as I take everything in. "This is amazing. I wish I had the talent to paint. If I had a space like this, maybe I would have forced the talent onto myself." I chuckle as I pick up a small leather sketchbook.

"Oh. I wouldn't touch that." Hana rushes over. She takes it from me without explanation and places it over on the coffee table. "So, let's get messy, have some snacks, and enjoy the calm before the storm."

I can't help the curiosity that blooms, but I brush it off instead of asking about it. "I can get behind that," I tell her.

She gestures for me to sit next to Ru and goes to a cabinet to pull a few canvases out.

It's not long before the three of us are painting our version of the hillside outside. Hana's and mine look less than desirable. Ru's, on the other hand... "Holy Toledo, kid. That is looking amazing!" I give him my biggest smile.

"Thank you, Dahlia-neesan. Ren-oji always takes time to paint with me when we visit. He tells me I'll be able to out-paint him soon!" he exclaims excitedly.

It's heartwarming to see him so happy about this. It makes me wonder what Ren is like when he doesn't appear stern or closed off. Clearly, he's close with his nephew. Or at least somewhat close to spending this kind of time with him. It's hard to picture him expressing anything other than disdain or the neutral look he gives everyone.

The way I view the room shifts slightly as I consider that thought. At first, I was so in awe of all the supplies and the space that I failed to notice the artwork itself—the work that Ren created. *His space.*

The canvases visible are all swirls and blocks of deep tones, with the occasional highlight to break up the darkness. It's like a small looking glass into his head, but from the darkening colors and obscure shapes, I realize I may have been wrong in my first impression of him.

My experiences with most military men were similar, so I kind of categorized him in the same group. Although he obviously struggles with whatever invades his sleep, he doesn't freely give away the pain that's there. Considering these pieces tells me he's more complex than I initially thought.

One piece stands out amongst the others. Partially hidden behind a larger canvas, the painting is a realistic depiction of a young woman with red splattered across her lightly bronzed skin and ocean-blue eyes. Her mahogany waves fan around her face with the same splatters obscuring it.

Curiosity almost gets the better of me, but I refrain from asking the first thought that comes to mind. *Did he have a woman in his life?*

A pit in my stomach forms, but I'm not sure why that made me uncomfortable. *Probably because you've checked him out a few times, but you don't need the complication. You're leaving, remember?*

"Does Ren-oji have any sketchbooks I can use later?" Ru asks Hana as he sets his finished painting against the window.

Hana gets up but looks at me. "Would you want one too? Something to maybe keep you busy later?" The glint in her eye and her smirk makes me nervous, but what harm would giving me a blank sketchbook do?

"Sure," I say.

While she walks back towards the cabinet, she ruffles through a few things on the table next to it. I take the time to help clean up our mess, but we're interrupted when Reiji walks in.

"*Otousan!*" Ru runs up to his dad, but Reiji has to hold out his hand before the kid runs into him. "Look at what I painted this time."

I almost expect him to get annoyed, but his face lights up when Ru pulls him to the window. Something about it shocks me but I can't put my finger on why. It isn't unusual for a father to be excited for his son or proud in the way he's beaming, but it's unusual when I picture the man who walked into the room seconds ago.

A tailored man bearing the same stone expression his brother has. He radiates authority and if I were to be honest with myself, he makes me nervous. Even Ren doesn't elicit this type of nerves from me, and I can clearly see *he's* dangerous. Fuck, he nearly killed me in his sleep.

"This is wonderful, Haruto. You should be proud." Reiji crouches down to eye level before ruffling his hair and standing back up.

I still can't help but feel like I walked into a parallel universe. It's clear they're all close, if not very family-oriented.

Reiji casually rolls up his sleeves before he straightens his light blue dress shirt. His smile disappears, which only makes me more nervous. *Shit. Should I have left, after all?*

"I haven't introduced myself yet. Reiji." He offers his hand, which I tentatively shake.

"I'm Dahlia... uh... sir." I swallow, trying to put as much strength into the handshake before pulling away.

Hana blatantly guffaws. "Oh, please. You don't need to all be so formal. Just get to it before you make her pass out, Rei."

His face slightly softens before he clears his throat. "I wanted to thank you for what you did for my son. You have my family in your debt."

My eyes bug out. I get the feeling this isn't something I should brush off but what do I say to that?

"Breathe, hon," Hana says, beside me now, putting her hand on my shoulder. "What my brother is saying, should you need anything, let us know. Yeah?"

What do I say to that? "Thank you." *Smooth.* "I'm glad he's okay. I should be thanking you for giving me a place to rest before I leave."

Reiji looks to his sister with raised brows but gives me a slow dip of his chin.

He doesn't say anything else but gestures for his son to follow. When they are out of the room, I turn to Hana. "Thanks for keeping me distracted. I'm going to make sure all my stuff is ready to go for later."

"Wait!" She grabs a sketchbook similar to the one she took from me earlier, but this one is a little larger. "Here. Keep it and use it whenever you get bored. I need to talk to Rei, but I'll find you shortly so we can eat." She also hands me a few pencils and erasers.

Giving her a small smile and saying thank you, I follow her out of the room and back to my guest room. I clutch the sketchbook until I'm able to shut the door and breathe a little easier.

I quickly finish packing and check my phone once more before confirming it wasn't just glitching. Grumbling, I shove it into my backpack a little too roughly so that the sketchbook falls off the bed.

What the...

While I bend down, the open, filled page stares back at me. It's a set of eyes, and a partially complete bridge of a nose covered in freckles, but something about it causes fluttering in my chest—a soft, giddy sensation I have no business feeling.

The eyes are so detailed that they look almost crystalline as I fall transfixed by them. They feel too familiar, but I slam the book before I let that thought take off.

Hana must have accidentally given me Ren's sketchbook instead of a blank one.

I hold the book out with shaky hands, hesitating to return it. *It isn't yours.*

I can't say what compels me, but I shove it into my backpack.

Maybe it was the one page, so she let me take it. If it's a full book, I can return it before leaving.

But somehow... I don't believe that.

Chapter Sixteen

Ren

Despite all the shit we've dealt with so far, it doesn't take long to reach the end of West Hillcrest Drive. The last stop we have turns out to be a Target. I was afraid to go to such a big store for multiple reasons, but we need other things that a supermarket won't have. Like nails, for one. We managed to scavenge some bats at a sporting goods store, a couple of crowbars, and some tire irons from a few automotive shops. I also decided to grab a few jerry cans and shove them into the bed of the truck, plus a few other little things we could use for the cars.

At least the jerry cans will come in handy. Getting gas isn't going to be easy, especially when it starts to expire. That thought alone makes me feel as if we need to move more urgently.

I slowly drive the truck into the parking lot and circle the building a few times, noting emergency exits while trying to determine what we may be dealing with. Satisfied there are no alarming amounts of zombies outside the building, I drive back around and put the truck in park right in front of the entrance.

"I don't want to be inside long. I know there may be a large chunk of supplies, but I don't think clearing the whole area with just us will be possible." I glance back at the building. "Although it may be a shit idea, we should split up. Juan, take food and beverages. You can take A5 with you, but remember, we need to stay quiet. Bludgeon when possible. Matt, look for what we need for the weapons. I'll raid the pharmacy and surrounding areas."

All nodding in confirmation, we exit the truck as quietly as possible.

Hesitating, I shove the truck's key under the driver's seat. "Better be here when we get back," I mumble. I want to get this over with so I can get back to my family.

The front of the building is large, with two separate points of entry on each end and double doors specifically for shopping carts in the middle. The entrance doors are completely shattered, while the exit on the right is unmarred. They're automatic sliding doors, but the intact one is pushed outward. I know it's meant to be able to be shoved open in case of an emergency but that doesn't stop it from looking unusual opened like that.

Stepping over glass and trash, we make our way into the store, weapons raised and at the ready. We each clutch a bludgeoning weapon along with our firearms, hoping to stay as quiet as possible.

We each grab a few bags from the closest register and head to our designated areas.

The store reminds me of what a place would look like after an actual riot. Registers busted open, trash and merchandise littering the floor, and what's left of a few bodies lying motionless by the exit.

As if a hurricane has swept through, the off-white shelves are busted or tipped over. People have already grabbed what they could—although I don't see how housewares would be necessary at the end of times, but who am I to judge? Who the fuck knows, maybe those Martha Stewart wannabes want to go for an edgier home look. Nothing says welcome home more than stolen merchandise with blood on it. *The apocalypse collection.*

Turning the corner to reach the health aisles, I'm faced with a handful of zombies. They all turn and run towards me, a few with limps, others missing limbs altogether. There are four of them so far, but none make much noise.

My first reaction is to bring the gun up, but I manage to stop myself. Instead, I raise the crowbar I'm holding. A short-statured zombie reaches me first, blood coating the front of its baseball jersey. It goes to grab me, but I shift left and bring the crowbar down on its head.

I move towards the second zombie without hesitation. The crowbar meets its temple when a pair of hands grab at my leg. Kicking out and swinging at the same time throws back the other zombie, which skids into a now empty end-cap.

The last zombie reaches me only to get its head smashed in just as quickly.

Dreading that there could be more, I walk faster towards the pharmacy. I can handle a few of these things, but what if there were more fast ones? Fighting a few of those alone would be a death sentence.

The pharmacy's gate is still open. Relief hits me when I find partially full shelves. Not everything was taken, but I hope to find a few of the medications on Hana's list.

I may give her shit for it, but I'm thankful she created it in the first place. Pharmaceuticals aren't my specialty. I wouldn't know any other medication to look for besides maybe Morphine and a few generic antibiotics.

I take a few steps down the aisle and notice two boxes of protein bars lying flat on the metal shelf. Grabbing them, I shove them into my shopping bag.

Not bothering to open the door, I hop over into the pharmacy.

The dead zombie wearing a white and red pharmacist coat lying on the ground takes up most of the space in front of the registers, his head leaking blackish-brown blood that reminds me of tar you'd find on the beach. The funky odor its body emits has me covering my mouth as I walk by. These things don't all smell as you'd think, but once they die, it's as if the festering that occurred in their living body has finally caught up to their dead one. It's an off smell and not quite the sickly sweet and rotten smell you'd expect, but instead, it has an undertone of something acidic underneath the foulness of decay.

It takes me a while to go through the pharmacy shelves with prepackaged medications, wanting to make sure I don't miss anything. I do manage to find a few Hydrocodone bottles, Norco, a higher milligram Ibuprofen bottle, and a few other stronger pain medications. Hopefully, we won't need these, but I'd be an idiot to leave them. I'm also able to find a handful of different antibiotics. Most of them are general ones, but a few are ones they use to treat more specific things, according to Hana's note. My sister is the one who would know. Suddenly, I'm even more grateful for her list as I grab boxes and bottles.

Once finished, I go through the aisles and grab anything that was forgotten, like a few bars of soap, toothbrushes, and some toothpaste. On the floor are some gauze pads, one bag of cough drops, and even a box of condoms. Not that I plan on needing them, but a few couples in our group may appreciate them. I don't want to travel with a fucking pregnant woman in this hell storm, but who knows when people will manage to find the time to *get* pregnant.

Not finding much else that can be useful, I head over towards the grocery aisles.

Shuffling sounds behind me.

Seconds later, I'm being shoved into an aisle and toppling the shelves. The air rushes from my lungs as I land hard. The zombie above me lands as disheveled as I did, giving me an opening.

I kick up, pushing it off me before bringing the crowbar up. Blood splatters across my cheek, and once again, I kill a zombie closer to my face than I'd prefer.

Taking a second to even out my breathing and take stock of my battered body, I stand up and look at the bag I managed to keep in my grip. Nothing seems to have fallen out. Thank fuck for that.

"You good?" Juan whispers as he walks over, pushing a shopping cart with a case of water and some dried and canned foods. It's not enough by far, but it's something.

"Yeah. These things can honestly sneak better than I'd thought. My ego may have been battered by how many damn times I've been tackled." I peer farther down the main aisle. Matt turns the corner and waves before heading down the next aisle. "Let's load this up. Hopefully, he'll be done soon," I say as I turn and walk towards the exit.

It's so strange how there aren't as many zombies as I'd have expected. We have a large population in Southern California. Even Los Angeles County has an overwhelming amount of people. Where did they all go?

We make it to the truck quickly and load up as fast as we can. Once loaded, we both turn to go help Matt when a gunshot has us both crouching, raising our guns in defense on instinct while our eyes scope the area.

Another shot rings out, hitting the side of my truck near my head. "Where the fuck is it coming from?" Juan says as he eyeballs the store and parking lot. We both move and crouch behind the truck when more shots continue to fire down on us.

There! One on the roof, hiding behind an HVAC unit.

Juan pats my shoulder and aims his weapon before fisting his hand with one finger up. In the direction he's pointing his rifle, there is somebody crouched almost out of sight behind a hitched trailer across the large parking lot.

Shit, about a hundred meters. Barely at max range for the pistol.

As I stand and take a shot at the one closest to us, the racking sound of a gun pulls me to a stop. Swallowing, I slowly turn to see three men pointing a variety of weapons at us. The pistol closest to my face is the one I draw focus on.

Farther away, loud screams are coming in this direction. No, not screams, but the damn shrieks those zombies make. The gunfire is drawing them towards our location, like ringing a dinner bell. The dead zombie inside and the lack of some of the zombies nearby now make sense if these guys already came through here.

"Now, I don't want to get acquainted with you, so let's make this fast before we become an all-you-can-eat dinner. Drop the keys and walk."

I take a moment to determine our chances of being able to get out of this with all our shit, including our lives. A fourth man walks up and draws up short when our eyes meet. Or rather, *eye.* He has gauze, a bandage around one eye, and a black patch to hold it in place. The bridge of his nose is bruised and causing the other eye to appear a little swollen.

Of all the places to run into this fool.

"Well, what the hell do we have here?" He laughs. "Damn. You know, we thought we got lucky with a working truck landing on our laps, but to run into you? Tsk. Of all people."

Snorting, he comes closer and smiles as if I just offered him gold on a silver platter. "Now, is that bitch with you? Because damn, I would love to repay the favor." He points to his bandaged eye.

My eyebrows lift in amusement and surprise before I can help it. I school my features quickly, but not quick enough.

"So, she was one of yours. I was right about the kid then. My brother is going to be ecstatic to know we ran into you. I don't know if he would be happier if I ended you now or if I brought you back to give him the honor." He paces slightly, rubbing the back of his neck.

"You see, you guys killed a fair amount of our men. I'm assuming it was you lot. I doubt the *sohai* had the gall to do it herself. I can't believe we ran into you." He dramatically points and shakes his gun at me. "We started to travel outside the city because of the gun stores not far from here, and it looks like that worked to our advantage." The smirk on his face couldn't be any more smug.

Damn, does this idiot ever shut up? Trying to remember his name, I think back to conversations I've had with Rei. He dealt with these morons a lot more than I ever did. Jace? Jason? Jay, I think. Yeah, I think his name is Jay.

Damn. Dahlia did that to him? I laugh, unable to help myself. Fuck, she may appear quiet but, hell, does she have fight in her. The reluctant respect I have for her is growing the more I stare at this guy.

"Sorry, I just can't help it. I have to say, I'm impressed with the new look."

Juan side-eyes me and rolls his eyes, but he can't hide the small smirk.

Jay's hand whips up and smacks me in the head with the butt of his gun. "Fucking *puk gaai*."

I clench my jaw and ignore the pulsing throb accompanying his hit.

So, the Yeun family is still alive. And from the looks of it, they still have a decent-sized crew with them. I wonder how many others they have hidden somewhere. He mentioned they are traveling, so I can't imagine too many more. His brother isn't here; that is obvious. While I continue to try to remember what I know about his family, I realize he's still talking. "I think we'll bring you along then."

He looks over at one of his guys and jerks his head towards Juan.

"We can kill him, take this one, and throw him in the bed of his truck," he says before he walks off towards another vehicle.

In the distance, the screeching is louder, closing in at an alarming rate. I hadn't noticed before, but beyond the lot, slower zombies are making their way towards us, too.

The man with the gun pointed at my head lowers it slightly, aiming it at my chest while he motions for me to move.

He breaks his attention from me for a second to look around nervously. A sheen of sweat on his brow becomes more apparent as his nerves rise. "*Bai gaa fo,*" he says to himself. I don't speak Cantonese, but from the look on his face, I can tell he's worried.

Looks like they don't like the zombies any more than we do.

A few shots go off as they reach us, which only spurs Jay's other men into action.

One of the others goes to grab Juan when suddenly he's staggering back, red painting his face with the acquired loss of half his forehead.

The others take cover, confused about where the shots came from. Juan and I, knowing damn well where it's coming from, take advantage of the confusion and bring our weapons up and fire in quick succession. Then, we take aim at the men who are now in a more visible line of sight. As they go down, the squeal of tires makes me turn around. Jay is once again running away like the coward he is. The remaining men follow, all jumping into their cars and peeling out of the parking lot.

"I hope we don't have to deal with that shithead again," I mumble as Matt comes running towards us, a few bags threaded on his arm, a new bat in one hand and his rifle in the other.

"Well, if you don't think my timing is perfect, let me tell you." Matt snorts out a laugh and hops into the truck. Juan and I waste no time in following.

As the back door shuts, a loud bang sounds near Juan's door. A zombie is bashing its head into the window, causing the panel to shake. I turn the engine on and drive forward when another bang from the other side has the whole truck shaking.

Multiple loud shrieks rent the air, so loud I'm surprised my eardrums are still intact. My foot hits the gas as if made of lead, and I turn the wheel towards the exit. Up ahead, at least twenty more have made their way over, all speeding up at the opportunity for fresh meat.

"Shit, you're going to have to ram them or turn, man, but behind us is no better," Matt says.

Glancing in the mirror, I can't control the curse that slips past my lips at the sight. We are beginning to be surrounded.

Pushing the gas as hard as possible, I prepare to slam into the group coming towards us. I have seen what a deer can do to a windshield; I sure hope I don't find out what a body can do.

As if the universe gives us a break, the exit behind the building is clearer, and not as many are coming from that direction.

"Hold on."

I turn the steering wheel sharply, almost to the point I think we'll tip. The noise probably doesn't do us any good about drawing more attention. Still, it doesn't matter as more zombies reach us, ramming into the truck like battering rams, unaffected by the fact that the force is literally tearing their bodies up and throwing them back away from their so-called meals.

There are fewer zombies, but I can't help the one that runs directly in front of us. It hits the headlight and gets dragged under the tire, causing the right side of the truck to jolt upward twice before settling.

All I can think about is how damn happy I own a slightly lifted truck and that we didn't take one of those eco-friendly cars after all. If I drove any other car, we would have been royally screwed. I wonder when our luck will run out.

I turn onto the street behind the Target, trying to get my bearings to get us home, when I realize I may have spoken too soon. Three zombies come sprinting directly in front of us, not slowing down despite the threat of being run over.

Before I can swerve out of the way, the first hits and blood splatter rains over the windshield, obscuring my view of the road. When the next one hits us, a huge crack now adds to the blood.

"Shit. Shit. Shit!"

Not able to see, I swerve a sharp left, trying to look out the driver's side window, when the third zombie comes straight for my side.

Before it can slam into the window, I swerve again, searching for another turn in the road. I slam on the brakes, and it runs past the truck before I step on the gas. It takes a moment for the zombie to turn, but I only drive a few feet before it's already on us, jumping on the bed of the truck.

"The fuck. Was this thing a damn track star or something? Shit. Slam the gas! I'm going to try and nail him!" Juan shouts, rolling his window down and slipping partially out of the car.

He jolts back. A slightly slower zombie reaches for him, and he shoots it in the head. The once-woman falls, causing the others who are gaining on us to trip. The larger group is all slowly falling behind, except for the fast one now trying to crawl on the truck.

Juan pops back out the window, bracing with one hand to keep himself steady while aiming at an awkward angle. The first shot is disrupted by the truck lurching over a pothole, but the second seems to draw the zombie's attention towards him, giving him a better angle. The third hits it between the eyes. Juan quickly slides back in the truck and rolls the window up, continuing to look back at the others farther down the street now.

"Shit. That's the most we've seen in a while. Just so fucking weird they go into hiding or something," he says.

I focus on driving, having to rely on the small patches through the windshield not covered, and my window to the left. We drive around thirty minutes before I pass an empty gas station and risk stopping.

Pulling up, we all scope the area before feeling confident enough to exit. Matt and Juan take position, weapons ready, while I keep the truck running and hop out, walking to the station that I hope still has a solution to clean the damn window.

Thankfully, it does—barely—so I pick up the squeegee and quickly work on the window. Although it has begun to dry, I do manage to clean enough to see through on my side. When I get home, I need to wash the truck to get most of the blood off, but this will have to do.

Since we are here, we decide to go inside and see if there is anything of use, although if the stores have already started to get picked over, I doubt there will be much here. It takes us all of ten minutes to go in and find nothing before we are back in the truck, heading home. Although that didn't go how we hoped, we at least aren't empty-handed. That's all we can honestly wish for in this new hell.

I can only hope we manage to survive long enough to find safety and food.

Chapter Seventeen

Dahlia

Did they die out there? If that's the case, then how the hell do I think I'm going to travel that far? *Alone.* No matter how hard my father drilled into me to be prepared for things, I'm no match for what's out there. Those men have experience, and still, they could be dead. What chance do I have?

I knew I should have left earlier. Now, the longer I wait, the more my chest tightens, and the possible scenarios of me dying out there alone play through my mind on repeat. Or the thought of never seeing my best friend again rears its head.

"You're pacing again, hon," Hana says softly. She gets up from the kitchen barstool and comes up behind me, placing a hand on my shoulder. "You're only stressing yourself more."

"Sorry, Hana." I give her a small smile and cover her hand with my own, squeezing it before letting go. After painting, Hana insisted she check the wound and told me it looks as it should. She helped clean and dress it for me before we ate a snack.

As time passed, Hana's mood started to decline, which was odd at first but understandable. She's usually so full of positive energy that it rolls off her and wants to latch onto everyone in the vicinity. Seeing her so tired and almost at her wits' end makes me hurt for her.

Without even thinking about it, I pull her into a hug. "He'll make it back. It's probably taking a long time traveling with so much in the way on the roads. Don't worry." Pulling back to look her in the eyes, I smile again, bigger this time, trying as hard as I can to believe what I am saying, more so for her sake. Not that I don't care if he's okay, but the anxiety and hurt clutching my heart to think that I may never make it to my only family left is debilitating. It also doesn't help that I actually *do* care and have been worrying about their safety.

Hana snorts at that and walks across the kitchen. She opens one of the cupboards to reveal a variety of alcohol. She finds a bottle of red wine on a built-in rack and gestures to the cupboard closest to me. "Can you grab some glasses?"

Without saying anything, I open the cabinet in search of two stemmed wine glasses and walk back over to where she is uncorking the bottle. Once ready, she pours us each a generous glass and walks out to the patio, taking the bottle with her.

Stepping through the French doors and around the corner, there are plush, comfortable patio lounge chairs facing the most breathtaking view I've seen by far. The sun begins to drop, causing the shore in the distance to glisten in oranges, reds, and pinks, reflecting the swirling clouds. The hills off to the side are covered in foliage, almost causing me to believe we are on holiday, enjoying a secluded stay far away from our mundane troubles.

"I was always jealous of his house. He got this place for a steal. This kind of view alone is worth every penny I have. You think?" she says as she sinks into the cushion and looks off into the distance.

The shore crashing against the cliffs in the background and the trees rustling in the breeze slowly help me relax. I take a sip of the wine, surprised by the earthy but tantalizing flavor.

"I won't lie to you, Hana. I'm genuinely surprised your brother not only has beautiful art in his even more beautiful home but even has a Sangiovese in his cupboard. I would think he'd be all beers and well..." I pause, tapping my chin to find a way to finish my sentence, when she interrupts me by giggling.

"Oh, hon, our little Ren is a paradox for sure. When he joined the military, many people were shocked. As a child, he was an incredibly gentle kid." Her eyes grow distant, lost in a memory. "He loved spending time among the trees and doodling. He was quiet but so full of life. Just not in the outgoing sense as myself or Haru."

She chuckles as she sips more of her glass. "But Ren..." She pauses and sets her glass on the table between our two chairs, looking back at the shore before continuing, much quieter. "Only my family knows, but Ren was with our mother and father when they died, and it was incredibly violent, especially for our mom. After that, well... he became even more reserved. Rarely spoke. When he grew old enough, he—" She stops abruptly as if she were about to reveal something she shouldn't.

"When he joined the military, my brother and I weren't at all surprised. Reiji wanted our brother to go back home and work with him, but Ren refused. I think he just wanted an escape, you know?"

She picks up her glass and takes a long swig, downing the rest, and I do the same. The heaviness that drapes over us makes me want to pour a second glass.

Hana must have the same idea. She fills both our glasses.

In the back of my head, I know it's probably not a good idea to drink, but I can't help but seek the relief it's starting to provide, masking our reality with a blindfold. If I can't feel it, it's not happening. At least, that's what my mind wants to believe. To stay ignorant in this new horror show. If only for one night.

"Anyway!" she says, having to force her normal perkiness. "He never lost those interests. He loves edgier things at times, as you may expect, but he's still that same boy underneath all his broodiness. As you saw, he's still invested in his doodles." She laughs. "He goes to auctions often enough and likes to spend a lot of time outside. He just tends to do it all alone." She shrugs, side-eyeing me as if searching for something.

I don't know what to say. I want to tell her it's a pleasant surprise if I'm being honest. It's nice to see some men can take pleasure in the arts and the natural world around us instead of wanting to either play sports or bang heads all the time. What do most men around here do? I don't know. I can't help the snort I let out at the thought, causing Hana to give me a funny look.

"Sorry, my thoughts ran away from me," I say as I take another large sip.

"Damn, you are quiet. I can see your mind moving a mile a minute, but you don't say what you're thinking." She laughs, this time with a genuine smile. "How about this— tell me, what have you been doing with yourself before all this hell broke loose? You came from the airport. Where'd you come back from?"

The alcohol's warmth is starting to loosen my muscles and, quite frankly, my mouth. I don't drink a lot anymore, but when I do, it does manage to get more words out of me.

"I was in Hawaii with my friend," I say, smiling. "She recently moved across the country and got married to her high school sweetheart. We decided that a little getaway was worth the money, so we splurged. She even surprised me with an extravagant spa experience."

I finish my wine, trying to brush the emotions that come with that thought. With my glass empty, Hana pours another. She's about to get me drunk at this rate.

But then you can forget. One night of drinking is fine...

"Oh, I love Hawaii! It's been years since I've been, though. Such a beautiful place. You traveled a lot growing up, yeah?"

My smile widens. "Yeah. My dad and I traveled a lot since he was in the service. Once he became an investigator, though, we started to settle. Which was kind of nice since I was getting older."

She stretches her arms above her head before pulling her feet up onto the chair and wrapping her arms around them, still holding her glass.

"What about your mom? Was she not with you?"

She must have noticed the wince because she speaks up before I can respond. "I'm sorry. I didn't mean to be insensitive if that's not a good topic. I get it," she says.

"It's okay. My mom left my dad soon after I was born. I don't remember her. It was just my dad and me. I'm lucky, though. He looked out for me as best as he could, and that was enough."

I smile, thinking about my dad. He was my rock. I couldn't have asked for a better man to raise me. He was as hard as steel to most of the world, but when it came to me, he knew how to soften up, showing me that sensitive heart of his. It couldn't have been easy raising me alone.

With those memories comes the reminder of his loss and the feeling of never getting the chance to make him proud. *What would he think of me now in all this?*

"Sounds like he was an awesome person. I'm sorry he's not here with you," she says softly.

Not wanting to dwell on his absence, I just whisper, "He was." I pick at a loose thread on my shirt while trying to think of something else to talk about. All I want is a distraction from the loss of my dad and not being with Meg.

We sit with our thoughts for a moment, sipping our drinks before she speaks again. "Did you have anyone else? A boyfriend or someone you need to get back to?"

I choke on my wine mid-swallow. This wasn't what I meant by distraction.

She reaches over to pat my back until the coughing fit goes away.

"Ugh. No." My chuckle is strained. Awkward. "I haven't been dating much. Not for a while at least..." I clear my throat." I don't have anyone other than Megan."

That loose strand on my shirt looks awfully interesting. I don't want to get into my dating life or lack thereof. Meg is the only one who I have ever felt comfortable talking about my past with or about the pitiful times I tried to go out with men.

How do I tell someone that I have tried seeing people but would end up getting ghosted? Or how do I mention that one of them must have had such a shit time with me that they acted petrified of me when we ran into each other. I still can't figure out why he acted that way, but it must have been something I did or said. Nothing else makes sense.

Regardless of why, how do I mention that without sounding pathetic?

Hana must sense how uncomfortable I am because she changes the subject. She sticks with small talk, keeps me chatting as we finish the bottle, and opens a second. We continue like that for a while.

The alcohol has my head swimming, and my nerves finally relax. We fall into silence again as we enjoy the night. The sun has long since set, and it's starting to get chilly, but it's a refreshing calm from the past few days.

"I'm sorry. You know—about my brother," Hana says abruptly. When I give her a questioning look, she clarifies, "I mean for a couple of things, actually. First, I'm sorry my brother came into your room when you got out of the shower." She chuckles despite her serious apology.

I raise my hands to stop her. "Oh no. That's fine. I mean, embarrassing, but it's not something you should apologize for," I tell her.

She dips her chin with a slight smile. "I swear he forgets that not everyone was in the military or values privacy. Those guys got used to living in close quarters a little too comfortably for my taste." She drains the last of her wine and sets it on the table next to mine.

"But I'm mostly sorry for when he almost hurt you. I've mentioned it before, but I still can't help but feel bad. I know he wouldn't ever do that intentionally, but he still messed up. I hope he apologized."

I rub my upper arms to try to warm myself up. "He did when he told me to wait here for a bit," I say.

"Good. He can be a bit broody and, in all honesty, can scare people sometimes with his intense expressions alone. I can't imagine what you feel after all that. So, I'm sorry if he scared you," she finishes.

I can see why people find him scary, but even with the intensity of his expression, he's still hands down the hottest man I've ever met. His intensity and the dangerous but protective vibes he gives off somehow make him even more attractive to me. How my brain can overlook that incident is beyond me, but somehow, it did.

Loud, boisterous laughter has my head whipping up. Hana is doubled over with tears in her eyes. "Oh my god, that's amazing. Oh, hon!" She's still laughing and wiping her eyes. "You find that ass-hat hot?" Her laughter dies down, but she's still beaming.

The blood drains from my face when I realize my mistake. Horrified, I ask, "I just said that out loud, didn't I?" I don't think my face could get any more hot and flushed.

"Yup," she says, popping the P with amusement.

I was wrong.

It can.

Oh. My. God.

I cover my face with my hands and slouch forward.

Even as embarrassing as it is, I meant what I said. I can tell with just a glance that his figure isn't only from working out in a gym daily. It was muscle honed from the real use of his body in either work or action. I've been around enough military men and women to know when one was from their mandatory physical training at the butt crack of dawn and the ones who used their bodies for more than paper-pushing or whatever their military occupational specialty, or also known as their MOS, entailed at their duty station.

There is also something about him that tells me he's capable, and he's clearly confident. Someone you could genuinely depend on. That speaks to me more than his appearance alone, making him even more attractive.

Too bad we'll go our separate ways. Otherwise, it would be nice to dive a little deeper into why I find him so attractive despite everything that's happened. Although, I should've learned my lesson by now about dating military men.

Hana's voice pulls me out of my wandering thoughts. "It's okay. I actually kind of figured. I just never expected to hear you say it. That makes me happy, considering he pushes most women away." She leans forward and rubs my shoulder, meaning to comfort me. When I uncover my face, she's still smiling. "Let's finish this inside. I want to raid his pantry," she says, thankfully changing the subject.

Before we stand, an alarm wails from somewhere in the house.

My heart flies into my throat, and we both jump up out of our seats.

"What is that?" I ask. The sound is loud but not as loud as some home security systems I've heard. It sounds more like a personal detection system than something to scare the perpetrator or call for authorities.

"Shit. That's one of his perimeter alarms." Hana scans our surroundings, squinting into the dark yard. "Crap... Inside. Now," she commands. Despite the glassy eyes from alcohol, her demeanor transforms completely. Somehow, even drunk, she remains calm and escorts me back inside. Some of the men file outside and begin fanning out around the property.

My head is spinning from the alcohol and the new fear coursing through me. "Why would that be going off?" I ask her, hoping she'll tell me. Did those things make their way here? Are we no longer safe?

Our gazes clash at the sound of a truck pulling up the driveway and our eyes widen. We take off for the front door.

Hana peeks out the window before inhaling sharply and flinging the door open.

The truck is pulling in front of the garage as we rush outside, the alarm long forgotten. The motion-sensor lights go on to reveal the once-pristine truck. The windshield is cracked and what looks like dark blood is coating the front and side of the vehicle. There are holes in the exterior, which causes my blood to run cold.

The guys all climb out of the truck, looking beaten and exhausted. They're covered in grime and dried blood and appear not to have slept in days.

My eyes zero in on Ren. He's covered from head to toe. It looks as if he tried to clean himself up but only made it worse. He normally appears put together but now it's like he's minutes away from toppling over.

With the alcohol fully in effect, I rush to meet him while he starts walking up the steps to the front. But before Hana and I can ask him what happened, he notices the alarm.

Despite his evident exhaustion, his eyes are sharp as he scans the yard. "Matt. Juan," he calls them. "Help my brother's men search the perimeter. Something's breached the property. I'm taking them inside."

Hana and I don't get a chance to say anything. He grabs us by the arms and starts pulling us inside the house. When Hana trips and sways a little, he audibly curses. "Jesus, Hana." His voice is laced with irritation, but he doesn't stop.

He's taking us inside when Reiji enters the family room. His face slips for a second when he sees the state of his brother. Instead of mentioning it, though, he focuses on the present. "Haven't found anything yet. I set Haru in your room for now until we secure the garage."

Ren only responds with a soft grunt before continuing to rush us down the hall. It's not long before he pushes us into his room and shuts the door behind us, leaving us alone with a drowsy Ru, who's sitting in the chair.

Hana isn't having any of it, though. "Can you stay with the kid?"

"Sure," I say. My nerves are making it hard to speak.

She may be visibly drunk, but she opens the door and walks out of the room with a determined look on her face.

I turn around and sit on Ren's bed, glancing at Ru. "You alright, kid?" I ask him,

"Yeah," he responds sleepily. "Do you know what's happening?"

"I don't." I glance back at the door. "Your dad and uncle have it covered though, whatever it is."

Just then, Reiji walks in. He grabs Ru's shoulder and looks at me. "We're bringing all the kids into the garage. You're welcome to join them. It'll be more secure there until we know what set the alarms off," he tells me.

"I may go back into the guest bedroom, but thank you."

With that, him and Ru leave, not wasting any time.

It may be safer to go with him, and I know rationally I should, but the alcohol battling my healthy logic is winning. Instead, I walk down the hall back into the room I'm staying in. My head still feels like it's swimming. *Ugh, why did I drink so much?* What kind of idiot gets drunk at a time like this?

Taking a seat on my bed, I pull the sketchbook out of the backpack. The book isn't as empty as I thought it would be but instead, almost filled. I flip through the sketches of landscapes and a few portraits. Most of the portraits are of the same woman. The longer I take them in, I see more and more similarities between her and Ren. The last sketch I find of her, the resemblance is blaringly obvious, and I realize this might be his mother. There are a few sketches of his siblings and Ru. There is one other sketch of a man before I flip the page to the incomplete set of eyes.

Someone is shouting something about checking the other side of the property and heavy steps running inside the house. I glance up, and at the same time, someone is running down the hall, his gun in his hand.

What the hell is happening?

My pulse is racing at the thought of having to run again. If not zombies though, what could it be. Could it be other people seeking out safety out here in the hills?

A soft rattle reaches my ears. It's barely audible against the still blaring alarm from somewhere inside the house so I brush it off. My eyes stray back to the sketchbook.

I only hope the alarms aren't loud enough to attract more zombies. It's louder inside, but from outside it hadn't been as bad. Hopefully, that's a good thing.

Another rattle sounds behind me just as Ren walks through the door.

"Where the hell is—" He stops. His attention is stuck on something behind me.

He moves too fast for my inebriated eyes to follow.

Grabbing me, he pulls me up from the bed and shoves me behind him.

Dread settles in my belly. There's a man there.

It's so brief, but I almost believe the pair of eyes staring back at me are familiar.

He's gone before my cloudy brain can fully register the thought.

Ren's own weapon is raised as he moves to the open window.

Everything happens so fast and slow at the same time while my body fights to sober up.

Ren, not having been quick enough to reach whoever was outside, shouts to someone down the hall.

The alarm finally turns off, and his friend James peeks his head into the room. "We saw someone hopping your fence." His eyes flick to me before settling back on Ren. "It was only one person, but they're gone. I think we spooked them."

Ren clenches his jaw. "Check the property again. Have Dirk help double-check the fences. The ones facing the hills should have been turned on."

Turned on? Like what... an electric fence?

"You okay?" Ren asks me.

He steps up closer, his brows furrowing when I don't respond immediately.

I slightly sway, and by the annoyed expression that crosses his face, he must have realized I'm not sober.

"Seriously?" he asks incredulously. His face hardens slightly while he waits for me to say something. Instead of acting mad, he almost appears resigned, his exhaustion weighing heavily on him.

Up close, I can make out the scratches on his face underneath the dirt and blood. My drunkenness forgets the commotion and the threats outside when I take this all in. I can't hide the concern that flares to life as I boldly touch his shoulder to look at him. His arms are also cut up, but it's hard to tell the extent of his injuries with the grime caking his body. My hand reaches his cheek as I lean in for a closer look at a particularly deep scrape on his neck. "You're hurt," I say softly.

Surprise flashes across his face, but he doesn't pull away. Instead, his eyes bore into me. His hand reaches up to mine, still slightly cupping his cheek.

Butterflies erupt in my belly as my eyes break away from his injuries and meet his gaze. He may try hard to appear unfazed by everything, but his exhaustion allows the uncertainty and what I think is confusion to mar his face. His Adam's Apple bobs as he swallows, and he gently removes my hand but doesn't let go. "I—"

He's cut off as Hana barges into the room and he lets go of my hand quickly as if he was caught doing something he shouldn't be. Hana's just as drunk as I am, and with her ever-steady fear that has been growing over the past few days, she must have finally reached her breaking point.

Her eyes are watery when she regards her brother. "What the fuck, Ren. Where were you?" It's like what just happened didn't faze her, as if the house wasn't in a panic only moments before. She's solely focused on why her brother was gone so long.

He sighs and rubs his forehead. "Hana, I feel like roadkill. I need to make sure everything is safe, and get myself cleaned up; then we can all talk." He directs his gaze to me. "Can you guys just hang out on the couch in the living room?"

Was his voice softer with me than when he spoke to his sister?

Nope. You're drunk. Just your mind messing with you. Like how you almost believed you saw who you thought you did outside. Only your imagination.

Shit, I need to sleep this off.

Still in a daze, I dip my head and walk out of the room.

It isn't long before Hana and I are curled up on the couch. I try to keep my eyes open as Reiji and a few others discuss what happened, but the alcohol finally wins its battle.

Chapter Eighteen

Dahlia

A swaying motion has me struggling to open my eyes. Failing, I slip back into my drunken slumber.

A soft groan next to me makes me open my eyes, and I'm met with Hana touching her head.

"Damn. I should have at least had a snack or some water," she croaks, rolling to her back. "Never let me talk you into wine without food. Ever. Again," she emphasizes.

I chuckle only to then clutch my own achy head. It doesn't escape my notice that we're in Ren's room. I sit up and ask Hana, "When did we come lay down?"

Or what I actually want to ask is, why here?

Audibly groaning, the blanket that was covering me falls to my lap when I sit up. I need to finalize my plans. Maybe I can even try to leave today if I'm not feeling like death incarnate.

I raise my head when there's a soft knock, and my pulse quickens as her brother strolls in.

He's now in clean clothing, with not a speck of blood on his body. He's wearing a black long-sleeve shirt and faded gray jeans that fit him perfectly. Although he's covered, it doesn't hide how his muscles slightly strain the fabric on his sleeves or chest. It only makes me curious what he looks like from behind.

The sight distracts me long enough not to notice their other brother walking in behind him. He's dressed like he just got out of a business meeting instead of surviving the apocalypse. He's sporting a white dress shirt, cuffs rolled up with the first button undone, and nice slacks.

I get the feeling he doesn't know how to unwind, although the colorful tattoos covering his arms only litter my mind with questions regarding these mysterious brothers.

"How's the head?" Ren smirks at his sister.

She groans and throws her pillow at his head, only causing him to chuckle when she misses.

I sneak a peek to see him giving her a playful smile, which then shifts to concern.

My breath catches at his smile and then again at his obvious love for his sister. This man, who appears to be nothing but a stoic rock, looks at his sister with such affection that it almost steals my breath altogether.

"You worried me there. You never drink like that, Hana. You passed out as soon as you sat down." Ren walks over and sits at the end of the bed. Their brother leans against the wall near the door, eyeing Hana.

Not wanting to be a part of their family heart-to-heart, I quietly get up to make my way to the bathroom down the hall. I'm too afraid of using the one attached to the room.

I do a quick mental checklist of things, like getting dressed and brushing my teeth, but also clean my car and ensure I have everything ready to go. But before I can even make it off the bed, a hand grabs mine, pulling me back.

"You don't have to leave. You're welcome here, hon. Also, if they lecture me, you being here lessens the blow." She winks before looking at her brother, whose attention is now solely on me with his usual, cool gaze.

"Anyway, we were worried about you, jackass. So, I decided we could take the time to get to know each other better over a drink and temporarily forget that my idiot baby brother decided to go out and gallivant around the city of the dead as if it was the Vegas strip!" She throws up her hands in exacerbation. "Plus, we didn't plan on getting drunk, but we hadn't eaten and lost track of time. I know it's incredibly stupid to drink like that right now when we may never be safe again, but I guess I wasn't thinking."

I chuckle despite it not being funny. She is right; it was stupid. Even if I'm still unsure as to what actually happened last night, it's the perfect example of why we shouldn't drink. I guess I had been too eager for the temporary escape to think it through. If my point hadn't been made to me by now that I wouldn't survive out there alone, that should do it.

Reiji straightens as he addresses his sister. "It *was* incredibly stupid, Hana. I hadn't been aware you both were drinking that heavily." His eyes flick to me for a second before returning to her. "I'll skip the lecture, but I need to know you won't make poor decisions like that again. I need to know you'll be safe." His tone is low but firm. Somehow, it packs more weight than if he shouted.

"It won't happen again." She lowers her gaze while guilt plasters her features. "I'm sorry, Reiji-sama."

My brows scrunch at that. I don't think I've heard her address her brother like that before.

When Rei doesn't respond, her head comes up, and she looks to her other brother. "Anyway, sorry we fell asleep. What the hell happened to you, Ren? I was worried." She grows serious again, tears welling in her eyes.

Oh damn. This is why I didn't want to be present. Not that crying makes me uncomfortable. I mean, I cry. But this is family stuff. I'm here for the ride temporarily.

"I'll spare the details, but we're going to have a meeting with everyone. Have you gotten around to asking?" He stares intently at Hana.

She shakes her head, and I swear he rolls his eyes at her response.

He runs his hand through his hair before glancing at his brother. "We were talking, and we have a proposition for you." His eyes meet mine this time, raising his eyebrows as if in question.

"For me?" I ask in confusion, looking around as if someone else was in the room.

"Yes, you." He pauses and rubs the back of his neck. "We wanted to come with you. In short, we want to get home but haven't found a safe place for our pilot to land yet."

I just stare at him, a little dumbfounded.

When I don't say anything, he keeps talking. "You told me where your friend is, that it's currently safe. Since it's a small town, it may stay that way for now."

I probably look like a deer caught in the headlights. Can't they go anyway? Why do they need me for this venture, or why tell me at all?

Hana's warm hand squeezes mine reassuringly, making me realize I still haven't said anything.

"This might be a good thing. You can come with us if you'd like. Your friend, too," she says, looking at her brothers like she's confirming that it is okay.

"We don't *need* to travel there, but knowing it's a safe place for now is a good enough reason to risk the distance to get there," Rei explains. "Nothing here will be as safe since we are surrounded by busy counties. I also told you that we are in your debt. I want to extend the invitation for you to come with us." He offers me a small smile, which surprises me more than their proposal.

They're offering me a chance—a real chance to survive this and not be alone while trying to get to Meg. I can't survive this alone. I was already thinking this before they got back, but seeing how disheveled they were on their return was confirmation enough. It doesn't take more than a second for me to respond.

"That would be amazing," I whisper.

My eyes mist over from relief and from knowing I won't have to do this alone or give up trying to get to the only person I have left.

Grinning, I turn to Hana who is also gifting me with her warmest smile. "Good! Now, let's go get some Tylenol and water, yeah? What's for breakfast?" she asks, her perky attitude in full swing.

She gets up from the bed and leaves the room with Rei on her heels, trying to slow her down.

Ren shifts slightly where he's seated, reminding me I'm not alone.

He clears his throat. "I'm sorry we took longer to get back. I know I asked you to wait a day, but things took an unexpected turn out there." He tilts his head, giving me a sideways glance. "I also wanted to have time to think it over and then speak with Rei."

"No worries. I'm just glad you guys made it back alive," I tell him.

Memories of last night flash to the forefront of my mind. A pang of embarrassment hits me square in the chest, but I don't have much time to dwell on it when Ren speaks up again.

"Are you sure you're fine with us tagging along?"

Planting my feet on the ground, I slowly walk around the bed to face him. I wish I could say how terrified I was about venturing out alone. I would have died, most likely immediately. Even with them, I could still die, but my odds are a lot better.

He pushes his disheveled hair out of his eyes. He usually has it styled with the top slicked back. Now, it's a loose mess falling into his face and giving him a rougher, albeit sexy, look.

"It would be pointless for us to aimlessly search for another place a plane could land. It would most likely get everyone killed and waste any resources we have," he says, like he's just talking about the weather and not everyone dying. It almost sounds like the resources are more important than those lives.

I wince, not able to control it at the mention of more violent deaths in such a nonchalant manner.

"I'm sorry," he says. There's sincerity behind his words but also a bone-deep tiredness.

Something about the way he sits there, giving me his full attention, has my heart racing. Being alone with him makes me more comfortable than I thought possible with a man. In each encounter with him, there is never that normal uneasy feeling from being too close or even touching. There's something about him that makes me feel like he wouldn't judge or ridicule me when I speak my truth.

Testing out that theory, I decide to say what's on my mind. "I was terrified," I whisper. "I've been thinking that if you and your friends couldn't make it out there, then I have no hope whatsoever. I won't survive. Even though you guys made it, how you looked... Well, it scared me. It only proves my own point and makes everything even more real. This is all real." I wave my hand to indicate the situation around us.

"I'm not strong enough..." Once I started, I couldn't stop the word vomit from spewing.

His eyes bore into mine. Unflinching, he says, "Somehow, I doubt that."

His stare is unyielding until his eyes drift across my reddening face. If I didn't know any better, I would mistake the way his gaze dances along my skin as a mix of longing and lust. But instead of elaborating on what he just said, he walks away.

He isn't one to continue conversations, I guess. Usually, that wouldn't bother me, but for some reason, it does.

Maybe I just don't want him to leave.

I follow him out but make my way back to the room where my clothes are. After quickly dressing in jeans, a soft purple T-shirt, and a hoodie and using the restroom, I walk back out to the living room.

Everyone is gathered, some snacking on small bags of chips or crackers while talking amongst themselves. Five women are crowded on the couch and chairs in the family room while the kids are all sitting on the floor near them. The men are divided into two groups between both rooms. Matt and Ren's other friends are together while the others speak with Rei.

From the sounds of it, everyone is trying to plan their next steps. My eyes roam the crowd before I find Hana sitting at the kitchen island. Her eyes meet mine, and she waves me over with a smile.

Walking over, some of the other conversations around the room become clearer. Although everyone is whispering, it seems that many of them want to stay here.

Hana pats the bar stool next to her and passes me a bag of nuts, two Tylenol, and a bottle of water. I gratefully take the snack and medicine, pull the stool out, and sit. Since there are so many of us inside the house, we have already run out of most of the food in the fridge.

"So, what's the plan then," I ask before I swallow the pills. Her eyes flick behind me towards everyone else.

"I think Rei wants to leave tomorrow or the day after. We need to make sure we have anything we can use since we can't come back. I guess most of these people don't want to travel. Rei is going to talk to them soon as a group." She grabs another handful of nuts.

Why would anyone want to stay? I understand it may feel safer from the zombies, but there's no food or water. Once you run out, that's it. There isn't a lot of space to plant food here or at least space where it would be easy to and from what I've seen so far, no fresh water sources. They would need to find somewhere with fresh water, at least.

Also, do they all not remember last night? I was drunk, but I caught on enough to realize someone had broken onto the property before running away. More people could come but not be spooked away the next time.

"Seriously?" I ask.

"Rei is going to give them the option to follow along, at least until we find them somewhere safer. He's worried about the ones with their kids; otherwise, he'd let them make that choice. He's all tough exterior, but the biggest softie when it comes to children."

I can't help but be surprised by that. I've seen how he is with Ru, but I still can't picture him as a family man. However, I agree with him in that respect. The kids would be safe here for a short time before they starved. And that's if no other people intervened first. Hopefully, they can stay safe in a group until they find somewhere to settle and fortify.

Instead of verbally agreeing, I grab more nuts. My stomach is protesting the little food I've already neglected to eat.

"We'll need to get food soon," I mumble.

"Don't worry, Dahl, we'll be good." Smiling and getting up, she pats my shoulder and walks over to grab a water bottle. On her way back to her seat, she stops to look behind me again.

"We have a plan laid out," Rei says from the living room.

Everyone focuses on him where he stands in the middle of the room. I'm now noticing Ren is off in the corner, arms crossed, leaning against the wall.

"We plan on making our way to a small town in Utah that we have under good impression is safe right now. I know this length of travel is scary and has its risks. On the other hand, what we need can be found there instead of taking twice as long and twice the risk to aimlessly search for what we know is available elsewhere.

"I understand some of you have concerns, but I assure you, staying together will be safer. At least, long enough until we come across somewhere you want to stay."

He makes eye contact with everyone, taking a second on each face. "It may seem safer to stay here, but from what Ren has told me, it won't be. Either there will be no food or water and nothing within miles to scavenge, or others will take notice of the homes out here and want to take them for themselves. They won't hesitate to kill for it. Don't let last night fool you. One person breaching the property will be the least of your worries should you stay here."

A few soft gasps and murmurs follow his declaration. I study Ren with curiosity, wondering what actually happened out there.

My eyes linger on how his shirt stretches tightly across his chest and then trek up to his face. When they clash with his, I gasp and turn in my seat like I got caught with my hand in the cookie jar.

I wasn't expecting him to be watching me, especially with that same look he gave me last night. It was curiosity and confusion all bundled together. My cheeks heat, knowing he caught me checking him out again.

I risk another peek, but his eyes are on his brother now. His expression has shifted back to his normal one, just as intense as usual. If anything, it may be a bit more intimidating. If I had to guess, it was because of how many people are in the room. From what I have seen and heard, he doesn't trust easily, and I can't imagine he likes sharing his home with so many people.

"We mapped out a set of meeting points along our route to Parowan. Should we ever get separated, we can use those points to meet. The trip by car would normally be seven to eight hours, but we expect it to take at least a couple of days."

"Days?" one of the women asks, interrupting Rei.

Don, I believe his name is, speaks up. "Tobi." He glowers at another man among their large group.

"Apologies for the interruption, Reiji-sama," Tobi says. Glaring at the woman who spoke, he gives her a silent shake of his head. Her face closes off before she dips her chin with an eye roll he doesn't notice.

Well. That's weird.

Reiji speaks up, not seeming as annoyed by the interruption as Don was. "I know you all have questions and concerns," he addresses everyone. "From my understanding, the roads are more congested, and because sound attracts attention, we'll need to go slow. It'll be a long trip." He looks over to his brother in silent communication.

Ren takes a step forward. "The groups we went over last time will be important. When we need you on fire watch or going on supply runs, you'll need to step up. We have to work together to ensure we survive. I added a few of the men to help you ladies with the children." He directs his attention to the group who hadn't wanted to volunteer for anything.

Although I don't know if I can handle some of the tasks we may face, I was surprised that most women just wanted children duty. Just the thought of needing to keep them all safe has my anxiety tap-dancing in my chest.

"Dahlia." My stomach does a little flip when Ren says my name.

"Hmm?" I meet his eyes again.

"Since you'll be with us, you'll be helping us with supply runs and with the kids."

Those little flips in my stomach turn into an anvil. The responsibility alone is like a dead weight on my shoulders. I want to be a help to the group, but I'm terrified of screwing up.

"Is that alright?" Ren asks when I don't respond.

I swallow. "That's fine," I say, the pitch in my voice heightening.

He gives me a nod before giving the floor back to his brother.

Would it kill him to actually speak instead of silent gestures? And why is that so annoying to me?

Rei pulls our attention again with his authoritative voice. "If you have questions or concerns, don't sit on them. Speak up. To stay alive, we need to work together and not hesitate. Let Don or Ren know if there is something you need to say. We plan on leaving tomorrow at dawn. Get some rest and be ready." With that, he leaves the room.

"Ever the serious one," Hana whispers behind me with a snarky snort. "Come on, I overheard one of the guys mentioning prep work. We can help."

She grabs my hand and drags me off towards the garage.

Prep work turns out to be cleaning out all the cars outside, including mine, and organizing and evenly distributing supplies amongst each vehicle. Ren suggested I keep anything I already had in my car, including the little food and provisions I have.

Before we get started on prepping weapons, I take a break to grab something from my freshly organized car. To my surprise, someone has left the supplies I asked for on my driver's seat. Knowing it was probably Ren, my stomach flutters with nerves, especially after seeing the light I hadn't asked for included in everything.

Later, while we work on more prep, I try to add the modifications to my shotgun. The bayonet was precisely what I was looking for, but I can't get it to mount properly, so I put it aside to ask for help later. Although it will be embarrassing, I'm hoping I'm an idiot in this case and there isn't something wrong with the lug.

The other weapons we have to prepare are the bats. Ren's friends, James and Juan, are helping Hana while I hammer nails into the wood. The other women helped briefly but ended up sitting in the living room with the kids. With the excuses they gave, it's like they just didn't want to work, but it's not my place to say anything. The others are helping Ren and Reiji finalize things like finishing up packing the cars and going over their plans.

"I guess work is too much for them." James snorts as he starts hammering a nail into his bat.

Juan shakes his head. His disheveled curls bounce with the motion, and his dark eyes are full of amusement while he gives his friend a sideways glance. He reaches over the table to grab some of the larger nails, his muscles straining against his tight, light blue T-shirt as he leans forward. The color is soft against his olive-brown skin and the contrasting deep-colored tattoo on his left bicep. My eyes zero in on the small Marine Corps tattoo amidst the others decorating his upper arm, but it's not an insignia I am familiar with.

James' laugh has me glancing up. "Looks like someone's getting distracted." He elbows Juan. "Maybe our man got some competition."

Their laughs make my cheeks heat.

"Nah, *hermano*. I saw how she ran to him and how she watches him. We're chopped liver," Juan says with a chuckle.

"Way to break my heart," James says with his hand over his heart. "You break a man's heart, freckles. You sure you want to keep eyeballin' that sad asshole? The dark side isn't very fun." He smiles. "We have jokes and real smiles over here." He laughs at himself, and Juan grins in amusement.

They both must see how bright red I'm getting because they stop chuckling. The fact that they noticed me practically running at Ren and have caught me staring is mortifying. It's already embarrassing enough, but more so when I don't even know how to feel, but they call me out on it anyway. Embarrassed, I hammer the nail into the bat.

"Sorry, *Chula*. We're only messing with you. If we're embarrassing you, just say so. I can smack James for you." Juan leans down and tilts his head to come into my line of sight from the other side of the table. He gives me a small smile before they both get back to work.

"Crap," I mumble. The bat beneath me is split from where I hammered the nail. I shove the embarrassment aside but only replace it with irritation. *Can't I even do this right?*

The bat is an older one that someone found in their car instead of one of the new ones. The nails are too thick, and the wood is too brittle, but I can't help but still feel incompetent, as the others are nailing their bats without issues.

Reaching across the table, I grab a few thinner nails and duct tape. Hopefully, the tape will keep the bat from splitting further.

I wrap some tape around the bat a few times to keep the split form from worsening. As I hammer in the smaller nails, I notice they're barely large enough, but they will have to do. It'll still be better than having no weapon.

Once that's done, I move on to the next one. The guys go on talking, but I keep to myself.

Thankfully, I only messed up on the first bat, but I can't help but feel irritated at myself. We need functional weapons, not something that will break at first use.

Once we finish the bats, we move on to the last task. The guys found grip tape on their run, so they applied it on all the tire irons, crowbars, and even the bats. I have a crowbar and a rusty tire iron myself, which I happily used the tape on.

Going through all our prep work lasts most of the day, and once we are done, we are all ready to relax before we leave tomorrow. Although we need to start rationing food as best as we can, we collectively decide we can indulge ourselves a bit. We don't know what awaits us behind those doors tomorrow. We all want to have one last meal at least and to fall asleep feeling safe and with a full belly.

It's hard to imagine that it could be our last night, but the more I let the thought sit, the more it feels like the truth.

Chapter Nineteen

Ren

My mind is a whirlwind of chaos, my anxiety threatening to pull me into its grasp while the past few days finally catch up to me. I'm going through the last of my things, making sure I don't leave anything I may want to take with me behind, but my exhausted body just wants to lie down.

It's like I've been dragged through the dirt and thrown over a rocky cliff. Exhaustion can't even describe the weary state of my body right now, not to mention my mental state. I lie down, confident enough that I should have everything ready. If sleep would claim me, I'd be happy. Instead of sleeping, though, my mind keeps racing.

We managed the run, although there were hiccups, but to come back and find someone had breached the property and got away? It pissed me off. Pissed that I didn't do anything to catch the person. Pissed, they almost managed to get into the house. And just overall pissed at our situation.

I thought I would be used to this feeling of being in a state of survival and readiness for a prolonged time. The perpetual fighting and running. Although there were times that would be considered rough in my past, like being starved, sitting in a damn hole with nothing but my rifle, rats, and brothers for company for days on end, this still seems to top any experience.

The difference now is that there's less hope of returning to something better at the end of it. Deployments weren't easy. The shit I've done would never be considered easy, but I always had the knowledge that I'd get to go home if I lived long enough. There was an end in sight. Not to mention, it's not just my men and me anymore. It's my family that I need to protect against the world now.

Another sobering thought is that this has only barely begun. We still have food, water, and relatively safe walls surrounding us. Once we walk outside tomorrow, we may never find that safety again. We'll be living day by day in constant fear.

My nerves are flaring to life at the reminder that my family's safety will be in my hands completely. This may never end. We may not even make it out of this city, let alone the state. Every time my thoughts go to Haruto, I swear my heart almost stops. For him to have already seen what awaits us is enough to make my damn head hurt but to make him go back out there and face it again?

Sighing, I brush my hair out of my face and close my eyes.

I'm finally dozing when laughter outside the room jolts me awake. We all agreed to let everyone enjoy this last night. Rei and I both warned them not to have too much fun, though, because nobody wants to allow a nasty hangover to cost them their life. We'll have to be focused when we leave and at our best. We emphasized that to Hana and Dahlia.

When I realized they were both drunk, I almost lost it. I know Hana can take care of herself, but Dahlia? She was so intoxicated that she didn't even notice the man halfway through the window of the bedroom. The fucker had a balaclava on, covering his face. His eyes were intent on Dahlia before he booked it, which only set me off. I couldn't help but feel like he wasn't only there to steal from us, but he was gone before we could question him.

I'm hoping sleep will find me when a soft knock disrupts my efforts, and the door opens.

I should have started locking my door.

"Don't bother, Hana. I'm trying to sleep." I cover my eyes with my arm.

The soft footsteps stop, but she doesn't respond. My annoyance flares. Can't she give me five minutes alone? I move my arm and sit up, ready to tell her to get the hell out, but it's not Hana.

"I'm sorry," Dahlia says. She's standing in the middle of the room, clutching something behind her back. "Uhm. Hana wanted me to come ask you if you'd like to join us, but..." She trails off, looking everywhere but at me.

I can't help but scoff. Of course, Hana sent her in to do her dirty work. "I'm trying to get some sleep," I tell her.

"Uhm. Yeah... Sure. Uhm." Her gaze finds me for the first time since she came in. "I also wanted to return this." She reveals my sketchbook from behind her back.

My anger only worsens. "What the fuck? You stealing shit now?"

She flinches and takes a step back. "No. I'm sorry. I meant to give it back sooner, but things were crazy."

"That doesn't explain how you ended up with it," I say, narrowing my eyes.

She shifts from foot to foot before placing it on the bed. "Hana accidentally gave it to me instead of a blank one. I'm sorry..." She looks down at the floor. "Honestly, I didn't mean to bother you or take your stuff."

Some of the anger subsides, but I know full well Hana doesn't do things like that without it being intentional, and it still simmers beneath the surface.

Instead of responding right away, I stand up and walk over to the closet to throw on a shirt.

Grabbing a black long-sleeved t-shirt, I turn to Dahlia. I don't miss the way her eyes automatically take in my bare chest, skimming my skin with heat behind them. Her eyes cast a trail of flames in their wake.

I try to brush off the way her gaze has my pulse racing. "Sure, *angel*," I say the pet name with a sneer, unable to help myself. I believe her, but her eyes singe my skin, so I direct my irritation at how my body responds and how my sister wants to meddle at her.

"That's not fair," she says. Her voice is still quiet and a little tentative, but it gains some strength as she keeps talking. "I know you don't actually know me, but I haven't done anything to deserve your snarky remarks. Take it out on your sister. Not me." She storms off with her back a little straighter, more confident.

That little fire shocks me. I may even admire it a little, not that I'll tell her that. "Wait!" I call out, pulling the hem of my shirt down. "Look, I get it was Hana. She likes to meddle in shit she shouldn't be putting her nose in."

She stops by the door and whirls around. "I can see that." She snorts. "I get the feeling there was an ulterior motive for talking me into coming in here instead of her."

My chuckle surprises me, but it comes naturally. "Most likely." I sit on the edge of the bed. "Just let her know you tried, and I told you I only want to sleep."

"Okay. Well, goodnight." She's out the door without another glance.

If the zombies don't kill me first, it'll be Hana. She has a way with people. Even when she's torn to shreds inside, she still manages to stay positive, always wanting to make new friends. She also has a way of getting people to follow along with her wild ideas. She probably got the shy new girl to come in here without much of a fight.

My sister is smart. Rei was always proud of how well she used her innocent and friendly personality when it came to not-so-friendly people. Although, it seems she can persuade the nice ones just as easily. She isn't someone to mess with, that's for sure. Although she could never officially be a part of the family's clan, she started to dabble here and there when she realized her position in a hospital someday could be valuable for the family. I need to keep an eye on her; otherwise, she's going to get herself or Dahlia in trouble.

My mind tracks back to the way Dahlia looked at me and the way my body reacted. I can't ever remember having a woman look at me like that. Lust but intertwined with something else. Something I'm not used to.

My eyes catch on the sketchbook. Did she open it? She must have if she knew it wasn't blank. Grabbing it, I open it to the last page I had drawn. The image stares back at me. Realization dawns when I continue to take in the details of the sketch. *Fuck. I drew her, didn't I?*

Laughing echoes down the hall, reminding me that everyone is enjoying what could be their last night.

Our last night.

Groaning, I get back up and decide to join my family.

I shut my door behind me and walk down the hall, only to stop short. Dahlia is standing there, transfixed on an art piece. The painting is one of the few copies I have, not an original. I had it professionally commissioned years ago to support an artist and thoroughly enjoy it.

It's a depiction of Van Gogh's painting, *Skull of a Skeleton with Burning Cigarette*; one of my favorites.

She has a ghost of a smile as she observes the piece of art, lost in thought.

I can slightly make out her eyes as moonlight seeps through the windows, surrounding her as if with purpose. They almost seem to change every time I see her, from green to blue and back again. I think that's why I started to draw her. It was the first thing I noticed when we found her.

Now, in the dim space with the moon's cast, they remind me of a shadowed forest of lush green, contrasting against her skin and freckles. Her red hair also looks darker here, causing her eyes to strike me harder. My gaze tracks down her hair as if snared in a waterfall, slowing as I take in her curves.

I'm unable to look away as I catch her hourglass figure, falling to hips that elicit images of my hands running down her waist and hips. A myriad of thoughts of what I'd like to do to her body flash before my eyes like a movie reel. My heart is racing again, my whole body heating with the memories of how her eyes lingered and drank in my bare chest.

I continue my perusal, trying to shake the feelings she unknowingly elicits. I stop again on the splash of color tattooed on her right arm: a full sleeve of wisteria and other flowers, butterflies, and a few other things I couldn't make out without closer inspection. Blues, violets, and deep reds blend with shades of greens and black. It only makes me want to pull her closer to have the opportunity to appreciate the beautiful art painted on her skin.

Forgetting why I was even in the hall, I walk up beside her, staying quiet as I take in the way she studies the painting. She doesn't notice me until I stand beside her, shoulders brushing. My pulse increases with the warmth of her body. Shit, I hope she hasn't noticed me watching her.

"Sorry, I didn't see you there." She smiles shyly at me before returning her attention to the painting. "I was looking at how incredible this was painted. Someone must have studied his work to the point of obsession. It's beautiful." Her smile grows as her eyes meet mine. "This was always one of my favorites. Reminds me of a *memento mori,* a reminder of death. Some think it was painted as a joke, but I don't know." Her eyes trace the small image, taking in every minuscule detail as her face alights with wonder and equal contemplation. "Either way, it always gives me a lot to think about."

I can't help the ache in my chest as I continue to watch her. Somehow, she surprises me again. I can reluctantly admit she's beautiful, especially here, staring at one of my favorite pieces with real appreciation.

Clearing my throat, I excuse myself before I do something stupid, like continue my earlier thoughts and act upon them.

She may be beautiful and thought-provoking, but it doesn't change anything. I don't need the complication. I need to focus on my family's safety and not allow my thoughts to run away with me about some girl.

When I step outside, Reiji, Hana, and Haru are all lounging around the patio chairs. Rei is leaning against the window while Hana and Haru share one of the chairs.

I sit down at the edge of the lounger when Hana says, "Finally! I knew she could do it." She glances towards the door. "Where'd she go?"

I jerk my head toward the house just as Dahlia steps outside. I move to stand, but she quickly says, "You're fine. I can fit." She climbs on the lounge chair, trying not to bump into me, and sits against the back cross-legged.

Although we both can fit, I choose to get up anyway. "It's alright," I say and move to stand beside my brother.

Hana immediately jumps into the conversation, although it's mostly one-sided from the sound of it, while Hana talks Dahlia's ear off.

Rei pulls a pack of cigarettes out of his pocket, accompanied by a lighter. Our eyes meet over the soft glow of the lighter's flame as he inhales. To an outsider, they would think we're only looking at each other, but Rei knows I am silently asking a question. *Are you okay?*

He only ever smokes anymore when he's nervous about something. He was never a regular smoker but quit altogether years ago when his son was born. His smoking gave him away. His silent answer to me is to look at Haru, who is now giggling at something Dahlia said as she sips a glass of wine Hana poured her.

Flashes of last night come to the surface. Dahlia touching me, expressing real concern for *me*. She may have been drunk, but I can't forget the look of worry that flashed across her face when she ran to meet me when I got home. I think about her lying with Hana, passed out on the couch with the pink tint to her flushed cheeks. Of how I picked her up from the couch to take her to bed. She tried to burrow into me while I laid her down next to my sister. Then, I think about her admiring the art.

Since meeting her, she has never once looked at me in fear. She doesn't know about me, but most women steer clear unless they want one thing. A night they think is them stepping out into the wild side of life. It's not because I try to be scary, but somehow, I bother normal people. Or maybe it's because that's all I allow to come out of most encounters with women who do approach, not bothering to give any of them hope that it could be more.

I've never come off as the white picket fence type, which typically leaves many only coming around for that one thing. Instead, she looked at me last night as if she were scared. Not at me but *for* me.

That nagging feeling of her being a burden continues to grate on me. Last night, her being drunk hadn't helped. But, when we spoke this morning, and she said she wasn't strong enough, somehow, my mind rebelled against that. Her kindness may be a weakness, but I don't see her as weak. That little fire she displayed in sticking up to me proved that. I also get the feeling she doesn't normally stick up for herself, yet she did with me.

I force my gaze away, now realizing I was staring at her.

Turning away, I catch Rei still watching me from my peripheral. The butt of the cigarette burns brighter, and the wispy clouds of smoke drift between us in the still air carrying the heavy scent of tobacco. Haru's laughter pulls both of our attention.

"*Otousan!*" Haru calls when he stands and runs to his dad, not noticing the smoke surrounding his father. "Can I please ride with Dahlia-neesan tomorrow?" he asks as he jumps up and down.

His resilience to our situation is incredible and humbling. He shouldn't *have* to be resilient at all and instead get to live his life like any normal child. Yet, living in a literal horror story, he's holding on to his innocence despite what the world is telling him. If he can continue to hold onto hope and happiness, we all should be able to.

Reiji assesses Dahlia and Hana before glancing at me for a second. "That's fine. If, for any reason, I tell you differently, you do not argue. Understand?"

Ru agrees, still beaming.

What? My eyes fly to Rei in question. Is he serious? Haru should stay with one of us. What if something happens?

My brother stares back at me almost in challenge, waiting for me to question him.

"I can ride with them," Hana says, interrupting the building tension as we continue to stare at each other. "I planned on riding with Dahlia anyway."

My sister pours a glass of wine and hands it to Rei. She then offers me a glass before pouring one for herself.

"Thanks, Hana," I say, more thankful she'll stick with the kid than the glass I take from her.

"Since we didn't get to honor her in the proper way, a toast to Sayuri-san," Hana says, raising her glass, drawing our attention.

Swallowing a sudden dry throat, I raise my glass as Dahlia does the same.

"To Sayuri-san," my siblings and I say in unison.

"To Sayuri," Dahlia whispers, staring into her glass.

We all fall silent, allowing Sayuri's memory to linger.

"Sorry, I didn't mean to cause the mood to shift. I was just thinking about her," Hana says. With a sideways glance, Dahlia wraps her hands around her stomach and peers out into the darkness.

"When we get home, we can take the time to honor her," my brother says before taking a sip of his drink. "Are you all ready for tomorrow?"

He regards each of us before his eyes fall to his son.

"I'm scared," Haru speaks softly. I'm taken aback by his honesty. He isn't one to shy away, much like his aunt, but it's still surprising compared to his father, who is more reserved.

"It's normal to be scared right now. I think we all are, but instead of letting it impair us, we need to allow it to fuel us. We are all here with you and won't let anything happen to you," my brother replies.

"I'll be honest, kid, I've been terrified since the beginning, but you know what? We're all in this together. We'll make it somewhere safe," Dahlia says as she squeezes his hand. She smiles, but it doesn't reach her eyes. Maybe she doesn't quite believe it, either.

I'll do everything in my power to keep my nephew safe, but even I can't stop the doubt from slowly creeping into my thoughts. The fear is real, but maybe Reiji is right; it's to be expected.

Haru seems comforted by her words and smiles back at her before going on about something off-topic with Hana.

After about an hour, I stand to leave before Dahlia almost trips over me as we both head in the same direction.

"Shit! I'm sorry. I'm not drunk this time. I practically nursed that glass." She chuckles shyly as she brushes hair behind her ears, my eyes following the movement. My gaze lingers on her face, taking in the reddening of her freckled cheeks before I dip my chin in acknowledgment. The urge to brush my thumb across them is strong, but instead, I turn and walk back inside. I'm ready to rid myself of these feelings she's stirring inside me.

I don't need to be her friend. Even if she, for some unknown reason, seems to give a shit if I die or not—if her expression yesterday is anything to go on. Even if, for an instant, she surprisingly brought out a part of me where I wanted to stay and talk about what thoughts the painting had provoked in her. Or even the fact that she reminded me of someone I don't want to be reminded of. The nightmares do that enough. It was a bittersweet moment I needed to walk away from.

So far, she seems to be someone who doesn't speak up but cares about those around her. Taking care of Haru is a perfect example of that. I can even admire that. I've met a lot of people who seem to have a hero complex but don't care about anyone but themselves.

She has opened up in the few days she's been with us. She's appeared more comfortable. I push those thoughts away. Who she is doesn't matter right now. Tomorrow is what I should be focusing on.

Walking to my room, I notice the crowd has quieted down. Mostly everyone has decided to turn in as well. Although that is a good sign, I can't help but wonder if everyone will be ready for what awaits us.

Chapter Twenty

Ren

The sky is just beginning to lighten, turning a dark gray as we climb into our cars. Yesterday, Dirk and Juan helped me examine the truck to ensure that most of the damage was cosmetic. Thankfully, it was, but driving with a broken windshield will be stressful.

Although my brother seemed fine with his son riding with Dahlia and Hana, I also asked Matt to sit in with them. I would have myself, but I wanted each of us in our own car, giving us more options if we needed to abandon one of the vehicles. In the worst case, Hana can leave Rei or me behind if something happens to us. Rei probably doesn't like the idea of Haru not being close to him, but I think he's also scared. Who knows what the right decision could be in this situation? Anything can happen out there, and we can't ever be fully prepared for it.

I take a moment to look back at my home, knowing it will be the last time I do. I took anything with any sentimental value but unfortunately left behind most of everything I own. Other than necessities, weapons, and some blankets, I grabbed a few photos of my family and a few things that were my mother's. I decided to keep those in the pack that I'll keep on my person most of the time. It takes an unnecessary amount of space that could be used for more important things, but I know everything we have now may need to be left behind with no more than a second's notice. I don't have the heart to part with these yet. Especially my mother's small sketchbook. It was only partially filled out, but it's the only thing I have left that allows me to feel connected to her. It's as if she had just drawn inside of it instead of over twenty years ago. I refocus on the truck as I climb in and start the ignition.

James chose to ride with me since he drives an electric car. Pretty soon, it'll be useless. Dirk is also leaving his muscle car, saying it wasn't practical, and is riding with Juan. We may all swap around to allow each of us to rest, but we want everyone to be paired up for now.

Don, one of Rei's men, is riding with him. Don has worked for Rei for years, but recently moved here to act as a liaison of sorts for my brother's business here in the US with his girlfriend, Jen, and their kid to accompany him. I don't know him well enough, but Rei trusts him. That alone isn't good enough for me, but Rei won't hear of my paranoid assumptions about other people. I suggested to Rei that he leave the car and stick with me, but he wanted each of us to have a mode of transportation.

We drive in silence for a while. The sun is finally making an appearance, casting soft light on the bloody nightmare ahead of us. I liked the slightly secluded location of my home. Now, not so much. It's going to take a while to clear the canyons and get us to the 101. When we went on our run, it took time to bypass some of the roads and this time will be no different.

Sighing, I take in the smaller towns and homes we pass by. All abandoned. A few bodies, unrecognizable, litter the roads, and buildings are scorched from fires. I had hopes that people managed to board up their homes and businesses to wait whatever this is out, but as we continue down the street, that hope dwindles. It's worse than what the other parts of town looked like the other day.

"It's so weird. I don't know if I can get used to it being so empty outside. Or the fact there aren't zombies wandering around," James says quietly, still looking out his window.

I don't think I can get used to it either, but we don't have much of a choice. "I'm hoping they stay hidden even if it makes me more nervous," I respond.

I remember that first night when it was still full-blown mayhem outside. People running in the streets—a bloody massacre. Complete anarchy. Some people were taking advantage of the chaos, burglarizing businesses only to end up dead under a zombie. It spread quickly, leaving devastation in its wake. Now, there's nothing. No signs of life or zombies. I can't tell if that makes me relieved or more tense.

We continue to drive slowly for a while, only coming across a few small groups of slow zombies or roadblocks we can deal with easily. It's not long before we finally turn into another canyon road. There is only a newer gas station and carwash before we're met with the drying brush of the hills.

Following Rei, we all pull off the side of the road, keeping our distance from the gas station. James arms himself with his firearms and knife. I do the same before hopping out.

We all make our way towards Rei quietly. Once we are all huddled together, the others from our group follow. My brother speaks as quietly as he can but loud enough for everyone to hear.

"We should try and rest up—just for a short time. Let's see if we can siphon some gas here. It's secluded enough; hopefully, there won't be many threats around," Rei says

Our sister saunters over, taking a long pull from her water bottle before recapping it. "Can we let Haru stretch his legs a bit? He wanted to see the other kids," she asks Rei, but he is already walking away. She asks me the same question.

I glance back towards their car, where Dahlia's standing by the open tailgate, talking to Haru. He's still inside, resting his arms over the seat. As if she senses my gaze, she looks over, smiling and giving an awkward wave before focusing back on the chatty kid.

"That's fine, but make sure they stay here. We don't need them venturing off."

I turn to go while Matt and James catch up. A few yards ahead, Dirk and Juan are already nearing the building.

Matt pats my shoulder and motions back towards the cars. "Since they're over there, I'll stick back. I think Rei had Don stay back, too, but I don't trust any of those other shitheads."

I pat him on the arm in agreement before he walks away. I hesitate a moment, wondering if I should stay with them as well, but when I notice how many men Reiji left and how quiet it is, I try to relax a little. *They will be safe for now. I can't be in two places at once.*

As I approach the gas station, I take note of my surroundings, straining to listen for any sounds other than our group. Thankfully, everyone is whispering, and the further I walk, the less I can hear them. Somehow, the children in the group are doing the same.

The gas station door opens, and Dirk walks out with a small bloodstain on his white and gray shirt. "There was only one," he says, unable to hide his disappointment.

I shake my head with a smirk as I brush past him. I'm not holding out much hope anymore that we'll find much, but I still grasp that small sliver.

The shelves inside are mostly bare. We can take a few things here and there, but not much. One of the coolers in the back still has a few bottles of Gatorade and some soda. Soda isn't the best thing, but I grab a few bottles anyway and stuff them into my backpack with the Gatorade. Walking further in, I spot a door open near the restroom. Taking a closer look, I can make out a small table and vending machine.

"I already broke the damn thing; there was nothing inside," Dirk says behind me, slightly startling me since I hadn't heard him double back. For such a broad man, he can sneak like a damn thief.

"Then there isn't much else then. What about siphoning the gas?" I ask as I walk back towards the counter where the register is tipped over, open and empty. Crouching, I dig around behind the counter, finding a few packs of cigarettes. I pocket them as an idea comes to me.

I know Rei may want a pack or two, but I can use these as a form of currency. Money is next to useless now, but besides the obvious food and water, any alcohol, pills, and cigarettes will most likely hold the most value. That and ammo.

I took any remaining alcohol from my house and packed it away for that same reason.

"Rei, James, and Juan are already out back. They found a generator and are going to see if they can get it to work. Maybe we can fill up the normal way. Otherwise, it may be hard to find a way to rig the underground gas tanks," he responds.

I almost thought he hadn't heard, but he's just focused on reaching for something under one of the shelves. When he comes back to his knees, he flashes me a peek of the container. I can't help but snort when I make out what it is.

"You should quit at this point, man. Finding dip is going to be harder and harder as we travel," I say, standing and brushing debris off my jeans.

He only chuckles and pockets his new pack of chewing tobacco. He, along with a lot of guys we worked with, enjoyed their chew or pouches. There were a few reasons why so many chewed instead of smoked. I know a big one for my friends was that it curbed their appetite during deployments and was also easier since you can't smoke in most public places, especially on base. They've told me the regulations and designated areas were just a pain in the ass. Either way, I never took to either.

After combing through the store again, I am about to walk back outside when Hana pushes the door so hard it almost looks like she ran into it.

"The kids. Haruto! Dahlia and Matt were helping Yuna and Ann change a tire, and I turned away for a second—"

I'm already running out the door. "I don't know where they went. It couldn't have been far; there's nothing here!" Hana cries.

She looks around in a panic. She must have come straight here first instead of looking. I know she can take care of herself well enough, but I am glad she doesn't choose to do anything reckless like going half-cocked on her own. Rei runs over, having heard Hana. He addresses Dirk, "Have everyone ready to leave in the cars. Now."

Dirk takes off without a word.

Maybe they decided to play hide-and-seek or something. They could be hiding in one of the cars. We continue to pick up our pace when a scream makes me pull up short, and I try to gauge where the sound came from. It was one of the kids, I am sure. More screams come from the car wash on the other side of the lot. The kids are all running out frantically, screaming and crying.

"Hana, get the kids to the cars. Now!" I shout as I search each of the children's faces, but none are Haruto.

"Shit."

Time seems to stop.

Haruto is tackled to the ground. The thing was once a woman with broad shoulders and twice his size. It has him pinned, attacking hungrily.

My blood runs cold. My veins feel as if they've iced over.

I pump my legs harder. *I won't make it in time.*

I'm still too far away to get a shot—at least if I don't want to risk the kid.

He's at the other end of the carwash near a Sedan that looked to have been stuck inside mid-wash. He's frantically trying to use his arms to keep it from biting him.

A loud shout echoes off the walls.

There's a blur of movement. It's thrown to the side and behind the car.

I can't fully make out what's happening until I get closer. The zombie's head is being bludgeoned.

Dahlia.

She threw herself at the zombie to help the kid.

She gets up, heaving before crouching down, motioning for him to get on her back. Before he can get on, she straightens in time to shove another zombie away, swinging a crowbar at its head. It doesn't seem to kill it, but it trips over the other body and falls.

A loud shriek brings my attention behind them, where three more come sprinting for Haruto and Dahlia.

Where the hell did they come from? Was there a home or something behind here we didn't notice? Rei starts shooting, not caring anymore about being quiet.

This gives Dahlia a chance to put Haru on her back, piggyback style, before she starts running.

"Are you bit?" she yells over her shoulder, and to my relief, he shakes his head as if she can see his face and says something only she can hear.

I follow Rei's example, trying to cover them while Dahlia runs as fast as she can with the added weight. When she notices me, I swear there's a flash of relief in her eyes before she pushes forward. More zombies appear behind the car wash, attracted to the commotion.

Fuck. There must have been something we missed. They couldn't have made it through the hills that fast unless they were wandering around.

As Dahlia reaches us, Rei tries to grab for Haru, but she keeps an iron grip on him as she keeps moving. "You both have guns, I don't; it's safer if I take him and you cover. It's harder to shoot while holding him!" she snaps with an irritated expression and keeps running at a surprising pace.

Rei spares me a look of surprise before focusing back on the zombies gaining speed. We both turn on our heels, shooting at any that get close enough while we retreat to the cars.

From ahead, James and Dirk join in, giving us cover. I inwardly cringe when I think about how much ammo we are using, but I can't concentrate on that now. All I can think about is getting us all to safety as more emerge behind us.

Dahlia makes it to her car, which is already running with Matt at the wheel, ready to peel out. She ungracefully shoves Haru in the back and hops in. Rei checks all the cars, making sure we have everyone. When he is satisfied that we aren't leaving anyone behind, he hops in his own car. I get into the truck, still shooting at any zombie close enough before we all finally reach the road at breakneck speed.

Thankfully, we managed to pick off the fastest ones, allowing us to leave them all in the dust as we get the hell out of dodge.

"What the fuck happened?" I ask James.

He releases the magazine from his pistol to check his rounds. "When I helped Hana load the kids in their cars, Matt mentioned that Tobi's woman asked if they could help change their tire. Apparently, they were running on a flat for the last mile but were too scared to pull over. The jack they had was busted, so Dahlia went to grab hers but then never came back," he says, shrugging before replacing the magazine and putting the gun down. "When we stop next, we can ask 'em, I guess." He chuckles. "Not going to lie, bro, that chick hauled ass. Freckles makes me look like a fucking out-of-shape bastard." He laughs as he looks out the window.

It shocked the hell out of me, especially how she didn't seem to care how she spoke to Rei. Her usual quiet and awkward attitude went right out the window, revealing a take-no-shit type of woman.

She was right about where we needed to keep our focus. Although Haru explained how she carried him to safety before, it's still surprising to see it first-hand. Also, when we found her at the clinic, she looked scared and almost defeated, yet she put her life in danger without a second thought when someone else's life was at stake.

My attention is refocused when Rei pulls off again, now farther onto the canyon roads, away from any homes or businesses. When we meet him outside, he looks about ready to shit a brick with how stressed he is.

As Hana comes over, Haru breaks away and runs to his dad, eyes rimmed red. Reiji wraps his arms around his waist and lifts him up, cradling him as the poor kid cries. He rubs Haruto's back and shushes him as he looks at Hana, waiting for an explanation.

"He's fine. I checked him over, no cuts or bites." She stares down at her hands, her own eyes welling with tears. "I turned away for a minute. Haru asked me for something to snack on, so I went to look in the back for something." Sniffing, she crosses her arms. "When I turned back around, they were gone." Her sobs are muffled as she covers her mouth with the sleeve of her sweater.

Haru sniffs and looks at his dad. "It's not her fault. We saw a cat, and the others wanted to follow it. I told them that was not a good idea, but they went anyway. I tried to go and stop them, but they wouldn't listen." His breath hitches. "They found the cat, and it was acting funny. Tommy kicked it and laughed. I told him it was mean and dumb. I kept telling them we needed to leave, but they didn't care. Then he dared Rachel to open the door. She did it before I could stop her."

He's breathing harder now, getting angry again, thinking about the other kids. Haruto has always been mature for his eight years and experiencing what he did this past week seems to have aged the poor kid further.

"There was a monster inside, but it was stuck. They all started screaming and running, and then it broke free from the seat." Tears run down his face again before he buries his head in his dad's shirt.

"Shh. You're okay." Reiji rubs soothing circles on his back. "Next time, if those kids want to make a stupid choice like that again, I know you mean well, wanting to protect them, and I admire that about you," he says, gaze fixed on his son's puffy eyes. "But your life means more to me than anything else. Instead, tell one of us. Don't put yourself in a situation where you could get hurt again. Even if it seems it's all quiet. You saw what can happen. Anything can happen anywhere and anytime in the blink of an eye."

It's always strange seeing this side of my brother. I know for a fact he's only soft with his family. I remember the one time someone tried to exploit it and use it against him. Rei didn't give him a chance but instead made an example of him. His men know he won't fuck around. No. He cuts you off at the legs and reminds everyone else who he is.

Rei puts Haru down and crouches down to eye-level. "You scared us to death. I don't think I have been more afraid in my entire life except these two times now when you could have been hurt. Ren and Hana are also here. Go to them if you need to. I don't care, as long as you are safe, and you turn to one of us." He hugs him before standing back up.

My nephew looks down, still silently crying and sniffling. "Sorry, *otousan*," he says. "I am sorry Ren-oji, Hana-oba. I didn't mean to scare you," he sobs before running to hug Hana, who squeezes the poor kid, most likely suffocating him.

"I'm sorry too," she says to Haru but focuses her gaze on our brother.

"You need to keep a better eye on him. I need to know my son is safe." He looks off into the distance before lowering his voice so only I can hear him. "I don't give a damn about anyone but us right now. I don't want to see those other kids hurt, but I care more about my son and you both. I'll make rounds and talk to everyone with kids. They are all responsible for their own children, and if that kind of shit happens again, I don't care who they are; I'll leave them all if it keeps my son and you both safe," he says softly, but he can't hide the menace leaking through his normally stone-like expression.

It's moments like this that remind me exactly who he is away from his son and wife and, I'm grateful he's my brother and not an enemy. He values family, unlike the others in his type of business, cutting ties altogether if they aren't associated with their clan.

"Understood," I say as I turn away to walk Hana and Haru back to the car.

The adrenaline is still coursing through me as my mind replays what happened. If it hadn't been for Dahlia, *again*, Haru would have died.

Maybe. Just maybe I can rely on someone else to protect my nephew. Dahlia managed to use her own body to save him. She wasn't as big of a liability as I thought she'd be.

I don't want him to be like Sayuri, dying because of my own inability to accept the help. *Maybe it'll work out if I trust a little more. Take the offered help.*

The closer we get, the more I hear Matt and Dahlia arguing inside the Plymouth; Dahlia's in the passenger seat with her back to me. Matt looks flustered but when he notices me, he says something to her that has her stiffening. In my peripheral, Hana's face scrunches up. Interesting.

"She was quiet the whole drive," she says as we make it to the car. Haru, still sniffling, opens the liftgate and climbs in through the back, not noticing the tension between the two, who are now sitting quietly in the front seat.

Matt, still flustered, climbs out and walks towards me, stopping and waiting for Hana to climb in and shut the door. "Don't blame her, man," he says.

"Why the hell would we blame her?" I ask him, glancing at the car. She's still facing away from me.

"She thinks you guys are going to want to leave her, thinking she almost got the kid killed or some shit. I tried to explain to her it won't be like that, but she's worried. She said she saw the kids walking into the car wash and took off to get them to come back when shit hit the fan." He sighs, pulling his hair and securing it back into a bun.

Curious, I ask, "You didn't see what happened yourself?"

"I didn't notice. I was helping the idiots who didn't think to flag anyone down before we stopped. They didn't even have the proper equipment." He rolls his eyes before letting out a heavy breath. "Anyway, she's worried even though I told her you guys are pretty cool about not jumping to conclusions," he says.

I can't help the annoyance that flares about her expressing anything to him. Why not come to me about it, to begin with? And whatever gave her the impression we'd just up and leave her for saving Haru's life?

"I need to go make sure the tire held up. We found another jack and barely started tightening the lugs when things went to shit," he mentions before walking back to where the others are beginning to huddle together.

I stare at them for a moment, debating if I should bother talking to her. It doesn't matter, but I also don't want Dahlia to do anything foolish, like sneak off because of some stupid misunderstanding. She would get herself killed, which, in turn, would lead to my sister killing me.

This right here is one of many reasons I don't like dealing with people. I don't want to have to comfort or make someone feel better because they can't be upfront about their feelings. Does that make me an asshole? Probably.

I lightly tap on the passenger window before I can talk myself out of it. Dahlia's head whips around, eyes wide for a moment before opening the door. She slips out and surprisingly keeps her chin up and eyes on me instead of looking down. That spark of annoyance surfaces again, and I can't help the small smile playing on my lips, which seems to piss her off more. Her face hardens and her eyes squint a little, her brows slightly furrowed. I hate to admit it, but it's cute.

She stares at me, waiting for me to say what I need to. What I can't understand is why she is annoyed to begin with. I understand her being scared but is her reaction to fear to get pissed? I don't think so; she hasn't given me this irritated look before, and I'm positive I have seen fear in her eyes a few times. No, it almost seems like she's getting more comfortable around us and can't stop herself from showing her thoughts. If only I could read that mind of hers.

We continue our stare-off before she finally looks down, losing some of the fire. Her shoulders slump slightly. Not wanting to antagonize her further, I finally speak.

"Look, we don't blame you. If you didn't run off when you did, it may have been too late for us to help anyone." I run my hand through my hair and look away. "So, thank you. I mean... it was reckless to run off on your own, but we can't be upset. If you hadn't, I would have lost someone important to me. Next time, try to grab someone on your way, okay? If you got hurt, well..." I pause for a second, clearing my throat. "There are people who would be upset," I say, failing to mention it would upset *me* despite not understanding why.

Her brows wrinkle slightly as if she didn't comprehend what I said or maybe she just doesn't believe me.

"Alright. I'm sorry. I—" She drops her chin. "I'll do better. I shouldn't have left him. What we've already seen, I can't help but feel like this was my fault." The more she talks, the more her voice takes on an edge. "So, I'm sorry." She finally meets my gaze, fire reappearing in her eyes as if challenging me that she's wrong in needing to apologize.

"Like I said, Dahl, we don't blame you. If anything, you might as well be his damn guardian angel since you seem to be good at getting him out of tight squeezes." Giving her a small smile, I turn, leaving her wide-eyed as I return to the truck. I called her angel once before, using it as a term to mock her, but the more I think about it, the more I realize that she's like a guardian angel for that kid.

My smile grows as I think about that small little fire that seems to be slowly growing within her. I may not understand why, but it has me looking forward to the inferno.

Chapter Twenty-One

Dahlia

"You know why I had to intervene, right?" my father asks as we pass through the gardens. He took me to one of my favorite places. A butterfly conservatory. Maybe he thought it would lessen the blow.

"I think so," I tell him. I don't really, though. I'll be eighteen soon enough. Dillon isn't that much older than me. Only three years.

My father's sigh is heavy when he sits on a bench, glancing up at the serene picture surrounding us. "Look, sweetheart." He pauses, scratching at his freshly shaven chin. His light brown hair is cropped short like I've always remembered it. "I know it's hard right now, but it won't last. That man may not be more than a few years older than you, but he knows better. You're still underage. He could be court-martialed. He's lucky I haven't reported him yet."

My eyes well with tears at his words. "But Daddy, I'll be eighteen at the end of the year. He's been nothing but amazing. I love him..." I sniffle, rubbing my eyes with my sleeve. "What will I do without him? I'm nothing without him," I say, looking down at my feet.

He won't understand. He's still so angry over Mom, and it's been years. Is that why he's doing this to me?

I almost miss the way my dad's jaw clenches when he turns his head away. "Things don't stay nasty forever, my little butterfly. Stop quitting on yourself. You don't need a man to be happy." His soft voice conflicts with the storm behind his gray eyes. "When you're older, you can find someone who makes you happy, but they shouldn't be the foundation for that happiness."

He stands, grabbing my face in his palms. "You have such a bright future ahead of you, baby Dahl. You've been excelling in your dance classes, ranking well in your competitions, you've taken so much interest in your JROTC classes; I can't wait to see where that all leads you." My gut clenches at the thought of the Junior Reserves Officers Training Corps program I'm in. I love the time on the range, but other than that, the idea of a military career makes my stomach churn. I only joined for my father, and when he lit up at the news, I knew it would make him proud.

He brushes his thumb over my tears as his eyes stare into mine. "I promise it'll get easier. I'm always here when things get tough, okay?"

My father's voice echoes in my mind as I stir awake in the back seat of my car. I wipe my wet cheeks and eyes while I sit up.

Somehow, I would have preferred a nightmare over that memory. It was the last full day I had with my dad, and I was upset with him for most of it. Back then, I couldn't understand where he was coming from.

You won't always be here though...

"You okay, Dahlia-neesan?" Ru whispers in the seat beside me. His aunt is asleep in the front seat while Matt stands outside the driver's side, leaning against the car.

It's hard to smile, but I try for him. "Just a scary dream. Nothing to worry about."

"I don't like seeing you sad," he says before leaning over to hug me. It's a little awkward trying to hug in the backseat, but my heart swells regardless.

"I'll be fine. Thanks, kiddo. Now try to get some sleep, okay? I'm going to step out for some air."

He pulls away and shifts in his seat to get more comfortable. I cover him fully with this blanket and bend to grab my backpack and the shotgun before climbing over the driver's seat.

I gently tap on the window near Matt, who then opens the door and helps me get out. "Thanks."

"You good?" he whispers.

Not wanting to converse, I say, "I'm fine. Just going to sit against the wall. Need some air."

We've stopped to rest for the night—or at least to try to rest. From the looks of it, most of us are up. The guys on watch are all out of their cars, keeping their flashlights on our surroundings while the others whisper inside their vehicles.

I pull out a flashlight from my pack and glance around. The guys have been thorough about keeping watch, but I can't help but be nervous after the gas station. Not seeing anything except the few abandoned cars and the guys in our group, I walk around the car to sit against the wall. I decide to try to mount the M9 and tactical light, although if I couldn't get it right the last time, I doubt I can this time.

My father's memory drapes over me like a shroud as I fiddle pointlessly with the bayonet. *Can't I at least do one thing, right?*

Soft footsteps crunch against the gravel. Ren crouches in front of me, jerking his head at the weapons. "Need a hand?" His voice soothes some of the weight bearing down on my shoulders.

"If you can figure this out, sure. I know my dad had one mounted before, but I can't get it on the lug," I tell him.

He sits next to me, close enough that our bodies are brushing. Thank God it's dark because my face has probably turned into a tomato.

He sits his rifle against the wall and shifts to pull a multitool out of his pocket. He takes the shotgun and the M9 bayonet from me to look them over.

After a few minutes of trying to determine what the problem is, he begins using the file tool to shave down the part of the M9 that attaches to the lug.

"I've seen this issue before. This isn't the best solution, but we don't have any other option," he tells me.

I watch him as he works. Slightly fascinated, I lean into him. Something about him doing this for me has my lady bits in a frenzy. Like I noticed before, he's capable—someone to rely on. Not to mention protective of his loved ones.

What would it be like to be with someone like him?

I didn't realize how close I was leaning into him until he tilts his head slightly. Our faces are inches apart. Close enough to feel his warmth against my cheeks.

I move away too fast, hitting my head against the wall. "Shit," I say while rubbing my head.

His chuckle is like a satin balm. It surprises me how much I love hearing it. "You okay?" He smirks. Although it's dark, his amusement is obvious.

"Yeah. Sorry," I mumble.

He brings his attention back to the file. "You took good care of the shotgun. You mentioned it was your dad's?" he says, although it's more of a question.

I try to hide my surprise, mostly because he's initiating conversation, but it's also surprising that he's asking something about me personally. "Yeah. He called it his lucky one."

He tilts his head slightly as if to look at me but keeps his eyes down. "Why's that?"

The memory comes back easily. It was one my dad used to boast about a lot. "He said it was lucky to be there in the right moment... to keep me safe." I smile. "We lived off base in North Carolina at some point. I was still under a year old." I picture my dad when he used to tell the story, making my smile widen. "He needed to put me in a little rocker seat in the bathroom so he could shower. He was always strict about locking his guns away, especially once I was born. But that day, he left it out to clean with all the supplies on the bed. That's why he said it was lucky."

My focus gets caught on Ren's hands. There's something about seeing him use them, even for something so simple. *Who knew you could like a man's hands?*

"What happened after?" he asks.

I turn before he notices me being a weirdo and staring—although he probably already noticed.

"He was barely getting out of the shower when he noticed movement out in the hall and heard banging inside the house. We lived alone, so he immediately knew something wasn't right. He ran out of the bathroom to the bedroom—butt ass naked—he grabbed the shotgun from the bed, and when he found two burglars inside the living room, they all but pissed themselves. One had a handgun, but when they mentioned having it, my dad just looked down at them and told them." I snicker, thinking about it. "Mine's bigger."

I have to hold back the laugh and cover my mouth with my hand. My dad told me he knew right away they didn't know what they were doing with the gun and looked scared shitless when they saw him. Even as naked as he was.

When I was older, he admitted he laughed when he said it, too. *What a child*, I think humorously.

"My dad wasn't a violent man, but better believe he would have shot those guys should they have tried anything. They were only two stupid kids, though, mixed up in the wrong crowd. They ran away. The best part was that he chased them out the door, not caring that he flashed the neighbors walking their dog that evening."

Ren's chuckle is soft, but something about it has those pesky butterflies going ham in my tummy. "He sounds like a funny man." He blows on the handle of the bayonet. "Sounds like he'd have done whatever he needed to protect you…" He pauses to look over his work. "I can relate to that."

Forget butterflies… It's almost painful how my stomach just flip-flopped. *Chill, Dahlia. Stop overthinking. He's talking about protecting his family… Don't take it out of context.*

"This should do it." It doesn't take long before he can slip the handle in and secure the bayonet on the lug.

"I can get that light on there for you later, alright?" He hands the shotgun back to me.

I don't know what to say. My cheeks are hot, but I'm grateful for his help.

He doesn't make an attempt to move; he only raises his feet to plant them firmly on the ground and then rests his forearms on his knees. His flashlight follows his line of sight while staying vigilant.

Another pair of footsteps breaks the silence before James sits on my other side. "I'm over this shit already," he says. "I'm craving a damn cheeseburger right now."

I try to contain my chuckle to stay quiet, but it's a challenge.

"What? You can't tell me you wouldn't kill for a double-bacon avocado cheeseburger right now. Oh, man." He moans softly. "With grilled onions and onion rings."

My hand covers my mouth, trying so hard not to laugh.

"I mean. He's not wrong," Ren says, chuckling softly alongside his friend.

"See? My boy knows what's good for him." He playfully elbows me and looks between us. "I mean… sometimes." His wink catches me off guard when his gaze settles on me.

Ren reaches over me to smack James on the back of his head. For a brief second, I'm completely engulfed in him. The woodsy scent surrounds me as his body drapes partially over mine. It's the briefest moment, but my heart is still galloping.

Even joking around so quietly, it's still a wonder to see Ren more laid back. He's not smiling fully, but I can tell he's amused by the crinkle of his eyes as he listens to his friend. "You wouldn't know what was good for you even if it had a fucking for free sign in bold letters in front of your face," Ren says.

James' smile is blinding. As he talks to Ren, I can see the respect and adoration even behind his soft eyes. "Yeah, maybe. But same with you, bro." He turns his attention to me. "This dumbass is the most stubborn man I've ever met. Don't let him get his way. He needs a good challenge every now and again."

Although I'm not quite sure how that involves me, I respond anyway. "I'll keep that in mind."

"Good. Now, back to that burger. Honestly, I think that's what I will miss the most about the normal world. What about you, Freckles?"

Ren uses his flashlight to keep our surroundings visible, but with a sideways glance, I find him watching me instead of the stream of light.

"Honestly?" I pause, genuinely thinking about what I will miss the most. Instead of letting that question become a heavy topic, I keep it in the realm of food. "I think fresh coffee from a café. I'd kill for some good coffee right now."

He snickers and looks to Ren. "What about you, man? Those matcha chocolate wafer things you used to be obsessed with?"

Ren shakes his head but doesn't respond. He keeps his eyes peeled for threats.

"Well, you're no fun." Groaning, James gets up and brushes his jeans off. "Fine. I see you're in your typical mood." He snorts. "I'll leave you be, you party shitter," he tells Ren. "G'night, Freckles." He brings the flashlight under his face to give me a maniacal smile before he walks off.

My own smile widens as I take in Ren's serious expression, his humorous attitude gone. "You really attract the talkative type, huh?" I blurt before I can stop myself.

He raises his brows and his lips curl slightly. He's still so close that even in the dark, I can make out the different tones of brown in his eyes. "Same could be said for you," he mumbles.

"Touché." I snort. "Well. Thanks for helping me with this." I raise the shotgun.

His only response is a grunt before he stands and offers me his hand.

Hesitantly, I put the shotgun down and place my left hand in his. His palm is rough against my own. He pulls me up with a little too much strength, and I brace myself against his hard chest. His other hand grabs my waist to steady me. "Crap. Sorry," he grumbles.

He lets go and picks up the shotgun for me. "Just be careful with this."

Instead of my cheeks heating in embarrassment, my whole body probably looks like a tomato now. I smile and thank him again before I walk back to the driver's side of my car. I'm ready to try to go back to sleep.

Matt opens the door, and his hand strays to the small of my back as I climb in. This time, I can't stop my reaction, and I shy away from his touch, although he doesn't seem to notice.

When the door is shut, I sink back into the seat while my eyes stare out the window. Ren is still near the other side of the car. It's harder to make him out in the dark, but his flashlight casts enough light to see his face. My mind is reeling with what-ifs, but the memory of my father has my rampant thoughts ceasing.

Haven't I learned my lesson already? I shouldn't be entertaining the thoughts of what it would be like to be with Ren or how it would feel if he was interested. He's dangerous. Not only because he clearly has some issues he needs to work out, but I've seen the cold precision he displays when he takes down zombies. He shows nothing to indicate that this affects him like it does me. He may be capable and protective, but he's the type of danger on a stick that ends up skewering you. And not in a good way.

Although my mind keeps trying to convince myself of that, a part of myself still rebels against those thoughts—so much so that I even wonder what my dad would have thought about Ren. Would it be the same as before?

He isn't Dillon.

He may be dangerous, but I've seen the way he cares for his family. Oh hell, his whole family is one big mystery that screams danger, but even then, there's just something about them.... Something I trust. Even Ren's brother, who is a paradox when it comes to his son, but it only makes me confident in my choice to stay with them. People who care for their families that fiercely couldn't be bad people.

I shove that thought aside. It's pointless. One, he isn't interested. Two, it's quite literally the end of the world. It doesn't matter. What matters is getting some rest and trying to get my shit together so I can be a help to the group without getting someone killed.

Great. Great plan. Now, let's see if I can follow through.

CHAPTER TWENTY-TWO

The drive so far has been awful. Not only are we all still stressed from the encounter at the gas station, but the trip has also taken longer than expected. We knew it would take more time than usual, but the chaos that erupted created so many obstacles for us to avoid, not including the zombies. But I hadn't expected it would be this bad.

We're finally making a little progress after intermittently taking the freeways and streets. We've needed to change our route a few times already, but we've thankfully avoided getting closer to central Los Angeles County. That would be a fucking death sentence. Instead, we've taken a route that puts us out of the way of our initial plan. Although it sucks, if it keeps us alive, we can't complain.

The journey out of state seems catastrophic with how slow we need to drive.

Besides the one stop we made to wait out our first night on the road, the other stops have been to either siphon gas, move blocks in the road, or find somewhere relatively safe for bathroom breaks. It hasn't been an issue for the guys, but most of the girls and kids are struggling to go next to the cars with possible zombies around the bend and multiple people in view. I don't think many of us slept either while we parked on the side of the freeway. For the few hours we parked, flashlights and movement flickered in all the cars the entire time.

The jerrycans have come in handy, though. I had some old tubing we brought, which has been a lifesaver when we siphon the gas. We try to keep the cans full any chance that presents itself.

My truck alone isn't the kindest with gas consumption, but thankfully, that isn't our main concern right now. Having a truck may be a pain in the ass for the next few days, but it also has its benefits. It's been the main hauler for supplies, although we tried to evenly divide them in case we need to abandon any vehicles.

Rei's car—a Mercedes Coupe rental—leads our caravan. He was excited to rent it, and even more excited it's his by default. Having another all-wheel drive vehicle will be helpful, particularly as we'll be traveling far and probably encounter rough areas or weather.

Up ahead, Rei slows down, eventually stopping. I pull up behind him as he puts the car in park and presses the brakes twice, letting everyone know there is something of interest we should check out. Following his signal, the sound of static from my small comms unit, or handheld radio, goes off before his voice comes through the comms. "May have found a good place to stop. Nothing out of place, so it should be safe to exit."

He isn't used to using the small device, but since our phones aren't working, he's SOL—shit out of luck.

We've been on the same highway for a few miles and there hasn't been much of interest but a few small towns to stake out. There are no lurking zombies around, so I hop out of the truck. Holding my knife in one hand and the other resting on my firearm holstered at my hip, I slowly make my way over to Rei.

Standing by his driver's side door, hand shielding the sun from his eyes, he stares off towards the exit ramp. I can't make out the town name, but I know we've barely reached San Bernardino County. Granted, that knowledge is a load of shit since the county is the fucking size of a small country.

My brother drops his hand to look at me. "This town might be a good place for a supply run and maybe a place to rest for the night."

I survey the area off the freeway and say, "We should find somewhere we can sleep. Maybe an abandoned house or something." Whatever city this is has many residential streets lining the freeway.

With the dip of his chin, he strides off to update the rest of the group before we return to our vehicles. We continue until the next off-ramp and drive through what is left of the town and into a more suburban neighborhood. With muscles tensing, I follow the car in front. My anxiety is skyrocketing. The idea of stopping has me on edge. We never know what to expect, especially in an unfamiliar town.

It doesn't take long before we turn into a cul-de-sac with a park at the end connected to another cul-de-sac beyond. A handful of the houses are adorned in harvest-styled decorations. A few even appear to have early Halloween décor on the lawns and in the windows. Some homes look empty, while others are boarded up from the inside.

Rei pulls into the first house on the right corner. No cars are parked in front of the home or the driveway. The double doors at the front are both open, and a duffle bag is abandoned by a pruned rose bush near the entrance. It looks to be vacant and I'm guessing my brother is thinking along the same lines as I do for choosing this one.

Following Rei's lead, I back in next to him in the two-car driveway as the others park nearby on the street, trying not to block anyone in but staying as close as possible.

Rei gets out, followed by me and the guys. Everyone else stays in their cars, leaving them running and ready to flee if needed.

We quietly approach Rei, who's inspecting the front door from the sidewalk. He gestures behind him to the deserted house. "We should clear this one and fortify it as best we can for the night," he whispers.

I glance over his shoulder to observe the place. It's a two-story family home with real shutters attached to the windows, which is incredibly odd for California but useful to us. Visible through the doorway, a few suitcases and bags are left on the floor as if someone gave up and left their belongings in favor of their lives.

Several cars are outside the other homes or on the driveways. One car is parked in the middle of the street, possibly in an attempt to block the road but ultimately failing.

This home seemed to be left and forgotten. Without another word, we all fall in line, weapons at the ready. Before we make our way inside, I lightly tap

Reiji on the shoulder. "I can take this. Stick with Haru in case shit hits the fan," I suggest.

He takes a moment to think about it, and I know he's about to say no when I speak up again. "Rei, this is what I'm good at. We made our groups and decided you'd stay back unless needed, remember?" I raise my brows.

When he put me in charge of grouping everyone, I told him it would be best if he remained the delegator, only helping in moments like this when it was absolutely necessary. He reluctantly agreed when I mentioned our group needs him, but his son needs him more.

I can tell this is a struggle for him. He's used to having his men do jobs for him, but it's different when your family is involved. No matter what we've both been through and despite my past in the military, he'll forever see me as his baby brother.

"The guys I have at my back are all men I served and trained with. We can work in tandem efficiently and quickly. Stick back. Please, Reiji," I resort to pleading.

"Fine," he says before returning to the cars. I let out a breath of relief, thankful I won't have to argue with him.

Taking point, I begin our trek inside, relying on instinct and muscle memory while going through the motions of clearing the home. We go room by room, allowing our training to take precedence. Juan, acting as team leader in this situation, follows in opposition to my movements as the others follow suit.

It doesn't take much time to secure the home, although we take a few extra minutes per room to check any spaces that could potentially squeeze a body. Although it seems to be a single-family home, it's much larger on the inside and has been newly remodeled. The second floor alone has three bedrooms and a bonus room, which is like a large second living room. The first floor has one bedroom, kitchen, office, formal dining, and family room.

Once the home is clear, we head outside to ensure everyone gets inside safely; I stop Juan and James and ask them to search around the perimeter. Although the house is secure for now, something about this street puts me on edge. It's like there are more people around in this neighborhood. I can't trust anyone not in our group to be friendly.

"Matt," I whisper as we walk down the few steps leading to the front of the house. He stops and waits for me to catch up. I continuously look around at our surroundings, unable to shake the unease of being out in the open and unfamiliar environment. I take a second to reel in my growing apprehension.

"Can you help the others inside? We can put the women and kids upstairs in that large room. The men can spread out throughout the house. I want to put my family in the primary bedroom upstairs."

He doesn't question my decision, most likely understanding the direction of my thoughts. The second living room is large enough and has a lock on the door. The primary bedroom has access to an attic and a door that opens to a balcony. The balcony itself is a foot away from a pergola, decorating their fenced-off yard, making it accessible to the roof if necessary. Worst-case scenario, there are options for running or hiding. Close to the primary bedroom, there is a Jack-and-Jill style room across the hall in which the guys can station themselves.

Once Juan and James finish their search around the outside of the home, they meet by Dahlia's car. Rei helps Hana and Haru climb out from the back while Dahlia hesitates before heading toward Matt. For a second, I wonder if I should call her back, but I decide against it.

No one speaks as we approach the house, afraid of making an unnecessary noise and attracting unwanted zombies. I catch up to Haru, placing my hand on his shoulder to direct him inside. I don't say anything as I stride through the home, passing the others who are making their way upstairs. As we reach the bedroom, I motion for him to take a seat on the bed and wait for Rei and Hana to catch up.

Rei closes the door, and he and Hana both take a seat close to the fireplace.

"I don't think we should try to make a supply run here. I can't quite say why, but something feels off," I say as I lean against the balcony door.

Rei gazes at Hana in contemplative silence before he speaks up. "I don't like it either. I thought this town might be a good place to stop, but I don't have a good feeling about it. It's like we are being watched. You feel that too?" he asks hesitantly.

I'm relieved he feels the same, and it's not just me. "I don't think everyone evacuated this area based on the number of cars and boarded homes. Not only that, there's just something setting my nerves on edge," I say as I focus on the dark yard beyond—nothing but some weeds and worn furniture.

A slight movement in the shadows pulls my attention to the yard connecting to ours. I strain for a minute, trying to determine what the movement was, doubting it was an animal. No sound or any new movement announces another presence but our own.

"Can we have Dahlia-neesan stay with us?"

The soft voice brings me back from my fruitless observations. Although Haru is clutching both elbows, appearing a little nervous, the look of resolve in his eyes makes my heart stutter. It's a look I recognize. His jaw is set, his shoulders square, and he doesn't look as anxious as his hands would make us believe.

Before I can speak up, Hana looks down at him. "Of course, kiddo. I wanted to ask her anyway." She winks at me. Ignoring her, I turn back to Reiji.

My brother's focus is on his son. "That's fine." He brushes the hair from Haru's face. No one else may notice, but I recognize the fear in his eyes as he peers down at him. "We need to get everyone set up. Will your men be taking watch then tonight?" he asks me.

He already knows the answer.

When I grouped everyone, I kept my own men for watch. It isn't that I don't trust my brother's judgment, but I know these guys. I know they will have my back, not to mention we're used to working together.

"Yeah. I was about to get with them right now," I tell him.

I won't lie—I'm surprised at how much he wants me to take the lead. I hope he sticks with making the large group decisions. I can help with tactical decisions, but I don't want to be the person making the final calls. I left the military. Leave the leadership to my brother.

"I'll help you check in with everyone barricading the place up then. I will have my men around the house. They won't be on watch, but I've already told them they need to be ready for anything." He pulls out a pack of cigarettes and starts walking towards the door.

"Sounds good," I respond.

My brother follows me out of the room when Hana gently shoves me with her shoulder. "I'm going to go get Dahlia. Walk with me?" She wraps her arm around mine, not allowing me to decline as we walk down the hall.

The guys have already started to board up the first floor as best they can. The shutters are closed over the windows, and furniture is being repositioned to block any potential exits and entrances. The front door is the only door currently accessible, although it looks as if they are planning to barricade it soon.

This doesn't completely abate my unease, but it does relieve some of the stress, knowing I have a few guys with me who I can rely on.

James walks up to us with an unusually grim expression, distracting me from my thoughts. "I'm sure you already have a hunch, but I think there are people in some of these houses, or someone is making it appear that way," he whispers.

My eyebrows rise at his observation. So, he feels it, too. That doesn't bode well for us then. I trust my gut and my brother, but hearing someone else mention it only solidifies my worries.

"You guys believe there are more survivors out here?" Hana asks us, still clutching my arm. Her face morphs into concern rather than fear.

"I wouldn't doubt it." I glance from Hana to James. "As much as we need rest, I think we should stick with rotations. I can take first watch since you've been riding with me. You rest for a few hours. I'll have Matt up with me and then rotate with Juan. Dirk can also help later. Rėiji is going to stay with my sister and Haru. We can set Don up with Jen and Liz in one of the smaller rooms if they don't want to stick to the living room."

With a mock salute and a chuckle, he says, "Rah, Major." All seriousness gone, James leaves to finish securing the front door, but Hana stops him before he makes it out of the room. "Have you seen Dahlia?"

Without saying anything, James gives her a smile and points behind us.

Hana releases my arm and quickly disappears around the corner and out of view.

Following my sister, I walk into the kitchen to find Dahlia awkwardly leaning against the kitchen island with Matt. He's leaning into her while speaking quietly. At first, an unfamiliar feeling pierces my chest. It shouldn't matter, but the idea of him being as close as we were yesterday irritates me.

It takes a second for me to shove those feelings aside enough to realize how uncomfortable she appears. Her arms are crossed, and she's staring at the floor as if it holds the world's most valuable secret. Instead of making me feel better knowing she doesn't like his attention, it has me clenching my fists.

I keep trying to remind myself that she isn't my problem, but her discomfort pisses me off. *Fuck, get a grip, Ren.*

She lifts her head, and her face softens when she sees Hana's smile.

"You'll be up with me tonight," I say to Matt while he straightens and shifts away from Dahlia. "I want us to stick with rotations. I'll have Juan and Dirk rotate with us later."

It takes him a moment before he rips his gaze away from her. "Sure, man, no problem. You already talk with James about his concerns?"

Uninterested in our conversation, Hana grabs Dahlia by the hand and leads her out of the room. My gaze tracks their departure until they're out of sight.

I clear my throat before sitting at the kitchen table. "I agree with him. I don't think this street is as empty as it may seem. It may be still and quiet, but it doesn't make it feel any less inhabited," I tell him.

"Well, I'm fine with staying up with you. I don't know if I can sleep anyway. So far, everything has been a fuckin' trip. Where are all the zombies or people?" He shrugs and slightly raises his hands in question. "I would think there would be more. Either way, some of the boarded houses are making me uncomfortable right now. People took the time to bunk down, so I doubt they left."

I consider the houses and the possible movement I caught outside. "We'll have to be vigilant. We can leave early tomorrow. Anyway," I say as I get up. "I'll see you then. I'm going to check out the front and make sure everything is locked down well enough."

I walk through the whole house, confirming that every possible entry point is barricaded before going through the familiar motions.

A few hours pass before Dirk finds me in the backyard. The only light illuminating the space is from the flashlights. The sky has grown gloomy, barely casting any moonlight. The chill in the air announces a possibility of rain or the start of cooler weather.

"Anything to be worried about?" Dirk asks as he walks up, whispering but still sounding too loud.

"Nothing. All quiet. You sure you want to take over? It hasn't been that long. I can stay up a while longer."

"It's fine, man," he tells me, looking around with a suspicion I'm beginning to think we all share. He claps me on the shoulder before walking away, not leaving room for discussion. I stare after him for a moment before movement on the balcony catches my attention. The flashlight doesn't reach as far, nor can my eyes make out the shadow looming by the sliding door to the room my family is in.

On silent feet, I cross the backyard and enter the house, heading straight for the stairs. When I enter the bedroom, my eyes take longer to adjust to the darkness. They didn't keep any lights on like the others did downstairs. A few people found candles in the home and decided to use them to light a few of the rooms. Taking out my weapon, I creep through the bedroom, squinting to make sure that everyone is asleep and well.

Reaching the door, I notice it's unlocked. Sliding it open, I raise my arm, ready if anyone is stalking on the balcony. I relax a fraction when I recognize Dahlia sitting with her feet up on a patio chair, clutching her knees to her chest. Surprised, she lowers her legs to the ground, ready to stand. I quickly raise my other hand to stop her. "You're fine; you don't have to move," I say as I position myself near the chair beside her. "Do you mind if I sit?"

Her eyes widen before she dips her chin slightly. "Sure, sorry, I can go inside if you want. I just sometimes feel like I need to be alone. I can't remember the last time I had to be around so many people for such a long period of time," she admits as she pulls her knees back up, directing her attention back out over the gray landscape.

"You don't have to leave. I can go back inside if you'd prefer." I just stand there, hesitating to walk away. I don't want to bother her... but something about sitting with her the other night makes me want to do it again. It's either that or sit on the floor in the other room while I fight my exhaustion.

A soft smile spreads across her face. "You're fine. I don't mind you so much. You don't try to bombard me with questions or make small talk. Don't get me wrong." She throws her hands up as if in defense. "I love your sister already, but damn, she can talk. I'm used to being alone." Her smile doesn't waver; I am drawn to it like a magnet. A little sunshine in the night.

Taking the invitation, I sink into the small seat. The chairs are placed close together, with a small wrought iron table between them. The balcony isn't large; the furniture occupies more than half the space.

She doesn't say anything but rests her head on her knees, seeming swept away with her thoughts. We sit in companionable silence, and I relish the unfamiliar yet pleasant feeling. Whenever I try to spend time with anyone, including my family, no one can sit without needing to talk. Most people find it awkward to sit in silence, so I tend to avoid trying. I let the comfort of the moment calm me, and for once, I find myself relaxing despite how my nerves have been on edge. It doesn't take long before my mind stills enough that I doze off.

Suddenly, I'm being shaken awake. I reach for my gun instinctively, but a hand gently grabs mine. My eyes struggle to focus; all I can manage to see is the violence that invades my mind.

"Are you okay?" Dahlia asks as she crouches in front of me. She doesn't remove her hand from mine but instead uses the other to grip onto my knee while she gazes up at me with concern.

It takes a second before I remember what I was dreaming about, realizing I had fallen asleep. It's the first time in a long time that I felt comfortable enough to doze off.

I sit up straight and run my hand through my hair. "Sorry, I wasn't planning on falling asleep."

She smiles at me again, the warmth in her expression clutching at my heart. When was the last time someone other than my family was worried like that for me? I can't tear my eyes away from her, but before I can respond, she looks over my shoulder towards the other yard next door.

"I didn't want to sound like I'm being a chicken or something, but I swear I keep seeing movement in the other yard. I know it could be a zombie, but I'm not sure," she whispers, brows creasing as she takes her seat again. I turn to investigate the yard adjacent to ours, but there's nothing but darkness—no shifting of shadows or any noise to indicate anything is back there.

"I thought I saw something in the yard behind us earlier, too. Honestly, something isn't sitting well with any of us. I don't want to scare you, but I think we should just leave." I stand up, stretching my arms above my head, trying to get rid of the stiffness from dozing off awkwardly in the chair. Her eyes follow the movement, drifting up my body, which causes a flutter of emotion I'm still not quite familiar with to assault my stomach. It's the same feeling she elicited the last time—a cocktail of lust and something else I can't name. Something deeper than the empty heat I've experienced with other women.

As I turn to go inside, I stop and rub the back of my neck. "Thanks for you know..." I trail off. Shit, how do you thank someone for just being a silent companion? "Anyway, have your bag or whatever you brought in ready."

I walk away before she can say anything. Probably a cowardly move, but it seems I am full of those when it concerns this woman.

After Rei agrees we need to leave sooner than anticipated, I spend about an hour rounding everyone up, making sure we search the house for anything useful. Then, we are all silently leaving while the sky begins to lighten.

As we pull out of the driveway, I swear there's another car engine off in the distance, but after a second, it's gone. Shaking it off, I prepare myself for the outside world once again.

We've only driven about two klicks on the freeway when my brother stops again. His voice is barely audible through the static on the comms, but I think I make out that it's clear.

The surroundings are quiet, and nothing seems out of place, but the other abandoned cars on the street block some of my view.

"What now?" I grumble to myself. Instead of relying on my S&W, I grab the A5 from my duffle and keep the pistol holstered. I leave the car door open as I get out, and when I round the Coupe, I realize why Rei has stopped.

People.

Four men in their mid-twenties to early thirties are spread out around their car in the middle of the highway. They all appear fit and knowledgeable in how they hold their weapons. The way the three surrounding the car are scoping out their surroundings with a ready grip on their rifles causes me to believe they may be military or law enforcement. Two focus on Reiji and me, while the other keeps his eyes on the road behind them. The fourth man is bent over the open hood of his car.

I bring my firearm up, not caring if it appears hostile. If anything, I'd rather them recognize that I won't hesitate to act should I need to. Two of the strangers visibly tense and keep their eyes focused on my movements as I continue forward.

We've passed by other groups of people but haven't stopped for them. Nobody has tried to get our attention as we passed, either. Our last encounter with anyone else was back on our first supply run. Although we haven't come across that many people, I'm starting to wonder if I hadn't been imagining the sound of a car earlier.

The way they watch me, keeping their grips steady, makes me smirk. It's all too familiar. I would be surprised if they weren't military or some form of law enforcement. Even considering who they could be, I don't lower my weapon.

"Rei," I say in warning.

Rei doesn't look at me, but by the way he's silently contemplating something, I know he is observing the men closer and weighing up options. My brother also has his pistol ready. His men, Don and Ian, are also flanking him with theirs. The tension alone could kill as the strangers and our group all keep our eyes on each other.

Although their car is blocking most of the road between other vehicles, I would imagine there would have been another way than to stop for them. *Just what the hell are you thinking, Rei?*

James and Dirk fan out to keep an eye on the perimeter. Matt decides to follow, throwing a suspicious glare at the four men. They have a sharp eye on everything happening, but the two men still look uneasy. The other two seem relaxed, not surprised to see anyone driving by or having guns aimed at them.

That alone causes me to look at the scene closer. The hood of their car is propped up, smoke curling into the air. Knowing what dangers are around every bend, my anxiety would be spiked if my vehicle had broken down in the middle of the highway. Chances are, not many people would typically be driving by now.

Odd, that's undoubtedly a red flag.

The tallest of the four, who abandoned his attempt at checking over the car, steps up. The man has dark blond hair, shaved close to his head. He's wearing a t-shirt with quarter sleeves, revealing a few tattoos I can't make out.

"Price."

I stare as he extends his hand to my brother. "My name's Price," he clarifies as if we couldn't hear him the first time. Rei lowers his gun and shakes his hand with his usual confidence.

"Reiji." He gestures to me. "My brother, Ren."

"I can't tell you how relieved we are you stopped," he says a little too casually. It's as if he wasn't worried to begin with. "We've been debating on our next steps. The car broke down out of nowhere. Never had issues with it before. Oh, this is my buddy Klein." He points to a shorter and slightly thinner but toned man beside him. His short, auburn hair stands out under the sun. He also just stands there as if it's any other day, no concern marring his features. "And these two we picked up ourselves not too long ago. This is Jenson and Davis."

He points to the two other guys standing slightly off to the side, focusing on our surroundings. These two men seem more worried about their situation, in complete contrast to their companions.

Jenson has an Air Force tattoo on his forearm, and the last name greetings is all I needed to know. If I had any doubts before that they were military or at least have some kind of military background, I don't anymore.

"You can lower your weapons. We don't mean any harm." Price signals to his friends to stand down. When they do, we all follow suit.

While Price talks to Rei, I glance to where James is slowly walking back from doing a search around the area. He raises his hand, points his finger, and rolls his wrist in a circular motion, letting me know we can all assemble. *So it's just these guys then.* I turn and give the okay to everyone in their cars to get out should they need to. Hana will know to keep the kid at a distance.

It doesn't take more than a few seconds before the rest of our group makes their way over. Although Dahlia is smiling down at Haru, who seems to be rambling on about nothing and everything, she takes a couple of quick glimpses around as if she's worried something will jump out at her.

Rei is offering them help by seeing if any of us can look over their car when the others reach me. Dahlia chuckles at something Haru says before her attention strays to the strangers. Her eyes widen slightly, and she goes so rigid that if I gently push her, she'll fall like a loose piece of plywood.

I turn back towards the four men, ready to speak up so we can get back on the road. I don't want us to be out here for long. It's not safe and any threats can jump out on us at any time.

"I appreciate the offer, but unfortunately, this shit won't start up again. I'd need a garage and parts." Price gestures to his car. "Maybe you guys wouldn't mind sharing some space for a little while. Just until we can find a place to hole up. And before you shut me down, I get it." He raises both his hands up in placation. "I wouldn't want to take in strangers either. Especially when you have people to look after," Price says as his gaze tracks our group, then lands on Dahlia. His smile grows, and in my peripheral, she stiffens even more, if that was even possible.

His mouth opens, ready to say something else, when Rei cuts him off.

"That's correct. We don't particularly want to be letting strangers near our families."

His attention shifts back to Rei. "Sorry, I meant to say I get it. The four of us can lend a hand in protecting your family, if only for a ride. I wish I had a specific place in mind, but we haven't decided where would be safe yet. We were all military. We could be a huge benefit to your group."

Rei studies them for a moment before his focus shifts. His eyes linger on our sister and his son longer than anyone else. He typically plays things safe but occasionally will take a gamble if he believes the risks won't outweigh the reward. He would never usually gamble his family's safety, though. The fact he's even considering their offer causes my anger to slowly rise. These men could be anyone. They could have ulterior motives, and we wouldn't know until it was too late.

I'm about to walk away when he speaks up. "We can offer a ride only if you agree that our supplies won't be shared. Everything you eat, drink, or any other provisions you need, you'll have to supply for yourselves." Reiji pointedly stares at Price. "Second, we don't use guns unless it is *absolutely* necessary. My family is more important to me than anyone else's life at this point. Threaten or put their lives in jeopardy; your life is forfeit to me. Understood?"

Price's eyebrows shoot up, but his smile grows. "Understood, sir," he replies with a hint of amusement.

I have no idea what the fuck my brother is thinking. We shouldn't be letting anyone else in. We already have enough mouths to feed and bodies to protect.

"Who has space in their vehicles?" Rei asks our group. My gaze traces back to our people when Hana goes to take a step but stops. Her head whips down to where Dahlia has a vice grip on her arm. Hana looks up at her, confused, but must sense something since she doesn't move or speak up.

Interesting.

I notice Price watching Dahlia again. I wonder if they've met before. Glancing between them both, I observe them closer.

Something about how he's leering at her makes me itching to pull my rifle up. It pisses me off, but it has me almost sure they know each other. Maybe he's an ex or something. It wouldn't be surprising with the way he's eye-fucking her like he has the right to. *It isn't your problem.* I remind myself. *You shouldn't care about how another man looks at her.*

She seems uncomfortable but has a guise of familiarity in her expression as she stares at him. Unsure what to make of this, I ignore them for now. I shove my irritation aside and make my way back to the truck.

Rei will find me sooner than later, I'm sure. I don't give a shit about his explanations, though. We don't need any more strays.

A soft knock on my door has me looking over to find Davis and Jenson waiting. Clearing his throat, Jenson speaks up. "Your brother put us up in your truck for now. If you're fine with that," he says with a very slight southern accent.

With an audible sigh, I jerk my head towards the back seats. They don't need further direction as they climb into the truck and buckle in.

"We appreciate your helpin' us, man," Davis says as he clicks his seat belt in. "Not sure what we'd do if y'all didn't stop. We haven't seen any other people in some time. Price and the silent guy are the only ones we ran into that were willin' to help."

Through the mirror, he stares back at me with a genuine expression of gratitude.

Although they seem nice enough, my instincts are screwing my stomach into knots. My chest feels as if a weight is being pressed hard enough to cut off my oxygen. It's taking everything I have to calm my nerves without snapping.

The only few times I have ever gotten such a negative feeling about someone in particular, was overseas or when my mother woke me in the dead of night. Both gut reactions were validated in death.

I'm not sure if I should ignore this, but what more can I do other than express my grievances to Rei? I tell him, and then what? I'm sure he'll give me his reasoning, but I still can't shove away this gnawing feeling that's climbing up my stomach and into my chest. It's as if this anxiety grew physical talons that are taking hold of my organs.

I take a deep breath in an attempt to relax. There's nothing I can do right now except drive. I'll keep my eyes and ears open for anything that can identify why this new group of men is throwing my nerves into a shitshow. For now, I can get to know these guys while we drive and get a feel for them. Maybe they can shed some light on why I am feeling this way.

"So, where did you guys come from anyway?"

"We're both on leave. We came from Luke over in Arizona," Davis says while keeping his focus outside the window.

"Luke Airforce base? Both of you, then? What made you come over here to LA?" It's not unusual for people to travel to LA, obviously. Just curious if maybe it's important. Aside from our first venture out, they are the only active military I've seen, but there was no order even then. People were being massacred, and any formation or rank went out the window.

"We'd never been to California. We've been plannin' on visitin' for a while. A few clubbin' nights, girls, you know, a real Cali experience, we thought. Except our first night out turns into a fuckin' end-of-world situation. We came thinkin' we're gonna get lucky." He chuckles. "Some luck."

Jenson snorts. "More like SOL. We barely got out of this club we'd just managed to get into before hell broke loose. We were able to find our rental and book it, but eventually, the roads got so backed up that we abandoned the car and ran on foot. It was fuckin' crazy."

It seems that they were here to dab into the nightlife. They are young and obviously single then, so it makes sense.

"Anyway," he continues, rubbing his hand through his wheat-colored hair, disheveling his high and tight cut. "We made it out on foot for a few miles before roads started to clear with less and less of those creature things around. We eventually ran into Price and his friend. They had a functioning car and offered us a ride. I won't lie, I was a bit shocked, you know. So far, all we've seen are people carin' for themselves."

I know all too well what it's like. I don't blame anyone for that because I'm the same way. I only care about those close to me. I won't risk them for strangers.

"The car breaking down was random. It appeared to be running fine. We crashed in an abandoned house for the night before we left this morning. Thankfully, you guys drove by. I don't think I want to be trekking by foot again," Jenson says as he rubs the back of his neck.

They seem honest enough, so I jump into what I'm *really* curious about.

"Did Price or his friend talk about themselves much? What do you guys think of them?" Blunt and to the point. I don't want to dance around the questions. Price and this other man are causing my damn nerves to kick into gear, and I can't help but keep thinking of Dahlia's reaction. I may ask her later how she knows him.

Jenson and Davis stay silent but glance at each other. Jenson looks back at me and makes eye contact through the mirror. "They give us a bad feelin'. The ride with them was fine; they're polite, didn't throw us to the dogs, so to speak, but—" Davis cuts him off.

"We can't pinpoint it, but it seems so fuckin' weird how calm they are. I don't give a shit if you're special forces or some dang superhero or somethin'; these are goddamn flesh-eaters!" He raises his voice a little. "Who can stay calm? They act like they are on a damn Sunday stroll. It's weird, man. It's just off," he says while appearing flabbergasted. It has clearly been on his mind.

"You think they can be trusted to watch anyone's back?" I put simply.

They both shake their heads and, in unison, say, "Negative."

I don't know them. I barely spoke with them, but their honesty about their other traveling companions has me putting them in my good graces. If they can be helpful, I won't mind them tagging along. I can agree, albeit reluctantly, that we need abled bodies who know what to do in a flight or fight situation, but finding those types of people can be hard. If they can be honest and tell me they don't trust those other men, they have thought about it themselves.

"I'll be upfront with you both," I say as I stare deadpan at them in the mirror. "Any wrong move, you're out. Put my family in jeopardy; I'll kill you myself. Understood? If you can hold your own, watch our six; we'll watch yours. We don't have to like each other or be friends, but we can work together."

"Yes, sir," they say in unison, not in any way surprised or offended that I just threatened their lives. Another thought pops into my mind.

"Did Price mention knowing anyone from our group? I mean, I don't think you had much time to talk since we stopped but curious if he said anything or maybe you saw something."

One of them hums as they reflect on my question.

"Hmm. I don't think he said anything, but he was eyein' the pretty redhead a lot. But so was I, so I can't say that means he knows her." Davis smirks at me through the mirror. His hazel eyes squinting in amusement.

Rolling my eyes, I continue to follow Rei. Hopefully, I can get this growing unease to dissipate, and we can move on.

If only.

CHAPTER TWENTY-THREE

Dahlia

The farther we drive into San Bernardino County, the more spread out the terrain becomes. The desert hills showcase nothing but dry brush and different types of cacti and shrubs for miles between towns.

The freeways are starting to become less congested as we drive, but there are still abandoned cars littering the roads. Well, not quite abandoned, considering the blood stains covering the cars and asphalt or the mutilated body parts scattered around. It looks like the zombies got to everyone out here as well, although where they are is beyond me.

I clutch the steering wheel tighter, desperate to keep my eyes open. My body is exhausted, but I'm terrified to fall asleep. When I tried to nap earlier while Hana drove, memories kept resurfacing, threatening to drown me in old pain I thought I had shoved aside years ago.

"I won't stop." His hand clutches my jaw while he forces me to keep looking. "I've told you already. You belong to m—"

"Whoah!" Matts shakes my shoulder, jerking me awake. "Dahl, you, good?"

I take a deep inhale, trying to shove the memories away. "Yeah. Shit. I'm sorry." My eyes are glued to the road while Matt stares at me from the passenger seat.

"Are you sure, hon?" Hana asks from the back. "Maybe one of us should drive."

Body trembling, I grip the wheel tighter. I don't want to cause an accident, especially with the kid in the car but fuck... I don't want to sleep.

I take in another deep breath and pull off to the shoulder. The cars behind us follow suit while the ones in front stop when they see us pulling over.

We've needed to do this a couple of times—usually when someone needs to use the bathroom or swap drivers—so the other cars know to wait.

My hands are aching from how hard I held the wheel, and my eyes burn from fatigue.

Matt climbs out first, ready with his gun. He takes it slow as he scans the surrounding area and takes a quick glimpse under the car to our right. He walks around the front while continuing to keep his eyes peeled.

I don't bother getting out of the car; instead, I climb awkwardly over the center console.

It isn't long before we're back on the road with the caravan.

"Are we almost there?" Ru asks from the back

Poor kid. He's been glued to our sides since the gas station. The incident instilled some fear into him, making him not want to hang out with the other kids while we take small breaks from driving. I don't blame him, but I'm glad we can breathe a little easier where it concerns him. He's a smart kid.

"We still have a little ways. I know it's not comfortable to be in the car so long, but we'll get there and be able to rest before we get you home to your mom," Hana explains.

Haru mumbles something about missing her but I don't catch the rest of their conversation as my eyes droop. I shake my head violently. *Stay awake. It's not that hard.*

My eyes feel like sandpaper, and my body gradually gets heavier. I jerk my head again as I doze off.

"Why are you doing this?" I sniffle as tears stream down my face.

His gentle smile only manages to make him look delusional. "I've already told you, Dahly girl. How many more times do I need to show you?" His hand trails down my stomach. My body revolts at the idea of him touching me again. Why I used to love him touching me is a mystery. Now, his hands on my body feel like acid scolding my skin.

"I love you too much to let you go."

I startle. My head whips around. Matt is staring at me with furrowed brows. "You good?" He's standing outside, leaning over the seat with blatant concern in his eyes as he clutches my shoulder. "You were having a nightmare, I think."

My smile is awkward, but I try anyway while I dip my chin. He doesn't believe me if the raised brows are good enough to go on, but he doesn't say anything else when he lets go of my shoulder.

I'm just now realizing that we're parked in front of a diner right off the freeway.

Ren's friends are all spread out in the parking lot. Two of Reiji's guys, Chris and Kei, join them in securing the area. Ren and his brother are standing in front of the diner, arguing. I can't hear what they are arguing about, but Ren looks visibly pissed off.

"We already cleared the building," Matt says. "You haven't slept, so we didn't want to bother you."

I don't say anything. I glance back out through the windshield. When he realizes I'm not going to respond, Matt walks off, grumbling. My eyes find Ren, and as if he could feel my gaze, he turns his head to meet mine. He doesn't smile or show any acknowledgment except for a small nod.

Even as tired as I am, it still annoys me. *Wouldn't kill you to smile.*

Regardless of his expression, a thought pops into my mind.

What if I just told him?

Would he believe me, or would he be like the few people who weren't Meg? Those that brushed it off and told me I was crazy.

I wonder if he would protect me the way he does his family.

No, that's silly. You aren't anything to him, Dahlia.

Sighing, I get out to stretch my legs. Maybe I can ask him for help. I could let him know it would be dangerous for Ru and Hana. Perhaps then he'd want to help me.

I'm barely out of the car when Dillon walks up confidently, making me want to flinch back.

Turning, I walk around the other side of the car while Hana and Ru get out, but he grabs my arm to stop me. Dillon loosens his grip, and from an outsider's perspective, it would appear like he was stopping me for a friendly chat. He smiles at Hana, who gives him an assessing look before glancing at me.

I try to smile, but it only turns into a grimace. Thankfully, she doesn't say anything, even though I can tell she wants to. She holds Ru's hand and walks over to her brothers.

My eyes zero in on Ren again. *Maybe—*

"Don't think about it, Dahly baby." He pulls me around the car and out of view of Ren and his family. "I see that look." He cages me against the car as he leans in. "Think about the last time you let someone interfere."

My body shivers at the warning. I remember. I just wish I didn't.

"What do you want, Dillon?" I can't hide the tremble in my voice or from my body.

His chuckle grates on my nerves as his smile grows. "You say you don't care, but you still call me by my first name." He brushes hair away from my face and cups my cheek. "No one calls me that anymore. You know it's always my last name." His hand trails down my neck to the skin peeking under my V-neck shirt.

My body revolts at his touch. Bile rises to my throat, and I swallow to keep from throwing up.

Honestly, I have no idea why I still call him Dillon. It must be a habit. When we were together the first time, that's how I knew him, and from then on, I couldn't seem to call him anything else. Maybe it's a reminder for myself—a reminder that calling him something different won't change who he is.

Gaining a little courage with that thought, I plant my hands on his hard chest and try to shove him off, but he's like a boulder. He won't budge.

After a minute, he must want to humor me because he takes a step back. "Look, Dahl face. I miss you." His features soften, but I won't fall for it. "I'm sorry, alright?"

My jaw drops. He's sorry? Does he think that's going to make everything magically okay?

I don't even respond. I turn to walk back around the car. Ren almost comes into view, but Dillon stops me again.

Ren meets my gaze until his focus falls behind me. Dillon's arms wrap around my waist, and Ren keeps his gaze steady on the man at my back. He already looks angry from whatever he and his brother are discussing, but somehow his expression darkens.

You can't do this alone. Ren can probably help.

I may not know him well, but that gut feeling that I would be safer with him is relentless as I try to decide what to do. I should tell him. At least warn him that Dillon is dangerous. I don't know who the other men are with him or if they are just as bad, but I know for a fact Dillon will get someone killed if he doesn't do it himself first.

Ren's eyes find me again, and I wish that, more than anything, he could see the fear behind mine.

"I told you. Don't think about it." Despite the heat from his body at my back, my body goes cold at his closeness. "I apologized, but that doesn't mean I won't take matters into my own hands again," he whispers near my ear.

His threat leaves me frozen. My body trembles and chills break out over my arms and neck.

Ren reluctantly turns away when his brother says something.

Done toying with me, Dillon lets go of my waist. "Just remember that. But I want to make things right with you. We can be happy again. I can keep you safe better than anyone." With that, he steps away towards his friend Klein, who's watching us.

My feet are like lead as I stand there for a moment. It isn't until my body reminds me that I haven't used the restroom in a while that I finally walk towards the diner.

Dread weighs me down as I walk past Ren and his family. I can't remember the last time I felt so alone amongst so many people.

I just need to stay awake and figure out another way to keep Dillon from hurting anyone.

If only I could do that without getting hurt myself.

Chapter Twenty-Four

Two fucking days. Two agonizingly long days traveling. So far, there's been multiple attacks from zombies. Thankfully, it's only been a handful at a time. I was reluctant to have more people in our group, but the four men stepped up each time we needed to fight off zombies. The extra pairs of trained hands came in handy.

Regardless, I'm still pissed off at my brother. I finally got to hash it out with him at the diner, but he wasn't having any of it. Normally, he'll entertain my concerns, but with this, he brushed me off. He threw my need to protect my family back in my face when he told me that to do that, I need to rely on others. I don't understand how adding strangers to the mix can be helpful. I'm already trying to rely on our group, which is hard enough, but something about Price, in particular, is setting off alarm bells. I just can't pinpoint why.

Outside the diner, he seemed handsy with Dahlia but later, when I asked how she knew him, she brushed it off. All she told me was they had history. And when I asked if there was a problem, she gave me a nervous laugh, told me no, and that it was just weird to run into people at a time like this. I wanted to push it but thought better of it. Instead, I decided to keep an eye on him. Dahlia isn't my concern right now and I needed to remember that. If he isn't going to bother Hana or the kid, it'll be fine. *For now.*

Despite my decision, it's still pissing me off. It doesn't help I haven't slept properly in days. The longer I go without sleep, the more the anger simmers, threatening to boil over.

We have been traveling at a snail's pace, attempting not to make too much noise, only to encounter barriers in the roads, rerouting, or needing to get out and completely move the obstacle. Rerouting is becoming more tedious as we move farther from the more populated part of the county and onward. Getting gas has been a pain in the ass, too. There have always been cars on the road, but as we continue toward Victorville, there are fewer and fewer cars between the populated cities. The ones we have driven past were all empty.

The last two days have been horrible. At this point, I need something to get my mind off this growing irritation. Or a place to try to fucking sleep.

I snort at the thought. As if I'd be able to. Like always, sleep doesn't come easy, and when it does, it's been blood-filled, jerking me awake as quickly as it took me under.

Whatever will help calm this growing rage, I need it soon.

Up ahead is our next assigned meeting point, and Rei turns his right blinker on, directing us to an off-ramp. This is the first time he's decided to get off in a while, but it's starting to get late. The sun will be setting soon.

Rei drives a short distance before pulling up into a dilapidated motel parking lot. The lot is cluttered with trash, blood, a few bodies, and, lastly, a few dwindling zombies making their way to our vehicles. These ones are slow, and if I were a gambler, I'd bet they smell of decay.

Whatever the case, I can use this opportunity to let out some of this rage.

Opening the door and grabbing one of the tire irons, I get out and make my way to the first zombie. Without even thinking twice, I bring up the makeshift weapon and bring it down upon its head, releasing some of the pent-up energy wrecking my body.

Metal meets brain matter in a split second. I know later I'll regret the feelings coursing through me. Regret knowing that I let myself lose a little of my control, but I can't help the relief that slowly spreads as I direct this anger somewhere other than at myself.

I'm kicking it off and rounding to bat another. These few seem to be more decayed than the others we've come across. They aren't quite rotting flesh, but the way the crowbar sinks into their skulls smoothly feels like they're *softer*. These also have more of a decomposing smell.

A hand latches onto my ankle.

I ignore the detail of the zombie's state and kick my other foot into the face desperately trying to sink its teeth in. The zombie was once a teenage boy—no more than seventeen.

My foot connects with its chin, snapping its head back from the force of my steel-toed boots. Its grip loosens enough for me to kick it off a second time. My mind is a whirlwind of whys, only fueling my anger.

Why the fuck won't he listen?

My boot connects a third time.

My gut is never wrong. My chest heaves.

I bring the crowbar down.

Metal meets flesh with a sickening thud, my focus fading.

Why can't he see I only want to keep them safe.

I swing again, this time harder.

To not repeat our history.

Blood splatters my face, but I swing again.

"Ren. Baby, wake up." The ghost of her voice whispers. My chest constricts.

Piercing pain follows the memories.

I swing.

Her cries echo in my head.

Why?

Again.

Her blood coating the room.

Why?

The ache in my hand dulls the tightness in my chest.

Why can't you stop?

My vision darkens.

Stop.

Swing.

Fucking.

Swing.

Haunting.

Swing.

Me.

The metal hits the cement, completely splitting through its head. The connection between metal and concrete jars me out of the whirlpool of memories and the darkness that threatens to pull me under.

"Fuck," I say, my breath harsh as I gasp for air. My heart is like a war drum behind my ears. It's hard to regain focus with the throbbing and pounding in my head.

I stare down at the body, taking in the damage.

The head is completely split and mangled. No longer resembling a head at all.

My eyes close as I try to calm my breathing. I ignore the mumbles and what must be all eyes on me while I rub circles over my heart.

A hand on my shoulder makes me jolt around with the crowbar up and swinging down before I abruptly stop.

Hana brings her arms up and hunches back. "Woah. Chill. It's me," she says while she straightens. Her eyes take in the body and me, but she doesn't mention anything. She already knows I won't talk about it.

"What do you want, Hana?"

For once, she hesitates to say anything while looking at me like I'm a cornered animal. *I might as well be.*

"Can I speak with you for a moment?" She bites her lip nervously and looks around before pulling me back towards the truck. My sister pays no attention to the scene around us. She steps over the body, but her foot slips in blood. I instinctively reach out, steadying her while she mumbles a curse.

I'm about to ask if she's okay when she wipes her shoe off on the zombie's shirt. "Ugh, I really liked these shoes," she grumbles. "You didn't need to rearrange his brains, Ren. You owe me a new pair."

My eyes widen, yet somehow, I'm not surprised. Sometimes I wonder what dark shit goes on inside her head. She's a bubbly, talkative person most of the time, but the death surrounding us doesn't seem to faze her. Granted, she's related to me, and I can admit I'm fucked up, so maybe she is a bit too.

All of Reiji's men stare at me with unease as we walk back to my truck. I ignore the concern plastered on my friend's and brother's faces. Instead, I continue to breathe deeply in hopes to rid my body of this feeling. It's like I need to crawl out of my skin.

Hana climbs into the passenger side without as much as a word. With not much else to do, I climb back into the driver's seat.

Once the door is shut, she blurts out, "I need your help. Ugh. So, I'm not sure what's going on, but Dahlia isn't doing good. She hasn't been sleeping at all since picking those strangers up. She nearly crashed from dozing off. She's obviously tired, but she's acting like she can't sleep." The mention of the new group perks my interest as I turn to face her. "She *won't* sleep."

"What does this have to do with me exactly?"

She releases a heavy sigh. "I was going to ask if you could possibly have someone keep an eye on Dahlia or have someone stay outside our room?"

Room?

My expression must have asked the question.

"When you went all whack-a-zombie, Rei pulled me aside and let me know he wanted to try and barricade the top floor. We noticed that the stairwells are all indoors, with doors that lock. So, it may be worth it. Anyway, I need your help. Please? Maybe she'll feel safer knowing someone is on guard or something."

"And again, what does this have to do with me?" I raise my eyebrow, wanting her to get to the point. It isn't her fault, but the lingering anger is still there below the surface. I don't need another complication or something else to worry about on top of everything else.

She throws her hands up in frustration. "Ugh, Ren! Can you just trust me? Damnit. Look. I don't know since she hasn't talked to me. And yes, I mean at all since picking them up, but I've noticed some things. That new guy, the one with a money name or something." She waves her hand in the air as if his name isn't important. "He's been trying to talk to her and bothers her whenever we stop for breaks and rest. She's retreating further and further into herself, and it's weird, Ren. She was shy, but she was starting to make headway with me. Now, she's a ghost of herself. Even when she isn't driving, she's fighting to stay awake. It's as if she's terrified."

I peer over my sister's shoulder. Outside, Dahlia is leaning against her car, looking down at her hands as if trying to blend in and make herself small while everyone gathers by Rei.

Sure enough, as if he knew we were talking about him, Price appears. He walks straight to Dahlia and leans in close, bringing his face to her neck as if whispering sweet nothings in her ear. She shrinks away and tries to walk around him, but he grabs her wrist roughly, stopping her.

What the fuck. My hand is already on the door handle when my gaze catches Haru walking up from behind her, and Price releases her. My nephew, not noticing, grabs Dahlia's other hand and asks her something.

"See? It's weird. She's petrified. I don't trust him. And... at the last stop, he grabbed her like he did just now but purposely pulled her away from everyone's line of sight. She went so pale when he touched her, Ren. She's trying to run from him.

"I don't know what's happening, but I can't leave her alone. I want to tell Rei, but after he shot your concerns down, I worry he won't believe me." She glances down at her hands before looking into my eyes. All I see is alarm misted over by tears. "I'm scared she'll only try to run. Getting back to her friend be damned."

My brows fall, creasing.

She isn't your problem, I remind myself. Although, no matter how many times I tell myself that, I don't believe it. I hate to admit it, but she does feel like my problem. Like I want her to be. *Fuck. Don't go there. You know you can't.*

Groaning, I realize she's right about this guy. This man is going to be an issue. I could sense it before, and now I have a tangible reason to believe it.

"We can't afford to have someone only look out for one room. We need to worry about other threats." She goes to argue, but I hold up my hand. "But I'll keep an eye on him. If you're comfortable with it, I'll stay with you guys tonight." I rub the back of my neck. I can't help but be worried about falling asleep in the same room as my sister or nephew. *What if they try to wake me up? What if I hurt them?*

Hana touches my shoulder. It's as if she can read my thoughts as plain as a book in front of her. "I'll be sure to keep Haru from waking you up. Just don't sleep with weapons near the bed. Yeah?"

This exhaustion is going to kill me. The exhaustion from trying to reel in the anger, anxiety, and fear. It's too much. But my sister's visible relief at knowing I'll help makes it a little worth it.

I may not like it, but I'll help with this. Staying in the same room won't complicate anything for me as long as I keep my distance from everyone. Including Dahlia and the fucking whirlwind of emotions she brings with her. And it'll allow me to keep a better eye on Price.

She gives me a relieved smile. Although she's a bit fucked up like me, she cares deeper for others than I'm capable of. She actually wants to help people. Hana is a rare little gem in this world. I don't know if we'll ever be able to separate her from Dahlia now that she has her sights on her.

Before I can change my mind, I get out of the truck and open the back door.

I glance back to see if Dahlia is still there with Price, but it looks like he moved on. I've noticed that when he's not with Dahlia, he's with Klein off to the side somewhere. It's odd, to say the least. Jenson and Davis both have done well integrating themselves into our group. Juan and the guys adopted them into the fold easily enough.

Rei approaches as I grab my bag from the back seat floor. "I want us to clear the second floor of the building furthest from the street. There are only a few units in each building," he says as he points in the general direction. He doesn't mention my slip of control. Either because he doesn't think it's an issue or he'll quietly keep a closer eye on me.

I turn my attention to the motel. It appears to have four unattached buildings creating a U-shape surrounded by parking and a pool in what would be the middle of the U. The pool looks as if it wasn't cleaned often prior to the outbreak. The water was too green. The parking lot looks to have only one entrance and exit, which brings an idea to the forefront of my mind.

"We should all park behind, close to the pool. Maybe see if we can block off the exit with a few of the cars abandoned here," I tell him. If anyone happens to drive by, our vehicles shouldn't be noticeable but even if they are, we will hear or see them trying to clear the barricade. The barricade itself may cause people to look twice unless… "Maybe we can try and make it look like an accident."

"That works," he says, and walks back to his car without saying anything else. He's still not happy with my questioning him before. He's used to giving the orders and making the final decisions. He forgets I don't play by the same rules as he does since I'm not a part of his organization. I'll respect him in front of his men, but when it's just the two of us, I'll be honest and to the point.

I've said my piece, so I'll leave it be and let him deal with it, even if thinking about it sparks my irritation. I know that if something happens because of Price, he'll have to deal with me reminding him to trust my gut just as much as he trusts his own.

I don't need him ending up like our parents because he doesn't want to trust me.

I won't let it happen. I *can't* let it happen.

Otherwise, I have nothing.

CHAPTER TWENTY-FIVE

Dahlia

God, I just want to sleep. I can't even describe how desperate I am right now. Desperate to find somewhere I can barricade myself in to sleep away from Dillon. The fear is the only thing keeping me from falling asleep on my feet as we stand in the parking lot. They're all starting to discuss a plan to clear the building, but I'm barely keeping my eyes open.

Dillon is talking with Reiji and giving pointers as if he cares about what happens to the group. His charming personality only hides the ugliness underneath it all. He's all smiles and false concern while he plans with the group.

I notice the way Jenson and Davis side-eye him, though. They must have sensed something was off with him when they were traveling.

"Alright, hon. Let the boys plan." Hana gently pulls me away from the group by my arm. "You look like shit, and you haven't been sleeping." We walk a few feet away, just far enough where our whispers won't be noticed. "Now, tell me, what the hell is going on?"

My eyes widen. I can't help but be surprised at her forwardness. My gut tells me I can trust Hana and her brothers, but as that thought passes, my eyes find Dillon over her shoulder. His smile betrays nothing but the way he eyes me has chills crawling up my spine.

Hana's brows furrow, but before she can move to see what I'm looking at, I grab her shoulder. "I'm fine, Hana."

Her snort is her only answer.

"I promise I'm fine. I'm just worried about our situation. After the gas station, I've been worried about the zombies and stuff." I wish I could say that with more conviction. *I* wouldn't even believe me.

She rests her hand on her hip and bites her bottom lip. "You know, I have a strong feeling this has to do with that man who hasn't taken his eyes off you the entire time I've been here. Or the entire time since we picked them up."

Swallowing, I resist the urge to glance back at him. "I don't know what you're talking about."

Her laugh lacks all humor, and she throws her hands up, not bothering to be quiet now. "You can play dumb all you want, hon, but I'm not stupid." She sighs. "Fine. Don't tell me. But I'm worried about you and if there's an issue, you can come to me. You know that, right? We may not have been friends long, but you're stuck with me now, Dahl. You better get used to me. When they get this place locked tight, you'll be with us." She nudges my shoulder before returning to Ru and the group.

As if he's been waiting, Dillon excuses himself and walks over to me. He has already antagonized me once since we stopped, but I shouldn't be surprised he'd keep coming back. He loves to play his games. Loves it when I squirm.

"You're being so good. I'm surprised. It's like you finally know what's good for you." Grabbing my hand, he intertwines our fingers and walks back to the group while dragging me along. I try not to make my fear and annoyance obvious as I gently pull away, but he holds my hand with a tight grip.

When we're all back together, I pull my hand harder this time, finally slipping from his grasp. I don't say anything, but if his chuckle is anything to go by, he's entertained by my resistance.

All I want to do is get away from him. I'm going to fall on my ass any minute from exhaustion, but there must be a way to get away from him. At least for a little bit.

"So, it's settled," Reiji says to the group. "Ren, you'll lead our fire-watch group on the north side. The rest of our supply runners will be on the south side with Juan as lead. Price, you and your group can help them on the south side."

Ren mumbles a quick, "Sure." He seems tense. More so than usual. No one has mentioned anything about him going berserk on that zombie. It was as if he completely lost it for a minute.

Even with the blatant display of red flags, somehow, I find myself wanting to stand next to him, away from the complete black flag next to me. I may be losing my mind in wanting to find safety with a man who quite literally split a zombie's head in half, but even when I stood watching in complete shock, there was something there that spoke to me. It was the way his expression completely broke. It was anger at first, but then he looked like he was in pain. *Tortured.* It's probably foolish, but that somehow made it not scary to see him that way. It only made me want to help him. To be there for him. Has anyone ever just been there? To truly see him and still offer comfort and support?

"Dahlia."

"Huh?" I'm pulled from my thoughts to realize I am still staring at Ren. Considering how everyone is looking at me, I don't think this is the first time he's said my name. Cheeks heating, I say, "Sorry. Yeah?"

"Someone's lost in thought there?" Dillon sneers under his breath so quietly as if he wants to remind me that he's there.

"Originally, you were okay with being a part of the supply runners." Ren's brows go up, but he's not looking at me. His eyes are on Dillon before they come back to mine. "If shit happens, we won't always be able to save you. You can sit out from this if that's what you want."

"I'll help," I say rashly, almost shouting it. If I help, that means I'll get away from Dillon. It's dangerous, but so is he.

Wait. Shit. He's with the supply runners. "Actua—" Ren cuts me off before I can change my mind.

"You can stick with our group then." His eyes still shift between me and the snake beside me as he speaks. Can he see that I'm uncomfortable? Did he make that choice on purpose or just because?

The familiar butterflies in my stomach take flight at the prospect of him purposefully helping me. I know it's unlikely. He probably just wants to keep an eye on me, but I can't help but think he wants me to be safe. That he cares to some degree.

Ren's eyes take everyone in. "That goes for all of you. If you aren't confident in this, sit back. Otherwise, you may get yourself or someone else killed."

No one decides to stay back, but a few of them look like they may want to.

As they continue to talk, Dillon lowers his voice. "I'll be finding you later. I've missed you, Dahl." His thumb brushes my chin as he tries to cup my face, but I pull back. His smirk lightens his face as he walks away.

"With that taken care of, we need to go over a few other things and then get this going," Reiji says to the group.

I ignore the rest of their plan while I watch Dillon walk over to his friend, my stomach dropping at his threat.

Maybe I won't be able to rest. Maybe I won't be able to run from him at all.

Chapter Twenty-Six

I'm doing a quick walk around the building before we go inside. Call me paranoid, but I don't want anything or anyone sneaking up on us. Rei is finalizing any plans and trying to come up with a way to block off the lot's entrance.

My mind keeps redirecting itself to Dahlia during the meeting. Her eyes were trained on me. I don't know if I've ever seen that look on her face before. It was as if she was seeing something for the first time.

Then there's the way that prick keeps grabbing her. I don't understand why I care, but I do. I'm not sure if it's because I don't like him touching her or if it's the way she shrinks away from him. Or maybe both.

Shit, I just want her out of my head. It's too much. My head is already a fucking disaster, yet she's coming in and wrecking me further.

I try to shove those thoughts aside as I reach the middle of the lot.

Rounding the corner, the pool comes into view more clearly. A few straggler zombies are inside, unable to open the unlocked gate. Having them inside the pool enclosure will further give the impression that the motel is abandoned, but we need to make sure the gate is secure.

As I pass the enclosure and walk around to meet the group, there's a voice rising, irritation lacing his tone. "We shouldn't be wasting our time trying to fortify this place if we are only going to leave. It's a waste of energy," Tyler, one of Rei's men, speaks up. He'd been quiet the entire time we talked over our plan. Why the hell speak up now?

"You a fool, man? We need to be takin' a lot of precautions from now on. If we don't, we die," Davis responds, quieter than the other idiot.

Tyler only recently started working for my brother. If I remember correctly, he didn't have an important role in the business or the clan yet. He doesn't have any family with him either. I was slightly surprised Reiji even let him come along since he had no real importance. I can't even remember what he did at my brother's hotel and casino. Maybe he was just there for muscle... he isn't very bright.

It appears this fool is the only one arguing. He's about to speak up, arms out in the air as if he wants to shout again. "I wouldn't do that if I were you," Dirk softly says, placing his hand on the man's neck firmly from behind. Tyler stiffens and lowers his hands.

Swallowing visibly, he speaks quieter. "Alright, alright. Never mind, then. I just thought it was a waste of time. I guess I'm the only one who thinks that. I'll stop." He swallows again, a bead of sweat gathering at his dark brows.

Dirk smirks. "Good. Your loud fucking mouth is going to bring more of the dead here, and then no fortification will be good enough." He releases him with a shove.

Rei clears his throat, and everyone looks over at us. "Tobi, you and Michael will be assigned to block off the entrance with other cars while we clear the building. Try to make it look like an accident. It doesn't have to be perfect. I know we can't create a lot of noise, but throw some of the bodies or something on the cars."

A few of the women flinch—probably disgusted at the idea of using the dead in such a degrading way. I bet they're not used to the darker side of the business that their husbands or boyfriends are involved in. Ignoring them, he continues. "Chris and Kei will stay and keep an eye on the perimeter."

Jen and Maria, who volunteered for kid watch, agreed to help, although they look about ready to bolt. It's understandable. They have no affiliation with my brother's work and the violence that accompanies him. Most of these men kept their wives and girlfriends in the dark.

It has me wondering about how things will continue to play out. We'll do our best to teach and train them, but will that be enough?

Reiji's men have so far been capable, but they don't have the type of combat experience that my guys or I have. They're familiar with violence and getting their hands dirty, but training them further is going to take a lot of *doing* and not *explaining*.

It's not my problem, quite frankly. I'll do my best to help, but I can't stress about it. It sucks, but my family is the only problem taking precedence. Hopefully, we find a safer place soon for the ones who don't want to come with us. I don't know how much longer I can travel with such a large group. Yeah, numbers are great, but just now, someone disagreed with something and got too loud, too reckless.

He risked everybody's life, and for what, because he's fucking lazy? I'd rather only be with the people I marginally trust or at least with people who have common sense—those who will step up and protect themselves as well as their neighbor.

Rei finishes talking, although I missed most of it while observing our traveling companions.

He's waiting, staring at me in expectation as if he asked me something.

"Yeah?" I question.

If he's annoyed by my zoning out, he doesn't show it. "Anything you want to add before we start?"

I rub my hand on my chin, scratchy against the few days-old beard growing in. I could seriously use a shave. I wonder if I'll find some razors somewhere inside.

Maybe. It's a motel that usually has complimentary toiletries.

Rei clears his throat, regaining my attention. I agreed to take point, if only to make sure this goes smoothly, although I can't help the tightness in my chest. Taking leadership with the guys I've already trained and worked with for years isn't ever an issue. Hell, I was opening a business where I'd do just that. It's when I need to lead others who are at a higher risk of getting themselves or someone else hurt or killed. I don't want to oversee more than a handful of people. I don't want to be responsible for more lives.

Stepping forward and shoving my reluctance away, I give a few last pointers to the less experienced people in our group.

My eyes fall on Dahlia. She looks like she's about to pass out, yet she's clutching her weapons, ready to go inside.

Hopefully, this goes smoothly, and no one gets killed. Hopefully, *she* doesn't get herself killed. If only so Hana doesn't decide to murder me in my sleep.

Do you actually believe that?

Fuck do I know?

Breaking into our designated groups, I lead us to the north stairwell with James and Rei. I ended up sending Dirk and Matt to help the other group. Although she looks like she will fall over at any point, Dahlia follows along.

Hana and Haru are hanging back with the rest of the kids and their mothers. Although I would prefer Rei or myself to stay with them, I know we need to be able to clear this place out fast. My brother had Don stay back to help Hana keep their group in line. I lent Hana the S&W and gave Don one of the axes we found at the fire station, should they need them. I hope they won't.

Since being on the road, nobody has slept more than a few hours at a time. Granted, my guys and I are typically fine with that, but the others are not so much, which is why we need a place to rest that is somewhat safe. Also, we want to be able to go on a run and take more time looking for supplies. Every time we've stopped so far, it's usually quick ins and outs so we can get back to the road quickly without attracting too much zombie attention. All small liquor stores or gas stations. Not enough to sustain our group for long.

If we want to make it to our destination, we all need to be in good health, meaning food in our bellies and actual sleep. Sleep deprivation can cause people to act careless or downright stupid.

On our first look around, we lucked out and found a few sets of keys in the office—all were keys for the inn's employees. They should allow us through the stair doors if they're locked and into the rooms. Without power, the electronic locks are useless, and we don't want to have to bash into the rooms. It makes unnecessary noise but also defeats the purpose of sleeping somewhere you can close and lock a door.

James unlocks the stair door and grabs the handle before he uses his other to ask a silent question. *"Are you ready?"*

After I return the gesture in confirmation and signal to move forward, I lift my knife in my right hand and my Sig in my left. We all agreed to use bludgeoning weapons or knives instead of guns. If we hear gunfire, then we know someone is at serious risk.

As he opens the door, I sweep in, shifting right and left, scoping for any threats. The stairwell only leads up from this point and is on the narrow side. Only two of us could stand side to side to go up, and even then, it would be a tight squeeze.

I advance up the stairs, turning left before reaching the next flight. There are three in total to get to the second floor. Once we reach the door, James repeats our steps and opens it.

The screech is so loud I wish I could cover my ears, but I ignore that initial instinct. Although we all expected zombies, my head isn't in the right mindset. My exhaustion and overall stress are starting to wear me down. "Fuck."

James shoves the zombie from the side before it reaches me. Broken from my initial shock, I turn and stab it in the eye as James jumps back from him.

"You alright?" I ask James.

He gives me a 'Really, dude?' look and shakes his head. I don't blame him. I acted like a fucking rookie on first day of basic training. Those fucking screeches are loud as hell, and I've gotten complacent. We've been coming across more of the slow and smelly assholes. I run my hand through my hair and continue forward, determined not to make that same mistake again.

This building only has about twenty units on the second level and a couple of storage closets, giving us ten units, give or take, and some closets to clear while the other group clears the rest. We all have a set of keys, so we decide to go into the rooms separately. It's a bit risky, but I doubt there will be more than a handful of zombies in any room unless we encounter people hiding out. If so, then we know to throw out a whistle. Down the hall, the other group is entering the rooms. We split off, and each take a door. At the same time, I have a few standing in the hall to stop any that could get past one of us or watch our six in general.

I take a moment to listen against the door to see if any shuffling sounds can be heard, but I don't hear anything other than my pulse. I need to pry the plate off but as soon as I do, the keyhole is visible directly under the electronic key slot. Once unlocked, I step inside.

The room is small, a typical motel room. It has two full-size beds, a bath, and an older flatscreen sitting on a worn, flimsy table. It takes only a minute to glance over and walk through. There is no closet, only a single-door wardrobe. I double-check inside anyway, as well as the shower. Crouching down to look under the bed, I find nothing but questionable stains on the carpet. Satisfied, I head to the next room.

The sound of a struggle a few doors down makes me pause. I'm about to ignore it and go into the next room when a loud shriek reverberates in the hall. *Fuck.*

I run to the room and notice four zombies inside. In the doorway to the bathroom, Dahlia is struggling to shove off the screecher trying to make dinner out of her.

Without thinking, I rush over and stab my knife through its temple before whipping around and stabbing the next one trying to reach us. In my peripheral, Dahlia jumps back in and hits the third with a crowbar. The fourth one rushes me, not as slow as the last one. I bring the knife up to kill it when blood splatters across my face.

The zombie drops with a chunk of its skull caved in.

"Thanks," Dahlia says. She has blackish blood on her cheeks and forehead, covering some of her freckles. Her eyes have a slight bluish tint under them, giving away her exhaustion, but they don't take away the beauty from her eyes. My gaze falls to her full lips. She's smiling slightly but then I realize she said something.

I clear my throat and nod despite not hearing what she said. This isn't the time to get distracted. I walk back out into the hall and to the room I'd been ready to clear before I heard the struggle.

Opening the door, I focus ahead and then turn to my right, where the bathroom connects to the room with the door slightly ajar. As I walk further inside towards the bathroom, something tackles me from the side.

The screech is so close to my ear I wouldn't be surprised if my eardrum burst from the onslaught. The zombie is putting weight on my knife arm, restricting my range of motion.

Panic slightly rears its head before I use the heel of my gun to hit it over the skull. The hit isn't enough to kill it, let alone injure it, but it gives me some leverage to free my other arm.

Its mouth snaps close to my face when I bring the knife up, stabbing it in the head. It immediately falls, bringing all its dead weight on top of me. Thank fuck I didn't get any blood in my mouth this time.

"Oh my god!" someone gasps before they rush into the room.

I push the body off me, and at the same moment, someone shoves it away from the side. The zombie rolls off, and I am greeted by Dahlia perched over me. She's crouched down, worry etching her features. "Are you hurt? You weren't bitten, were you?" she asks, biting her bottom lip.

Damn. I peel my eyes away from her lips, not wanting to delve into what that stirs inside of me. "Yeah, I'm good."

"Alright," she responds, although she doesn't look like she believes me.

I ignore her concern while sitting up and taking stock of my arms. I know I haven't been bitten, but I wanted to be sure—a few scratches, but nothing to worry about.

Relief floods my system but doesn't eliminate the electrifying feeling of adrenaline rushing through me. Is this how life is going to be from now on? Will I be in a constant state of adrenaline?

Maybe I should start wearing a jacket. It'll suck in hot weather but might be smart when up against these shits when they come out of nowhere. At least it'll protect me from any more abrasions.

Dahlia stands up, brushing imaginary dirt off her jeans or, maybe, the blood. Not that that's going to help. She stands there awkwardly for a moment, probably trying to determine how to interpret my silence.

"I think the guys already finished clearing the other rooms. I'm going to go check on Hana and Ru," she says softly. I'm still seated, which gives me an eye-level view of her ass as she walks out.

Hot damn. Shit. No. *Fuck.*

I shake my head, trying to clear the inappropriate thoughts flashing through my mind.

Seriously, not the time to be thinking with my dick.

It's been a while since I've been with anyone, so I guess it's fair, but *damn.* The world legitimately ended. Not the time, and even if it was the time, I don't need to complicate our lives further.

I wasn't typically a relationship type. Yeah, I hope to have a family someday, but have never quite met anyone who sparked that interest. I tried a few relationships, but they never lasted. I would hook up and leave.

With Dahlia, it's not like I can go my separate way after since we are traveling together. I don't want to deal with the awkwardness.

Would it be awkward, though? There's something different about her from the other women I've been with. Something different in how she makes me feel.

Even with her in my home, it didn't bother me as much as I thought it would. I was more pissed that it *didn't* bother me.

I never brought anyone to my house. Anytime I met someone, I would usually end up at theirs. A few times in a car. Tacky, but my house was my sanctuary of sorts. It was a place I never wanted to tarnish if I ever did meet someone. It's a pretty ridiculous thought when I put it like that.

Admitting that to myself makes me feel like an idiot. Maybe I just don't want anyone to get the wrong idea. I don't want to share a bed after the fact.

I don't trust myself not to hurt them by accident. Shit, look what happened with Dahlia. It's a real fear whenever I try to sleep while people are near me.

Yet she doesn't skirt away from me.

"You good, man?"

Matt is standing in the doorway with his brows raised in question. Realizing that I am still down on my ass, I stand up and try to shake the aftereffects of the adrenaline and fight.

"Yeah, just got lost in thought. Everything good up here?"

Matt still stares at me questionably before he smooths out his features and gives me an update on how everything went.

"Yeah. Most rooms were empty, but we had a few zombies. No screechers. I heard them, though, so I guess you guys did. Did find one in a closet. That must of fucking sucked to die in a damn linen closet. Anyway, other than that, we're all good. Dirk is grabbing some furniture with Juan to barricade the stairs once they lock the doors."

We walk towards the closest stairs when I notice Rei coming down the hall.

"We are clear to bring everyone up. I'll be in a room next to you. Hana told me you'll be rooming with them?" he asks as he stops and leans against the wall.

"Yeah... I know there are enough rooms, but we should try to keep as many people together as possible. If shit hits the fan, we need to be able to get out fast. We don't want to leave anyone."

Although he's still annoyed at me, he smirks, and his brows fly up. He doesn't believe my reasoning, but he probably has the wrong idea. I'm doing this because our sister asked me. Not because I want to be any closer to Dahlia.

"I think we should allow everyone to rest tomorrow. The next day, we can send a small group to scout and scavenge. We're fine right now with water and food, but pretty soon, we'll need more. I'm worried we may have to start rationing everyone even when we have enough."

I roll my eyes. I already told him this in the beginning: We'll never know when we'll have access to food and water. There was a stent on one of my deployments, where we ended up half-starved when we needed to bunk down for a few days. We were able to manage since we had a small water source where we hid. It was since then that I always tried to be prepared for anything. Clearly, it wasn't enough this time since we needed to leave the house.

"Acting like a child won't solve anything, Ren. I made the decision so our group can be well-fed. I'll tolerate your disrespect behind closed doors, but not here," he seethes. His glare is cold as he narrows his gaze at me.

Reiji and I have always been close, even when we lived so far from each other. Our childhoods were not normal even before I moved to our grandparents but despite that, he always found a way to still be there for me as a brother.

This whole situation has us both on edge, and his anger is only nudging my own, even if it's unintentional. I hate it.

I understand his viewpoint, but the simmering anger won't let me relax.

"Don't give me that bullshit, Reiji. I understand you're used to being in charge. And honestly? I don't give a fuck about your status or your clan. I only give a fuck about my *brother*. About that kid and our pain-in-the-ass sister." I ignore the last person who comes to mind, not wanting to admit it. "If you could trust me the way you give your trust to those men who aren't your blood, you'd maybe realize I can keep you guys alive."

He doesn't say anything. His jaw clenches to the point that I think his teeth will crack.

I blow out a heavy breath and run my hand through my hair. I'm angry and lashing out, but I know my brother won't tolerate it. "Look. When we send a group out, I'll head out with them. We'll go out a few times and fill the truck bed if we can." I turn back to him. "Maybe hold off the rationing until we get to a certain point."

He gives me a stiff nod, but I know that's not the end of it. Not by a long shot. "You may not give a fuck, Ren, but I do. You may have a warped sense of trust and a belief you have to do it all on your own—" I raise my hands, about to interrupt him, but he keeps talking. "—but I won't risk my son or my siblings because my brother can't get his head out of his ass."

"Look, Reiji—"

"You can challenge me all you want," he says, still ignoring my protests. "I don't know why I put up with it, but you're my brother. Despite what you think, I do trust you. I also know we can't do this alone." He steps up closer, lowering his voice. "But when you challenge me, it's away from my men. Understood?"

"Yes, sir," I bit out. I don't believe that he trusts me, but I won't keep pushing it. I'm afraid that if I keep going, I'll lose it. Despite my anger, I love my brother, and I don't want to do something I'll regret.

He steps back and tucks one of his hands in his pocket. "After tonight, Haruto can stick with me for a while. I appreciate you looking after him." He pats my shoulder before disappearing behind the stairwell door.

In other words, he misses his son. I feel a little guilty for not having thought about that. Since all this started, he's been the one in charge. His son has been stuck to our sister's side, away from him.

I follow suit and step outside. The sun has started to slip beyond the horizon, casting a pink and red tinge on the sky. I find Hana still in the truck with Haru, playing a game in the backseat. Don is in the front with his wife, Jen, and his daughter, Lizzy, sitting on her lap in the seat next to him.

"All good, yeah?" Don asks from the driver's seat.

"It's cleared," I tell him.

That's all he needed to hear. He helps his daughter and wife from the front seat and walks to another car to grab their things.

"We're all set. Let's go get some sleep," I tell them. Haru and Hana are already getting out and grabbing their stuff before I finish my sentence. Hana gives me a smile and squeezes my hand.

"Thanks for doing the hard work so we can be spoiled and lazy," she laughs jokingly. "Is Dahlia alright? She checked on us but then took off before I could make sure she was fine," she says while pulling on her backpack.

"Yeah, should be," I say. I don't need to add more worry to her plate by explaining that she almost wasn't or even that I almost wasn't.

This was the third time I had been brought to the ground and almost eaten. I hope this lucky streak keeps up, or at least I stop making novice mistakes and acting as if I have no clue what I am doing.

Haru takes my hand, holding a bag and blanket. I lead us up the stairs and head to the first door on the right. This was the first room I cleared, but I still sweep it again anyway and check every damn nook and cranny before having Hana and Haru step inside.

"Didn't you just do this?" she asks with an incredulous smile. She snorts. "Anyway, I am going to go find Dahlia, so she knows which room we are in. Are we safe to walk around up here?"

Thinking a moment, I rub my jaw. "Yeah. We'll have everything locked with people on the exits. Just don't be loud or hang around outside a room."

She takes off without another word. Haru puts his stuff on a small chair in the corner and climbs into the bed furthest from the door with his blanket.

"I'll be right back. Do not leave this room," I emphasize. "Hana will be back in a minute."

He smiles and tells me he's fine before I leave the room, shutting the door gently. I only want to make sure everyone is set before I can even try to sleep. If I don't know who is on duty, I won't be able to rest.

Matt and Juan are talking down the hall, and they both glance over when they hear the door close.

"We're just talking about who'll be on tonight. James volunteered, and so did Dirk. One of Rei's men did, too. None of them have driven much, so they said they didn't mind takin' this," Matt tells me as I cross my arms over my chest.

"Alright, are we planning on having someone on all night or swapping shifts?" I ask.

"We plan on staying on all night. Since you guys have been taking most the driving and guard load. Figured we can let you shits sleep."

I shift to look at James and Dirk walking over. James smiles. "That fine with you boss?" he asks.

I take a second to consider it. "Yeah, that should be cool." I already know I won't sleep. Although Hana mentioned she'll keep Haru from waking me, I don't think I'll rest much.

At least it'll allow me to watch over the kid myself tonight instead of having to put someone on their door. I trust these guys when it comes to me. I know they'd have my back, and I would never intentionally hurt Haru or my family. They would do what they could, but I can never get that nagging feeling inside of me to believe anyone would put their life on the line for them. It's confusing since I know they've done that kind of thing in the past for other people, yet I can't get my brain to accept it for my family. Just my fucked-up self seeping through.

I can hear Hana and Dahlia speaking in hushed tones down the hall, followed by the click of the door.

"If you need me, I'll be with the kid tonight." Thinking for a moment and wondering if I should let them in on what Hana told me, I decide it's probably best if they know what to look out for. "Also, Hana mentioned something to me before. Just keep an eye out on Price for me. Something isn't right with him, and I guess he is taking a liking to someone in our group," I say quietly, not wanting anyone else to hear.

"You mean Dahl?" Matt asks.

Ignoring the way he said her name so casually, I continue, "Keep an eye out. Hana mentioned he's been approaching Dahlia aggressively" Their expressions harden.

"Yeah, man. I don't like him. Couldn't tell you why, but that makes sense," Juan says.

At least there will be another extra set of eyes for me. "Well, if you guys need anything later on, let me know." Turning, I head back down the hall to our room.

When I walk in, Dahlia startles on the bed closest to the door, wide eyes staring back at me. Hana is already asleep with Haru on the other bed. The kid is somehow hogging most of the mattress. How they managed to fall asleep so fast is beyond me. "I'm going to crash here tonight if you're cool with that."

The little chair in the corner is piled with everyone's packs. I lock the deadbolt and take a last glimpse around the room. I'm tempted to keep my weapons close, but I walk over to the chair and place them with our things.

I walk back over and sit on the floor against the door when Dahlia says softly, "You can sit up here if you're not uncomfortable with it. I'd feel bad if you slept on the floor."

Taking in her disheveled appearance, she's already half asleep. She's exhausted. She's managed to hide it well, but having that lock on the door must have helped her nerves. "Also..." She looks down as if contemplating if she should continue. "Never mind, but I honestly don't mind," she whispers.

I wonder if she wants me to but is too scared to ask. Maybe having someone else around will settle her fears.

I stop that train of thought before it runs wild. "It's fine. Used to it. Just get some rest."

Besides the thought of settling her fears, the thought of lying with her heightens my own. Not because of the feelings she's been stirring inside me, but the fact I could hurt her. I don't need that on my conscience. She's too fucking *nice*. That kindness will only kill her if she doesn't take my reactions in sleep seriously.

The room drapes us in darkness and a silence I haven't experienced since we were back at my home. I sit there, listening for anything beyond the door. It's about thirty minutes before I doze against the cool wood.

A whimper startles me, my heart rate racing as I strain to see across the room. Another whimper sounds before Dahlia screams, turning abruptly in the bed. She's having a nightmare.

She screams again, still not waking up.

Fuck. She's going to attract zombies.

Getting up quickly, I walk over to the bed to wake her. I check on Hana and Haru, but they're still asleep. *Seriously?*

I climb onto Dahlia's bed and gently touch her shoulder. Her face is wet from tears, and there is a light sheen on her forehead. She stops screaming, but she's slightly thrashing her head, fear plastered on her face. I've seen her fear, but this is something different altogether. It's worse than fear. It's like she's experiencing impending doom.

"No. No, please," she mumbles in her sleep. "Stop." The last mumbled words are a defeated plea.

Something about that and the look on her face has my chest in knots. Laying down on my side facing her, I don't even think about it. I reach out and rub her shoulder. "Shh. You're safe. You're safe, angel." The pet name slips out before I can stop myself.

I keep gently rubbing her shoulder. She finally calms down, and I find myself staring at her. I'm probably a creep, but I can't help but brush the hair sticking to her skin out of her face.

Her brows scrunch up again in fear, so I return my hand to her shoulder and rub her arm. "It's alright. You're not alone. It's safe."

I don't understand why I care, but I'm glad she can rest. I know what it's like to be in survival mode for long periods of time. I also know better than most what it's like to fear your own dreams. It's draining, to say the least. Something about being the reason she can sleep feeling safer makes my stomach flip.

I keep whispering nonsense before I can fight my own exhaustion and doze off.

Blood covers the floor. My mother's sightless eyes are staring back at me.

"M—mama?" I stutter.

Why is this happening?

Her body twitches before her eyes transform to blood red.

She's up and on top of me, going to bite my face before I realize what's happening.

Is this real?

This isn't what happened.

"It's okay. You're safe." There's a voice in the distance. It sounds familiar.

A melodic angel amidst the massacre.

My eyes don't want to open as I slip from the dream. I shift and lean towards the voice, wanting to wrap myself around the warm feelings it's giving me.

I drift back to sleep with someone whispering, "Sleep well."

CHAPTER TWENTY-SEVEN

Ren

The harsh sunlight streaming through the nearby window has me waking, slightly confused. I don't remember falling asleep.

With bleary eyes, I try to move my hand to shift my erection, but something is weighing my arm down.

What the...

Oh fuck.

I groggily try to move, but Dahlia softly hums. *Crap.* I don't want to wake her.

My eyes drift shut while my sleep-addled brain tries to assess my situation.

Dahlia is in my arms, her back to my chest. Our legs are entwined, and my right arm is draped over her possessively while her head rests under my chin. Her messy hair tickles my nose, and I need to blow out a harsh breath to push it away.

The weight of her against me feels right despite the muffled whisper in my head trying to convince me otherwise.

She shifts slightly with her hips rubbing against me. I bite back a groan at the friction.

Trying to calm my suddenly racing heart, I continue to take deep breaths. Regardless of my exhaustion, my dick only hardens more when I get a waft of her scent.

How did I end up like this? I don't remember falling asleep with her.

I try to sort my jumbled thoughts.

She had a nightmare.

That's right.

I try to open my heavy eyes, but my mind is becoming hazier. I'll wait for now. Maybe she'll move enough so I can slip out from under her soon.

Her smell reminds me a little of flowers, but I can't pinpoint which kind. The scent alone is comforting, but my disheveled mind can't figure out why.

I don't think I've ever *cuddled* anyone before. I have certainly never fallen asleep with a woman before, and although I keep trying to think otherwise, my thoughts drift to how she feels flush against me. My mind whirls, picturing a plethora of images of her naked. What would she feel like underneath me? As I slip in and out of her?

Jesus, Ren, stop.

I focus on my breaths, trying to ground myself, hoping to reel myself from where my thoughts are headed.

Instead, her warmth only causes me to drift back to sleep.

"Wow. Never thought I'd see the day," Hana whispers and snorts quietly.

My eyes snap open. She's standing over me. My first thought is why she's whispering.

She has the biggest shit-eating grin but isn't looking at me. I follow her gaze to Dahlia, her head resting on my chest and shoulder, arm and leg draped over me.

Memories of earlier this morning come rushing back. "Damnit," I mumble to myself. I fell back asleep instead of trying to move. Hana chuckles, reminding me of her presence.

Goddamnit. I want to throw something at her while she stands there with her annoying ass smile. I also don't want to wake Dahlia up.

My annoyance grows as I take in the situation, not because of the woman in my arms but because of my sister. The moment feels too intimate for her to walk in on when I can't even grasp how I feel about it in the first place.

If not for Dahlia still sound asleep, I'd snap at my sister to get the fuck out. My glare must convey my message because she snickers before tiptoeing out of the room.

Knowing her, I'll never hear the end of this for the rest of my life.

"Great," I huff quietly, but it causes Dahlia to stir. She softly moans, which only verifies that my dick is still hard. She buries herself closer before stiffening.

Her eyes fly open, and she jumps up so fast I can't see her expression before she turns away. Her hands are on her face when she apologizes, muffled by her palms.

"Oh my god. I am so sorry. I—"

She peeks at me through her fingers. She's wearing sweats and a tight tank top without a bra, putting her breasts fully on display beneath the light-colored shirt. Her nipples are hard, pebbled against the thin fabric.

Fuuuck.... I need to hold back the groan and avert my eyes. It certainly doesn't help with the hard-on I'm trying to hide.

I can't say what my expression reveals, but whatever she sees causes her cheeks to flush even more. She throws another apology over her shoulder as she grabs her backpack and books it to the bathroom.

Groaning, I throw my head back.

Well, I was certainly not planning on sleeping, let alone falling *back* to sleep a second time. I don't sleep in usually. Even before my nightmares started to get worse, I hadn't been someone to lounge around in bed. I must have been more worn out than I realized. I don't want to admit it, but... damn. I can't quite say it was the best sleep of my life. I still had my usual nightmares, but I felt *comfortable.*

She must have spoken to me in my sleep, trying to calm me the same way I had for her. I didn't hurt her, though. Instead, I gravitated towards her and pressed us flush together as if seeking that unfamiliar comfort.

I need to stop thinking about this, or I'll still have a damn tent under the blanket, and I don't want to scare her. Crap... the thoughts of holding her won't relent.

No. Don't go there. This kind of shit can't happen again. I may not have hurt her now, but what about next time?

Grunting, I shift the front of my pants to relieve the pressure. I wonder if the water is still working. A very cold shower sounds good right about now.

As if the universe is listening, the shower turns on. I'm sure the water will be freezing, but still, that's exactly what I need. Who knows when we can get another one anyway? Hopefully, Dahlia will take a quick one so I can hop in. With my luck, the water supply will be gone before she gets out.

My thoughts immediately drift to her in the shower. I bet she's even more stunning without the tension she's been carrying... or clothing. She is incredibly beautiful. Her body...

Shaking it off, I get up to find a change of clothing. When the hell did I turn into a pubescent teenage boy? I don't usually allow myself to get distracted like this, yet she threw me off my axis completely.

A knock at the door blessedly pulls my thoughts away from Dahlia. It opens, and although my back faces the door, Matt's voice announces his presence. Pulling clothing from my backpack, I turn around to find Matt showered. It seems like he slept as well, which is good. We all need to be at our best now; rest when we can. We can never tell what will happen at any given time. Life will be high stakes for who knows how long.

"Shit, who knew Ren could sleep in," he says, laughing. "I honestly can say I'm jealous. I would still be out if I could, but we need to start planning our run today. I know we meant to let everyone rest for the day, but I already know you, so here I am." He's smiling at me as if waiting for me to confirm his assumption. He isn't wrong. I wanted to go out today regardless of everyone taking a break. But before I can speak up, the bathroom door opens, revealing Dahlia, dressed in a soft gray t-shirt and dark blue jeans, hugging her curves. She stiffens for a second before she realizes it's just Matt in the room. She gives him an awkward wave and returns to towel-drying her hair over one shoulder.

After getting sleep and being able to shower, she's practically glowing. Her eyes seem brighter, and there is a lightness to her now when there was only visible anxiety yesterday. A peculiar tightness grows in my chest, but it's not like the other times I'm used to, and I'm not sure what it means. All I know is that I can't tear my eyes away from her. It's as if I am seeing her for the first time.

She's fucking breathtaking.

Matt's also staring and gaping like a fish out of water. Clenching my jaw, I speak up. "I'm going to shower first. I can meet you outside at the truck."

His attention flicks back to me, slightly dazed as if deep in thought. "Yeah... sure." Waving at Dahlia, he walks away while I grab my clothes and shut myself in the bathroom.

This shower better be arctic.

Chapter Twenty-Eight

Dahlia

Sitting on the bed, all I can do is obsess over my embarrassment. I was praying so hard that he wouldn't be in the room when I got out of the shower.

Oh god. I can't believe I was basically on top of him, and that look he gave me. I can't decipher what that look was. Anger? Probably. So far, he either doesn't notice me or acts like he doesn't like me much. He seems to only care about his family, for which I can't blame him. I can feel how red my face is right now. In the shower, I couldn't stop thinking about how his body felt. He doesn't slack in the muscle department, that's for sure, but it was more than that.

I have no idea how I ended up cuddling him. I don't even remember him coming to the bed in the first place.

Cringing, I get up to grab my wide-toothed comb. I remember a nightmare and trying to calm him. Apparently, sleepy me thought it would be okay to grab onto him.

What is wrong with me?

I quickly brush out my hair and pull it into a high ponytail. Everything in me wants to run away and ignore him, but I know I need to apologize again. I need to act like an adult, even if I'd rather run and hide like the giddy inner child I'm behaving like.

If I'm honest with myself, I felt safer with him here last night. I also admit I have been unbelievably attracted to him from the get-go, but I don't know how to talk to him.

Do I want to talk to him? I don't like that I was so grounded next to him. That feeling of security was surprising. I do want to, I think, but I don't know how. In most of our encounters, I'm awkward; the only time it felt easier to talk was when I had alcohol.

I just need to get this over with. When he comes out, I'll apologize and tell him he doesn't have to worry That I don't know why it happened, but I'll take the floor if he ever sleeps in our room again. I don't mind, or maybe Hana will share the bed with me.

I can't help but snort at that thought. Like it even matters anymore. He won't stay here again. Who would? If I were him, I'd run for the hills. I probably came off as some clingy woman who was too afraid to sleep alone when I told him he could sleep on the bed; then I all but straddled him in his sleep when he was probably trying to wake me.

I *was* terrified, though. Fuck, I'd been surprised but also so relieved when he said he was going to stay with us. His presence alone blanketed me with the security I needed to sleep.

"Thought you left."

Ren's husky voice pulls me away from my fearful thoughts. When I raise my head to find him by the bathroom door, my fear goes out the window. Instead, my heart kicks up its pace, ready to beat through my chest. He's only wearing black jeans with no shirt. My mouth drops open for a second before I can stop myself.

Did the room just get twenty degrees hotter? My skin and face feel as if I just opened a burning oven.

He has tattoos covering his arms, chest, and half of his torso. Most of his tattoos are a blend of traditional Japanese art, except for the full-sleeve of black and white designs on his right arm and pecs. I am drawn to what I think is a dragon cradling a skull on his left side. It appears to be one tattoo, starting from his wrist, winding up his arm past his pecs, covering his side before disappearing under his jeans. The dragon faces a winged creature, but I avert my eyes before I can figure out more of the designs in detail.

Instead, my gaze travels down, and my eyes widen. *Good god.* He even has the sex line abs where the front of his jeans rest, creating a delicious V. I turn my head away frantically, although this time, he most definitely noticed I was ogling him.

Oh shit. I push my loose bangs from my face as I get up from the bed.

"You alright? Your face looks like you just spent too much time in the sun," he says humorously.

Great. He's laughing at me.

Steeling my nerves, I stand up straighter and look him in the eye. Although he sounded amused, he doesn't smile, his expression like stone.

Does he feel anything, or does he just believe he is too good for anyone? For some reason, this only pisses me off, but I shove it down when I remember how I woke up.

My embarrassment dampens the irritation. Taking a deep breath, I tell him what I wanted to say initially.

"I just wanted to apologize fully for… you know." I gesture to the bed. "I don't know what happened, but I was afraid last night and must have felt safe or something. If you stay with us again, I can bunk with Hana. Not that you would want to…"

He stares at me, his gaze tracing my face and then lowering. If my face could get any redder, it would now. His expression doesn't change, but I swear there is something different in his eyes—as if there was longing there.

Wishful thinking. I roll my own at myself.

His eyes come back up to me slowly, and he nods.

I scoff. I understand that I struggle talking with people sometimes, but I try to change, and he just nods?

He tilts his head and steps forward, causing me to bump back into the bed. He doesn't stop but instead pushes a stray hair out of my face. His eyes meet mine, and he holds my stare. Nerves rattling me, I drop my gaze, but his hand drifts to my chin, tilting my head up as he leans forward.

When I meet his eyes, his brows furrow as if confused. It's as if he's fighting a silent battle, and I am only here as a witness.

Instead of leaning further in, he takes a step back and clears his throat. "Are you still up for going on runs? I know I helped you out yesterday with the screecher, but you dealt with the rest well. More than well, actually, since there were a few. Do you think you'll manage on runs?"

The change of subject takes me aback. Runs? I haven't thought about it since leaving his house. I haven't had to help them yet with anything other than clearing this place.

I knew I would have to go on supply runs when I thought I was going alone, but now that we have a group, did I want to go if he was giving me the option? I'm not very good at fighting. I can use a gun decently, but I feel like I was only lucky with the other zombies yesterday. That's all. Until now, I have only been lucky and managed to run instead of fighting.

I think about my father. My stomach churns with the reminder that he isn't here. Would it make him proud if I stepped up?

It may be a poor choice, and despite wanting to make my dad proud, I do want to be able to contribute. I want to survive in this new world; the only way is to hit this head-on. "Yeah, but I won't lie to you. I don't know how to fight. I sort of feel like I was lucky up until this point. I am good with a gun. Well, I am decent, but that doesn't help us much in terms of stealth," I say with an awkward chuckle.

He considers me before rubbing his stubbled chin. "You don't need to know how to fight; just bludgeon or stab if you can. For the most part, we will watch each other's back, but you need to understand the risk. We won't always be able to save you. If you put yourself into a situation that endangers the group, we'll leave you behind. Same goes for everyone. If that bothers you, I recommend sticking with the others."

I flinch. I can't help it. Even if he means it, I can't help but feel he sees me as a liability. For some reason, that hurts more than it should. I know I'm not the strongest in this group. I don't have much to offer, but I want to try.

Thinking about staying behind also makes my skin crawl. I don't want to be left unaware when Dillon is around. Even if he doesn't like me, Ren's presence makes me feel safer. If I go out with them, I'd rather be with him and the zombies than here with Dillon.

As if reading my thoughts, he says, "I won't be taking any of the new guys we picked up. I don't trust them. I don't know you well enough either, but you took care of Haru. Figured if you want to start getting practice at making these types of runs, then with us is your best bet."

He places his hand in his front pocket and leans against the wall beside me. His muscles flex with the motion. Before I get too distracted, I peer into his eyes instead.

"Yeah, I'll join you guys."

I also want to say that I don't feel safe here alone, but before I can look up at him, the door opens.

"Oh! I'm sorry if I am interrupting," Hana says with a huge smile and her hands up as if trying to placate someone. She doesn't seem sorry in the least.

"When you're done, meet us by the truck. We're going to head out soon," he says before donning a shirt and his pack and walking outside. When the door clicks shut, Hana sits down next to me.

"I can tell you this now: my brother never, and I mean never, sleeps with women. Well, I mean literal sleep. And he certainly never *cuddles* anyone." She wiggles her brows at me.

She knows? I groan loudly so she gets the picture. "I'm so embarrassed, Hana. You're not helping," I say as I focus on my hands, nervously picking at my shirt.

She reaches around my shoulder and pulls me into her. "Girl, why be embarrassed? You weren't the one doing the grabbing." She laughs out loud as if she just let me into the funniest joke she's ever heard. She must read the confusion in my face because she continues between snorts. "I woke up a few times. You guys were both having nightmares. What a pair you two make." She chuckles again, still latched onto my shoulder.

"Anyway, he pulled you in at some point. I think you were too tired to realize when you were over there shushing him back to sleep." Her huge smile gives me the feeling that I won't hear the end of this for a long time.

"This makes me happy. My plans worked. Two birds, one stone and all." She winks at me.

Huh?

"Alrighty! I hear you're going to go with them today. Be careful, yeah? I don't need to lose a friend when I just picked her up. Oh, also, can you be on the lookout for tampons or those cups, any warmer socks, and lastly, baby wipes? I have soap, but I don't know when the water lines will shut off or whatever supply this place has access to runs out. Honestly, I don't know how it works here. Whatever, that is beside the point. I plan on using soap and baby wipes solo when that happens until we have access to water." Her face scrunches up, revealing her thoughts on that plan.

Not able to help it, I laugh. "Yeah. I needed to find some of that stuff anyway. I always have a bug-out bag in my car, but my stupid brain forgot a lot of shit I didn't realize I'd need. Like tampons." I smack my forehead for emphasis.

Satisfied with my answer, she releases me and heads to the bathroom. "Be safe, baby Dahl!" she says perkily as she shuts the door.

I can't help but smile. Hana reminds me a little of Meg, only a lot more outgoing. She seems to hold on to a positive attitude, not allowing anything to bring her down. Her personality makes it easier for me to talk to her. She's incredibly welcoming, and it makes me want to be her friend all the more. It's funny that she truly seemed happier about her brother in bed with me than upset. Wouldn't most people be appalled, or is that just me?

Grabbing my crowbar, backpack, and shotgun, I make my way to the door and out. Ready to face the next challenges coming our way. As I slip outside the room, my thoughts stray to Meg. *God... Please be okay. Please... We're coming*

The sun is out with a vengeance today. It's definitely going to be a hot day. Not a cloud in the sky or a breeze to lick the heat. How it goes from feeling colder one day to blazing hell the next is beyond me. California is one of my favorite places, but I would prefer colder weather or, at least, somewhere not as moody. It may be a benefit, though. We won't freeze to death without electricity. But maybe we'd only cook ourselves instead without our air conditioning. Even when we had no AC, we always had the option to spend a day at the library or walk around inside a mall or something. Now, we don't.

Voices up ahead pull my attention to the present. A group of guys have gathered near Ren's truck. I guess none of the other women in our large group want to learn to be useful. No, that's not right. I guess most of them have children. A few don't, though, and yet they aren't here. Hana mentioned she wouldn't mind stepping out but also wants to watch their nephew.

I am starting to realize that they don't trust outsiders much with their family. Ru is always with one of them. I was the exception since I kept him safe, but even then, he hasn't been alone with me for long periods.

I don't fault them, though. Especially now when the world will only chew you up and spit you back out. I can understand why they want to keep him close. Not to mention the incident with the other kids. I can't blame them for wanting to be cautious.

Seems it will be Matt and Ren's other friends. They have all been nice the few times we've talked, although I haven't really interacted with Dirk yet.

"Hey, Dahl," Matt says as I shuffle over. My smile is a tad awkward, and my wave is even more so.

Matt has been sweet, but he's a bit intense. We share a few things in common with some of our music and clothing interests, but that's about it. I never liked the guys in similar scenes I hung around. I may like edgier clothing, but I love art, reading, and other creative outlets. Throw me in the woods to go camping, a good book, and some coffee, and you have a happy woman.

"It will only be the six of us for now," Ren says. "I don't want to hit any of the larger retail stores. We can scope them out and mark them down to return to later, but I don't want to risk running into large groups of zombies or even unfriendly people holed up. We need to keep a sharp eye out in our surroundings." He regards each of us to get his point across.

"When we go anywhere, we should stay in groups of two. When we clear places, Matt, you're with Juan; Dirk, you'll be with Dahlia; and James with me."

Matt glances at me before looking back at Ren, who continues: "Remember, we don't want to use guns, but we need to be prepared for the worst." He asks me, "Do you mind if we take your car? Juan will be taking his, and Matt will be taking Rei's rental. I want to leave the truck for them in case they need to split."

"Sure," I respond, not minding at all. Matt, on the other hand, gives Ren a confused look but doesn't say anything.

"That's settled then. I figure we can meet at the shopping center which is about two klicks east of here. It may work in our favor to take different routes, scope out what else is around," he tells us. "There is a smaller market we can check out and a few mom-and-pop shops. Once we get what we need, we can move on and scout the larger retailers and see if there are any that might be safe to enter." Ren looks at us once more before asking if we have questions. When none of us speak, he takes that as a no.

"Alright then. Let's head out," he says and walks to my car without further explanation.

I stand there a little dumbfounded. If he was pairing me with Dirk, wouldn't we all drive with our groups? Not understanding his logic, I follow.

"Keys?" he throws over his shoulder as he walks. Shifting through my backpack again, I find the keys and pull them out. As I'm about to look up, he's already grabbing them out of my hands, unlocking the driver's door, and then climbing in.

What the hell?

"You're planning on driving?" I ask, slightly annoyed. I don't mind him driving, but the part about not asking is what irks me. And mainly just him. Yup. It's just him that irks me. The way he thinks he's commander and chief over us all. Well... when he's like that with *me*.

That, and my mortification from earlier following me around like a cartoon rain cloud. He did ask if we could *take* my car, so maybe it was supposed to be implied. I still can't help the annoyance flaring to life.

"Problem?" One of his brows goes up, and I swear one side of his lip twitches as if he wants to smirk. Is he teasing me now? Asshole.

Rolling my eyes, I walk around to the passenger side and get in.

He reaches over to place the shotgun in the back seat. "I'll put that light on when we get back."

"Thanks, I appreciate that," I say. "I tried to figure it out, but my dad was the one to do all the mods and whatnot."

I peer out the window, not wanting to talk about it. I'm still embarrassed about earlier, and now I've just admitted to another reason why I am basically useless to him. He already had to put the bayonet on, but I can't even figure the light out. These guys know what they are doing. They can probably take my damn shotgun apart and put it back together again, blindfolded. He says nothing as he starts the car and begins our drive. It was only a brief reprieve, but I forgot about the reality surrounding us now.

A jolt of fear causes my pulse to rise. We could be attacked at any moment. I keep my eyes fixed on our surroundings, not wanting to be the weakest link. I can at least be alert and ready. As we slowly drive down the road, I take mental notes of any stores that may be worth a shot to look through.

I notice a pharmacy in the back corner of an abandoned lot. That may be somewhere to look.

When we make a right turn, the car jolts to a hard stop, flinging me forward and catching on the belt and Ren's extended arm.

"The fuck?" Ren whispers. He puts the car in reverse and turns his body in the seat to peer behind us. My eyes track back to what he'd been focused on.

At the end of the road are at least fifty zombies aimlessly wandering around. They remind me of the Hollywood zombies —the gory, mindless undead. Some appear more decayed than some of the others.

I realize I'm holding my breath; my lungs feel like they are expanding to excruciating lengths. We are backing away so damn slowly.

For a moment, I think we have been quiet enough and in the clear, but then one of the zombies looks directly at me. "Oh crap," I whisper, so softly I could barely hear it.

The large group of undead all turn in sync. Then, they start running towards us.

"Oh shit!" I don't hold back my fear any longer. Ren pushes the gas and somehow manages to turn the car around without crashing into the lamp post or sidewalk and is flying down the street, avoiding cars and other hazards on the road. I turn back to look and see they are all following us. Thankfully, they aren't as fast as the screechers, but they are managing to make those lame gaits look deceiving.

As we make another turn, I spin back around, confused why we aren't taking the same way back. "Oh my god."

The roads are flooded with them. Everywhere. We've been so used to them being hidden away or in small groups that I couldn't imagine so many would be in one place. How stupid was that assumption? The ones in the city must have had food sources to run to. The buildings were probably flooded with them. Here, not so much.

Would the cities be looking like this now?

Oh god. All around us, it looks exactly like a scene straight from *The Walking Dead*. Zombies are around every corner—most of them exposing traumatic wounds to the elements. A few with missing limbs or large chunks missing from their bodies are crawling on the sidewalk. Close to us, there is one with its intestines hanging out of its stomach and dragging along the cement as it reaches for us.

Bile rises to my throat. Panicking, I try to find something to vomit in. I find a small bag from the liquor store on that first night and hurl as soon as it's close enough. I can smell the decay through the window now, causing me to vomit more.

I dry-heave for a moment before I can get my stomach to settle. Ren pays me no mind as he keeps driving.

"I can't tell where the others went. They hadn't gone down that road," he says. His gaze searches frantically, trying to figure out where the fuck to go.

He curses again before I hear and *feel* a huge thunk under the car.

"Was that a..." I trail off, not actually wanting to know; otherwise, I'll vomit again.

Ren answers regardless. "Yes. Shit!" He swerves hard. "We need to find a way out of here. If we can lose them, we can go back. Otherwise, we're screwed."

Something hits my side of the car, causing me to shriek. Ren swerves away from the zombie and manages to give it the slip before almost running into another group of them standing dead center in the street. A bloody handprint mars the window, while beyond, more are fighting to get to us.

I can't help but fully panic now, my eyes turning into saucers on my face while my skin drains of all color. Even when we were booking it out of the city, it had been chaotic. The people running outside of their cars on the road made it easier for us to drive out with less attention on us. They were unknowing and unfortunate distractions.

Distraction.

"We need to distract them. They respond to noise. Is there something we can do to create enough noise away from us?" I ask.

Ren takes a moment to think before saying anything. "I doubt it. We'd need to expose ourselves, and they could grab us too easily. We need to find somewhere they can't follow. Fuck, I don't know." He runs his hand through his hair while he looks around.

I feel deflated. My sliver of hope has dwindled. Even he seems at a loss for what to do. Is he overwhelmed? I mean, he is experienced in war, or I think he may be, but this isn't war. This is just mindless, hungry death closing in from all angles. These things will continue to chase us until they are satiated on our flesh, regardless of our strategies or how many times we shoot back. Wrong, they will never be satiated, so they will never stop. Not until they are killed.

He makes a left turn. There are fewer zombies on this street, but we still have a tail of them. "Wait! Look!" I point off to the right. It appears to be an auto shop or something—one of those where there is an entrance and exit you can drive through.

"Maybe we can get in there and close the gates. Maybe rig something up to make noise while we drive out the other side? A distraction."

Although he glances at me quickly, he takes that turn without hesitating. It's a stupid idea. I don't know how we will cause a large enough distraction, especially with the electricity out, but we can try. Let's hope there aren't many zombies inside, and we can close the gates before this horde catches us. He must have the same thought since he speeds up.

Let's hope I didn't get us killed.

Chapter Twenty-Nine

Dahlia

Driving closer to the auto shop, it doesn't appear to be crowded inside. A handful of zombies notice us and exit the building in pursuit. There are four gates in total. Two are open, and one of the back gates is partially pulled down, or at least that's what it looks like from here.

"Since we want to make noise, cover me. Use the shotgun," he says as he drives up the curb. We don't have any chance to back out now. Ren drives us through the gate at a questionable speed before slamming on the brakes. He's out the door as soon as he throws the car in park, causing me to jerk forward. I falter momentarily, allowing the situation to sink in until I hear my name.

"Dahlia, come on!"

I can't help the tremors coursing through my limbs as I slowly grab the gun and get out of the car. The horde is making its way quickly toward the building, and the few already inside are moving to grab at us. I lift the shotgun, trying to remember what my dad used to tell me about firing it and the many times I have used it, and I pull the trigger. Pain lances up my shoulder, but I don't think about that when I realize my mistake. I shot too low and wide, barely clipping the torso of the closest zombie.

"Fuck. Ren. I haven't shot this thing in years!" He's trying to pull the furthest gate down when he stops and runs back to me. He grabs the shotgun out of my hands and swaps it for his handgun.

"Do you have other shells on you?" he asks as he pulls the trigger, completely blowing off the head of the zombie ten feet away.

In my panic, I take a second to figure out what he's asking me before I run back to grab the handful of shells in my backpack. I had more somewhere in the car, but this is clearly one thing I did not prepare myself for. Bug-out bags?

Yes, always. Having ammo at the ready in case of an angry zombie-horde invasion? Nope. Not in the slightest.

I hand him the shells, and he clips off the closest zombies before he needs the ammunition. He makes his way back over to the gate. "I fucking hope you can shoot that better than this. Shoot at their heads!"

All his comment manages to do is piss me off. I used to be a pretty damn good shot with that shotgun back in the day. It's been years since I have had the practice, and I wasn't fearing for my life while using it. All but ready to prove I am not as useless as I feel, I shoot the closest one making its way to Ren.

My first shot clips the shoulder, but my second hits between the eyes. I prefer rifles, and I've never worked on moving targets, but I finally get into my groove, picking them off somewhat quickly. More and more are rounding the corner street, though, at least a hundred now.

"Oh my god. Hurry!" I shout as I aim for another, missing again. My panic flaring to life causes me to keep missing my shots instead of hitting true.

Fuck this. I grab the crowbar from the seat of the car and walk to the gate. I step closer to the exit and shoot another one in the head.

One charges at me, it's jaw hanging at an odd angle. I swing with the crowbar with as much strength as I can. It jolts back in time for me to bring the gun up and pull the trigger.

Ren finally gets the first gate down and runs to the last. He raises the gun. Thrusting forward, he stabs the closest zombie. He uses his boot to kick it off before he shoots another one close enough to reach us. Once they're down, he wastes no time before getting back to work on the gate. We can hear screechers approaching our location, putting more pressure on our efforts.

Just as Ren finally pulls the gate down, I clip off the last zombie who managed to slip inside.

I take a breath of relief, but suddenly, I'm hurtling forward. The gun slips from my grasp. Landing hard, I skid before my head slams into a mounted lift. Spots obstruct my vision, and it takes me a second before I realize someone is on my back.

No, not someone.

A zombie.

I buck my hips wildly, desperate to get it off me. Screaming, I push up to try to spin around. My heart is in my throat as I panic.

I succeed in flipping myself over and kick it hard in the chest. My arms awkwardly hold my weight while I try to crab walk backward.

It lunges and lands on top of me. My hand comes up underneath its chin as it looms over me. The eyes, once brown, look milky, and every vein is bursting a brownish red. It's snapping frantically like a rabid animal.

The only thing I can focus on is keeping my hand under its chin, terrified of slipping. I feel awful thinking about it, but why couldn't I get attacked by one that was smaller than me? If I were standing next to it, it would tower over me.

Its body weight is beginning to constrict my air as I struggle. My feet won't find purchase on the wet ground to buck it off.

Is this how I die in an abandoned auto shop mauled by a dead woman?

It couldn't have been more than seconds, but wrestling with this creature feels like an eternity. My arms feel heavy, and my vision darkens.

The erratic growls sound further away—like someone's turning the volume down.

My arms are weakening. My hand slowly loses purchase. *Oh god…*

Suddenly, it's being ripped away from me.

I gasp and cough, desperate for air.

My lungs and arms burn, and my face is wet. From blood or tears, I'm not sure. Probably both. I continue to cough and roll over to get up, but it takes me a long time to find my strength with my shaking limbs. My gaze falls to the zombie. Its head is unrecognizable after being bludgeoned on the mounted lift I was acquainted with. Bile rises to my throat again, my stomach feeling nauseous from the sight, or maybe it's the head injury.

"Did it bite you?" Ren asks. "Fucking hell." He grabs my arms to inspect them before looking me in the eyes. He gently brushes my bangs behind my ear to reveal where I hit my head and cups my face with his other hand.

"Shit. Do you know how not to get injured every time you go out?" He tilts my chin to get a better look despite the limited light from the high windows.

He spins me around and brushes my hair away over my shoulder. The warmth of his fingertips on my skin is a drastic contrast to the cold wracking my nervous body.

He gently turns me back around, inspecting every inch of me for bites when I finally respond. "You know, how else will I keep things entertaining?" I say dryly, pushing back the nausea. "Where did she come from?" I ask while I pull away from his hand and look around. I didn't see any zombies slip past, but everything happened fast.

"I think she crawled under that other gate," he says, pointing to the one behind us.

Right. It was partially opened. That was incredibly careless of me to forget. I assumed driving up was enough to get the others to come out. I didn't look around or even consider the other entrance behind me.

"Go sit down a moment. I will look around and ensure nothing pops out at us before we figure out how to make enough noise to make a getaway."

He walks off before I can say anything. Not caring, I walk over to the car so I can sit.

Here I was trying to be useful, but instead, could have ended up getting killed. Again. I could have gotten him killed for not being more aware of our surroundings.

God, I can't get anything right.

Groaning, I sit and pull the sunshade down in the car to use the small mirror.

"Oh crap." Right above my right eyebrow, a colorful bruise is forming, and a small gash bleeds down my temple. The cut is small but looks deep enough that it might need stitches.

I'm still healing from my last injury, and now I have another. With this one, I most likely obtained a concussion. I remember the last time I got one. Just thinking about it has my face reddening in embarrassment.

During one of my dance classes, our instructor had been running late. I hadn't been paying attention while I was talking to one of my friends. The other girl wasn't either. I ended up getting kicked in the head when the girl was practicing her grand battements across the floor as she focused on herself in the mirror instead of her surroundings. You never know the strength of a dancer until you get a pointed foot to the head. Downside of being short in a ballet class, I guess… I'm at foot level.

Great, just great. I close the mirror and flip the shade back up before double-checking the rest of myself. Thankfully, she didn't bite me, which is surprising. It happened so fast, and she could have gotten me in the neck if I hadn't moved quickly. At least I managed to do *something* right.

I can't help but bristle. Snorting, I sarcastically say, "Wouldn't Dad be so proud? I managed not to get bit." *But you almost fucked up and got both of you killed.*

The clamor of the zombies from outside grows as more reach the building, pounding on the walls and gates, trying to get in—a constant thumping and thrashing to keep my heart racing and my anxiety at a breaking point.

Ren's voice makes me turn my head to look out the driver's side window. "It's clear. You good to look around?" he asks me.

Without the gates open, there aren't many windows except a few small ones closer to the ceiling, which doesn't help prevent darkness from draping the room. "Yeah," I call out.

I reach down by my feet and feel around until my hand clasps around a flashlight. Turning it on, I make my way over to Ren. He's inspecting another car that's parked at the far end of the shop. I hadn't noticed it before.

"If it runs, we can park it and put something heavy on the gas. Maybe something on the horn," he says, and opens the driver's door to find the keys in the ignition. The car turns on without any issues.

What luck. Inside an auto shop, it most likely could have been a dud. He turns the car off before standing up straight and observing me intently. "Help me find something we can throw on the gas. I'm going to see if there are any supplies to grab. Once that's done, I can play around and see if I can rig the horn to go off."

"Sounds good to me." I turn and walk away.

There is a large worktable on the right side of the shop, closest to a door that must be the offices or the guest service entrance. Tools galore fill the surface—most of which I don't recognize, let alone can name. I pick things up to feel the weight before I find one that feels heavy enough.

Thinking, I put it down and run back to my car, grabbing the vomit bag. Ren gives me a questioning look which I ignore.

When I open it, I cringe and throw the heavy tool into the sick bag, tossing in a few other heavier ones before it becomes one large weight.

When the bag is full, I bring it to the other car and place it on the seat. Turning, I make my way back to the office and peek through a window into the building. There is one zombie moving slowly around the small room, but otherwise, it's empty. Maybe there are at least some water bottles or even instant coffee inside. Every time I went to get my oil changed, they always had those things available in the waiting room.

"Hey Ren, I want to check this space out," I call out over my shoulder. "Maybe they have some water or snacks or something. I can't tell if there is another open door, though, from here. I'm going to tap the glass, so be ready in case," I say, before waiting for his grunt of approval. I raise my free hand, still clutching the crowbar in the other hand. Ren's gun is in my car on the seat, and I resist the urge to facepalm myself. I need to get in the habit of always keeping my weapons with me.

Ren quietly comes up behind me, close enough that the heat of his body warms my shoulder. He gently grabs my arm to stop me before I can knock on the window. He proceeds to pull me back, position himself in front, and then lightly taps the glass.

The zombie inside looks straight at us. It was once a middle-aged woman. The clothing still looks pristine except a red bite mark through the wrist of its tracksuit top, and its dark hair is still pulled up in a bun at the top of its head.

It's slightly unnerving. If I didn't see the bite, I would have thought it was human. Or at least until I looked closer at its face and saw the ash-gray tinge to what was once a warm-brown shade. Or saw its glazed over eyes. All the blood vessels have burst, so the white of the eyes are nonexistent. Another obvious giveaway is the smell. Even from here, I can catch the slight putrid stench coming from the room.

"I wonder if the ones that seem more dead are ones that haven't… uh… eaten," I whisper, thinking aloud. The once-woman reaches the glass, its hands slamming against it, causing the panel to shake. Ren waits to see if others come into view before going to the door. He slowly pulls it open while raising the shotgun.

The zombie is so distracted with clawing the window in front of me that it doesn't notice Ren. Its head explodes against the glass, chunks of pink and red splatter across the surface with a sickening splat, and I unintentionally duck with my hands up to cover my head. I turn and fight back the need to vomit again. It takes me a second before I'm able to stop gagging.

I can't help but mourn the person it once was. One moment, she was someone's partner, friend, or daughter. She was important to somebody. Now, she is lying there with no one left to mourn who she was.

"I don't know if I can get used to this." My voice is a whisper, but Ren hears me all the same. His expression softens slightly as if he wants to say something, but instead, he walks back to the room and disappears into the doorway.

The shotgun firing startles me. My feet are already running before my mind can catch up.

Around the corner and down a small hall, Ren is kicking a now-dead zombie to turn it onto its back.

I'm not sure what he is searching for, so I call out, "Are you okay?" I walk towards him without thinking about it, hoping he wasn't bitten.

All he gives me is a nod.

Does he do anything other than nod or grunt? I roll my eyes when he goes back to examining the body.

The hallway has only three other doors, but they're all closed. *Wait.* "It didn't follow the noise but waited," I ask, although it's more of a statement than a question. They can't open doors—or so we believe—which means it waited for us to come inside. Or did it not hear all the commotion?

"I came across one like this before." He pauses. He may be looking directly at me, but his gaze is far off as if reliving the memory. "Just the one, but it's odd. It waited for me to be in a position where it would have an advantage. I nearly got bitten that time. I also discovered scratches won't turn you."

He looks down at the zombie. "I got blood in my mouth, but I have a strong feeling vomiting so soon was the only reason I didn't turn..." He rubs the back of his neck and meets my eyes. "But I'm not sure what would happen if blood got into a wound or if maybe I was only fucking lucky. I don't know, but I don't want to find out either."

He had been that close to turning? My eyes widen at the thought.

"These are the ones we need to be careful with. It was slower than the other one I came across. What you mentioned about them eating. You may be onto something. The one I came across before had a firehouse buffet full of his buddies."

I cringe at his description. "Maybe they start to internally decay and weaken when they don't have a food source? The one in there only has one bite. Maybe it turned this one." I motion to the body near my feet. "Maybe it started to get weaker."

Although, wouldn't it have eaten him?

I wish we could find people who knew what was happening. Someone who knew what we were up against. Can we wait this out? Will they eventually die? I can only hope so.

"Possibly. They don't seem to be rotting as you'd expect. It's fucking weird. I'm hoping we pass a still functioning military base or a facility where they are trying to fix this or find answers," he says, mirroring my thoughts. "I am going to clear the other rooms. Just stay in here and see what you can find."

He walks further into the hall, leaving me to search the sparse room.

The space is small, just enough to fit a three-person couch, a desk, and a water jug with a cup holder attached. The water jug looks full. The far-right wall has the door to the outside, which is mostly glass. This allows a clear view of the horde beating on the gates outside only a few feet away.

Oh shit. How did they not hear the shotgun or notice us yet? Although I won't complain if they never do.

I move as quietly as possible, not wanting to draw attention to myself, still flabbergasted that the shotgun hadn't already. If only a few pushed on the door, the glass could shatter. Or, with my luck, it's unlocked and can be forced open.

With that in mind, I slowly walk to the door and find a deadbolt. I switch it closed, although it seems pointless with a fragile door. I notice a black pull-down curtain and waste no time tugging it down in place. I can only hope being out of visual range will deter them from noticing us. The loud cacophony of their fists against the metal gates must have drowned out our presence from the closest zombies.

I turn back to the water jug and gently push the whole thing to the side, not wanting to spill too much water or make a lot of noise. Less than a quarter of the jug is missing, and it's not actually as full as I originally thought. At least we have one win from this unexpected detour. It's not a lot, but it's something.

Sighing, I scoot the jug closer to the door we came through and walk to the desk, which has two sets of drawers on each side. Thankfully, it's a simpler one without locks.

Opening the first on the left, I find nothing but receipts and your typical office paraphernalia. As I go through the drawers, I discover nothing of value to us until I open the last drawer on the bottom right. There are a few protein bars and what looks like a half-eaten sandwich in a Ziplock. Ignoring the moldy sandwich, I pocket the four protein bars.

I close the doors and head towards the hall where Ren disappeared. He hasn't come back out, but I haven't heard any form of struggle, which I hope is a good sign. The first of the three doors reveals a cluttered office with nothing but a filing cabinet, desk, chair, and a safe built into the wall, which I pass by without bothering to look. Money is worthless now.

The second room is a single bathroom. I slip inside and grab the toilet paper. On the wall by the door is one of those outdated machines where you can put a quarter in for a tampon or pad.

I inwardly cringe at the cardboard applicators as I picture what this machine might offer. Before I can get my mixed hopes up, I find it empty. I guess I won't be that fortunate. I hope we don't need these soon because I only have a few in my car glove compartment.

Groaning to myself, I search the basic bathroom. The only things I find of interest are a small first aid kit and toilet paper. Don't these places have to be up to compliance? Where is the better first aid crap? Clearly, they aren't up to passing any inspections.

Continuing to the last room, I find it's a break room of sorts. There is a fridge on the back wall, a long counter with cupboards, a four-person table in the center of the room, and a small sofa on the wall closest to the door. There is a coffee machine on the counter and a few disposable cups.

Ren is already going through the cupboards, pulling anything edible and placing it on the counter.

I close in on the fridge. I'm not sure if I want to take the risk, but maybe people had lunches packed and stored inside. I sometimes would put my whole bag in the fridge, even if there were dry goods inside.

"Fair warning, I'm opening the fridge," I call over my shoulder before holding my breath. To my surprise, it's mostly empty. A few cans of soda, and Tupperware containing some mystery entree that I am not curious enough to investigate.

"You'd think they would have a vending machine or something," I grumble as I grab the sodas. What a bust. Granted, we aren't inside a grocery store. People come here to get oil changes, not gourmet meals and beverages.

"I agree with you there. I did manage to find some instant coffee, an unopened variety box of chips, and a box of crackers. That's it, though," Ren says as he picks up the items from the counter.

"They aren't getting a good Yelp review for this. Maybe I should start a thread online titled, *Places to find all your needs during a zombie apocalypse.*" I chuckle.

Ren snorts and gives me his back before I can fully see the slight curve of his lips.

So, he does have different expressions other than a robot. Who'd have thought?

Smiling, I help pick up some of his finds and the sodas. We bring everything over to the car and load up, including the water jug, before finding anything we can use from the garage. We don't find anything else besides a clean tire iron, which I grab, and a fire extinguisher. I open the last drawer to one of the smaller worktables and find a lighter and a pack of cigarettes.

Not a smoker myself, I think about what someone would do for these bad boys if they were. While I pocket them, I find Ren's eyes on me. *Was he already watching me?*

His expression asks me his unspoken question.

"Hey, they aren't for me. Money is worthless. A little jail currency might be worth something later."

He gives me a look I can't quite decipher before he refocuses on the car we plan to use as a distraction. Eyeing the lighter, an idea comes to mind.

"What if we set the building on fire? Or pour oil on the car and let this place blow," I say. That might be enough to drag more zombies from the surrounding neighborhood. "I didn't see much except industrial buildings around here, so maybe the fire will spread. It could clear us a way today or even tomorrow, too."

Ren stares at me as he mulls it over. His brows furrow while he rakes his hand through his hair. I'm noticing that is his tell sign that he's thinking something over. It's tempting to run my fingers through it, to feel how soft it is, but I restrain the inappropriate urge.

"That could work, but we may need to be ready to leave the motel tomorrow. The fire could spread and go in the direction we're hoping, but it could also be unpredictable, flushing us out." He pauses to pick something up from the floor but throws it back. "Even if the fire isn't close enough to hurt us, the air quality will be just as bad as the flames." He tilts his head, contemplating the idea. "But... I think I can take that risk. Maybe we'll be lucky and can make another run tomorrow then."

It's slightly startling to hear him talk so much. He's been responding to me and not with grunts or nods. Well, not *only* grunts and nods.

Granted, we are in a crap situation, but it's nice, nonetheless. Usually, he gives short, clipped responses and doesn't give an explanation or any observations, as he did just now. I wonder why.

I shake that thought off and focus on what we need to do now.

I search for oil cans or anything flammable that isn't gasoline. I don't think I saw any but if we do find some, we would want it for the car. Speaking of… "Should we siphon the gas?" I point to the Sedan we plan on blowing up.

Ren just shakes his head but doesn't clarify.

I spoke too soon. I can't help but roll my eyes.

I manage to find some cleaning products and synthetic oil, all of which have flammable warnings on the bottles. Ren hops into our car and pulls up as close as possible to the exit with enough room to open the gate.

We pour the flammable finds around the opposite gates and furthest away from our car. Then, we pour some near the Sedan and then inside the car, making sure not to allow the liquid to connect with the area we plan to burn first. I don't want the car to catch fire while we are still inside. Maybe that's why he wants the gas to stay in the car—bigger boom.

Grabbing the lighter, I make my way to the first puddle but stop when Ren walks up behind me. He leans in and reaches around me to grab the lighter. His chest presses against my back as his hand brushes mine.

"Just head to the car. I can drive us out. You hit your head. You shouldn't try to make a run for it with that." He points to the wound. The lighter slips into his hand without much restraint. Wondering if he can see my blush turning a new shade of red, I slip around him to go to the car, picking up my new tire iron from the table on the way.

Sitting down in the passenger side, I take stock of myself again. My head is throbbing, and my body aches all over. The nausea is slightly better, but Ren is right. If I needed to run right now or even smell burning fumes up close, I may pass out or vomit.

I try to shove that thought away and focus back on Ren. He's messing with the wires under the dash as the car's horn blares so loud that my hands instinctively go to my ears. My head feels like my pulse is beating a drum behind my eyes and against my skull.

He gets out of the car quickly and pulls out an old, crinkled receipt he must have grabbed from the office. Flicking on the lighter, he puts it under the paper to set it on fire.

Throwing the flaming receipt into the puddle of liquid, he runs without checking if it works. The floor, drenched in all types of cleaners and oils, lights up in a blaze of glory. It catches instantly with a loud whoosh.

Ren is struggling to get the gate back open. "Fuck," he curses. It looks like the latch is stuck.

When our eyes meet through the growing haziness, he's unable to hide his panic. It's only for a split second before he schools his expression and runs back to the car. "I need the crowbar," he says in a rush.

I reach down between my feet to grab it and hand it over. Before I can say anything, he's running back to the gate while covering his mouth with his arm.

The whole room is starting to fill with smoke, so much so that it's becoming difficult to see. My eyes adjusted to the dimness a while ago, as there was still some light filtering in, but now the smoke is depleting what is left. The fumes are a cocktail of mixed chemicals and burning debris.

My lungs are burning, and my eyes are watering. Breathing becomes a struggle as my body fights for oxygen, and I cough relentlessly.

Oh, fuck, did we just kill ourselves?

I'm about to hop out of the car when the gate flies upward. The bright light momentarily blinds me while Ren jumps into the car. He switches on the engine and hits the gas without wasting time. He doesn't seem to care about the zombies in our path. Thankfully, most of the horde is on the other side of the building, but the noise attracts them like moths to a flame. Or, in this case, zombie to a flame.

Ren is quick enough to swerve but still hits one, dragging it under the tire. "Oh shit!" I yell, my adrenaline back to kick me into gear.

What feels like hours turns out to be five minutes, but we manage to get away from the building and the growing horde of zombies without any other issues. Screechers can be heard in the distance.

Before we need to worry if the car horn will be enough to draw their attention, a loud explosion rocks behind us.

I duck. Ren leans over, draping his arm over my head until the sound dissipates. His hand shifts to my thigh when we straighten, gripping it as if to assure himself or me that we're alive. If we didn't just survive the inferno on our heels, my heart would cease to beat from the intimate contact.

My neck whips around, and in the growing distance, the fire is raging, spreading to all available buildings in its path.

"It worked," I say, slightly dumbfounded. Ren's eyes flick to the rear-view mirror before returning to the road. I think he's heading back to the motel, but I'm not positive.

"I figured we wouldn't try today, but will we try again tomorrow if the fire sticks to this location?" I ask.

"Maybe. Let's focus on getting back. We need to make sure no other horde hits the motel. I'm starting to worry that with less easy sources of food, they'll start looking for one. Hopefully, this fire is a big enough distraction..." He drifts off for a second in thought. "It's as if they were all inside the buildings, but now, they're deciding to wander back outside."

In the background, the horn still blares, despite the car being blown to shreds. The explosion also triggered other car alarms, causing an orchestra of sirens. I didn't think about that, but other cars had to be parked nearby. That alone should be enough noise to pull the dead in that direction. Hopefully, there weren't any survivors in any of those buildings. My chest tightens at the thought.

"You okay?" Ren asks softly as he glances over at me. His expression looks suspiciously a lot like concern, but I can never tell with him.

"I don't know," I say honestly. My voice is hoarse, and I can't take my eyes off the scene in the mirror. "I was hoping there weren't any survivors in any of those buildings. If there were, my idea killed those people or forced them out to be surrounded by the dead..." I drift off.

His own eyes flick to the mirror but he doesn't respond immediately. Instead, he appears almost thoughtful as he thinks about what I said.

We drive in silence for a while, passing less and less zombies. After a few minutes, he finally speaks up. "Don't put that on yourself." He squeezes my thigh. Goosebumps break out over my arms as my face heats. "We do what we need to do to survive. You also don't know if there was anyone alive around. I doubt it. Even if there were, they weren't safe there, regardless. You can't blame yourself for that." His grip on my thigh tightens again. It has my heart beating rapidly, which doesn't help the dull headache.

His answer doesn't help either. I almost get the feeling he says he doesn't care to make himself believe it, but the look on his face as he continues to eyeball the mirror says otherwise. He probably has the same thoughts as I do right now. Or is it just wishful thinking that he cares more than he lets on?

"Also, maybe if someone was inside, they have time. The fire is spreading, but maybe that'll give them the opportunity to get out. They could've even been stuck until that fire. You never know."

Now, he's only trying to make me feel better. It works a little, but the only thought going through my head is that I hope we didn't murder anyone.

Chapter Thirty

Dahlia

The ride back to the motel is silent, both lost in our own thoughts. When the building comes into view, it's as if a weight is lifted from my shoulders—if only temporarily. It's not safe, but it is the safest place we have right now. A place to return to after the chaos.

As we pull up to the motel, the first thing I notice is that no one replaced the cars in front of the entrance. A spike of anxiety rises before the guys we got separated from come into view. They stand in the lot next to their cars, staring off into the distance, where the fire is currently blazing. The sound of our car brings their attention to us, and the relief on all their faces is palpable.

Jenson and Davis help move the cars back while Ren pulls up in our previous parking spot. His friends are racing over, and they open our doors before we have a chance to get out.

"Holy shit. We saw the fires and were ready to go back out there!" Juan says as he pulls Ren in for one of those hugs where they pat each other's backs as if a normal hug is too weird for them.

"What the hell happened? When you didn't make it to the shopping center, we thought you guys got killed. We started to clear the place and grabbed a few things before we realized you were taking too much time. When we started to look for you, we saw a huge horde heading away from us, and then a fucking explosion happened," Matt says.

James walks up to Ren and pats his shoulder before pitching his questions. "Seriously, was that fire you guys?"

Ren takes a moment before grabbing our backpacks and walks towards the motel, not saying anything. I believe he won't answer them as we walk upstairs to the room, but finally, he says over his shoulder, "Just give us a moment. I want Hana to look at Dahlia first, and then we can meet up."

He keeps walking, not waiting for them to respond. They all glance at me again, finally noticing I have an egg-shaped bruise and gash on my head.

"Fuck, what happened, Dahlia?" Matt reaches up to brush my hair away when Ren is suddenly behind me, grabbing my hand to pull me along.

He still doesn't speak, but the others act as if that isn't unusual. Matt gives us a peculiar look but doesn't say anything else. Focusing back on Ren, we reach the room we stayed in the previous night.

Ren shuffles me inside before letting go of my hand and closing the door behind us. He doesn't move from his spot. I can't make out his expression as he leans against the door, looking down at the floor.

"Are you alright?" I ask and step towards him. I hesitate but still take the chance and place my palm on his left shoulder. He doesn't react. Instead, he acts as if I'm not standing in front of him or touching him at all.

I pull my hand away, unsure of what to do. He's not usually one to talk, but I can't help but feel bad. I don't know what's upsetting him, but seeing him so affected by whatever it is makes me sad. We haven't known each other long, but this seems so strange coming from him.

Before I can move away, he grabs my hand to stop me. My eyes widen as he pulls me closer and lifts his gaze. Silently, he rests my hand against his chest, holding it hostage. The strength of his steady heart beneath my palm and the warmth of his hand against mine send heat throughout my body. His eyes shift between mine as if entranced. His seem to darken, the browns with flecks of gold and the hints of red blending to create a swirling depth I want to get lost in.

His usual expression is gone, but there's something else there instead. It's a blend of worry, exhaustion, and relief. My heart races, and the familiar butterflies take flight in my stomach. My eyes fall to his lips, and I wonder what it would be like to kiss him. To be lost in this moment. In *him*. I bite the inside of my lip with that thought, and his eyes follow the movement. I almost expect him to lean forward, and I *want* him to.

He just holds my hand as we stay like that, suspended in time, before he squeezes and slowly lets go.

"Ren—" He abruptly walks around me and heads to the bathroom, shutting the door behind him. I'm left standing there in shock and confusion. The butterflies melt into a sinking feeling as I push back the hurt from him walking away.

What the hell just happened? I don't move but instead stand there in disbelief.

He's only in there for less than a few minutes before the door opens, and he steps out. His face betrays his feelings, but I can't decipher them. Is it guilt? "Sorry. I shouldn't ignore you. Everything's fine. It's just now that we're in a relatively safe space; I feel like I needed a few minutes before having to answer any questions."

We both stand there for a couple of dragged-out seconds, only staring at each other. Finally, I walk over to the bed and sit.

"Is there anything I can do?" I ask, unsure of what he's trying to say. Was he coming down from the adrenaline, or was it anxiety from the continuous life and death situations? The constant need to be in survival mode? Had it taken a toll on him, and now he could finally breathe?

I wonder what that moment was between us then. For a second, it felt like more than that.

He waits to respond until he's seated on the opposite bed. "No. Thanks, though..." He rubs his hands over his face. "It's been a while since having to be in a situation where not only my life is at risk but when someone I... I mean, in the beginning, even with Haru's situation, I still felt like I was in control. Like I could protect him..." He drifts off briefly. "Today, it was different..."

Not sure what I'm doing, I decide to move across to the other bed. I sit down next to him, our shoulders brushing. Instead of feeling butterflies, my heart aches for him. He seems conflicted, but he finally speaks up again.

"When we were in the car, I almost panicked, not knowing where to go. I don't like the feeling of not knowing what to do. Then when I couldn't get that gate up, I was sure we were about to die from smoke inhalation or get ourselves blown up because I couldn't open a fucking door," he says, and I can hear the anger behind his words. "I almost got you killed..." he whispers the last part, shocking me further. I'm trying not to read into it, but my heart flutters at the thought that he cares.

I sit there. Stunned. Was the auto shop what broke him? Was that the final straw?

And he's opening up to you...

I don't think about it when I place my hand in his. His head snaps up, and our eyes clash. There's a vulnerability in his gaze. The man who never allows his features to express anything but indifference is displaying the man underneath—the one I'm beginning to suspect feels as deep as the sea. Something about knowing that pulls at my heartstrings.

"You got us out of there. If it weren't for you, we would've died. I never noticed that you were feeling unsure at all," I say quietly, with a small smile.

He *did* keep us alive. If I had been driving, we would have been goners. To top it off, he also saved my life and stepped up when I should've been covering him instead. I squeeze his hand and pull away, but he tightens his grip, keeping me there. My head spins, and my heart picks up its pace. I can't remember the last time I've been so close to a man so much in one day as we've been today. His hot and cold demeanor is throwing me for a loop, but those damn butterflies continue to assault my stomach. A voice whispers in the back of my mind, telling me that none of this matters right now. It's the end of the world; stop getting your panties in a twist—literally.

"Thank you," he responds in a quiet voice, almost to the point where I'm unsure if I heard it at all. This time, when his gaze lands on my lips, he moves his hand to the base of my neck and leans forward. Those butterflies mutate into a full-on hive of hornets while my nerves go haywire. Closing my eyes, I lean into his touch and follow the pull towards him.

His breath caresses my lips. Barely a ghost's touch.

The bedroom door slams open against the wall, startling us both.

Ren jerks away and stands. Not recognizing who it is at first, he positions himself in front of me, blocking me from the nonexistent threat. I stand up and gently push on his arm as he goes to raise his weapon. *Where did he even grab it from?*

"Oh my god! I heard you guys were in a fire?" Hana barges in, unaware of the moment she so ungracefully interrupted.

When he notices who it is, he sighs. "I'm going to get cleaned up," he grumbles before returning to the restroom. I don't want to assume, but it almost feels like he needs space from his family, too. But he was comfortable with me... I wonder what that means.

Hana gives me a confused expression before saying, "What's his prob— Oh my god, Dahl! Your head!" She rushes over to grab my arm and forces me to sit back down. I don't even have time to speak before she starts poking and prodding.

"What happened? How the hell are you conscious? This looks awful!"

I flinch when she gingerly touches the bruising around the gash.

"Wow, you have amazing bedside manners," I say dryly, not able to help myself. Instead of being offended, she laughs.

"Don't remind me why I'm not a doctor!" She laughs. "I'm kidding. I was so close to finishing school," she says and retrieves her bag from the floor by the window.

"Oh, come on. What happened? It must have been intense to put Mister Cool and Collected in a heap," she says as she points her thumb toward the bathroom.

"It's been a long day, Hana. I hit my head on one of those car jacks mounted on the floor. A zombie almost got me."

A shiver wracks my body as I remind myself how close I was to getting killed. Hana takes a pair of gloves out of a box from her backpack and slips them on. Then, she pulls supplies out of her bag, including a small flask.

"I don't have a lot of disinfectant, so I'm improvising." She pours the alcohol onto a gauze pad. "I need to clean that up before I can stitch you up. Have you had any nausea or vomiting?"

"Yeah." I tell her about how I had already been vomiting before the head wound but that I was also nauseated for a while after. Although she was laughing a moment ago, as soon as I start talking about the injury and how I obtained it, she switches into nurse practitioner mode. She asks questions about how I have been feeling as well as things like my name and location while she checks my pupils. Finally, she starts putting in a few stitches.

"I'm like Sally from that *Nightmare Before Christmas* movie. At this rate, I will have most of my body restitched up," I say jokingly, trying to break the growing tension.

She chuckles but surprisingly manages to keep her hands steady.

"At least you're prettier," she says with a wink. Before I can respond, the bathroom door opens, and Ren appears, still in the same clothing he was in earlier.

"The water shut off. Shit timing. I smell like a zombie bonfire."

That causes laughter to rise and burst out of me like a balloon. Shockingly, Ren responds with a rare smile. It softens his face, making him even more attractive, if that's even possible.

"Is she going to be alright?" he asks his sister as he sits on the other bed.

"She'll be fine. Normally, I'd say try and stay awake a while so I can monitor you, but you're not exhibiting any serious signs of a head injury other than the obvious here. Your memory and cognition seem intact, and I don't see any pupil dilation, balance, or mobility issues. You should be fine. I wish we had some instant ice packs. The swelling is a bit gnarly." She eyes it with disapproval.

"Again, with the bedside manner," I say, chuckling. "You make a girl feel so damn beautiful," I retort sarcastically.

She laughs along with me before finally finishing her work and patting my arm.

"That should be it. If you feel any dizziness, sensitivity to light, or anything that seems off, let me know," she tells me. "Now, what about you, Ren?"

She places her hand on his shoulder, looking him over to assess if he has any wounds. He grunts and shies away from her touch.

"Alrighty then. Oh, you mentioned the water." She walks over to the trash and tosses away the gauze and gloves she used. "If you hadn't seen it, in the shower, there are three buckets I managed to partly fill before the water shut off. I wasn't excited about using baby wipes, so I tried to get as much extra water as possible. Just save me at least a bucket, yeah?"

She packs up her gear before leaving, not saying anything else while Ren follows her out.

"I'll be back. Go ahead." He gestures to the bathroom. "I'll go after you. I'm going to give the guys an update." He is gone before I'm able to respond.

Although the idea of using a bucket to bathe isn't the most appealing, it's still better than a baby wipe. Once we need to resort to that, the car rides are going to suck being so up close and personal with everyone.

Not wasting any time, I go in search of the buckets.

It looks like they're usually used for cleaning, but thankfully, they don't seem dirty or worn. Shutting and locking the door, I grab one of the pails.

Just as Hana said, they are all partially full. There may be an easier way, but I decide to pour one of the buckets into one of the others, filling one completely and only leaving a small amount of water in the one I plan to use. Quickly stripping out of my soiled clothing, I throw my undergarments in the sink. I can try to recycle the water to clean them.

I grab a clean washcloth from the sink counter and dip it into the water. Grabbing a small bottle of liquid soap, I give myself a bird bath. Washing my hair proves to be a challenge, but I manage to get the blood out. Once clean, I wring the washcloth and grab a clean towel before wrapping it around myself.

I pull the drain stopper up inside the sink and pour the water I bathed with inside. I add a little bit of the same soap to wash my undergarments. I could have probably used more water, but I want to make sure Ren and Hana have enough to use later.

While hanging my clothes over the shower door, the sound of the bedroom door opening makes me pause. Was Ren back already?

"I am almost done!" I call out, putting my shirt and pants in the sink to try and wash them as best I can. After debating for a moment, I decide to use more water—only enough to fill the sink all the way. I walk back to one of the other buckets.

A shadow from under the door catches my eye, and I stop. There's someone standing there, not moving. I call out, "Is everything okay?"

Nobody responds, so I reach for the lock but stop as the doorknob rattles, the lock catching in place.

What the hell? "Ren?"

No response.

I freeze. Realization hits me.

It's not Ren inside the room but someone else. A pit lodges in my stomach as my fear rises and my breathing becomes erratic. I clutch my chest, trying to ease the tightening and the claw-like feeling sinking into me.

Ren wouldn't just stand there, let alone try to come into the bathroom. I stare at the lock, triple-checking that it is in place. I search for clean clothes before realizing I forgot to grab any.

"Shit." Fear courses through my body. I already know who's standing behind that door. Since his return, he has been relentless. I don't know how I forgot about him being here. I should have made sure someone stayed in the room or locked the door until I was done.

I am alone, naked, but for a towel, and I left my weapons in the other room. Standing still for what feels like hours but realistically minutes, the shadow disappears, and the sound of the bedroom door closes.

Did he leave?

Chills break out over my bare skin. Dread fills me as I remain frozen. *Is he just playing with me?*

I don't see any movement under the door. Still, I don't move for a long time before finally straightening my spine and unlocking the bathroom door. Slowly, I edge out.

I freeze. Like a deer caught in the headlights.

My skin prickles like there's a thousand spiders crawling up my body. The blood must have drained from my face because it feels numb. Dillon stands there, leaning against the other door.

You should've known better. He won't ever leave.

If running for years and getting a restraining order hadn't stopped his obsession, why would I think he was done toying with me now?

My body moves before my brain can catch up. I back up to slam the bathroom door but I'm not fast enough. His boot-clad foot stops the door's trajectory, taking any chance at safety away. I can't help the short scream that leaves my lips as the door hits his boot.

Forgetting the door, I clutch the towel against my chest and back up until I hit the shower. My body shivers. Not from the cold glass against my skin but because of the feeling of impending doom shrouding me. *No. No. No. No.*

"Tsk tsk. Dahly. You know better than to run," he says as he walks into the bathroom. "I told you I'd come. I would've loved to be with you last night." He steps right in front of me, reaching out to grab my chin, pulling my gaze up to his in a painful grip.

"I plan on us leaving tomorrow. Once we're done here, you can go start getting what you need. If you utter a word to them, you know what will happen," he threatens. "I don't like how that one looks at you." His grip tightens before drifting down my neck towards the towel.

His threat brings back a harsh memory I'd rather forget.

I struggle in his hold as he pulls my back tight against his chest. His other hand grips my face to keep my eyes in front of us.

My friend Ricky. Sweet Ricky... "Please, just help him. Please just stop. He didn't do anything." *Tears stream down my face as I beg.* "Please, Dillon. Just help him."

"I won't stop." His hand clutches my jaw tighter while he forces me to keep looking. "I've told you already. You belong to me." He doesn't let up his hold as he forces me to watch my friend bleed out slowly on his bathroom floor.

My voice hiccups. "We aren't together. Please. He's only my friend." *A friend I've known for years.*

"Tsk. I've seen how he looks at you, Dahly..." He lets out a long sigh. "Fine. Only on one condition will I call an ambul—"

The hotel room door catches loudly on the security bar, startling me from my past, which is threatening to overwhelm me. Dillon stops, his hand clutching the front of my towel.

"Dahlia," Ren calls out.

Dillon's hand comes back up towards my throat, squeezing slightly while his other hand touches my lips, ordering me to stay silent.

"Dahlia," Ren says again, louder this time.

From the other room, the sound of the door getting slammed against the security bar causes me to flinch under Dillon's hold. If the door is barred, Ren won't be able to come in.

While Dillon's partly distracted, I shove against him, causing him to slip back. With one hand still clutching the towel, I race forward. Before he can get to me, I slam the motel room door closed. I almost crush Ren's fingers in the process but I'm able to flip the security bar lock open.

A hand grabs the back of my head, tangling in my wet hair as he wrenches me back. My fingers barely brush the door handle. My feet slip, and I fall back while my towel comes loose in the struggle.

He releases me just as the door flies open. Ren's features are like ice as he glances from me to Dillon. He's clutching his weapon tightly but doesn't have it raised.

He must know something is wrong, right? Clutching the towel to cover the front of my body, I jump to my feet and rewrap the towel around myself. Dillon just smirks at Ren before speaking up. "Sorry, man, just having some fun. Didn't want anyone to interrupt, you know? I've always loved the cat and mouse games," he says as he winks at Ren. "A little role play, if you catch my drift."

Ren looks at the two of us, but his face is unreadable, nothing to give away his thoughts. I try to plead with my eyes, too afraid to voice my fears. I've never wished for someone to be able to read my mind as much as I do in this moment. I know I couldn't prevent Dillon from acting out if I speak up. I wouldn't put it past him to hurt Ren or even kill him if he got in his way.

Will he think that we are a couple and decide to leave me alone with him? *Oh god. He can't believe we were role-playing... right?*

I'm shivering harder, and there's no doubt I look like a ghost right now. I don't want to be left alone with this person or to leave with him, but I do want him to leave. How can I tell Ren or even Hana that this man isn't safe to have around? How can we get him out of the way before he hurts someone? I don't want to risk the kid or anyone else, but I also can't stay quiet for much longer. If I do, I may end up being the reason they die.

"Alright, well, Price, if you don't mind, I want to get cleaned up. Why don't you go see James and Matt? They're in the room two doors down. We need help planning the next run," Ren states with an edge of command laced in his tone.

Dillon smirks, as if he's the cat that got the cream. "Sure," he says in amusement before grabbing my chin and crashing his lips to mine.

I flinch and shove him away. He gives me a look. One that I know all too well. He will make sure I pay for that later.

Ice-cold terror wracks my body with that thought.

Ren speaks up, his voice laced with venom. "It's time for you to leave." He steps closer. "Now." His voice sounds deeper. He takes another step, suddenly exhibiting an air of dominance. He still doesn't raise the gun, but his grip on the weapon makes me believe he might.

Dillon takes a step back, eyes widening before replacing it with his trademark smirk.

"See you later, my Dahly girl."

Suddenly wanting to vomit or cry, I hurry back into the bathroom, closing the door. Running over to the toilet, I dry-heave, but there is nothing in my stomach to throw up. It takes me a moment to calm my breathing, which doesn't do me any good.

My body is trembling so hard, chills skidding up my spine, and my stomach feels like I swallowed razor blades. *I will never get away from him.*

Memories threaten to consume me... Memories of the moment he came back into my life right after my dad died, the way I ended things. The way he kept coming back... All the times he refused my rejection.

The door opens, but I ignore it. I keep trying to calm the sudden dread and panic, which causes me to hyperventilate. I can't go through this again. I thought I got away. It's the end of the world, for fuck's sake; why do I have to deal with this crap again when I already have to worry about getting eaten alive.

Ren's hand hesitantly touches my bare shoulder. Crouching down, he pulls my hair back out of my face as I still dry heave and struggle to calm my rapid breaths. "Did he hurt you?" He's speaking so quietly, gentle even. I'm slightly taken aback.

The relief is so intense; it's like a weight has been lifted from my body. He did see, then.

"Not this time… yet," I whisper, meeting his gaze. My breath hitches. This close, his eyes appear pained as he takes me in. He grabs my hand and pulls me to my feet as he guides me into the other room while I continue to clutch the towel.

"Get dressed. I'm going to get cleaned up, and then we can talk."

Before walking into the bathroom, he locks the deadbolt and security bar lock on the motel room door.

The stark relief and the tension leaving my body surprises me. I have never relied on anyone but myself for protection or the feeling of safety since my dad died. It's a strange yet reassuring feeling to know there's someone else I can rely on besides myself. Maybe that's why I'm so drawn to him. He offers a rare form of security—something I haven't found since losing the only man that ever mattered in my life.

Not wanting to waste any more time, I walk to my backpack and look for a clean T-shirt and a pair of black yoga pants, not caring what I wear right now. I only want to be comfortable. I'm also running out of clothing. I kept a few changes of clothes in my car regularly besides what I threw in my backpack, but now I'm down to one other clean outfit left. I'll have to try to wash the others from the last few days or find new stuff soon, which reminds me to finish washing the ones in the bathroom. Embarrassment overtakes me when I remember my underwear and bra hanging in the shower. Groaning, I try to push that thought away.

I quickly brush my teeth and use the trash can to spit out the toothpaste since the bathroom is occupied. After Dillon touched me, I feel dirty all over again. *I wish I could take a normal shower.*

Once I get dressed and brush my teeth, I sit on the bed, bringing my knees up to my chest and allowing the tears welling up to finally fall.

The feeling of hopelessness is overwhelming. My new friends need to know what happened. They at least need to know we can't let Dillon stay. He'll end up hurting someone or getting someone killed. There's even the very real possibility he'll do it intentionally. He's crazy. A genuinely evil man.

What makes me terrified is that he was a horrible person before the zombies came. With the new world, normal people will be forced to show their monstrous tendencies. What will it cause him to reveal? He won't have to worry about law enforcement or anything to stop him from doing whatever he wants. If he could do what he did while there *were* laws, what would he do now?

I thought maybe avoidance was the answer, but what else can I do? If I don't go with him tomorrow, will he hurt someone? Or what if I just tell Ren? Maybe he can help me.

Fuck, what do I do?

I know I should tell them, but... it's not only that I fear for their safety, but because I'm afraid of admitting what happened. Of admitting that I'm a coward.

My father's words come back to me again, the same ones that have been on repeat since this all started. I can't help but wonder... *What would he do?* I realize I already know the answer. He'd seek the help offered.

Tears continue to roll down my face, but I find my resolve.

I can't do this alone. Not anymore.

Unable to settle my nerves and the relentless panic rising, I start pacing around the room. The tears have dried, but my heart feels like it'll beat out of my chest as I think about what I'm going to do next.

I wish Megan were here. I wish I could talk to her. She would know exactly what to do. She wouldn't be afraid of confronting Dillon herself. Or Ren and the group for me.

Oh god... I hope she's still safe.

No. Don't go there, Dahlia. You've cried enough today.

I try to redirect my thoughts back to the problem I can actually do something about.

Should I talk to Hana about this… or Ren?

A part of me wants to talk to Hana because I'm scared of what Ren would think of me. Would he find me weak and agree that I'm a coward? My breath hitches. Maybe I can't do this. Maybe I can run—

"Hey," Ren says, startling me.

He steps into the room wearing nothing but jeans. Too embarrassed and ashamed of the memories swarming me, I avert my gaze.

He walks over, crowding my space. I don't have the opportunity to step away before he gently grabs my fidgeting hands. "Why don't you sit down," he tells me while he pulls me towards the bed.

Sitting on the edge, I keep my eyes focused on the floor instead of the man who sits beside me.

"Look…" He rakes his hand through his wet hair. "You don't have to tell me anything. But I need to know if that man is dangerous."

It's like I lose my voice at his question. My throat dries, and I'm unable to speak. I lick my lips and try to swallow to work myself up to telling him. *I guess I'm talking to Ren then.*

You can do this. He won't turn his back on you.

Although I'm terrified of how he'll look at me after, I know I can trust him. Even if he sees me as weak, I know he won't just brush me off. Despite trying to make everyone think he doesn't care, I don't believe him. Instead, I see someone who cares too much.

Something about him makes me crave having someone to finally lean on. To have something more…

"Is he dangerous, Dahl?" he asks again.

Taking in a deep breath, I nod. The back of my eyes sting, and I need to blink rapidly while those memories threaten to drown me.

Dillon's touch scolding my skin like dry ice… the horror of watching my friend almost die. The terror when I realized he would never leave me alone.

Remember, you can't do this alone. I take a deep breath. It's now or never. Just tell him. At least enough so he'll understand.

"Uhm..." I wring my hands in my lap. "I met Dillon, or Price, in high school. He was only a few years older than me, freshly enlisted." I didn't understand back then how inappropriate that was. "My dad intervened when he found out that we were dating." I'm still not sure why my dad *didn't* report him.

Ren stays silent while I talk. I don't look up, too afraid that if I see the judgment, I will fall apart.

"Right after my dad passed away, Dillon came back into the picture. At first, I was flattered, you know?" God, I was an idiot. So stupid... *So naïve.* "After some time... well... I started to notice things I didn't like." I wish I saw the signs the first time we were together. Signs that pointed to his obsessive and controlling behavior. The way he wanted to *own* me. "My friend, Meg, finally talked me into leaving, so I did. Except..."

My breath hitches. I still can't believe that after all this time, he keeps coming back. I just don't understand *why.* Why won't he let go?

I rub my eyes with the back of my hand while I take deep breaths. Ren's silence allows me to keep going. His presence is somehow comforting as I relive some of my worst memories.

"He started to show his true colors, and it scared me. A lot happened after that. He followed me everywhere. People got hurt...and he even..." *Assaulted me.* I can't say it. It's still too raw. I sniffle, wiping both my eyes hard enough to splotch my vision.

Ren is stock-still beside me. The only indicator I know he's listening is his gaze staying intently on my face, but I refuse to look. I'm scared to see his reaction.

I inhale. *One. Two. Three. Four. Five.* Counting to five and holding it for another five. When I'm done, I continue.

"He was deployed when I finally graduated. As soon as I could, I ran. He found me a few times, but he was still in the service and would have to leave not long after. I kept moving around until eventually, I didn't hear from him for a long time..." My voice hitches. "Until now. I honestly thought maybe he'd given up and moved on. Or he died or something, I don't know." I shrug. My nails are digging into my hands from squeezing them too tight. I relish the pain. The distraction from the deeper wound.

Ren shifts closer and dips his head to meet my gaze better. "Did he... hurt *you* back then?"

It's his tone that does it. The genuine concern with a hint of anger at the possibility of my answer. I completely shatter. The dam fractures. *Obliterated.*

My body trembles with the sob that breaks free. I try to cover my face with my hands as I turn away, embarrassed at breaking down in front of him. But instead of shying away, he tentatively wraps his arm around my shoulder.

The contact is a balm to my raw heart, and I twist into him. He doesn't pull away but holds me closer. I bury my face into his warm chest, and I let the tears fall.

"He won't hurt you again," he declares while he rubs small circles on my back. His words are soft, but they hold a weight that gives me no other option but to believe them.

He holds me as I take in deep breaths to try to calm down. I allow myself to focus on the way his body heats against mine. I soak in the feeling of being in his arms, completely engulfed in him. I savor how him holding me is like a quiet promise of safety.

The comfort he offers soothes the ache but also has my heart beating quicker for another reason altogether.

I pull away, trying to reign in the embarrassment and forget that I've been nothing but a mess ever since I've met this man.

"Are you okay?" he asks softly. With his forefinger, he gently turns my face to look at him. It's like I melt into his touch and momentarily forget the pain that has been weighing me down. He uses his thumb to wipe away the residual tears staining my cheeks. My face flushes at his gentleness, and when his hand drops, I can only think about what it would be like if he continued to touch me. His gaze is enough to distract me from the fear and pain. His touch, though... His touch has me wishing for more. But also, it has me missing what our world was like before. It's like a reminder that we're still human despite the end.

It's bittersweet.

And I crave more.

"Yeah," I whisper, partly dazed from his caress.

As if he can read my mind, his gaze falls to my lips for a second before coming back up to meet mine. He brushes a strand of hair behind my ear, and little goosebumps prickle my arms when his hand lingers where my jaw and neck connect. I can't help but lean into his palm, savoring his warmth.

Something shifts between us. The tenderness from moments ago now feels charged. Electricity coils inside my abdomen with anticipation. His intensity and the raw hunger staring back at me has me breathless while heat and desire spread through me like molten lava.

I bring my hand up to his face, allowing myself to forget everything but this moment with him. For a second, I only want to dive headfirst into the abyss his presence offers.

To forget. To feel like I matter. To feel protected. To feel *safe.*

His hand moves to the base of my neck and squeezes softly, sending a jolt of need straight to my core.

"Fuck it," he mumbles to himself.

He leans forward to meet me and pulls me in all at once.

I take that leap... and never has falling felt safer.

Chapter Thirty-One

Ren

Fuck it.

Ignoring the voice in my head telling me why I shouldn't, I bring my lips to hers. I don't understand what the hell I'm doing, but somehow, I don't care.

She shows no hesitation as I respond to her unspoken desire. I was shocked by her forwardness but when she touched me, my control slipped.

When I wanted to kiss her before, I'd been grateful for my sister's interruption.

Not only because I already know it'll be another complication but also because I'm not the type of man who deserves someone like her. She doesn't know the true nature of who I am or what I'm capable of. She won't understand the lengths I'll go to keep the people I love safe.

But something about her allowing me to see her this way... to be openly vulnerable... to *trust me*. It has those feelings she stirs soaring before I can even understand it. It guts me to see her this way, to hear her story, but I'm also elated to know that she isn't afraid of me but instead confiding in me. Instead of turning away, she sought me for comfort. For support.

Dahlia doesn't pull away from me as I move my lips against hers.

She parts her lips and tilts her head, inviting me to deepen the kiss.

One of her hands wraps around my neck, her other coming up to my chest. My skin feels seared beneath her palm as she curls her fingers like she wants to grasp onto me. Her lips are so warm and sweet, like a freshly baked Castella cake. I'm completely engulfed in her flowery aroma, and I can't help but soak in the warmth of her body, which is so close to my own. I can't help but savor the softness of her lips. My fingers entwine in her damp hair as my other hand goes to her hip.

My first instinct is to pull her closer, to taste her tongue, to taste all of her. I want to kiss every inch of her, feast on her until she screams for me.

If she saw the blood on your hands... Learns what you did...

That voice in my head keeps whispering warnings of what she would think when she discovers the type of person I am. She wouldn't be allowing me to touch her so intimately. I may not be the same as the man she fears, but I'm no better.

I'm more confused now than ever, considering I've never given a shit about what someone will think of me, especially since I don't typically get close enough for them even to get a chance to know me.

Although I continue to have those doubts, I can't stop myself from wrapping my arm around her waist and hoisting her onto my lap to straddle me.

She only kisses me deeper, harder, moaning softly when my hand in her hair tightens, and I continue to hold her with the other firmly. My tongue teases hers before she returns my advances with her own, submitting readily to my mouth and tightening grip.

The way she lets me lead has my jeans constricting, and more images of what I'd love to do to her fill my thoughts.

Her kiss is like a mind-altering substance that I can't seem to break away from. One taste, and I'm thoroughly intoxicated. Hooked. Wanting to chase that high over and over until I spill out over the edge of sanity. What started as a slow, sensual moment only grows hotter, like flint to steel.

Her hips grind slightly, rubbing against my now-straining erection. A groan leaves me at the friction. Her whimper causes me to almost forget why this shouldn't continue. Her little moans cloud my thoughts with nothing but images of her under me, her riding me, her tightening around my cock as we both come. If she keeps grinding her hips against my aching dick, I'm not sure how much more I can stay in control. Her presence alone clouds my judgment, but her kiss—her kiss blows my mind out of this fucking reality.

Completely lost in her, I kiss her jaw before reaching her neck. Her sigh is more like a soft moan, which has me reaching the hem of her shirt.

She doesn't stop me. She loosens her hold on me as I pull her shirt up and over her head, exposing her black bra contrasting against her freckled skin.

Dahlia grips my hair as I begin kissing down her neck to the tops of her breasts, peeking out of her bra. Before I can shove the fabric aside, she tugs on my hair to pull me up.

I'm about to ask if she is okay, but she interrupts that fleeting thought by crashing her mouth against mine in a desperate frenzy. She grinds herself harder against me, only heating the growing need to be inside her.

"Fuck," I groan against her lips. My hand on her hip moves to her ass, squeezing and pushing her down harder.

The clink of my belt buckle sends my mind reeling, disconnecting me from the present.

"No, man. No. No. No!" He fights the restraints on his wrists behind his back, the buckle scraping against the wall. My hand tightens around his throat to shut him up. The others have all been silenced, only leaving this one. But he isn't the one from that night.

"Where is he?" I ask him for the third time.

Instead of telling me when I release his throat, he tries to run. His mistake. I raise the gun...

It's like a bucket of ice water dousing the flames, and chills crawl up my spine.

Fear momentarily shocks me, thinking I'm about to have a flashback while completely awake, but Dahlia tugging at my buckle reminds me where I am.

I gently grab her hand to stop her before I get lost in everything that is her.

Instead, I force myself to remember where I came from. *Who I am.*

She deserves better than that. *I'll only hurt her in some way.* I can't risk it.

We're both panting as I break the kiss, and her hands are still on my buckle. I release my grip on her hair, allowing it to drift down her back before reluctantly pulling away. Unable to separate fully, I rest my forehead against hers as we both catch our breath.

She deserves better. What if you were to hurt her now or in your sleep? What if she learns the truth?

Questions and what-ifs continue to assault me. It only further solidifies why I can't keep doing this.

When I don't move or kiss her again, she must realize what I'm doing. She slowly disentangles from my lap before quickly pulling her shirt back on.

Whatever the reasons as to why this shouldn't continue, it takes everything in my power not to throw her back on that bed and lose myself in her hot center, to bury my face between her thighs and eat her like the starved man that I am. To be a selfish man and say fuck it completely.

Standing, I take a few steps back before I do just that.

In my peripheral, she's touching her lips, a look of utter confusion crossing her face. Or is that curiosity? Her cheeks are blushed, but when she watches me as I pull a shirt on, her face turns beat red. It's by far my favorite expression she has given me, especially with the look of desire still in her eyes.

Warring with myself, I turn around instead of striding back to her. I fix my belt buckle and try to adjust the erection that's become uncomfortably confined and painfully strained against my jeans.

The way she affects me is bothersome. Even worse, I can't remedy it without complicating my life or hers. It doesn't make sense to me, but I don't want to see her hurt. I also certainly don't want to see a look of fear directed at me or... *disappointment.*

"I'm sorry. I shouldn't have done that." I clear my throat. Kissing her was stupid. Especially the timing. It was selfish, not to mention she was vulnerable.

Shit. What the fuck were you thinking, Ren? "I don't want you to misunderstand, but..." I drift off. I don't know what I should say to not make things worse. "After everything today... I didn't mean—" She raises her hands to stop me.

The small smile she tries to give doesn't reach her eyes. "It's fine. I get it. It's been a crazy day. I mean, it's the end of the world." She huffs an awkward chuckle. "I understand..." She trails off, fiddling with her hands.

Shit. Now she thinks I only did that because what? It's been a stressful day? Well, yes, it has been, but hell, since I first saw her, she's been driving my equilibrium to shit. I may not understand it, but I can at least admit that

I want her. I have never wanted anyone like this before. She reminds me of things I hadn't realized I was missing in this world, plus a million other fucking things I'm not ready to acknowledge.

Realistically, though, she's a *good* person. Me, on the other hand? I'm screwed up. I don't just have skeletons in my closet. I *create* them.

I have a lot of blood on my hands. People fantasize about men like me, but when they finally see the blood we're willing to shed, they run screaming. Men like me don't get the happy ending. Women want a man who can protect them, but they don't want to see the lengths to which we'll go and the reality of what we'll do to keep them safe. Most women especially don't like men who do questionably violent shit inside and outside of the law.

I run my hand through my hair before deciding. Maybe I can't have her, but I can at least look out for her. I have been, but begrudgingly. She deserves to be safe. If I can provide that, I will. Whether I wanted her with us at first or not doesn't matter. She's one of us now. She's proven she can handle herself in our group and that she'll do what it takes to keep the kid safe. Even if I can't have her, Hana for sure will never let her go.

"Shit, that's no—" A knock at the door interrupts me.

"Ren? Why's the door locked?" Hana whisper-shouts from outside, followed by more insistent light taps on the wood.

Sighing, I walk to the door and unlock it. She sure knows when to interrupt. Like fucking clockwork. Before my hand reaches the knob, Hana barges in. Walking past me, she stops short when she sees Dahlia.

Eyes widening as she takes in Dahlia's now ruffled appearance and swollen lips, she looks between us for a moment, probably drawing incorrect conclusions. Well, partially incorrect conclusions if my dick has any say in this or the way Dahlia was grinding on me moments before. Fuck. I need to stop thinking about that.

"Oh my god. I didn't know, I'm sorry I—"

I raise my hand to cut her off

"No, Hana. The door is locked because that prick came in when Dahlia was alone. If I hadn't shown up, I don't know what he would've done."

Her eyes grow even wider, shock and concern flying across her face.

"Are you okay?" she asks Dahlia before sitting next to her and drawing her into a side hug. She doesn't let her go; instead, she leaves her arm around her shoulder. Dahlia glances at me for a moment, cheeks still red, before focusing on Hana.

"I'm fine. Honestly."

My sister stares at her as if she thinks she's full of shit. Rightfully so.

Glancing at my sister, I say, "Hana, can you stay here with her? I'm going to check in with the others."

I don't bother waiting for Hana's response before walking out of the room. My nerves are ticked, and I can't stop clenching my jaw.

I'm pissed off. Pissed at myself for practically taking advantage of her just now, for what Price did to her. At myself. Why didn't I push her when I asked about their history? I suspected there was something off… I saw how she withdrew around him. Why was I so adamant about her not being my problem? *Fuck!*

It doesn't take long for me to reach the other room a few doors down. Everyone is still present. Juan, James, and Dirk are sitting at a tiny kitchen table off the side of the larger room, and Matt sits on the bed. Thankfully, Price or Dillon, or whatever the hell his name is, isn't here.

Dahlia is the only one who calls him by his first name. He introduced himself to everyone as Price first, but maybe he wants only her to see him as Dillon. It seems very intentional to show off their history.

I close the door, turning the deadbolt before I ask Juan, "Did Price ever come over here?" I walk further into the room, ignoring the confused looks they point in my direction. They all heard the scream. Most of them thought it was nothing, and Matt was ready to come with me to check on her, but I told him I'd shout if anything was wrong. They were all but forgotten once I reached Dahlia.

Taking a seat in the empty chair at the table, I pour myself a drink of what was left of a bottle of scotch they had been nursing. I don't particularly enjoy scotch, but it gives my hands something to do and replaces the bite of my nerves with the bite of alcohol scorching my throat.

"What the fuck happened? We came by, but the door was locked. When I caught up with Price, he said you guys were indisposed. The fuck did he mean by that?" Matt asks, appearing both confused and almost disappointed.

I'm not surprised. He's been pining for Dahlia this whole time, and she's barely glanced at him. As juvenile and petty as that is, I can't help but feel thrilled at that thought.

Not sure where to start, I tell them everything from when I left here to what Dahlia disclosed, minus the more intimate moment between us. Guilt tugs at my gut as I recite her story, knowing it wasn't given to me lightly, but they need to know that this man is a threat.

Once finished, they all stare at me with a mix of stunned and angry expressions coloring their faces.

"So, this guy is not only someone who preys on women but most likely assaulted her from the sounds of it. At the very least, he was stalking her for years," Matt says as he clenches and unclenches his fists.

James rubs the back of his neck and looks at me. "I mean, he hasn't done anything though. Innocent until proven guilty, bro. What will the others think if we lose a capable guy? It's her word against his, you know?"

Everything about his statement pisses me off. Maybe we can't prove his past indiscretions, but we can still clearly see what he's done in the short time we've known him. Dahlia's reaction was enough for me to believe her. Even her first response when we picked them up was enough. She didn't have to say the words aloud, but she painted the picture as clearly as the art she admired in my home. Why would she lie?

"I don't give a fuck about what anyone else believes. I know what I've already seen. I walked in there while she was clutching a fucking towel to her naked body on the floor. All while he towered over her." I bristle at the memory. "She hasn't slept for days. *Days* because she was *terrified*," I say, my tone quiet, icy, daring them to disagree.

Stepping forward, Matt places his hand on my shoulder. "We aren't disagreeing with you, man. We're with you. We just don't know what we can do about it right now," he says, continuing to keep his hand on my shoulder as if to placate me.

This.

This right here is the reminder that these men served with me but aren't like me in the slightest. They don't have the warped moral views I do.

They weren't raised with the family I had. Didn't grow up viewing things in a way that doesn't fit nice and snug in the socially accepted morals normal people cling to. Maybe I shouldn't have brought them into this. Otherwise, I could've handled the issue, and no one would've been the wiser. Even if they agree with me, they wouldn't understand the lengths I'll go to protect my own.

Am I claiming her as that now? *My own.*

Fuck. I run my fingers through my disheveled hair.

"I don't want that bastard around her or my sister. We need to do something," I say as I lean back in the chair, clenching my jaw. I take a sip from my glass, allowing the heat to spear through my throat.

There's an unfamiliar edge in James' voice when he responds. "Look, man, I'm not saying I don't believe you, or her for that matter, but—"

"*Callate,*" Juan interrupts, directing a scowl at James before he stands up. "Ren." He jerks his head towards the door.

In understanding, I down the glass and get up to follow him.

Juan closes the door quietly before we start walking down the hall. "I know what you're thinking," he says, keeping his voice low.

"And what is it that I'm thinking?"

He stops to pull out the keys for the stairs but doesn't answer until we're in the parking lot.

"Don't act like I don't know you well enough, *hermano.*" He side-eyes me as we reach his car. "You're thinking there may be a way to dump that fucker." He climbs into the front seat.

Sighing audibly, I follow. "I shouldn't have said anything," I tell him.

"I'm not expecting anything less," he says. He turns the car on to roll the windows down partially. "It just needs to happen when they don't suspect."

I glance over at him. "You want him gone too?" I don't know why it surprises me, but it's still a relief.

"Hell, yeah. Something's off about that one. Even his friend, Klein." He tilts his head as he glances out the window. "I talked to Jenson, and he mentioned the same shit."

It doesn't make sense to me how Juan and I, and even those two new guys can sense something, but the others don't.

"The others won't understand. At least not now… not yet. I have a feeling that with all that's been happening, eventually when the cruelty of our world catches up to them, they won't so much as blink. They can be ruthless in their own way, but they won't cross that thin line until they learn the hard way of what our lives have come to.

"But until then, you need to be careful. I don't want you to lose them. Right now, we need each other in this shit show, *hermano*, so whatever you're planning, rethink it. I'll help you keep an eye on him, or at the very least, on the girls."

Here I was thinking they were all different. I had forgotten about Juan. He may not have grown up in a family like mine, but he's known everything there is to know about me and my family since we first met.

He even helped me out of a few binds when we were in the military. He saved my ass before, quite frankly. I never understood why he accepted me, but he has, nonetheless. I have always kept him close. At first, out of fear that he could expose me and land me in prison, but then, as time went by, he became an unexpected friend.

"I don't like the prick, but for some reason, when it comes to *her*, I get even more ticked about the situation," I say honestly, admitting it for the first time. "I can't explain what I'm feeling with her, but I know I don't want her to get hurt. I want to keep her *safe*." Although it pisses me off, it's like she's a bit of light in my darkness, and I can't imagine it getting snuffed out.

No… more like my own little dream amidst the nightmares. "I was so close to filling him with lead right then and there, but I stopped myself. I was more afraid of her fearing me and running than the repercussions of everyone finding out."

It's as if I'm baring my soul with how hard it is to say all of this out loud, but I'm taking a chance with him. I hope he'll understand why I need to do what I need to do.

I'm also admitting the truth that has been grating at me. I let this woman get under my skin. Her quiet yet blazing bravery, quick thinking, and, as cliché as it sounds, her heart. She may not say the words, but I see how much she already cares for my nephew and sister.

For fuck's sake, she had the same damn idea about the cigarettes as I did. It's a small thing, but it shows that she tries to think of the possible scenarios we may get into in the future—she's savvy and innovative. She's a lot smarter than she lets on. She intrigues me, and the fact that she's a beautiful woman doesn't even hold a light to her damn person. She brings painful memories to the surface, not in a way that hinders me but in a way that reveals a longing I hadn't noticed was there, deep within myself. She makes my fucking head hurt, but I don't even care.

She's not the liability I thought she'd be.

"Ren, I get it," he says softly, pulling me back to our conversation. "Andrea and I barely just started dating, but damn I knew Ren. She was for me. We were only together for a few weeks. I didn't talk about her to anyone yet. I wanted to give her the privacy she asked for while we got to know each other. When this started going down, I lost contact with her. I drove out to her home first before meeting you guys."

He pauses, wiping his eyes and breathing in deeply. "I found her. At first, I thought everything was going to be okay. She *was* okay. She was hiding in her room. She was telling me that her neighbor attacked her. I must have gotten there just as it happened because I only had a few minutes with her. She started to tell me she felt funny..." He pauses. His gaze looks distant... "She turned. I didn't even understand what the hell was happening before she started attacking me. I didn't want to hurt her, but she kept trying to bite me and was raving like a rabid animal. I shot her in the head." His breath hitches slightly before continuing.

"I understand that feeling of wanting to keep someone safe. It's like maybe I could've done something if I'd gotten there sooner, but..." His voice betrays the pain burrowed deep, making him sound far more exhausted than he let on. "I know I didn't have control over that. At least with this, you have a chance."

Not knowing what to say, I place my hand on his shoulder in silent support. I had no idea he was battling with this. This entire time, he was having to deal with a devastating loss and doing it alone.

"Saying sorry only feels empty or cheap because it can't bring Andrea back."

He flinches at the sound of her name. Guilt pierces me to see him so defeated.

"I am sorry, though. Thank you for telling me. I hate that you went through that, man—more than you know," I say quietly.

"I know." He wipes his eyes again. "I'll do what I can to help you. Just don't do anything rash. Let's wait it out."

We stare at each other for a few seconds before I relent.

"I won't. For now, at least." We get out of the car when I change the subject. "Were you sure you didn't want me to be on watch tonight?"

"It's fine. Just stick close to the girls and that nephew of yours, too. We'll be good. James is gonna swap with me later so we can all get some sleep tonight."

Slightly relieved, knowing they will all get a semblance of rest, I begin my trek back to the room. Movement on the other side of the lot catches my attention, but whatever it was is gone when I turn to check it out. Was someone trying to listen in to our conversation or is my mind playing tricks on me?

Changing direction to investigate, I pause when Juan stops me. "Ren, I forgot to mention that Rei asked to see you. Sorry, man, it slipped my mind. I think he wanted to talk about plans for the group that wanted to settle."

Great... I return to the motel and seek out my brother. Might as well get him up to speed. I'll let him know my concerns again, but Juan's right. I need to play it safe. To wait it out before I deal with Price. I can still at least keep my brother informed and even ask him to have someone keep an eye on that asshole for the time being.

Thinking back to the last argument I had with my brother about the additional members of our group has my nerves on edge. This isn't a conversation I want to have tonight, but I might as well rip off the metaphorical band-aid.

Chapter Thirty-Two

Dahlia

I jerk awake at the screams outside, adrenaline surging before I can process what's happening. Ren startles next to me, jumping out of bed quickly to grab his weapon. I hadn't even realized he'd been sleeping next to me.

He scans the room, checking on Hana, who's somehow sleeping through the screams. Ru looks up with dreary eyes as Ren shakes Hana awake.

"Hana! Get up. We may need to leave," he says. He's moving fast around the room, grabbing all our stuff and throwing it on the bed. "Grab your stuff and make sure you have weapons ready."

My mind is still trying to catch up with what's happening. How does he manage to be so alert so soon after waking up? Ren's shoving his backpack on when a loud pounding at the door has us all swinging around.

Amongst the screams and shouting, familiar voices yell for us to open up. Ren hurries over, and when he opens the door, the rest of our usual group rushes in. The only one missing is James.

Ren also notices. "Where's James? What happened?" He moves to the back window facing the parking lot and looks out. "Shit."

Juan speaks up first. "He was making rounds. What's worse..." He pauses, rubbing his palms over his face. "Some of the doors up here were somehow opened..."

"Wait, the doors were open?" I ask.

"Yeah, and from what we saw, the stairwells were left open. When I started watch, everything was locked up tight. It's as if someone intentionally opened some of the doors before they were spooked by us coming around," Juan says, grief-stricken. "I hate to leave the rest of the group, but we need to get out before more come. The noise is going to be a huge problem."

He's not wrong. The screams must be from those whose doors were left open. Nausea assaults my stomach when I think of the families in our group.

"I agree." Reiji stands, but from his appearance, he doesn't seem as affected by the news of abandoning most of our group as I would have thought. Or maybe he and his brother are just good actors.

Ren glances at Hana and Rei, then pauses on me for a long moment before coming to a decision. "Alright." His eyes don't break from mine. He may not display it in obvious ways, but there is a lot of tension in his shoulders. He's scared for us, and despite the shit situation, my stomach flip-flops with that knowledge. "Do you think James is out by the cars?" he asks his friend.

Juan almost appears haunted. The pain etched on his face swirls in his dark eyes as his face hardens. "I don't know. We didn't see him anywhere on this side, so maybe."

Ren curses softly. "Make sure you have everything. We need to go now, and we can't hesitate. We need to be ready as soon as we're out that door."

"I'll grab Don, I can't leave him if I can help it. I'll be back," Rei says.

I try to hide my surprise by double-checking I haven't lost anything. He didn't seem like he cared about leaving everyone else but maybe I was right. *Great actors.*

Ren hands his brother his rifle and motions to Matt, who must have understood some silent communication with the gesture. He follows Rei out the door, weapons ready, without a word.

As we all wait for them, I collect all my belongings and find my shotgun fitted with the tactical light alongside the bayonet. I'm not sure when he found the time to add the light, but the gesture causes butterflies to flutter in my tummy all over again.

I throw my black jean jacket on while we wait. It feels like hours, all in anxious silence. When the door opens, Rei and the others run in and slam the door.

We all take a second to collect ourselves before Ren directs us on how we will line up once clear to do so. He wants the trained men to all go, fan out as much as possible to clear a way before we form a line.

Opening the door to join in the chaos, they all jump into action. Juan, Matt, and Dirk follow Ren and Rei out into the hallway. They use their secondary weapons, stabbing or swinging until they give us the signal to move out.

Not ready in the least, I still manage to get my feet to step out the door, suddenly more terrified than I thought possible when the number of zombies surrounding the place downstairs and the numbers climbing on the second level become visible. They are all currently distracted by the screams of the other occupants closer to the other stairwell, fighting their way out or hiding back in their rooms. The scarier part is how dark it is outside. With no electricity, the only thing allowing us to see is what appears to be a full moon and a cloudless sky. If it were a gloomier night, we would have been more screwed than we already are.

How in the hell did they all get here, and what attracted them like this? Were they in the other motel buildings?

A few zombies lunge at us but are taken out by the men behind me. It doesn't matter though. More are coming from the open door we're trying to escape through.

"Crap," someone curses. Three zombies charge Ren and his brother. They're shoulder to shoulder, barely fitting in the narrow hall, but they act as barricades from the onslaught of zombies.

I angle my body with my back to the railing. I try to ignore the growing horde below. We're getting sandwiched in. The other guys are starting to get pushed back from the zombies down the hall.

"Fuck. We can't do this quietly!" Ren shouts at his brother. More are crowding the hall ahead. "Where did they all come from?" He swings his weapon at the nearest zombie, blood splattering his face.

Rei must agree because he fires the first shot, abandoning the idea we could draw less attention with bludgeoning.

Using the guns, we slowly inch forward.

I'm shoved forward and almost lose my footing. "Hurry it up!" Matt exclaims from behind me. He fires off another shot but bumps into me again.

"I'm moving as fast as I can, asshole!" I shout back, allowing my anxiety to talk for me.

He keeps firing off shots while he yells back at me. "I didn't mean you, Dahl. I mean, we can't keep these motherfuckers off your backs much longer!"

His words are chilling at how close we are to dying.

The stairs finally come into view, and thankfully, they are relatively empty, other than a handful of zombies. The small space limits their mobility as they crowd each other. The two brothers quickly clip off the zombies while simultaneously swinging their different weapons. Rei is shockingly deadly with the gun and axe together. It makes me glad I'm traveling with them and not alone.

We're barely exiting the stairwell until we're surrounded. I decide to try out the bayonet.

No time like the present.

The first looks to have been almost eighty despite its current speed. It slips through our tight formation too fast for anyone to notice.

I don't hesitate. I stab forward, trying hard not to think about who she may have been before this. Cold metal meets little resistance, making my stomach churn.

Hana swings one of the bats with nails at any others that get close. Her hits are precise and lethal.

We take off running as fast as we can while staying in a line until Ren directs us to form a circle with Me, Hana, Ru, Jen, and her daughter in the middle.

We finally gain some ground and reach the parking lot, but the air becomes thicker.

Darker.

Smoke.

It fills the air, and my lungs heave. My eyes wildly search for the reason.

Oh no...

Ren's truck and a few other cars from our group are all on fire.

Loud curses, mainly Ren's, reach my ears when the blazing vehicles come into view. More zombies surround us, but as a group, we drive them back as best we can.

The smoke thickens and spreads like dark, ominous clouds.

Whoosh!

I spin around at the loud sound, eyes widening as one of the buildings goes up in flames.

My eyes sting from the smoke, but I continue following the others. The fires aren't a good thing, but the light gives us a better view of the shit show surrounding us.

When the loud sound cuts through the other noises, my body shudders, and my fear spikes astronomically.

Screechers.

Nobody says anything, but we all feel the growing pressure. We pick up our pace, jogging and pushing ahead.

Dirk breaks away towards Juan's car and fires at a zombie struggling to grab at something. The zombie is thrown back, revealing James. He's panting from the fight. He has blood running down his head and neck from a head wound. It doesn't look like a bite but like he hit his head in the struggle.

Juan catches up and helps lift him, but all too soon, they're surrounded.

"Shit," Ren curses ahead of me. He kicks out at the nearest zombie, but his eyes are on his friends. They're so close to the car, yet they can't get a second to open the door.

Breaking from our formation, Hana is the first to reach my car with Ru. Matt helps cover while they climb in.

There are fewer zombies near my car, but more crowd Ren's friends as they struggle to fight them off. James is barely conscious. He's leaning against the car while the other two fight. He must be out of it because he hasn't opened the door yet.

"They need help! Just go, we got this!" I yell to Ren as we reach the car.

My bayonet slices through the last one on this side of the car. My panic doesn't subside, but I know we will be fine once we get inside. At least, for a moment, for him to help them.

My eyes fall on Ren. He seems pissed off. He fires another shot and looks back. He stares at his sister and Ru in the car before his eyes fall on me.

Confliction.

"Get in the car," he barks.

"Just go!" I yell again, ignoring his command.

Another zombie jumps out around the car. More are behind it.

Ren shoves me aside as he takes another shot at them. "Just get in the goddamn car, angel," he sneers. The way he uses that name pisses me off. It's as if he only likes to mock me. As if he sees me as incapable.

My anger slightly overrides the fear, but I climb into the car after Matt regardless. Ren says nothing else as he gets in and starts the car.

Shouting rises above the gunfire outside.

Davis, Jenson, and Susan, another woman from our original group, are all fighting to catch up.

Ren's eyes are focused on his friends still fighting while James finally manages to climb into their car. He visibly relaxes when Jenson and the others reach them. They're able to fight off the growing crowd enough to all get inside the vehicle.

I can't help but feel heartbroken for the other people we're leaving behind. There were families. I only hope the children were still in the rooms behind closed doors.

I'm unable to contain the sob and tears when I think of their small faces.

A warm hand squeezes mine, startling me. I give Ren a surprised look, although he doesn't notice as he scans our surroundings. Doing the same, I notice the cars we used as a barricade have already been moved.

Someone already left?

My mind immediately goes to Dillon, but I'm distracted by another scream.

"Wait, please. Comeback!" someone shouts. Their scream is loud enough to hear over the sounds of bodies hitting my car as we back out.

I turn my body at an angle to see the building we evacuated. In an open window, Maria, one of the women from our group, is clutching Luis while screaming for us. Guilt sharp as a knife wraps around my heart.

"We need to go back!" I shout, but Ren clenches his jaw and stares through the mirror. "Please, Ren," I say with a sob.

There's only a breath of a moment before he swears and shifts the car in reverse, still uncaring for the obstacles desperate to get to us. To my relief, Rei's car follows us back towards the motel.

Although the parking lot is small and near to the building, the trek feels like miles. Zombies continue to surround us, gaining ground before they are practically on top of us.

"Matt!" Ren shouts, relaying some unspoken directions just by calling his name.

Matt climbs to the back and opens the liftgate. He shoots at any zombies nearby and props himself out of the tailgate. Matt shouts out to the woman as we make it to them. "Hop down on the roof. We'll pull you in. Hurry."

The woman doesn't hesitate to hoist her children down by the arms. She only spares a second to whisper in their ear and to kiss their forehead. Once lowered, their feet barely reach us, just enough distance for Matt to touch their shoes.

He wastes no time grabbing the kids as they fall. The others from Rei's car give cover, and Ren, with his other hand, out the window. Once the second child, Laila, is in, Matt indicates for Maria to jump down but she shakes her head, sobbing. It's then I notice the blood streaming down her neck. Without another word, she closes the window. All I can do is stare wide-eyed as we drive away.

Ren doesn't remove his hand from mine but manages to drive one-handed, although there are so many zombies now; I can't help but remember the last time we were in this position. The fires must have attracted them like last time. I wonder if the blazing sounds attracted them or the light.

The car lurches over something, causing a loud thump.

Hana squeals slightly, and in my beyond-manic state, I chuckle. My nerves are at an all-time high. How this is funny, I can't understand. Have I lost it? Probably.

Ren's head whips around and back to the road so fast that I almost imagine the ghost of a smile on his lips.

The car in front of us slams on the brake. James tumbles out of the car, while the others inside are shouting something. Before I can process what's happening, he starts running back.

Did he forget something?

The relief in seeing him okay is short-lived.

He stops when he's close to one of the zombies and pulls out a gun. Instead of shooting the zombie as I would have thought, he brings it up to his head. His eyes stare in our direction, but his face gives away nothing.

He pulls the trigger.

Hana screams, and I shout, "Oh my god!" I cover my mouth with my hand, unable to process why this is happening.

Ren's hand on mine squeezes so tight my knuckle bones grind together. My panicked eyes search his face. His jaw is clenched, and his eyes are fixed on the rear-view mirror. James was one of his friends. He just witnessed his friend kill himself and now can't seem to tear his gaze away.

Morbid curiosity has me glancing back into the mirror on the right to see a swarm of zombies all huddled over what was once James. There are so many of them you can't see anything but bodies on top of bodies. My stomach lurches, although I still have nothing left to throw up.

Why did he do that?

Then it comes to me. He was fighting off a zombie when they found him.

He had been *bitten* and had decided to use his final moments to give us an opening to leave.

A sob breaks free from my throat as the tears threatening to shed finally spill over.

Hana is crying in the back, and I can hear Matt cursing, his head dipped, allowing the shadows to shield his features.

Ren removes his hand and squeezes the steering wheel so hard that his knuckles lighten. I'm almost positive his teeth are going to crack from how hard he's clenching his jaw. Some of the zombies continue to follow, but most are adding to the growing pile behind us.

We may have gotten away, barely, but what are we even doing? Will this be how it is from now on? Always running? Always barely staying alive?

The tears keep falling as we continue to drive.

I can only hope that we won't have to live on *barely* for much longer.

Chapter Thirty-Three

Dahlia

Inhale. One… Two… I try to still the trembling in my body. The adrenaline and fear are creating a cacophony of chaos in my mind.

"Are they gone?" Hana interrupts from the back.

Exhale…

A shot rings out. Screeches pierce the air, and at the same time, the car ahead of us swerves hard. They barely manage to miss the fire hydrant on the corner of the intersection. Ten or more screeching zombies are sprinting straight for us from up ahead.

My hand grips my gun tighter. I'm nervous about having to use it in the car. There's no way we can get away without shooting back. I'm about to roll the window down when Ren stops me by grabbing the shotgun gently and pushing it down.

"Here, take this." His eyes don't leave the road when he hands me a second pistol he had holstered. I'm grateful I don't need to try and shoot the shotgun in a moving vehicle. I roll the window down just enough to take a shot at the incoming zombies.

The other vehicles are all doing the same. Juan's car ahead swerves out of the way so not to hit the oncoming zombies but somehow manages to turn, facing us from the street on the right. They aren't moving, which is a tactic I don't understand. They're basically sitting ducks. Juan has an older Wrangler, but up against so many of these zombies, I don't know how they'll fare.

The thought has me remembering what Ren's truck looked like when they came home that day.

Clearing my head, I aim for the closest zombie and fire. The nerves in my body flare hot and threaten to paralyze me as the chances of survival become less and less likely. I'm terrified since it's so dark outside. Only the lights from the moon and our cars give us coverage to make out what we need to kill or outrun.

My heart flutters in excitement when my target goes down, glad I could be useful here. Immediately, guilt for that excitement overwhelms me. I shouldn't be glad that I managed to take one down. *They used to be people.*

I shove those thoughts aside for now and target another.

The car swerves. The sharp right jerks me hard enough that I almost lose my grip on the gun.

Something slams into the side of the car. It's hard enough to rock the whole vehicle before we swerve again.

I frantically search for the cause, only to find a zombie gripping the side of the car next to Ren's window. *How the hell is it holding on like that?* It doesn't fall but instead appears to climb with a tight grip. *Holy shit.*

Fear wracks my body as I stare in horror at the thing.

Hesitating, I swallow before taking my seat belt off and leaning over, almost entirely on top of Ren. I'm not confident enough not to hit him if I shoot from my seat.

"This isn't the time to be feeling me up, angel!" Ren snaps, shifting slightly to relieve the pressure off his lap. *Ouch.*

I move my hand down. I clutch his thigh while my other hand aims the weapon near the window, all while trying not to block Ren's view. "Roll it down on three," I tell him. If only I could still the shaking in my hands from the adrenaline. Or maybe it's only the fear.

The zombie slams its head into the glass. Then again, and again. Blood splatters across the dirty surface. Its face becomes more mutilated with each hit.

The panel shakes violently but, thankfully, doesn't break. *Yet.*

"Oh my god. What the actual fucking hell is it doing?" Hana shouts from the back.

Ren doesn't respond, but for some stupid reason, he trusts me. His hand goes to the window crank. He's driving and trying to avoid the abandoned cars in the street with one hand.

"One…" I take a deep breath.

Slam!

"Two…" Shit. Shit. Shit. He cranks the window a little.

Slam!

"Three!" I shout. My nerves alight as I focus on my one task. *Please don't fuck up. Please don't fuck up.*

He cranks the window down harder. It goes down so slowly that it's almost comical. Well… if we weren't about to die.

As soon as there is space, I shove my hand out. I don't think about how close my fingers are to its face.

I fire.

Time stands still. My breath stops altogether.

Is there a new wound? Did I miss?

I hesitate, only for a split second. But I lean closer, ready to shoot at it again.

Suddenly, a fresh line of blackish liquid seeps from its darkening eye.

The zombie's hold slips. It falls to the street and is run over by the car behind, which isn't able to swerve in time.

Shifting back into my seat, I notice that it's Juan behind us. The zombies are all between the two other cars now. They somehow managed to draw enough of them to their car and swung back, allowing us to lead without the small horde in front.

Matt is still shooting from the back of the car out the liftgate.

We continue to drive at a reckless speed with so many parked and discarded cars on the road, which is now all silent other than the gunfire and a few screeches behind us.

The gunfire stops after what feels like an hour but may only be minutes. No more shrieks resound in the background, but it's like we're collectively holding our breath, waiting for more to follow in search of noise. My body breaks out in chills when we hear them again, this time sounding from behind.

"Shit," Ren curses. "We need to find somewhere to park. Otherwise, we'll run out of ammo while we keep drawing more out," he says, focusing on our surroundings for a possible hiding place. It reminds me of the last time we were in this predicament.

We continue to drive, and after a few minutes, we hear more gunfire. The pressure to find somewhere is building to explosive heights when I spot a police department.

"The police!"

Ren gives me an incredulous look.

"A little late for local police intervention, you think?" he says, flustered. His normal expression slips, revealing a more stressed and annoyed Ren underneath.

I can't help but grit my teeth. What a fucking asshole.

Can't he see that this is the only shot we have?

I speak up before I can stop myself. "No, asshole." I turn to glare at him. "The police department has a gated area where they park their cars, and they most likely have an entrance where they unload and book their detainees," I say as I point in the building's direction. "It should have a slide-down gate, like the one at the auto place, or some form of enclosure. In this town, it may not be big enough, but there's still a chance it may be. We can close the gates and hide there."

I give him a pointed look when his brows fly up.

"Oh, and who knows? Maybe we find some useful crap. Like ammo and weapons." I don't bother hiding the eye roll while mumbling, "Ass."

I don't usually get sassy with people, but he doesn't have to be a jerk. I don't need him questioning my competence. I already do that enough as is.

He gets under my skin like a damn fishhook.

His chuckle, however, surprises me. I was half expecting him to give me a scary broody look, but instead, I'm graced with a rare smile. My heart flutters despite my irritation.

Changing lanes, he heads towards the police department. I guess he's trusting me again. Let's hope my gamble pays off.

At first, I fear I'm wrong, but we find an entrance half-hidden by the trees lining the street. When we drive through the gate, we can make out the police department on the left and a connecting drive-thru structure that leads down a level. Although it's an incredible risk and possible there's no way out the other end, we drive in and head down anyway.

Adrenaline and fear course through me, but despite my body shivering, my eyes stay fixed ahead. It's so dark that we can only see what the headlights cover. If there are zombies down here, we are done for.

He must have the same thoughts because Ren flashes the high beam lights, illuminating the space.

The relief when we find exactly what I was expecting, is so palpable, I swear I can taste the sweetness of it. And thankfully, the space is large enough for all of us. That had been the real gamble.

On the left is the entrance to the holding cells, and up ahead is an exit that looks already closed off. No patrol vehicles are inside either, which makes sense when I think about it. When shit hit the fan, the police would have been out dealing with all the emergencies. I try not to think why they never made it back, but their misfortune may have been our saving grace.

Again.

The sorrow and guilt that latch onto my chest with that realization are unbearable.

Ren pulls forward, giving the others room, and then puts the car in park but doesn't shut the engine off. He grabs the shotgun from me and climbs out, turning a flashlight on. In a matter of moments, he's already sweeping the area and running towards the gate behind us.

A few shots can be heard, and the noise echoes loudly inside the garage-like building. A loud grating sound follows before something heavy slams against the concrete. A few other banging sounds resonate in the space, causing my heart to pick up again.

We wait in silence, clutching our weapons, while we wait for Ren to come back. A shuffling noise in the back pulls my attention as Matt hops out through the liftgate, leaving the five of us alone. He slowly walks back to the other cars, and whatever he sees, his shoulders relax, but he doesn't lower his weapon. Instead, he sweeps the area Ren already checked, being extra cautious.

Each car has its high beams on, which all but blinds me when trying to look in the mirrors. However, it does create a lot of light throughout the space and also a lot of odd-shaped shadows. From what little I can make out, everyone is crouching low, checking any place a body could fit and even some smaller areas to be safe.

It must be at least thirty minutes of us waiting before Ren returns and knocks on my window, causing me to jump. When my hand hits the button to unlock the doors, he wastes no time and opens it. "It's probably best to stay in the car. We are going to investigate where this door leads and make sure it's somewhere safe to hole up. Maybe we can find more flashlights. It won't be the most comfortable, but there will be beds inside the holding cells. Maybe even some provisions."

He closes the door before Hana or I can speak. I almost want to tell him I can come and help but can't chalk up enough courage. If I'm honest with myself, I don't want to. Exhaustion and fear have created a cocktail of misery, threatening to send me spiraling. *Breathe, Dahl. Just breathe.*

I inhale deeply through my nose as I close my eyes. My chest is tightening, and my limbs won't cease trembling. It's taking all my effort not to picture what they're walking into or the threat continuing to slam against the entrance.

It's like the stillness now is worse than the chaos moments before. Having the time to think about our situation is debilitating.

My heart races and my lungs fight to take in enough oxygen. *Fuck. What are we going to do? How are we going to get out of here?*

Are there people barricaded inside or zombies? Were the people in those cells left to die?

My mind chases question after question, which only fuels the rising panic. Chest heaving and physically aching, I rub circles around my sternum. *Breathe. The guys inside will be fine. We will manage to get out of this.*

Just inhale...

"Here." Something shiny reflects the car's interior lights in my peripheral. Hana is reaching over the center console to hand me a protein bar. "You should try to eat something. I know we need to ration, but you're practically starving yourself."

Silently grateful for her distraction, I grab the bar with a shaking hand. "Thanks," I whisper, afraid to speak too loudly despite the banging on the outside gate. No sound will make a difference right now.

I twist further to get a full view of the back seats where the two kids huddled together softly cry while Ru rests his head on Hana's lap, fast asleep.

"Damn. I wish I could sleep as easily during all this." I laugh softly, taking a bite of the peanut butter flavored bar. Hana smiles down at him, brushing his hair off his face.

"I know. I am almost thankful he is sleeping, though. He has already witnessed too much. Poor kid."

She joins me and starts snacking on another bar after offering some to the children. We're all silent other than the soft sound of our chewing. Eventually, the two other kids find a fitful sleep, and my eyes drift to the door to the building.

A shot rings out from inside. I gasp, startled. We hold our breath, but there are no more. *They're fine. They are going to be okay.*

"Do you think they're okay?" I ask despite trying to tell myself they are.

Hana's face slips as her eyes stay fixed on the door. "They should be good..." She clears her throat and looks to me.

"Let's not dwell… Yeah?" She pauses before she snaps her fingers. "I know a perfect topic to distract us. How 'bout you spill."

My brows furrow at her. "Spill? Spill what?"

"I need some good tea in my life, and unless you have a damn kettle to brew some real tea, you aren't getting out of the gossip-giving kind. What's up with you and my brother?"

Her question catches me off guard. "Hana, I don't know if you've noticed, but there's no new gossip since zombies started trying to kill us… Unless you think one of those things was eyeing us because they want to ask us out instead of eat us…"

She snorts. "If that was the case, they'd still be trying to eat us." She wags her brows. "But I can't get behind the rabid behavior. I'm no expert, but that's certainly a red flag."

Jesus. I chuckle. "Morbid much?"

"Maybe. But you're the one trying to change the subject." She leans forward. "What *really* happened with you two?" She gives me a look that tells me she knows something *has* happened and won't take a lie as an answer. "Come on. It's a perfect distraction, and who else can you talk to?"

My face grows hot, and she can probably see my blushed cheeks even in the poor interior light and all the shadows cast.

I turn away, hoping she didn't see, but unfortunately, my luck ran out tonight. "I knew it!" she half whispers, half yells, trying not to wake the kids. "I could tell from how uncomfortable he looked when he saw me and that red face and messy hair of yours. Dead give giveaway." Her smile only grows when I don't meet her eyes. Her hand grabs my shoulder, tugging me so I'll turn back.

"Give me something here, Dahl. I know something happened. Did you kiss? I mean, you were still clothed, but who knows… maybe before I came in?" With a sideways glance, I can see her wagging her brows again. "Plus, I don't know if I've ever seen such a flustered Ren."

A loud bang outside the building has me startling. *Fuck they need to hurry up.*

I try to take deep breaths, but Hana isn't patient. "Come on. It won't hurt to talk about it."

It's weird expressing anything out loud. Especially to Ren's sister. Although, she isn't that far off. I do want to talk about it. At least to say it out loud and get an idea of why Ren is so hot and cold. He confuses me and excites me all at once, and I don't know how to feel about it all. It's starting to bother me.

Sighing, I brush my hair behind my ears and look over at her. "Well..." I glance up and bite my lip, trying to think what I should tell her.

Hana makes me comfortable talking and being more open, but this is her brother. Won't she find that odd? Also, it makes me feel like I'm back in high school again, gossiping about boys and not the twenty-seven-year-old I am.

Something about her saying she's never seen him that flustered has me relenting.

Maybe getting it off my chest will ease the weight of all these confusing feelings. Or perhaps it'll keep my mind off Ren inside right now. Possibly fighting for his life.

Groaning, I scrunch my nose and bite my lip, too nervous to say the words out loud.

I didn't think her smile could get any wider, but I was wrong. She looks like a kid who just walked through a magical wardrobe into a damn all-you-can-eat candy buffet. Her brows raise in question, wanting more.

Flustered, I huff. "There isn't anything to tell. We kissed, kind of intensely until he abruptly pulled away... But I got the impression that it was more the emotions or adrenaline running high. Not him wanting more to come of it. Otherwise, he probably would've said something about it instead of 'sorry' and 'I don't want you to misunderstand.' He seemed ready to leave it where it lay as if it was a huge mistake." I dip my head and try to hide my disappointment and the embarrassment of admitting that out loud.

Her chuckle has my head flying up. She keeps laughing softly but doesn't enlighten me on what she finds so funny.

After a moment of her contemplating, she speaks up. "Knowing my brother, he doesn't beat around the bush, so to speak, but he also never dates or, for all I know, has ever had feelings for someone before. If that's the case, he may be clueless, or he can't figure out how to handle it."

My face scrunches up, and I don't feel any better after her statement, but before I can respond, her hand comes up to stop me.

"Oh, but Dahl, he wouldn't have stopped himself or apologized if it was just some high emotional or adrenaline thing. He would have gone with it and moved on without thinking twice." She leans forward and rests her arms on the seats. "No. I think he's trying to figure you out or, more like, figure out why you make him feel the way he does. And as for the misunderstanding." She emphasizes the word as if she does not agree with me at all. "I think maybe he wanted you to see that it was not in fact a high emotions thing. Or, more accurately, it *was* an emotional thing, him actually having them. He probably just has no idea what the hell he's feeling."

She shrugs and looks at the door, smile faltering. She stays silent for a few minutes while staring at the entrance.

"I'm trying very hard not to worry, but... it's incredibly hard," she whispers now, changing the subject. Thankfully.

Unfortunately, it is a less desirable one, causing all my anxiety to rear its head once more.

My eyes return to that dreaded door and stay rooted there, willing it to open and discover everyone safe. Not surprisingly, it doesn't open. I push my seat back slightly, still giving them room in the back, and close my eyes. I'm not expecting to fall asleep, but I need to try not to think of what could be happening to them inside or if the gate will even hold while the zombies outside continue acting as battering rams with their unrelenting assault to get inside.

If only we could discover more about what caused these zombies and learn anything else about them that could help us. It's been pricking my mind for a while now and the differences between these things are giving me a headache but also making me more worried. If some are different from the majority, does that mean there are others out there that we haven't encountered yet?

My biggest fear is that they will continue to change for the worse. The fact that there are differences at all is worrisome. That means they could theoretically evolve. At least, I think so. I'm no science major. But if that *is* the case... then we're fucked.

How can we find all this out? I wonder if once we get to Meg, we can look into a way of finding some of these answers. *If we make it there at all.*

Being unable to call or text her is harder than I ever imagined. I never noticed how accustomed we became of having easy communication at our fingertips. Hopefully we make it. And that she's still alive.

A soft rattling noise draws my attention back to the present, and my eyes open, seeking out the source of the sound. From the inside of the car, there's not much to look at in front of us. I squint, trying to see past the glare of the car's lights behind us. It's hard to make out, but it almost looks like someone has got out of their car.

Wait, no... That's not right.

It looks like someone is *crawling* under the car behind us. What the hell?

Straining my ears and eyes, I focus on the movement. Hoping to hear or see something to indicate what it is.

My pulse pounds harder, and my breaths come up short. A slight movement under the car has my attention, but I can't make out more than a shadow. "Oh my god," I whisper. Is it a zombie under there, or am I seeing things?

What can we do if it is? Once someone opens their door and steps out, they won't have a chance. If I blare the horn, they'll likely still jump out of the car. Not to mention, the horn will bring more attention to our location. I don't know how much weight the gate between us and the zombies can hold before it caves in. If more zombies come our way...

Shit.

If I roll the window down and yell to stay inside, that might draw attention to us. My attention shifts to Ru and the two other two clutching each other. What can I do without putting the kids in danger? I think I remember Ren having a walkie-talkie. Had he left it in his truck? Crap, I think he did... or he has it. *Fuck...*

What if I didn't actually see what I did…? Maybe I am just so stressed that I *am* imagining things. It wouldn't be the first time my anxiety caused foreboding feelings that made me overreact.

But what if it was *real*? I can do something about it before someone gets hurt. Oh god, what if there were more? What if one is under our car?

Crap. It's like I touched a live wire with how my nerves are lighting under my skin and how my body won't stop the relentless shivering. My panic rises as my eyes stay glued to the shadows under the car.

"What's wrong?" Hana asks, giving me a frightened look.

I take a second, wondering if I should speak up and scare her or ignore it. But before I think better of it, the words are spilling out. "I swear I saw a zombie crawl underneath their car." I point as if she won't understand what car I'm talking about. She looks back a second and then glances at me.

"Wouldn't they have attacked by now? Usually, they just run and bite."

All I can manage is a shake of my head. Some *are* different. Like the one Ren mentioned. My blood runs cold when I realize that if I'm right, it's been waiting intentionally. Slowly stalking its prey like a panther.

I can't help my hesitation, although I already know what I need to do. I can't make any noise to warn them otherwise I risk someone getting killed. Or the zombie attacks us instead with Ru and the others in the car.

Before I can allow my fear to paralyze me—although I half-wish it would because I don't want this responsibility—I take my jacket off, hoping it'll allow me to feel less constricted. I throw it on the floor and reach for the door handle. Once it's open slightly, I use my leg to push the door fully open. I don't want to die, but I also don't want anyone else to when I could have prevented it.

"Stay here," I say before clutching the pistol Ren lent me, a flashlight I fished from my bag, and the crowbar. I put the flashlight in my mouth, unable to manage all three with any grace and open the door fully. Most likely looking more like a fool, I jump as far away from the car as I can, instead of stepping out. It reminds me of playing the floor-is-lava game as a kid or being afraid that the boogeyman under the bed would grab my ankles.

I shudder at that last thought. "Oh shit. Oh shit," I whisper to myself. Facing the car, I raise my hand in a stop motion before realizing that if any of the veterans are still in the vehicles, they may understand a different gesture better. I fist my hand at eye-level, hoping I remembered enough from my dad, and mostly just hoping they understand what I mean. Who knows, maybe I'm not giving the correct 'stay the hell back' sign and look like an idiot, but no one opens their door, so that's a plus.

I back away from the car, trying to distance myself in order to draw the zombie away from everyone. I take the flashlight out of my mouth while trying to hold it in my hand and shuffle the crowbar under my arm. *You can do this. All you have do is make enough noise to draw it out. Simple. You got this.*

I blink away the tears and inhale deeply before yelling, "Stay in the car!" I lift the pistol, ignoring the increase of sounds from the zombies outside as they bang harder. It's an orchestra from hell sent to set my nerves ablaze.

My gaze stays fixed on the car. The sound a window rolling down reaches my ears. I raise my voice before anyone can say anything. I don't want them to draw attention to themselves.

"There's a zombie under the car!" I scream. My hand is shaking so hard I doubt I can shoot anything, even at close range. I stay still, hoping that it takes my bait or that I am wrong about it even being there. Trying and failing to steady my breathing and to slow my quickening heart rate, I wait.

I am almost starting to believe it won't take the bait and is fully dedicated to its prey before the slightest motion has me shooting without a second thought.

My shot goes wide, narrowly missing the front tire.

It's already out from under the car. Climbing to its feet, it comes towards me quickly. I freeze, wide-eyed at how spectacularly I failed and that I was *right*.

My hands are shaking too hard. It's getting closer. Just a few feet now. Raising the gun, I shoot again, this time hitting it in the neck.

"Fuck," I cry, shooting again, only to miss.

I drop the flashlight, impairing my vision. *At least I won't see the bite coming.* I grab the crowbar, swapping hands with the gun.

Oh god. It's almost on top of me. All my weight goes into the strike, hitting it over the head with a one-handed swing. It stumbles and falls back, but it's still alive.

I pounce, ignoring the sound of car doors slamming and the shouts surrounding me.

Once I'm on top of it, I shove the gun awkwardly with my left hand to its temple. I pull the trigger. Warmth splatters the exposed skin of my arms and neck.

This time, it lays motionless, empty, red, bruised eyes staring at the ceiling. My ears ring, and my vision tunnels while I stare at it.

A pair of hands grab my shoulders. Startled, I jump, ready to swing back, but his voice stops me. "It's just me," Ren says, releasing his grip on my shoulders. Grabbing hold of my elbow, he helps me up from straddling the dead zombie.

My mind is taking too long to catch up to what happened; my breathing won't calm, and my heart feels like it will burst any moment. I take in the zombie. Its whole mouth and neck are red, smeared with dried blood. Once a salt and pepper gray, its hair is coated in a black tar or gooey liquid.

I'm escorted back to the car, where someone helps me inside. Time passes slowly while I try to catch my breath.

I can't believe I managed that. I played the damn hero to keep everyone safe. I didn't want to, but I also didn't want someone to die. Then to carry that guilt for the rest of my now predictably short life. *But you did it. You actually managed it.* That thought relieves the weight that has been pressing down on my chest for a while now. Maybe I can do this. Maybe I can be an actual help to them.

"What happened?" Ren asks, so softly that I almost think I'm imagining it. His eyes betray his concern as he stares down at me. It's not his usual neutral expression or annoyance. "You weren't bit, were you?" His voice sounds strained at that question. He cups my face with his hand while his eyes take in the rest of me. He's probably remembering his friend no more than a few hours ago getting bitten and dying himself.

"No," is all I can manage.

He stares for a moment longer as if he needs to be sure before letting go. When he's certain I'm not hurt, he walks over to where everyone is huddled. A few of them are now peering under the car as if the bogeyman in fact will jump out.

Thankfully, no other zombie makes an appearance, and by the time everyone comes over to our car, my breathing has evened out, and I feel somewhat normal again. I'm grateful the slight panic attack didn't occur before I killed the zombie, otherwise I would've been the one to die. But I can't help but feel like I need to get myself together. I can't panic every time I have to kill a zombie. I've done it enough now. Shouldn't this pass?

"The holding cells and adjoining rooms are all clear. We found a small, busted generator that hooks up to this floor. It almost looks like they had the power gridded separately for this level. Not sure if that is normal, but it works in our favor if we can get it running." Ren gestures to his friends. "We already barricaded both the elevators and stairwell to the main floor. Same with the hallway; we should be safer inside," Ren says, paying attention to each of us and wanting to be sure we are listening.

"I don't know how long we have until the ones outside finally realize they can't get in, but prepare for at least a day. Once we rest, we can try to search more thoroughly for food, water, or anything else we may need inside." Ren turns his full attention to me and lowers his voice. "Are you fine to go inside?"

Suddenly, exhaustion catches up, and I'm more than ready to sleep like the dead. Pun intended. "Yeah, I should be. Thank you," I say softly, meeting his gaze.

He reaches over to help me out of the car, grabbing me by the waist to steady me. Regardless of how tired I am, it doesn't stop my heart from swelling at his attention. I grab his arms while I hop out, trying to ignore the warmth and hardness beneath my palms. I glance up at him to find him staring down at me. Even with shadows surrounding us, his eyes stand out to me. The little flecks of gold almost seem brighter with the car's lights beside us.

"Dahl?" he asks.

"Huh?"

Ren's lips curl slightly, and his features soften as if relieved. "You okay? You zoned out a little."

My cheeks heat as I mumble a yes. He removes his hands from my waist and steps back with a smirk.

I try to ignore the way he manages to make my head swim and step over to my fallen flashlight. Hana walks up behind me and grabs my hand, pulling me closer to her before telling me thank you.

"Next time, though, don't be a damn hero. You could have died!" She pulls me into a tight hug before we make our way inside.

Thankfully, my luck holds. I could have died, but I can't help but feel a little proud that I managed to keep everyone safe. Even if I could have figured out a better method, no one died because of me. We were safe.

For now.

Chapter Thirty-Four

Dahlia

We walk into complete darkness—so dark that I can't see my hand far from my face without light. My heart beats out of its chest. Although they came through here already, I can't help the rising panic at the unknown beyond the dark.

We all flip our flashlights on. The lights don't do the best to illuminate the whole room, but it is enough to see a slightly sectioned-off desk with a glass panel connected to the ceiling. I move my light towards the desk. The light reflects off a small camera perched on a tripod.

"How can we be sure there aren't more in hiding? I have no idea where that zombie crawled from," I ask Ren while trying not to flash the light in his eyes.

His face hardens at the question, jaw clenching while he keeps his attention on our surroundings. The shadows only obscure his features, adding to the ominous mood. "We did as thorough a search in the dark as possible, but be alert. If we can get the generator up and running, we can do another search," he says as he guides us through a hallway leading to the holding cells.

The first few are more like rooms in that they are fully enclosed and have doors that have windows. One cell is devoid of life but has some personal belongings, reminding me that California has the work release program. It's for people who committed minor crimes but can still work while incarcerated.

Flashing my light into the other cells, I find them bare, with nothing but a toilet, sink, and four beds or two bunks in each. All the cell doors are shut as we walk by.

I keep expecting something to jump out at me. Every little sound the others make has me flinching. *Shit, I just want this to be over.*

Ren opens the door to a cell on the left and has Hana and me step inside. Rei, carrying a drowsy Ru, walks into the cell next to ours and lies on the empty bed with his son.

It's strange how we've all fallen into this routine. As if it's becoming normal that we're on the run for our lives and now seeking shelter in another unlikely place. I can't pinpoint what about it that makes me sad, but it does. It's only another reminder that *this* is our life now.

Will we ever get back to our old lives? Or a semblance of what our old lives were? My mind goes to Ren... the kiss we shared.

Will we ever get to experience anything other than suffering? Experience something blossom, like a snowdrop within our harsh climate?

Don and his girlfriend walk by our cell. They're both holding the hands of the two kids, Luis and Laila, and their own child.

"Keep the door closed. I'll be back once everyone is settled," he tells me before leaving.

Shifting, I use the flashlight to illuminate the whole cell, wanting to see my new living quarters for the night. There are two beds, both attached to the wall. One blanket on each, no pillow. Having been the smart one, Hana had grabbed our bags and two blankets from the car. She tosses me my pack before fishing out a sweater from hers to use as a makeshift pillow. Reluctant, I flash my light throughout the whole cell again, wanting to be sure we don't have any unintentional cellmates, not that there was anywhere to hide here.

Being here brings me back to all the classes I took in school. When I was an eager girl who wanted to go into law enforcement until life shoved and battered me to the point where I lost all motivation for it.

Who am I kidding? I was *never* motivated. I had the idea that since I didn't enlist into the military, law enforcement would be another way to honor my father, another way to make him proud.

If the situation with Dillon hadn't occurred, I might not have been so beaten down and would have followed through.

Except with the pain and shame came the realization that following in the same direction as my father wasn't what I wanted. I was scared and paranoid for a while... I was—*am*—weak. That was the only thing Dillon taught me—that I wasn't capable.

Somehow, everything that has happened with the zombies makes me so thankful I never applied for the LAPD. I almost did twice, both times chickening out, creating poor excuses before throwing the idea out completely. I only kept telling myself it was what I wanted because I couldn't let go of the idea of disappointing my father even if he wasn't here anymore.

Unfortunately, I never figured out what I wanted to do with my life if I allowed myself to let that dream go. Not that it would have made a difference now. If I had been an officer during this whole end-of-the-world shit, I would have died on day one.

Although I'm glad I never applied, the twinge of disappointment mars the gratitude.

What would my dad think of me now?

Don't go there. You managed to do something right tonight. You kept them safe out there.

I try to shove those thoughts aside.

I wonder how many skilled doctors or first responders survived. They would have been doing what they trained to do and lost their lives for nothing. I'm sure most people didn't survive, and those of us who have, well, I don't think we have much time left.

The negative thoughts are relentless, but I manage to shove them away for now while I focus on menial tasks—like draping my blanket over the bed. It looks to have not been slept in, so hopefully, it was a fresh set of sheets. Not that I should be complaining, but it's better than the floor or the car or, you know, being zombie dinner. I place my flashlight on the floor next to the bed, leaving it on until Ren comes back.

Despite being a holding cell, it's surprisingly warm. Not warm enough to sleep without a blanket, but not as cold as I would have thought. As I try to relax, my mind moves a mile a minute, trying to make sense of what happened before.

Suddenly, we were overrun with zombies, but no one made an excessive amount of noise to attract that many. There were the fires, though, which were certainly arson. That must have been enough to draw them to us.

Someone started the fire and then intentionally opened some of the doors to our group's rooms. They didn't have time to finish the job before we realized what was happening. Who would do something so sick like that?

Dillon? I shudder at that thought. He wasn't anywhere to be seen when I think about it. He also had that other man with him who could've helped. He never spoke with anyone and stuck to Dillon like glue. The man with him wasn't someone I recognized, but Dillon obviously kept him close. What would have been the purpose of his action, though? Would he have killed some of our group but ultimately got me to flee with him? Or did his plan fall through altogether?

I should be relieved that Dillon isn't still with us, but for some reason, not knowing *where* he is only worries me. He made it sound like he had a plan, but then only to leave? It doesn't sit right with me.

Soft footsteps approach the grated door. The sound of poorly greased metal drags against the brackets. Ren steps inside and closes the gate. He walks over and sits against the wall between the beds. He focuses on Hana, who has shockingly fallen asleep.

Damn, nothing phases her, does it? Thinking about it, nothing phases all three of them. Yesterday, I got the impression that was probably the first time Ren felt the way he did. Like he was at the complete mercy of our situation. Not in control. Not being able to *protect...* Or at least, it may have been the first time he acknowledged it out loud.

And he admitted a little to you. What does that mean?

As if my thoughts conjure his attention, he studies me curiously before gesturing to the lit flashlight on the floor.

"You can turn it off. I wanted there to be light before you got back," I whisper, sinking lower into my blanket. I wish I grabbed my jacket from the car; I could have used it as a pillow.

He says nothing as he reaches for the light and switches it off. We sit there in utter darkness, the silence deafening. From here, we can't hear the zombies from outside; everyone is quiet nearby. The lack of sound itself feels overbearingly loud. It also makes me wonder when we'll talk about what happened tonight.

The rustle of fabric piques my attention before a warm sweatshirt is being pushed near my head. Shifting up slightly, I squint into the darkness. I can barely make out the shadowed shape of Ren as he adjusts his hoodie on the bed.

"What are you doing?" I whisper, wincing at how noisy my voice sounds against the silence.

"You're going to wake up with a stiff and sore neck if you lay like that." His whisper is somehow not as harsh to my ears as my own.

He's giving me his sweatshirt to sleep on. Won't he get cold? Before I can bring that up, he beats me to it.

"I'll be fine without it. I'm used to sleeping in less favorable places. Get some rest."

My eyes, straining to adjust to the absence of light, can make him out marginally better but still can't fully grasp his face. The sound of shuffling follows as he sits back against the wall, head against the cold surface.

"Was anyone going to work on the generator?" Repositioning my left arm under his jacket, my head sinks into its softness. Inhaling, the smell has me burrowing my face in its warmth. The first thought that comes to mind is a forest in the middle of winter. It's a crisp, earthy smell. I can't help but take in a deeper breath.

Momentarily distracted, his voice brings my attention back to him, thankful he can't see the embarrassed look that must have crossed my face.

"Yeah, Juan will take a look. He's the one who should be able to fix it if anyone here can. When he wasn't working with me, he was underneath a car or a bike. This shouldn't be much of a challenge." He pauses while bringing one knee up to rest his arm. "I'm more surprised it wasn't working. You would think they would've had things ready to go since they're in the emergency business," he says, something in his tone that I can't quite place. Almost derision.

We both fall silent. I'm unsure what to say. He's been more talkative with me, but I decide not to force a conversation. Instead, I close my eyes and continue to breathe in his unique scent. Curiosity has me wondering if it's a soap he uses to get this woodsy smell or if it's a cologne.

Although warm and comfortable, sleep doesn't claim me. The reminder that we lost someone today—many people—rears its head. Opening my eyes, my gaze immediately lands on Ren, sitting so close.

Close enough that if I just reach…

My hand finds his. It's as if it has a mind of its own.

Startled, his gaze whips to our hands before shifting to me. I can barely make out his wrinkled brows in the darkness, but I can't make out much more of his expression.

Clearing my throat, I whisper, "I am so sorry about your friend." I squeeze his hand, but he pulls away. A pang of embarrassment hits me, but before I have time to pull my hand back, he entwines our fingers and puts his hand back on his knee. He leans forward before resting his forehead against them. His eyelashes tickle the back of my hand as his breath hitches. We stay there, suspended in time, as he takes deep breaths.

My eyes mist over at the obvious pain overwhelming him. He doesn't sob, but the way he squeezes my hand and the occasional hitch in his breath tells me he's not okay.

Not sure what I'm doing, I slide off the bed to sit next to him. Our hands fall to my lap while I scoot as close to him as possible and lean my head on his shoulder. He rests his on mine while my other hand covers our entwined ones.

A tear tracks down my cheek as we sit there, lost in grief. For him, it's the loss of those he cared about. My grief is for him and the realization that maybe we won't ever get what we had back. How could we? By the time we get the chance, all that we ever were or cared for will be gone. Stolen by the death and decay racing to consume us. It hurts to know I may never see my best friend again, and even worse, knowing our futures aren't guaranteed.

My heart hurts for the man sitting next to me, but it also swells in the knowledge that I can at least sit here with him like this. To hopefully offer some form of comfort.

I'm not sure how long we sit like this. Hands entwined and leaning on each other while the world falls apart around us.

I think he's starting to pull away, but instead, he surprises me. Warmth spreads throughout my body as he gently kisses the top of my head.

"You should get some sleep," he whispers into my hair, letting go of my hand. He pulls away and rests his head against the wall, looking up into the darkness.

With bleary eyes, I climb back into the bed and tuck my hand under the sweatshirt.

I close my eyes and try to fight back the feeling of hopelessness. I bury my face into the warm fabric and allow the winter forest scent to bring me solace.

As sleep finally pulls its comforting cloak around me, there's the softest whisper that I almost miss before falling asleep.

Thanks, angel.

A bright light flashes under my eyelids, causing me to audibly groan as I pull the blanket over my face. Ugh, who turned the lights on? It can't be time to wake up yet.

A soft chuckle has me pulling the blanket down to stare daggers at whoever woke me up.

"If it's not even noon yet, I don't want to be—" I cut myself off when I remember that I am not in my own bed, and in fact, inside a jail cell with my apocalypse companions.

The chuckle grows to a full-blown laugh when Ren meets my glare. Embarrassed, I pull the blanket back over my face to hide my now-flaming cheeks. Usually, my brain goes blank and can't find topics to talk about with most people, but with Ren, somehow, I'm able to forget all of that. It's like I'm not myself.

No, that's not right. It *is* me being myself. As Meg or my dad would've seen me. What makes it more embarrassing is that he finds it all amusing. His laugh gets closer as he pulls the blanket back over my face. The most beautiful smile I think I've ever seen greets me as he crouches next to the bed.

"Morning, sunshine." He chuckles again. "I feel bad waking you. It's only been a few hours, but we want everyone to be awake and ready. You think you're up to searching, or do you want to stay with the others?" He motions to Rei, Hana, and Ru, sitting on the bed across from us. Hana looks as annoyed to be awake as I was, and Ru is falling asleep sitting up. Rei sits there with an amused smirk as he takes in the whole scene.

Knowing they're also in the room spikes my embarrassment further.

Thinking about it, I don't know what I want to do. A part of me wants to be lazy, stay here in my safe little bubble, but another part wants to try to be useful to the others. Last night, I proved something to myself. I was able to help, which has made me want to keep trying to be a better addition to our ragtag team. To prove to *Ren* that I can be a vital part of our group. Resigning to my desire to be of use, I say, "Yeah, I can help."

It'll be good to help them. Plus, maybe I can try to look more into that zombie from yesterday.

Sighing, I sit up and take in the room around me in the light, ready to start getting myself ready for my next task. Wait...

Light!

"They got the generator working?" I ask although the answer is clear based on the illuminated lights above us.

"They did. It's also light out, so where there are windows, it will be brighter. They're going to turn the generator off soon, though. We only have so much fuel for it," he says, continuing to reward us with his smile. He's expressing a part of himself that I don't think I would have ever thought existed.

After our moment last night, where he allowed his pain to be visible, and now seeing him like this, it has me suspecting that his normal, brooding appearance is a mask, one to hide the real hurt he must be feeling underneath.

Even after last night, I can't imagine how he's feeling after losing not only James but also Sayuri.

I hadn't known her for long, but even I could tell that Sayuri was a beautiful soul. James seemed like a really nice guy. He was funny, but unfortunately, I didn't have the pleasure of getting to know him other than a few interactions.

Ren is about to say something when a voice in the hall draws him to close himself off again, donning the mask that I have grown used to. Steeling his expression, he focuses on Dirk and Matt, waiting there in the hall for him to join them. "Grab your shotgun and crowbar if you want to help, Dahlia. Wear your backpack." He gestures to the shotgun, leaning against the wall next to the bed. He must have placed it there at some point since he had it last. I want to ask him if he'd let me use his pistol again, but I just stay quiet. I should just get used to using the bayonet.

I grab my things before following them out the hallway towards the garage area we started in.

As we pass the first rooms in the hall and the more enclosed cells, I push to peek inside one that has its door partially open before stopping short. I am unable to help but gasp when I find Juan searching the pockets on a body. When my eyes look past him, the other bodies come into view. All are covered to some degree with a sheet or piece of clothing—more than a few with crimson soaking into the fabric by their heads. There must be at least ten people who died here, and most of them looked to have been human... not all zombies.

"Did you guys find them like this?" I ask, slightly exacerbated. My eyes fly to Ren, whose face almost looks strained for a split second.

No one says anything for a moment, awkwardly shuffling before Ren finally speaks up. "No. We didn't." His hand rakes through his hair, eyes flicking past me into the room before meeting mine again.

"A few of them were already zombies. Most of them were on the verge of death from dehydration, and a few were already dead for the same reason," he says before walking down the hall as if nothing about this is wrong.

I spin around, taking in Juan, who now doesn't bother to cover his expression: sadness and resignation. "There was nothing we could've done for them, *chula*," he whispers, glancing down at the body he was searching. I recognize the uniform. It was an officer.

"They had all been locked up for who knows how long without water…" He pauses, clearing his throat. "It looked like someone was alive long enough to give them some before they ran out or were attacked. After that, it was a matter of time before their organs would've started to fail. Even giving them water, the little we have now, may not have saved their lives. Even if it did, they wouldn't have been able to recover from the damage with no medical intervention." He gestures to the bodies behind him and then looks up at me.

"I'm searching the ones who worked here. They were the ones already turned. Hoping to find keys or anything that can help us."

My feet are rooted in place as I try to reel in this new information. I can comprehend the words alone, and maybe I do understand what he means. Realistically, they were already dead, but to know that they killed these other people, *living* people. That Ren turned away as if it didn't mean anything. As if their lives were meaningless.

I hope that's not true. A part of me wants there to be another reason, and maybe someday I can gain the courage to ask. Instead, I speak up to Juan. "I know we need the supplies. I'm not stupid enough to pass up anything that can keep us alive, but this." I wave at the dead. "It feels so disrespectful. Please. Just…" I trail off and look down at my wringing hands.

"You know… Never mind."

I want to say to leave them be, but he's right. Finding keys could lead us to ammo or several other things we need. I hate that this is what we've come to. I don't even think I'm upset at them for this, not really. I'm only upset at the fact that this is our life now. A kill-or-be-killed world where we're forced to disrespect the dead in hopes of finding one small piece of something, anything that could keep us alive.

I turn and walk away, following the direction Ren had gone.

Not able to grasp the churning emotions spiraling within me right now, I try my best to ignore the knot lodged inside my throat. For some reason, I'm conflicted with the image I have of Ren. I'm trying to grasp the contrast between the man who fought his pain as openly as he did last night and the man who killed those people. Was it easy for him, or was that another reason he was in pain yesterday?

The more I think about it, the more I realize I don't blame him. There was not much they could've done, and that only adds to the misery of our situation. It only confirms what I'd been thinking.

I should have been angrier that we didn't do anything to save their lives instead of taking them. They were human beings—people who may have had a chance. We had Hana. She may have been able to do something, but there is this part of me that is trying to only focus on our small group. To focus on survival. The selfish part of me recognizes that only we can matter if we want to live.

But do we really?

I hate that we were thrown into this situation where we must fight so hard to survive that we almost forget what it means to be generous or kind and want to help others. Yes, we have very limited water and food, but would it have been bad to try? What is the point of surviving if we ignore our slowly slipping humanity?

And what does it say about me that in all my chaotic cluster fuck of thoughts, the only anger that rises isn't at my companions who did what I probably couldn't. I'm not even angry because we need to be disrespectful to the dead.

No, the real anger that rises is simple. The only thing I'm truly angry about is the fact that I'm *not* angry over the death. Or the fact that we didn't try to save them instead of ending them.

There's only relief that it wasn't *us*.

What does that say about me now?

I catch up with Ren, walking back out where our cars are parked beneath the small sliver of sun from the high, slim windows. In the light, the room is narrower than I thought last night. My thoughts stray far from the constructs of my moral compass to the zombie that somehow slipped past us.

Walking around Ren, I go to where I believe the zombie crawled from. The room isn't bright by any means, but with the artificial dim lights on the ceiling and the small amount of sunlight, I can see there aren't many places to hide. Last night, it seemed like the guys checked under everything someone could squeeze through.

I almost miss the spot until I pitch forward. I catch myself with my hands on the concrete. Somehow, I manage not to drop my weapons. Mumbling curses, I lift myself to my knees and brush my hands off my pants, noting the small streak of blood on the front of my fingers as I bring my hands up to investigate. I tentatively rub the minor scrapes. Why am I an injury magnet suddenly?

"Are you alright?" Ren hesitantly asks from behind me. His expression looks almost nervous as if expecting my hair to morph into serpents that will turn him into stone. As if he's slightly afraid.

What the hell could he be afraid of? I'm not the one who killed *people*.

Maybe that isn't fair. The zombies were all people once. I've managed to kill a few now. It isn't fair to him to lash out when I'm only mad at myself and this fucked up situation.

"I'm fine. Nothing but embarrassment here." I can't help the small smile, half laughing at myself for being a klutz in this moment, which isn't normally like me. Scratch that, maybe I've turned into one recently with all the injuries I've acquired. At my smile, I swear that his shoulders relax a little. "I tripped over something."

My gaze tracks my previous movements, now realizing there was a pile of packs blocking a row of lockers. The base of the lockers had been blocked by the packs, most likely blending in with the darkness last night. Easily missed. "The zombie must have hidden behind those packs, partially inside the cabinet." My brows crease as I continue to study the scene.

It *hid.*

"The zombie hid from us. Was it in here already, or did it sneak past us before the gate was closed?" I ask into the unnerving silence while Ren inspects the spot and the others walk over.

We've already seen a few zombies act in a sneaky way, but this is different. It wasn't instinctual but calculating and intentional in a way we haven't come across with them until now. Nobody says anything while staring dumbfounded at the cabinet as if it grew legs and spoke. "The ones we have seen so far that waited to attack, none were actually hidden, were they?" I ask quietly, unable to rip my eyes away from where it hid. No...

Stalked.

"You two are the only ones who have seen them so far." Reiji's eyes drift off, most likely trying to recall everything we have seen so far. "We have only dealt with the typical ones and the loud ones."

Sighing, Ren stands from his crouched position after having gone through the packs. Finding nothing of interest, he walks over to the cars. "The one that attacked me seemed to just stand there. I didn't notice it until it was on me, but I don't believe it hid. It was dark, so it was easy for it not to be noticed," he recalls, opening the trunk of my car.

I think back to the other one. The one at the auto shop. It wasn't hidden either, now that I think about it. It was out of sight and took the right opportunity, instead of jumping out at the sound. "The other one didn't hide either. It just didn't react to the sound immediately."

Fuck... It's like we are screwed regardless of what we do. These things are becoming more dangerous, and we are barely managing as is. What are we going to do if these things can hide from us now? It's as if we are no longer on the top of the food chain but mice in a house of cats. That thought has my anxiety clutching me tightly, making it feel as if my throat is constricting. With my heart rate increasing, an impending doom feeling seeps beneath my skin and into my bones. It's so strong, it's almost a physical sensation. I shift my crowbar under my arm and rub my chest, trying to rid the sudden tightness. *Just take a breath. You're alive. It's okay.*

I managed to avoid a full-blown anxiety attack last night, so why the hell am I on the verge of one now? Everything is going to be okay. Or at least... I hope it will be.

"Maybe it was stuck and only reacted when it got free," Hana says halfheartedly, not believing in her own words.

"I don't think so." I keep rubbing my chest but focus on those in front of me. "It didn't attack; it waited for a while and then hid under the car. Almost like it was trying to figure out the best way of catching someone by surprise. It didn't even react right away when I shouted." I shift my attention to the gun I'm clutching tightly in my hand, which feels like a heavy stone in my palm.

What the hell are we going to do now? These things must be able to see in the dark or have good enough senses because it knew where to go and where to attack.

No, don't think about it right now. Just breathe, Dahl. It's going to be okay.

Ren pulls one of the bats out of the car, and hands it to Hana. "No one goes without a weapon from now on. You sleep with it. You bathe with it. You eat with it. You never go anywhere without it on your person." His eyes land on Ru, hesitating a moment before grabbing another bat and handing it to him. His expression flickers for a moment, the pain plain to see.

This couldn't be easy for him, but what can he do? Even Ru needs to be able to defend himself. Ru's eyes widen as he reaches a shaky, small hand to grab the bat, looking larger next to his small frame.

"Just be careful with that. Please." Rei comes up behind him, also wearing a grim expression, and places his hand on his son's shoulder. It's incredibly sharp. We will all do our best so you don't ever have to use it, but we can start practicing," he tells him quietly, but we can all hear the strain in his voice.

My heart aches as they discuss the possibility of him having to do what needs to be done to survive. Although Reiji seems to be taking it hard, Ru appears to be handling it well. At first, he seemed nervous, but now he's paying attention to what his father is saying. A look of focus and determination colors his face.

I'm not only awed but also not surprised at this point. The kid has unfortunately been in the thick of things from the beginning and has already needed to take some situations into his own hands. It's sad that he needs to be resilient, but I'm also glad he's taking it seriously. It could be the thing that keeps him alive.

Momentarily distracted from their conversation, Ren gently taps my arm to get my attention.

He clears his throat. "I found this, but it's too small for me." He lifts his other hand, revealing a simple black belt with a small holster attached. Inside the holster was the pistol he lent me. "I noticed that maybe the shotgun isn't the best weapon for you…" He pauses, rubbing the back of his neck. "Well, at least all the time. The bayonet makes it a good one to have, but until we can find a strap for it, you should carry this."

Stunned, I don't move to grab it. He wouldn't have picked that belt up, knowing it didn't fit him. No. He had to have been thinking of someone specifically. *Me.*

Before I can stop myself, I allow my doubts to spew and ramble out. "Wouldn't it be good for Hana to have a gun? She only has a bat and maybe a knife. Also, when did you find that?"

He raises his brow, and then I remember where we are.

Putting my hands up as if to ward him away, I shake my head. "You know, never mind."

Hana should still have it. I also don't know how I feel about taking other supplies off the unfortunate people who didn't survive, but before I can turn around, Ren reaches towards me.

"What the hell are you—" I stop short when his arms wrap around me, strapping the holster on my waist.

"She doesn't need it. Either way…" His hands linger on my waist, sliding down to my hips, but he doesn't pull away. "It fits you."

My pulse quickens at the contact, and my mind floods with images of his lips caressing mine as he gripped my hips to pull me closer. The hunger was evident in the way he possessed me in those brief moments. But then my mind flashes to last night. Such a simple moment, yet it felt almost more intimate than the kiss.

His perusal stops on where his hands now rest before he pulls away reluctantly.

"Uhm... thanks." I give him a small, flushed smile.

"You're welcome..." He hesitates, as if he wants to say something else, but instead, he goes back to where his friends are gathered.

My gaze follows him while he walks away. I adjust the belt over my hips before pulling the gun out. I didn't pay much attention to it before, but with a closer look, I think it's a Smith and Wesson. I'm not an expert, so I can't determine which model, but it has an intense grip on it.

I can't stop the butterfly feeling in my stomach at the thoughtful gift. Because that's exactly what it is—he thought about me. It's stupid, but during the zombie apocalypse, that's basically giving me roses.

"You know what I would kill for?" Hana says behind me, her dark hair pulled up into a messy bun on the top of her head. She's sporting ashy gray jogger pants and a T-shirt. She has the bat, but now I'm wondering if she's had another weapon this whole time. I know Ren has two different handguns as well as a few rifles. Rei also has a small arsenal in his car, which I noticed once. If she was used to being around them, maybe she has something concealed, too.

"Caffeine. I want a damn latte." She groans as she wraps her arm around my shoulder in a half hug and a half 'I'm too tired to stand on my own' way.

I can't help the chuckle that breaks free at her nonchalance. It's nice to meet someone else who hates being awake in the early morning. Hell, in the daytime. I wrap my arm around her and walk us over to a small window that looks out towards the gated yard where patrol cars are parked. "You know, Hana, you are beginning to be my favorite person. I would kill for some damn espresso over ice. No cream or sugar, only delicious, tantalizing espresso,' I respond as I pull away to look out the window.

"As much as I'm enlightened to hear I'm your favorite person, I'm not foolish enough to believe you. Second, maybe, or even third. I don't know, Haru is probably cutting in close for second, but I know your first." She wags her brows at me.

"Anyways," I say, dragging out the vowels, fully intending to ignore her comment. "You know, I think there was a coffee shop around the corner. Maybe we can loot it. Find some bags of unopened coffee and make some DIY coffee bags using the filters. My dad and I would do that for camping trips."

"Oh! Maybe they have those packs of instant coffee. They aren't the best, but dang, I would kill for even one of those at this point. It's been days without caffeine." She huffs as she tries to peek out the window with me. The window is tiny, but we can make out the few abandoned patrol cars and a few shuffling zombies in the yard. From the lack of sounds, I assume the horde moved on from our lot. Hopefully. Maybe that at least means their attention spans aren't the best. Better for us if that is the case.

I ask Hana, "Were we planning on leaving today then if the zombies left, or were they planning something else?"

She keeps her gaze out the window—looking for what, I can't say. There wasn't much of a view from here. She stays silent, and I almost believe she didn't hear me when she finally speaks.

"I think they wanted to get into the upstairs building." Her scrunched brows give her away. She doesn't want to linger, either. We all need supplies, but the more we scavenge, the more likely someone gets hurt, or we all die from the zombies in hiding.

I place my hand on her shoulder and squeeze in a show of support. She usually seems unfazed by most things, even from the more violent comments or actions her family makes. It causes me to wonder what she was used to before all this, but the longer we are out here, the more I recognize the stress weighing on her shoulders.

"They will be fine. There might not even be many zombies inside. There were no cars in here, and the lot seems almost empty," I say, gesturing to the small window. "Everyone will be okay."

Her brows rise, giving me a dubious look. "You need to work on your pep talks, Dahl." She chuckles, then sighs.

"Well, while they go on an adventure up into the unknown, we should try and come up with a list of things to look for in the coffee shop. I also want to check on your numerous injuries, Miss Sally, and see how you're faring."

She gives me a large smile before she makes her way to the car, searching for paper and pens to write with. I thought we were just wishful thinking, but the more I genuinely think about it, looting a coffee shop sounds like the best plan either of us could come up with.

As if reading my mind, she says, "It'll be a good idea, and we'll get the good stuff. No decaf. Decaf leads to death. Caffeine is the key to staying alive in the apocalypse." Her voice is laced with humor.

Giving Hana my own wide, manic smile, I joke, "Agreed. Decaf equals death."

CHAPTER THIRTY-FIVE

Dahlia

As for bad ideas, this one takes the cake. This isn't even just bad, it's catastrophic. I had mostly been joking earlier or thinking we could do this later with everyone, else, but Hana has other plans.

Poor Don has his hands full with his kid, the other two poor children who have not stopped crying since waking, and his now hysterical girlfriend. The longer the guys are upstairs, the more she's panicking. We haven't heard any screams or anything that might suggest they're in trouble but the longer they're away searching the main building, the more worried everyone is becoming.

Hana pulled me aside and suggested this brilliant—and by brilliant, I mean stupid—plan. So here we are, having asked Don if he could watch Ru because we need to "use the bathroom" in private and that he should keep Ru literally locked up. Hana has recruited our newest group members, Davis and Jenson. Susan is staying and assisting Jen with the kids. She's been pretty distraught herself since losing her boyfriend back at the motel. Poor Don is so overwhelmed that he doesn't notice us slip outside.

"Hana, I don't want to question you, but this is the part in any horror movie where people call you too stupid to live, and then the murderer pops out of nowhere and kills you. The only things missing are ill-timed sex and suspenseful music," I whisper as Jenson closes the garage door and secures it.

I can't help but find this incredibly reckless, and rightfully so. Not only are we leaving without knowing if the guys are safe, but we're leaving her nephew with someone other than family, and I've gotten the impression that never happens. *Ever.*

Every cell in my body is urging me to go back and stay with the kid before Ren and Rei lose their ever-loving shit. I wouldn't even blame them.

Also… another tiny part of me is afraid of tarnishing the fragile connection that's been growing between Ren and me.

I wouldn't have agreed if I didn't feel certain Ru was safe where he is. They have water and some food, weapons, and are secured inside. When the guys went upstairs, we barricaded the door again, waiting for them to knock and have us let them back in. Ru is safe for now, but I can't help but worry that if something happens to his dad and uncle and then us, he would be alone.

"I always found it was more anticlimactic or lackluster than ill-timed in those movies," she whispers with a teasing smile.

My response is a deadpan stare.

"Oh, we'll be fine; we have these guys. They know what they're doing, and so do we. I'm losing my mind waiting around for them. I'm *always* waiting around for them to come back, and I'm more than a little tired of it." She throws her hands up. "I know it's risky, but I can't sit there any longer. I can handle myself. We both can. The coffee shop is only a few buildings down, and, so far, the streets are clear. We can do this if we're quiet."

I don't know what to say to that. A part of me believes that maybe she genuinely has no idea what we face since she was at Ren's house through most of this, but then again, we've been traveling for a while now. She saw the horde. She saw people die. So, I can't determine where this reckless behavior is stemming from. In my short time with the family, I've grown closer with Hana, but this wasn't something I was expecting in the least.

The four of us are partially crouched as we run across the now-empty lot. In the time we've been waiting, Hana has been staring out the window, watching all the zombies until they finally all wandered off. Something must have pulled their attention, although I'm not sure what. That's when she decided we should do something incredibly foolish.

Davis and Jenson were surprisingly up for the adventure. They've been keeping to themselves but helping with anything that needed extra hands. They wanted to help clear the building, but Rei wanted at least one experienced gunman to stay with us. Although I don't think this is what he had in mind, I try to shake my uncertainty as we approach the gate that separates the lot from the street.

From our little window inside, I couldn't see the coffee shop, but from outside, it's visible and a lot closer than I thought. Just as Hana said, it's across the street and a few buildings over.

Scoping out our surroundings, none of us find any zombies nearby, and we make our way across the road, avoiding debris and walking around an abandoned car that's partly on the curb. We all keep to a single file line with Davis in the front, me, Hana, and then Jenson in the back. Both the guys look alert, almost excited to be doing something other than sitting and waiting.

As we finally reach the other side of the street, I take a moment to check out the police department. From here, it looks unscathed, all the visible entrances closed. Hopefully, that is a good thing. I can't say the same for the building directly next to it. A car found its way into the front door.

My attention quickly gets redirected back to our small group, continuing down the sidewalk. I jog to catch up, repositioning myself in front of Hana.

Her brows scrunch in question, but she doesn't say anything. We all agreed to stay silent for fear of attracting attention.

It takes a few minutes, but we finally reach the coffee shop. We stand at the entrance for a moment, taking in the bizarre sight. The glass doors are intact, but the outside tables and chairs are all thrown around and toppled over. Inside, it looks the same. There are figures inside that lay unmoving.

Davis, on silent feet, opens the door slowly and motions us to follow. We all have our weapons ready as we go inside. The gun Ren gave me is holstered, but I've decided to use my bayonet as my primary weapon.

The crunch of glass forces my focus back to my surroundings, and before I can question my moves, I spin while raising my arms. Davis jumps back, hands flying up. I stop short before killing him accidentally. "What the hell, Davis? You can't sneak up on people!" I whisper harshly.

What the fuck. He takes a second to right himself, giving me a guilty smile that looks more like a grimace.

"Sorry. I was goin' to tell ya to let us take point," he whispers back.

Not responding, I motion him forward.

We each have our backpacks. We agreed that if we find anything large to take, we can leave it by the entrance, and one of the guys can carry it back, or we can even try to pick it up before we leave the station altogether.

Standing in the middle of the cafe, nothing but sorrow washes over me. How many of us used to go and grab coffee on a regular basis? The room looks like all the other coffee shops I've been to. I'm more than half expecting the aroma of roasted coffee beans to assault my nose any minute now.

Except it doesn't.

Instead, I'm greeted with what feels like an alternate dimension. Stanchions are tipped over but still in place to indicate where the line would have begun. The cooler is still surprisingly full, but the food in the glass barely resembles the delicious and overpriced food it once was. Everything is moldy and discolored.

My gaze falls back to the full cooler. Water bottles, juices, and other snacks and drinks are displayed. Some are expired, but the water and juice should be fine to take. There are even those kids pouches in a basket near the cooler. Although my first instinct is to start looting the place, we need to clear the building. Davis and Jenson are already behind the counter, walking towards the back room. I turn my attention back towards the only other door inside, the single bathroom.

Gesturing to Hana, I point at the door before making my way over. No matter how often we have encountered zombies, my fight or flight still kicks in. Mainly wanting to flee, I shove that urge back and push forward.

Before I can talk myself out of this, I lightly tap on the door, listening for any movement inside. Hana positions herself beside me, raising a small gun in her left hand, her bat in her right thrown over her shoulder.

The sight throws me off slightly. This woman who's always trying to be the half-glass-full, happy-go-lucky, and talk-your-socks-off woman is standing here looking a little scary. She's calm and collected, showing no fear as she waits for me to open the door.

Is this the real Hana? The one who only shows herself to those closest to her? I can't help but admire her even more as she stands here so bravely while

I stand here on shaking knees. It also makes me more than a little curious about who this family *really* is.

I raise my shotgun with one hand while I turn the handle.

The door creeks as I push it partly open.

A zombie lunges forward from the side.

My reaction is quick, but not quick enough. The blade of the bayonet slides into its stomach just below its name tag, which hangs off her green apron by a literal thread.

As it falls forward, I slip back, landing on my ass. I ignore the pain lancing up my back. All I can do is hold the shotgun up with the added weight. I bring my booted foot up to kick it off the blade.

It barely budges, but it's enough to dislodge the bayonet. I bring the weapon up higher just as it lunges. Its face meets the blade, slicing upward through its snapping mouth. With its weight and momentum, it sinks to the hilt, but it stills instantly. Inky blood drips down the barrel of the gun as its arms hang over me.

The poor girl looked to be my age or a little younger before she turned. She must have tried to hide inside the bathroom after everything hit the fan.

After ensuring I'm not injured, Hana walks past me slowly into the dark bathroom. The only light is coming from behind us. As my blade pulls out of the zombie with a sickening *plop*, a grunt has my head jerking up. Hana's bat is clattering on the floor as another zombie pushes her up against a wall.

"Shit." My feet move before my brain processes what's happening, but as I reach Hana, the thing is already collapsing to the floor, a small metal nail file sticking out of its eye.

Holy shit.

Dumbfounded, my stare lingers on the zombie. A soft chuckle pulls my attention. Hana crouches down to pick the bat up and then grabs for her nail file. She wipes it off on the zombie's shirt and pockets it. I stare at her with wide eyes. *Who the hell are these people?*

Had I thought a Barbie before? Nope. Not even close. She's a goddamn Apocalyptic Femme Fatale... and honestly, I'm so glad I'm her friend and not her enemy.

"I won't lie and say I haven't been waiting to try that." She softly laughs again before taking in the rest of the small bathroom before walking out.

She leaves me standing there in shock. It takes me a moment to shake off my surprise before I take a closer look around.

The bathroom has one toilet, sink, cabinet, and trash can. That's it. Were both these people hiding in here, but one of them was bitten? Or were they both bitten before hiding? It doesn't matter, I suppose, but what's bothering me now is that both didn't attack at the same time. What the hell is going on with these things?

Shaking off the thought, I walk back into the main room, where Davis and Jenson are waiting.

"All clear back there, y'all alright. Not bit?" Davis looks us over as we let them know that we're fine. "Good. Let's try and be quick. I'll help loot the back with Hana. Jenson, help Dahl clear up here," Davis says before walking back to the storage area with Hana on his tail. We all stay quiet, still afraid of any surprise customers.

I first direct my attention to the coolers, grabbing anything edible. The children's pouches don't need to be refrigerated, so I grab those, as well as the water. I double-check the juices to see if they need refrigeration before packing a few. Turning, I make my way behind the counter. I go through all the dried and baked goods to see what's still in date.

My backpack won't zip now because of all the bulky bottles, but I try my best to close it enough so nothing falls out.

Finishing up, Jenson finds me. "I didn't find a lot, but I did find a few unopened boxes of the instant coffee they sell. I also grabbed a few bags of coffee," he whispers, showing me the packages.

My heart picks up in excitement as I whisper, "We should grab some coffee filters if they have any here. Make coffee bags with them."

He responds with a dip of his chin before he walks back towards the entrance and looks out before returning.

What's up with men and silent gestures? For fuck's sake, it's almost as bad as a single-word text. Basically an anxious person's Achille's heel.

"Still clear outside, but I'm uncomfortable bein' here too long. We're too exposed. I'm goin' to keep an eye out for now if you want to find some filters and tell the others to quicken things up." He walks back towards the entrance, and I follow his direction in full agreement. I may have joked around, but I don't want to die over my caffeine craving.

Stepping over to the back room, I quicken my pace. It doesn't take me long to find a box with filters. I run back towards the cash register in the front and grab a bag to pack some as well as maybe a few other small finds. Back from the storage room, both Hana and David are carrying boxes. Hana has one box, whereas Davis has two.

"You can't be serious. We can't carry that, and honestly, I doubt we'll be able to come back for it," I say a little louder so they can hear me.

Hana only shrugs and walks past me, placing the boxes down by Jenson. Davis follows and drops the others. "If it's clear, we can try to walk it back and drop it if we need to run." He picks the boxes up again and looks outside.

The boxes look slightly heavy and awkward in size. Truthfully, I don't think it's a good idea to debilitate ourselves while being out in the open carrying something so bulky, but I also can't help but be tempted either. We do *need* supplies.

Sighing, I say, "Fine. Jenson, are we good to head back?"

He takes a while to respond, taking his time searching the street before answering with a thumbs-up gesture. "We'll be good, but we need to move fast."

We start walking back—Davis and Hana are in the middle this time, me at the back, and Jenson in the front. We both have our guns ready, keeping a lookout while the others carry the boxes. The added weight in all our packs is slowing us down a little.

Glass crunches, shattering the silence

We all stop in our tracks. "Shit," Hana mumbles softly. She slowly steps out of the glass pile before stopping.

We don't move, straining to listen for any zombies. Our eyes wildly search our surroundings, but when we don't hear anything, we keep going.

Although we're taking it slower, we're making good time nearing the fenced lot of the station. As the others pick up their pace, ready for the relative safety the station provides, a noise draws my attention behind me.

I stop and turn, but nothing jumps out at me. There's nothing obvious to have created the noise. My heart is pounding loudly in my ears as I glance around.

You're just hearing things. That's all.

Swallowing a suddenly dry throat, I slowly turn back and try to catch up with the others.

They are already on the other side of the road, almost inside the lot, while I walk by the abandoned car we passed earlier.

Fuck, how long did I stand there staring at nothing? "Don't let your nerves get the best of you, Dahlia," I whisper, picking up my pace to a slow jog.

Two steps forward and another rustling noise, like something scrapping against the gravel, make me whip around.

Oh shit.

The smaller zombie is getting to its feet before sprinting towards me.

The squealing shriek it makes has my heart nearly stopping.

It's not far, almost an arm's distance away, before I know what's happening.

My panic rises. It's too fast. Too close.

I fire the shotgun without thinking. I don't even have time to process how old they must have been when they turned.

As soon as I pull the trigger, I curse myself.

The shot hits true. The zombie jolts back forcefully with the blow, but as soon as I turn to run, multiple screeches announce our newest visitors.

All close.

Blocking my path are two zombies sprinting straight at me. Screeches pierce the air, all coming from down the road and from inside the other buildings.

"Oh my god." I search frantically for a clear path before I run back towards the car.

Without thinking about how stupid and possibly pointless it is, I jump up on the hood. It's a struggle to get onto the roof of the midsize car, with the backpack's weight hindering me, but I manage—barely.

Once on top, I reload and begin firing at the closest zombie, praying I have enough shells. In all the chaos, I almost forget the holstered weapon at my hip. I hope I have enough rounds, but as more zombies come into view, it seems hopeless.

My first shot takes out the head of one, but before I can shoot the next one in front, a loud bang jolts the car. As I whip my head around, my arms flail out to regain my balance.

Another is reaching for me now. Almost close enough to grab my feet. The car itself isn't large but gives me a hair's width of space from the hands around me. I try to shuffle forward before firing at it.

In the background of my rising panic, I can make out the sounds of more gunfire. I don't risk taking my eyes off the zombies. I'm too afraid of the closest hands within arm's reach, some managing to touch me now. I keep firing. Until— "Shit."

Until I run out of shells.

Cursing, I pull out the pistol.

With a shaky exhale, I pull the trigger.

"No," I cry. The shot barely clips the zombie's ear. *Breathe. Just breathe.*

I take another shot. My eyes well with tears and I grit my teeth.

My anxiety won't relent as I miss again. It's almost debilitating. *Come on. Come on. Come on,* I tell myself in rapid succession. I pull the trigger.

Yes! The zombie falls. *Finally.* I turn to the next one. Tightness in my chest only claws at me harder. It's painful now.

"Dahlia!" Someone yells at me, but I don't spare a glance. Instead, I focus on my target and pull the trigger.

Hands grab at my feet. None are tall enough to reach high enough, but knowing how screwed I am regardless doesn't allow that fact to be comforting.

"Dahlia!" The voice is closer now, and more gunfire finally draws my head up.

My breath catches at the sight of Ren, Matt, and Juan all getting closer. They all appear calm as they fire their rifles and fight the growing number of dead with eerie precision.

There are no other sprinting zombies on the road near them. Instead, they're all surrounding my perch, and the others in the street are still far enough away to not be a threat. *Yet.*

Ren's focus is entirely on me, not on the side of the street. He shoots flawlessly as they near, the others covering him and making sure no others get close. "I need you to jump down and run. Run!" he yells.

My gaze falls to the growing number surrounding the car. So many now. More spilling out from the buildings behind me. I know I need to move now before I get them killed, but how can I make it out of this alive with so many beginning to pile on top of each other?

I shoot another one directly below me, stretching its arm out towards my boot.

"Dahl." It's said quieter this time, but I hear it. Hear the desperation in his voice.

My eyes fly up to meet his. Right then, I recognize what he's trying to tell me.

To trust him. That he won't let me die.

That maybe he doesn't *want* me to die.

That he'll protect me.

I take a deep breath, release, shoot the zombie in front of me, and jump through the small gap.

I try to leap as far as I can, landing on my feet before falling forward onto one knee.

Hands grab at my feet, spurring me to act. I jump up and start running as fast as I can towards Ren, focusing solely on him.

He covers me as I run. His expression gives nothing away except his focus on the task in front of him, but as I get closer, I can make out the clenched jaw and the darkening of his eyes. There is a look of murder in his gaze—the expression of someone ready to burn this decrepit world to ash to keep us safe.

To keep me safe.

As he reloads his weapon, his muscles tighten and coil with the action. Clinging to the distraction, I allow myself to look at him; anything to keep the threat at my back from creeping into my mind like the poison that it is. My eyes are locked onto him as I take that final step. He reaches for my hand, intertwining our fingers as he runs alongside me. His grip is like iron, and he doesn't let go while he pulls me to safety.

Without Ren as my central focus, I notice a few of the others in our main group by the gate, all helping provide cover. Juan and Matt are now beside us, shooting any that get close, trusting the others to take the ones out from behind us. The way they work in complete synchronization only solidifies their history fighting together.

My instinct is to look back, but I know that would risk me falling or slowing us down, so I tighten my grip on his hand and run. Trusting them to lead me to safety. Trusting *him.*

When we finally make it to the lot, we all sprint to the garage, where Rei pulls the gate up and allows us to barrel in before he closes it. The only sounds I hear are the blood rushing to my head and the heaving breaths my lungs fight to take in. I break away from Ren's grip and clutch my chest. I wasn't in bad shape before all this, but I certainly wasn't in great shape. It doesn't help having the fear of death on your heels every other fucking day. My heart almost feels like it'll stop from the extreme exertion.

Before I can catch my breath, Ren grabs my hand again and roughly pulls me inside where the cells are. I'm jogging to keep up with his long strides before he slams open a cell door and pulls me inside.

"What the fuck was that?" he says quietly. His expression is all steel, but I notice the tick in his jaw and the fire in his eyes. I take an involuntary step back when I take him in.

If looks could kill.

"I—" I cut myself off to find my words. Not wanting to admit that he's starting to intimidate me, I try to square my shoulders and lift my chin before saying the first thing that comes to mind. "I'm sorry. I didn't mean to attract them, but my options were to shoot the zombie or get jumped. Which would you prefer?" I snap.

Not all of us have the cool and collected reflexes to kill so effortlessly, I want to say. Instead, I keep my mouth shut. I don't think he'd take that well.

He slams his palm against the bars, startling me. He doesn't even look at me as he paces back and forth. "You're sorry? You could have got all of us killed. You could have gotten Hana killed. *You* almost got *killed.*" Speaking the last word icily yet quietly, his glare meets mine, and my shoulders deflate while I step back intentionally this time.

No. He isn't intimidating. He's downright terrifying.

"Why the fuck would you go outside without telling us? Without a plan. Why the fuck would you put yourself in danger like that?" His voice rises at that last question, his chest heaving.

What can I say? I agree that it was incredibly reckless. It was either that or let Hana go alone. She was set on going regardless of me once she'd recruited the guys.

He takes a step closer, cornering me with the wall at my back. "You can't answer? You can't answer why you just put my sister and your life at risk? And for what? What was so damn important where your lives could be jeopardized like that?"

My chest tightens at the look he gives me. It's pure rage. He's allowing me to truly see him under the mask, but it's only anger. And it's directed at me.

My vision blurs with tears before they spill over onto my cheeks. Not because he's angry but because I can't help but feel disappointed in myself.

"Ren, that's enough. It wasn't her fault. It was mine. She didn't even want to go and only did because I was going to go without her regardless," Hana says firmly, causing him to partly turn and direct his attention at her.

While he's distracted, I slip around him and quickly walk out before he can continue making me feel even worse than I already do. The sad thing is he isn't wrong. I put everyone at risk, but it wasn't fair. I didn't ask for this. I could have let that zombie kill me, but was that fair either?

"Fuck. Angel— wait," he says but I continue out of the room and head towards my car. I need to calm down and collect myself. The more I think about it, the more enraged I'm becoming—numbing the fear, the disappointment, and any other feelings spiraling in the whirlwind of my mind. He clearly needs to collect himself as well. He has some issues he needs to work out, and I'm more than happy to allow Hana to point them out.

CHAPTER THIRTY-SIX

Ren

"You didn't need to be such a fucking asshole, Ren," Hana says harsher now that Dahlia has run out.

How could I blame her? The last time I felt fear like that was when I lost my parents, and even then, I had forgotten what that type of fear felt like. I thought she was going to be killed right then and there, and for what? Coffee? It triggered the hell out of me, and I can't help the swelling anger.

She didn't deserve me yelling at her, though. I was an asshole, and she most likely thought it was because I blamed her and was angry at *her*.

The reality is that I was afraid of her dying, and I'm angry that she came incredibly close to doing so. Raking my hand through my hair, I walk over to the bed and sit down while Rei walks in with Haru. He doesn't look happy either, but unlike me, his anger is directed at the right person. I'm sure he's already given the two other guys the third degree, too.

"Hana," is all he says as he directs an accusing glare in her direction.

"Look. I'm sorry. It was incredibly stupid. I get it." She raises her hands, palms out. "I was getting antsy, and I'm so tired of worrying about everyone else. I wanted to go out and be of use." Her voice is full of disdain, showing her own rising anger. "We found water and food. I'm fucking sick of you guys treating me like some delicate princess. How much more do I need to do to in my life to prove to you assholes that I'm capable? That I can be of use to you guys?" Her gaze connects with mine before she lifts her chin.

"If you're going to be angry, at least be angry with me. Not Dahlia. She only went because I insisted, and she's smarter than anyone gives her credit for. She knew I would have gone alone. She tried to tell me to wait, but I wouldn't listen. She didn't deserve that lashing, Ren."

Her breath is now heaving, matching mine from moments before. She looks as if she'd been the one running away from zombies and not Dahlia.

She's right, though. At least where Dahlia is concerned. "I'll deal with that, but that's not what this conversation is going to be about," I snap at her, unable to stop the irritation from lacing my tone.

"Ren," my brother says. "I'll talk with Hana. You go deal with your girl."

Your girl.

Mine...

Despite the rage still trying to claw its way out, something about that has my heart racing.

"Sure."

Standing, I stretch before making my way out of the cell. I need to deal with Dahlia, but I would be lying if I said I wanted to be involved in my siblings' conversation. Unfortunately, Rei and I both took Hana's word for it that she would be careful. I should have known better. She's a fucking cupcake for outside appearances, but she's also stubborn and likes to be involved with everything. Sometimes, I think it's because she's outgoing, but she's more like our dad than we would like to believe. She also tends to allow foolish ideas to lead her before she evaluates the risks. She's not stupid, but she can play like it.

She had been wanting to work with my brother, which shows that she likes to stay involved, and I overlooked that. His plan to integrate fully into the States was slow, but he was already planning five steps ahead. Having a doctor on your payroll was never a bad thing.

As I approach the garage, Dahlia's soft cries reach my ears. Someone's also speaking quietly in response. She's sitting in the open tailgate of her car, Matt leaning into her. The sight only pisses me off more.

I've had the suspicion that Matt has taken to Dahlia, but the way she leans away from him eases something I didn't want to admit and causes a sick satisfaction to run through me. I shouldn't care whether she wants him close or not. I shouldn't be feeling petty things like jealousy, especially at a time like this, but I can't fucking help it. She brings out a level of possessiveness in me that I'm not familiar with.

"Hey, Matt, can I have a minute, man?" I say as I walk up to Dahlia, who has her feet hanging over the edge of the trunk. She doesn't look up, but she stiffens at my voice.

My jaw hurts from how hard I'm clenching it. She's afraid of me. Because I lashed out at her. It wasn't only stupid. It was cruel and inappropriate. I let my control snap, and the impulsive anger won. No one deserves to be treated like that, let alone her.

Yet the anger still simmers below the surface as I stand there. It's at war with her almost dying and her being incredibly reckless.

Matt narrows his eyes at me, his hands fisted and his jaw tensed, but he walks away.

Smart man.

"You know what you did was fucking stupid. Right?" I say quietly.

Her brows rise, but she doesn't look at me. "I think almost becoming a Lunchable clued me in," she snaps back.

Just stop making it worse, Ren. Fuck.

I take a breath. I don't know what to say. I want to apologize for how I acted... how I am acting, but I'm struggling to control the consuming anger.

Turning, I pace, rubbing my hand over my face.

My mind tracks back to last night. The way she sought to comfort me before I spiraled.

The guilt had me in a chokehold as I tried to forget the look on my friend's face before he pulled the trigger. It was as if he had been looking directly at me through the mirror.

It was as if I needed another reminder that it was my fault. My inability to stop this obsession with protecting my family cost him his life. Matt was there to help them... I could have helped James. I not only caused his death but am at fault for Sayuri's too.

But the little dream climbed out of bed and warmed the ice threatening to freeze me. She gave me her silent support without expecting me to explain. She's done nothing but do that, hasn't she? She's been trying to just *be there*.

"Fuck..." I whisper. She still won't look at me, clutching her hands and staring like they have all the answers.

I get closer where I'd be slightly between her legs if I moved an inch. With my hand, I lift her chin to meet my gaze. Instead of fear in her eyes, though, I only see anger and hurt. I can't say that makes me relieved, but not seeing fear does something to me. It loosens the shrinking noose around my neck.

I swallow, my throat suddenly dry. "I'm sorry," I whisper. I want to tell her why I lashed out, but I don't want to sound like I am trying to excuse my behavior. It doesn't matter. I shouldn't have lashed out regardless or manhandled her.

I'm not sure I'm ready to admit that the simmering anger that's ever-present finally became unmanageable. I don't know if I'll ever be able to admit I have that anger to begin with. She's already seen the nightmares. How can I show her this, too?

Her red-rimmed eyes continue to track mine, her brows lowering as if searching for a lie. She says nothing, but she grabs my hand to stop me before I step away. With hers over mine, I allow myself to wonder what it would be like to be able to hold her again and not just her hand. To have those eyes staring at me again with something other than anger or distrust, with something *more*. Not lust, but something else.

Fuck. I shake those thoughts away, preparing to grovel if I need to.

"Why do you need to be such an asshole?" Her voice has an edge to it as she lets my hand go, her tentativeness forgotten. "Would it have been better to let your sister go alone, or would it have just been better to let that zombie kill me?"

I wince. I can't help it. "No. Fuck, Dahl–"

"No? Then what do you expect from me? I'm not one of your military buddies or your weirdly secretive brother who dresses like a businessman but carries guns. I'm not your sister who can kill zombies with a nail file!" she exclaims, her voice raised while tears slip down her face. "I'm doing my best here. Trying so fucking hard to be of help without falling apart, but I can't compare... no matter what I do..." Her voice breaks.

My brows furrow. I didn't realize she was feeling this way. But why am I surprised? Wasn't I the one who thought that she was a liability? That her kindness was a weakness?

Shit. Her kindness is anything but.

"Look..." I turn my head, trying to find the right words. I'm trying to overlook the anger and look at things with a clear head. It's hard, but I know she deserves no less.

I glance back at her and step between her legs. Grabbing her jaw with my palm, my thumb rests against her chin as I pull her gaze up.

"I'm sorry." She goes to say something else, but I press my thumb to her lips and keep talking. "You didn't deserve to be treated like that. I am an asshole, angel. I'm not a nice man." Her eyes widen. "You may not be like Rei or Hana, but we couldn't have gotten this far without you either." She's been caring for Haru, clearly helping Hana, and willing to step up when needed. How I couldn't acknowledge it better is my own fault.

I trace my finger under her bottom lip as my eyes follow the movement. When she starts talking, I drop my hand and meet her gaze.

"You're right. I didn't deserve that." She sighs and lays back, partially crunched over bags. "But I did deserve something. I just don't know what." She breathes out heavily. "What I did risked everyone. I didn't even mean to shoot the zombie, but it was so close I panicked and shot instead of trying to stab it." Her voice wavers a little. "I should have talked Hana into staying, but there was also a part of me that wanted to go. The only word that keeps running through my head is reckless, and because of me, I almost got you killed in a rescue attempt." She sits up again, meeting my eyes, this time with tears filling hers.

"But I wish you didn't risk yourself for me. You even said I'd get left behind if I did something that risked someone. I was screwed, and frankly, you guys were lucky to have made a clear enough path for me to run. I don't want people dying for me. Especially..." Her voice breaks a little, and she quickly averts her gaze.

"Especially what?" I ask her softly.

She stays quiet, fiddling with her hands as she stares at nothing, not intending to tell me.

"Yeah, it was incredibly stupid, and believe me, Rei is tearing Hana a good one, but it isn't unnatural to feel how you guys feel. I mean..." I glance up at the ceiling, trying to think of how to put this.

"This is so new. This life of ours. We were so used to coming and going as we pleased without having to check in with people or run it by them first. We could go outside without the risk of being mauled." I step forward again, wiping her tears with my thumb before letting my hand linger. "We want that semblance of freedom again. It's normal to want to go out and try to find what the whole group needs. To feel like you are contributing."

She bobs her head, indicating she is listening. I bring my hand back to her chin, forcing her to look at me as I speak the last words. "You don't have to be reckless to contribute. Staying alive and being here is enough. You both help with Haru, and you've already proven you will help with whatever needs to be done. You don't need to be a hero or do more than necessary. I'd rather you stay alive. Your life is worth more than coffee, food, or water. Your life is worth more to me than anything you can find out there." I whisper the last words, not having meant to say them aloud.

I can't help but be slightly hopeful she didn't hear them, but with her eyes widening, that hope is crushed. Although I recognize that something is changing within me, I can't allow it to develop into anything else. Nothing about being with me is safe, and the last thing I want is for her to get hurt.

That doesn't stop my eyes from falling to her lips, though. Or for my blood to heat and my heart rate to skyrocket. Shifting closer, her legs widen, beckoning me without words.

"So again, I'm sorry. I need you to trust me, alright? If Hana wants to go off on some half-cocked adventure, just tell me." Our eyes are locked in a standoff as I lean closer. "I want you both safe," I whisper.

"Okay, I promise." Her voice is soft, as if she's melting with my touch. The heat between her legs and just having her so close has me hardening. It takes all of my control not to push into her. To show her exactly what she does to me. She leans into my palm, her eyes slowly closing. *Fuuuck, I want to taste her again.*

Before I can close the distance between us, someone clears their throat behind us.

Thankful and slightly disappointed at the same time, I find Juan idling by. I turn back to Dahlia before addressing him. "We can talk more later if you'd like. You weren't hurt again, were you?"

"No, I'm fine. Thank you." Her eyes cast down again as she speaks softly but I don't miss the red tinge to her cheeks.

Pausing, I turn back to Juan but don't move away from Dahlia. He doesn't seem fazed by my behavior and comes over to sit next to her.

"We may need to leave soon. Once we made sure everything was secured upstairs, I found a way to the roof. I wanted to scope out the area, but there's another fire nearby. It looks to be heading this direction," he tells me as he puts one foot up on the car and rests his arm on his knee.

Dahlia's head whips around, a shocked expression painting her beautiful face. "Another fire? What could have caused it, do you think?" She looks at me expectantly. It has me remembering we all still haven't spoken about what transpired at the motel.

The fires at the motel were most likely arson, but is this one too? For some reason, it's like an odd coincidence. Either intentionally or not, but that means there are more people out there.

Shit. "Regardless of how it started, there may be others, and it could bring them this way if the fires don't reach us. We secured this building enough that it may seem inviting to some," I explain.

Juan glances to the side in thought before humming in agreement and hopping off the tailgate. "I'll get the others. We should have everyone here to decide what to do," he says before walking away.

Dahlia shifts, brushing her legs against mine, reminding me where I am.

"You don't think we'll be safe here?" she says as she leans forward to slide out of the car. I should probably move, but I stay grounded, causing her to slide down against me as she plants her feet on the cement and straightens.

Chest to chest, I lift my hand before my brain catches up and brush the hair out of her face and behind her ear. "No, I don't. I won't risk it either," I say. My eyes track the freckles on her skin, half expecting to find constellations on her pretty features.

This time, I need to remind myself why I don't want to allow things to develop into anything other than attraction. Even *that* is dangerous. All I need to do is remind myself of the way she looked at me when she saw those bodies. Remind myself how she would look if she knew my story. Those reminders act as ice water in my veins, convincing me to put some distance between us. For the first time, I hate myself for the things I can no longer change. I don't even know her well, but I can't help but be disappointed in myself. Why should I even care what she thinks of me? Maybe after some time, it won't even matter. Maybe—

"Ren."

My focus returns, and I turn around, not noticing I got lost in thought, just staring. What the hell is happening to me?

I raise my brows and lift my head to Rei to indicate I am listening. He gives me a peculiar look, glancing over my shoulder for a millisecond before casting his eyes back to mine.

"Juan let me know what he saw. I agree, I think we should leave, but I wanted your thoughts," Rei says. "We were planning on only staying a few days, but we have whatever this place has to offer, so it shouldn't make a difference."

As he steps through the doorway, the whole of our group follows.

Hana walks in last, her head held high, as if she hadn't just gotten the largest lecture of her life from our brother. When her gaze meets mine, there's a challenge there, and it causes my mouth to tilt slightly. Ever the troublemaker.

My attention is brought back once everyone is huddled in a partial circle around myself and Dahlia, who is still standing at my back. Although Rei has been calling most of the shots, he looks to me now to take the lead here. I can't explain the feelings that rise out of me. Pride, maybe? Because he respects and trusts me enough to let me lead *him*. But... there is something else. Something ugly beneath the surface.

Normally, I'd be used to being in a role of leadership, but right now? I'm still fighting the growing anger and other swirling mess of emotions the day has assaulted me with. I'm not sure I can deal with this right now. I'm on a precipice and the more I think about the gravity of our situation and the responsibility it is to hold their lives in my hands, the dread and doubt creeps in... Somehow, the weight of it feels heavier than if they had been soldiers or more of my brother's men.

Clearing my throat, I focus on everyone in our group. We have my family, friends, Dahlia behind me, and then Davis, Susan, Jenson, Don, Jen, and their kid. Lastly, the two kids we barely managed to save.

Sixteen of us out of the thirty we originally started with, and two of those came later. We lost half of our group in a split second, and we still have a long way until we reach Parowan. I try to shove the negative feelings aside and am about to speak up, but the open backpack on the hood of my brother's car catches my eye. I stop short. *James' pack.*

The sight of it is like the final nail in the coffin.

My body reacts before I can try to calm myself. The walls feel like they are closing in on me. My lungs respond as if restricted from oxygen, suffocation, and darkness swarming my mind and body in a silent battle.

Rei must have noticed how stupid his decision was to put me in charge right now because he steps up instead.

Although everyone's attention is on Rei, the oppressive feeling keeps tormenting me. I break out in a cold sweat as the dread sinks in. The only thoughts crowding my mind are the ones of my mother's lifeless body and the bodies of all the men and women who served with me. All who trusted me to keep them alive and who instead paid for my failures in death.

The families we just lost.

The image of James' face flashes before me. His bright eyes and big ass grin. *Fuck, I can't do this.*

Suddenly, I'm being pulled backward, and my legs bump into something solid. Dahlia's pulling my hand, motioning for me to sit with her. She holds my stare as if in a silent question. *You okay?* I think she means to ask.

Had she seen me start to spiral?

Grateful for the distraction, I hop up. She doesn't release my hand; instead, she scoots closer to where our legs and shoulders are touching and rests my hand in her lap. She doesn't look at me or show any ounce of pity or curiosity. She only keeps her attention forward, listening to my brother speak. Her touch alone grounds me, keeping me present and warding against the edges of anxiety.

I remember what I told her once before.

You might as well be his damn guardian angel.

But maybe she's mine, guarding me against the insufferable thoughts plaguing me.

"...tonight, if that horde out there clears. We didn't find much on the upper level. We believe it was already cleared out, either by those who worked here or another group. There wasn't so much as one zombie hidden inside, which makes me believe someone may be coming back." He motions to me. "Ren agrees, but we thought another night would be worth the risk. Now, not so much. Once you guys store all your belongings, we can split whatever our coffee looters found and pack the vehicles." He gives Dahlia a small smile before addressing Hana.

She steps up and forces a smile of her own. "We left the boxes over by the door if one of you can help sort it," she says to Dirk and Matt. They both go, and everyone else takes that as a signal to break away and make sure they have all their things. No one unpacked, but if we leave anything, we can't come back.

"Did you have anything inside?" I ask Dahlia.

"No, I already threw whatever I had in the car a while ago. Although have you seen my jacket? I thought I left it in the front seat." She throws her thumb over her shoulder, pointing at the front of the car.

Thinking back, I don't remember seeing it. "I don't think so. Maybe the kid snagged it again."

"Oh, you're probably right... Little thief." She chuckles softly. "Anyways, were you able to find ammo or anything upstairs?" Her expression is hopeful for a moment, but her smile falters when she realizes we didn't. I don't bother telling her that we found virtually nothing when she mumbles a few curses.

"What Rei said was true; it seemed like someone cleared this building. I'm surprised no one has come back yet, but we should leave, regardless. Either people are coming this way, someone may come back, or the fire corners us. Every possibility points us to needing to leave."

She glances at the now-darkening window. Squinting for a moment in thought. "I hate that we need to worry about other people in all this. I used to think that disasters brought people together. Yet it only divided us further. Who are the real monsters in the world now?" She peers at me intently. Not accusatory, but genuinely curious.

"I think we're all capable of becoming monsters...." I stare down at my palms. No matter how clean my hands appear on the outside, I see nothing but the blood that covers them. "Unfortunately... survival can bring out the darkness from most people, especially when it involves protecting those they love. If not, chances are, they're the ones being protected by those monsters..." I swallow and think about what I'd do to protect them. "The monsters who are willing to lose *everything* to keep them safe. I hope we come across good people, but I won't expect anything less than savage in this world. To protect my own, I'll be the monster."

My family, and now her, are the real reason I already am one. My family is what led me to be who I am, and now, as I speak the words, I see that I may not be able to hide that from her.

She holds my gaze intently, still no fear in her eyes. It pierces me deeply, to my very being as if she can see the intention and not only the actions. It brings goosebumps to my arms.

"So will I," she whispers before standing up and walking over to Hana, leaving me staring after her in surprise.

Chapter Thirty-Seven

Dahlia

Who knew the zombie apocalypse would be so boring at times. The drive has been slow as molasses. Had we been in the normal world, we would've made it to Parowan by now. Instead, we're driving through Barstow. It's taken another two days to get as far as we have, mainly due to the ridiculous congestion on the road. We've passed multiple groups now, all trying to do the same and pass the abandoned cars. We managed to steer clear of most of them, but there were a few times we would pull off to the side of the road to wait for those groups to pass.

Besides other groups, we've been delayed by multiple route changes due to congested highways, debris, or the occasional undead. The number of times we needed to stop to move cars is ridiculous. Considering how the roads are in some areas, it's hard to think everyone made it out on foot. Or if they hadn't, the zombies somehow followed their food source. It's the only explanation I have for why the crowded parts of the rural roads aren't swarming with them. Just a handful here and there.

So far, Ren, Matt, Hana, and I have all been rotating roles as drivers. Each car has been doing the same. We're all too afraid to stay still too long. We want to gain as much ground as possible, especially with how clear the roads have been recently. Sleeping hasn't been an issue for me other than nightmares.

Poor Ren has been struggling, though. Either he can't fall asleep, or when he does, he ends up waking himself up. He's starting to look like he's afraid to sleep with all of us in the car in the first place. It has me curious if he's dealing with what my dad did, if he was afraid of sleeping because he feared he'd hurt someone. It almost seems like what happened to James only made things worse for him. Although, I can't blame him.

Watching him tackle his demons alone breaks my heart, but what can I do? Since the police station, he hasn't said much to me. He's barely even looked at me. I can't help but feel like I did something wrong. It shouldn't matter, but it still bothers me. To say I'm confused would be an understatement, especially after the few moments we shared.

He's giving me fucking whiplash.

As he's been keeping to himself, I've been sitting in the back with Hana and Ru when I'm not driving. The other two kids are now in a different car with Don and his family. Sometimes Matt joins in on conversations, but he's distanced himself as well. I thought the end of the world would allow us to get over our petty social struggles, but I guess not.

"Want some?" Ru asks from my left, offering me a biscotti. Without missing a beat, I reach for it.

"Thanks, little dude. You ate one already?" He gives me a wide smile, revealing a few missing teeth.

"Yeah. They are super yummy," he says as he shows me a half-eaten one in his other hand.

The poor kid has been a real trooper throughout everything. He hasn't been talking a lot, but I can tell he's trying hard to get through this. I have caught him crying a few times, and when I asked if he was okay, he would tell me he missed Sayuri or his mom. I've heard them mention Emi a few times—I think that was what they called her—but no one has stuck to the subject. I can't imagine it's easy for Reiji.

Hana and I have been trying to keep Ru busy now, playing I Spy or any random game we can think of in the car. Next time we go searching for food, I want to try to find some cards or something for him to play with.

"What about your favorite uncle? Where's mine?" Ren asks from the passenger seat, pulling my attention to the front.

Ru giggles and stretches to reach for his backpack before pulling another out to share with his uncle. As Ren goes to grab it, Ru pulls it away in a flash. He giggles as he goes back and forth with him before Ren graces us with a huge smile. "You little bugger, fine, don't share." He feigns hurt, bringing his hand to his chest.

With another chuckle, Ru finally hands his uncle the biscotti. "Here, Ren-oji. Only because I don't want you to be sad anymore," he says innocently, causing Ren's smile to falter as he shifts back in his seat.

"Thanks, kid. This will certainly help." He shoots Ru another boyish smirk.

Before I can digest that interaction, we're pulling off the freeway, giving me a sense of déjà vu.

As we exit the highway, we drive for about a mile and then pull into a small, abandoned shopping center. Zombies litter the lot, but thankfully, they are all spread out, and there's not many.

There's a liquor store, a small outlet grocery store, and a laundromat. A few cars have also been abandoned, a few of which with their doors hanging open. There is even some slow movement indicating zombies trapped inside the vehicles. Shopping carts and trash litter the area too, creating a scene straight out of a dystopian movie.

"You think they want to search the store?" I ask.

Out the window, there are zombies slowly walking this way, but fortunately, no screechers. In the more rural areas we've driven through, we've noticed there are fewer of the faster, loud zombies. Same with the weird sneaky ninja ones, as Hana calls them. I just call them scary. Granted, they all are, but still, the ones that hide and wait are frightening. Thankfully, we also haven't encountered more since we left the station.

As Matt puts the car in park and removes his seat belt, Ren is already getting out. "Wait here, we'll go see what they want us to do."

Taking my own seat belt off, I clutch the crowbar and shotgun, although I ran out of shells. It's strictly a long-range knife at this point.

"Are we going to get more food?" Ru asks Hana.

She pats him on the knee and smiles. "Hopefully, kid."

We wait a few more minutes before Ren walks over, opening the driver's door. "We're going to try to clear these zombies in the lot. There aren't too many, so wait here. When we give you the okay, we can all huddle up," he says before shutting the door again and getting to work.

It doesn't take more than a few minutes for a few of the guys to go around with their bludgeoning weapons. It's surprisingly quick and without issues.

"Now, why can't it always be that easy? If that were the case, we wouldn't be having to run away." Hana says softly before pushing the seat forward to climb out.

"For real," I mumble.

Another few minutes and we're all huddled up between the cars, waiting on direction from Rei. "Hana, I want you to stay with Haruto in my car with Don, Jen, and the kids. The rest of us are going to help clear and search the market. I want everyone to try to stay with one other person as we go in." He pointedly looks at everyone. "I don't want anyone on their own. We don't want to use the guns if we can help it. I have no idea when we can find more ammo, so save it. Once it's clear, we'll spread out, but I still want you to stick close in pairs. Hana, if any trouble arises, you guys leave. Everyone remembers the next meeting point?"

When we all give our responses that we do, Rei directs us into groups before we make our way into the store. I don't know why I'm surprised he pairs me with his brother, but it does.

We all fall into our usual silence as we take in our surroundings.

There are handwritten quantity limit signs on the front glass doors, and I notice the number of shopping carts.

During the height of the last pandemic, people swarmed to their local markets and bought everything off the shelves in fear of mass store closures. Seeing how busy this small market had been, my hopes of finding much dwindle.

I wonder if people started to panic shop before the outbreak spread this far when they got word that something was happening around the country. I can't say how fast the spread happened here, but it's possible.

If it spread slower out here, that would also explain the chaotic and inconsistent amount of traffic blocks and the number of groups of people we've encountered.

With no understanding of what was happening, I can see why people would want to stockpile their supplies. Especially since no one told anyone what was happening on the news.

As we step inside the dark store, we all take a moment to turn our flashlights on. Although it's daylight outside and the store has quite a few windows, it is still dark enough that it will take time for our eyes to adjust.

As we walk further into the building, only the sound of our light footsteps can be heard. As my eyes adapt, I can make out the extent of the store. It appears intact, only shopped over instead of messy like the looted gas stations and liquor stores we've encountered since the beginning. It only confirms my suspicions.

The store is small, reminding me of a Dollar Tree or a CVS in size. We walk aisle to aisle, not encountering any zombies. The doors had been closed. Maybe they started closing the store when things started going haywire. It takes us no time at all to clear the main part of the building, but as we come across the entrance to the back room, we all stop. It looks to have been locked.

If they were closing the store, wouldn't the front have been locked, too? Or were they in the middle of closing before fleeing...

I guess we'll never know.

I turn to start following the others back to the front but stop when I hear something. My ears perk as I strain to pinpoint what it was. It was almost like a whisper of a groan.

"What's wrong?" Ren asks.

Weird. "Just thought I heard something."

He takes a second to scope out the area around us before he shifts closer to me.

"It may have only been one of us or something." I force my smile to hide my sudden nerves, and we walk back to regroup with the others.

"We'll look for whatever we can. Once everything is split between vehicles, I want to try to access the back room. That's probably where there will be more of what we are looking for," Rei whispers.

A little nervous to speak up, I take a breath. It may be good to voice my suspicions. "You know how people panic-shopped during the pandemic? I think maybe that happened here. They had signs all over about quantity limits, and the parking lot was full of carts. Almost looks like they were closing when they all just up and left," I say. "Something seems off. I can't put my finger on it, but I think we should grab what we can inside and leave. It doesn't make sense for that back door to be closed if the rest of the store was open. And there weren't any zombies inside."

Rei and Ren share a pensive look. "Let's see what we can find here first and if there isn't much, we'll check the back, but if we find enough, we can skip it. I agree, but we need food and water. We're already on slim rations," Rei says as he rubs the scruff on his jaw. Nobody has had the chance to find any razors in this fiasco, causing Hana and I to be grateful for jeans. The men on the other hand, their faces are all telling the story of the no-shave apocalypse.

Sticking with our original paired groups, we get to work and each grab a cart.

Although I know we need food and water, my first stop is the personal hygiene aisle. Ren sticks close, no more than an aisle away.

Surprisingly, the shelves are relatively full. I grab a few boxes of each period product still on the shelf, including some cups. Never having used one, I'm skeptical, but I grab them anyway. Hana and I have been lucky not to need any quite yet, but that time will come all too soon, and I don't want to be left empty-handed.

Continuing to look around, I also find some wipes. "Nice."

Besides our group's occasional footsteps and shuffling, the silence is heavy. It's like an uncomfortable weight bearing down on me.

Grabbing the wipes, I move on. I grab the few random finds littering the shelves, but my next stop is batteries if I can find any. I go aisle to aisle, trying to find any batteries on a side cap or anything else we can use, but ultimately, I find most shelves with essentials empty, including hand soap.

"Did people just never wash their fucking hands?" Snorting, I continue, only to jump when Ren laughs behind me. He walks up next to me with his mostly empty cart.

"I thought the same thing. If people always washed their hands to begin with, why'd they need so much soap?" He chuckles and inspects the items in my cart but doesn't say anything. I guess he's used to having a sister. I can't help but find that refreshing. How many grown-ass men have I been around that still acted like children when it came to periods?

"I think I may have been right. Everything has been picked over for the most part. I found some chips and two cans of soup just shoved next to a price scanner." I gesture to my finds. "Also, thankfully, deodorant and tampons. But other than that, nada." I shrug as I make my way over to the front, having already made my rounds. "Did you by chance find batteries?" I ask.

"None," he replies.

Well, that sucks. I hold back my irritated groan while I continue to the exit.

I stop abruptly. *That sound again.*

"Did you say something?" I ask Ren.

He stops in front of me. "No. Why?"

Am I hearing things? "Oh, never mind then."

We reach the exit and push out the front, keeping an eye on the clear lot.

"It's odd. Even in some of the smaller areas we've stopped in, there are more zombies. Not that I'm complaining, but this is making me more nervous than when there are groups of them," I say softly as I walk to Rei's car. As I get to the passenger door, I tap on the window.

"I found the goods," I say as I wiggle my eyebrows.

Hana opens the door with the biggest smile. "Bless you, goddess of a woman. Just in time, too. Gimme." We each take a few things before I put some aside for the other two girls in our group. Although I want to hoard everything, I can't help but feel bad. I walk back and open the back door, indicating for Jen to pick some stuff out.

"You have no idea how much I love you right now. Thank you so much. I was going to ask, but I felt bad since we haven't spoken much," she says as she grabs what she needs, leaving enough for Susan.

Wait. "Hey, I just noticed. Where's Susan?" I ask Ren. She must have split off when we went inside, but I don't remember running into her. I walked around enough to see everyone at least once.

Ren's brows scrunch when he glances back at the market. "I thought she was behind us. We can go back in when we're done." We walk our carts to the car and unload the rest of our stuff.

"Hey," Ren says while he shuts the passenger door. "Your jacket." He holds it up. *What the*— "Haru must have found it or something and threw it back in your car." Ren hands me the jacket, and I slip it on.

I can't help but feel uneasy. I didn't see the kid with it at all since I lost it. But what other explanation is there?

Instead of saying anything, I brush it off. We walk back to the store and run into Rei and the others as they are walking out.

All except Susan.

Before I can mention anything, Rei speaks up. "I was thinking we could drive around back and see if there is a way to get inside the back room from there. I don't want to have to break in in case it draws attention."

Something about going into the backroom makes me nervous. I still can't shake the feeling that the door shouldn't have been locked. I don't speak up, though. Instead, I mention our other concern.

"We haven't seen Susan. Ren and I were going to go in and look for her."

Reiji's expression falters for a moment, showing unease, before he quickly steels it again.

Juan steps up next to him. "Dirk, why don't you drive around back with them? I can help them look. We can meet you once we find her."

Dirk gives him an odd smile. "Kill," he says and walks back to the cars. I'm guessing that's some kind of slang?

I turn back to the guys. "Did you see her after we started searching?" I ask Juan.

"No," he says and steps in front to lead us back into the store. The three of us walk together in continued silence. Although we were just inside, I can't help but feel uneasy.

I swear I hear that sound again. I glance around, trying to pinpoint it, but it's gone before I can figure out where it's coming from.

My unease grows as I keep walking slowly down the aisles. I'm back in the personal hygiene aisle when Ren rounds the corner.

Crash!

Startled, I whip around. Ren positions himself in front of me before I can process what happened. It's Susan standing above a box she dropped. All the contents are scattered across the floor, and the cans of food are now dented or rolling down the aisle.

"What the hell, Susan? Where did you go? We were worried!" I whisper-shout, not caring if I sound like a jerk. This is not the time to go half-cocked and take off on your own. Her hands come up as if blocking an attack while she bends down.

"Whoa. Sorry. I got an idea."

I walk over and help her pick up the stuff she dropped. I lean in to pick up a box of noodles but stop. *What the... Is that what I think it is?*

The smell is overpowering while being this close to her. *Marijuana.*

My eyes narrow as I take in the woman. Not only does the scent waft off her, her pupils are huge, and her eyes are red as hell. *Is she fucking serious?* "What the actual fuck? Are you high right now?" I whisper-shout.

The smile she gives me makes me want to smack it off. Who gets high in situations like this?

"Nah, I'm fine. Anyway," she says, completely brushing me off and looks to Ren. The clear dismissal has me seething, and I'm about to say something when she keeps talking. "When I was looking around, I found the door to their cash office. It was open and empty." She raises her hand again to interrupt whichever of us was about to speak first. "And before anyone says it, yes, I know it was stupid, but I was fine and have a weapon. Look." She stands and digs in her pocket. In her palm is a set of keys. "The store keys. It should open the back room."

Although still pissed off, her idea isn't awful. She should have waited or told someone so they could go with her, and she certainly shouldn't have smoked weed. Ren isn't standing close to her, but he has to smell her, right? But he doesn't mention it. Instead, he just stares at her pensively. The key must be too good of a peace offering.

Shit, she better not fuck up again.

I finish picking up the last of the things she dropped and glance around. My nerves are on edge, especially after she made so much noise.

"The others went to drive around back. Maybe we can go and open the dock doors," Juan says as he walks up. I guess he heard what she said.

My stomach churns, nausea rising with my nerves. "Maybe we should wait," I say aloud before meaning to, but the others shrug it off as they start walking to the back. I understand they are more experienced, but can't they tell something is off?

For some reason, those doors being locked bothers me. It's not out of the realm of possibility that they only partially closed the store, but it seems odd to me, regardless. Do most stores lock their stockroom when the dock doors and emergency exits are locked at the end of the night? When I worked at a large retailer in college, we never locked the doors leading from the stockroom to the main floor... but maybe others do?

Still... I can't help but believe they usually wouldn't have those doors secured like that though. Especially when the front hadn't been locked.

Ignoring my relentless paranoia and ever-mounting questions, I follow.

Once we are in front of the double doors, Susan unlocks them before stepping aside to let someone else in first.

I roll my eyes and am about to open the door when Ren grabs my hand and pulls me back.

"I'll go in first," is all he says as he directs a cold glare at Susan. "Just stick with me," he whispers in my ear. Even the softness of his voice can't disguise the command. It should irritate me, but it doesn't. If anything, it makes me feel like I wasn't overreacting about Susan. He knows she's high, and doesn't give a shit as long I stick with him. He only cares about *me* right now and despite the fear still prickling my skin, a giddy feeling takes residence in my heart.

The creak of the door as Ren pushes it open drowns out the fleeting giddiness all too soon and replaces it with trepidation. I was expecting zombies to jump out at us. Instead, we're greeted with an unnerving silence.

Silence so heavy it could smother us. It makes the hairs on the back of my neck stand on end.

We all flash our lights into the darkened room. The glare of the lights exposes steel shelving and two long corridors running the length of the store on either side of us. The shelves are crowded with pallets and equipment.

Directly in front, there's a small light coming from somewhere out of sight on the right, indicating an open door or window. That must be where the trailer unloading area is. Maybe one was open.

We all take tentative steps inside while using our lights to look down both main aisles.

Besides the dusting merchandise, it's empty.

There is more than I would've expected. From here, I can see pallets of water and toilet paper. There must have been a delivery just before everything went down. We're going to be good on water if we can safely remove it.

That thought doesn't calm my nerves, and from the way Ren's brows furrow, it doesn't for him either. He points to the right with his knife, and Juan jerks his head as if to tell him to lead the way.

They walk ahead, and I am about to follow when another sound breaks the silence.

A soft groan-like growl from somewhere further inside.

I strain my ears, trying to make out what that was, but as fast as it came, it's gone. The only sound is Susan's shoes squeaking loudly in the otherwise quiet space. The guys are still walking ahead, their flashlights bobbing with the motion of their steps. *Did they not hear that?*

When I turn, I realize Susan had started walking in the wrong direction, staring down at something in her hands as she walks. She isn't paying attention to her surroundings.

Shit. What the hell are you doing, Susan?

I peer over my shoulder, but Ren and Juan have walked far enough away, I can only make out their lights. *Fuck, what do I do?* He told me to stay with him, but I can't just leave her either. *Shit.*

Not wanting to make noise, but needing to stop her, I follow Susan. Hopefully, I can get her to come back before she does something stupid.

My eyes frantically glance in every direction. My skin feels clammy, and I have to clench my jaw to keep from shivering.

I really hope I was hearing things before.

Slowly, I direct my flashlight around me, hoping nothing jumps out at me. The room shrouds us in darkness. Susan is only a silhouette against the sliver of light peeking behind a corner up ahead.

I try to pick up my pace without making noise, but my heartbeat and my own breaths are too loud; I can't tell if my feet are silent or slapping loudly against the cement.

Dread fills my belly.

That sound...

Growls and groans echo off the walls ahead.

Much louder this time.

More than *one*.

Surely she should have heard that... She can't be that stoned, right? But instead of stopping, she turns out of view around a corner. Crap!

I speed up to grab her. To make her stop.

Just as I take another step, she comes into view.

Oh my God...

I halt in my tracks.

Ohhh fuck.... My eyes widen in horror, blood draining from my face.

Susan finally looks up from her palm and falters when she sees it.

Biting back the curse that fights to break free, I take slow, quiet steps forward. I need to grab her.

And *run*.

I plant my feet softly, not wanting to draw attention to myself.

Mother fuckity fuck.

My body quivers while I take quiet steps towards her.

Nothing we've seen so far compares to this. Nothing.

What's happening right in front of us is a goddamn bloodbath.

The smell of death and blood hit me like a freight train. Something else putrid lingers in the air, too. It lodges in my throat, choking me. So potent that the taste sticks to the roof of my mouth. I need to swallow the bile that rises.

The trailer doors are pulled up and fully open. To the left, zombies crowd an open door. An electric pallet jack is in front of the door as if someone tried to block it off but failed. The crowd of zombies is piling on top of someone long dead. The others are focused on trying to push through to get inside.

To get to the *trailer*… where instead of merchandise inside… there are *people*.

Or what I assume were once people. Now, they are nothing but body parts being chewed on and consumed by the mass of the rabid creatures.

My eyes blur with tears. I have no control over the violent shaking of my limbs. It takes everything in me to keep my legs from giving out.

Nausea roils in my stomach while tears continue to slip down my cheeks.

It's a nest of them… A nest of zombies…

Blood coats the trailer, pooling beneath them and dripping like a stream off the ramp.

So many zombies. All piled on top of each other inside and out of the trailer.

Too many that I can't count. They are eating whoever tried to hide inside. If the number of zombies means anything, there must have been a large number of people.

The behemoth of bodies is so large that the zombies are biting and clawing at anything and everything. Including each other.

Clacking of teeth and sickening sounds of flesh being ripped from muscle and bone are as loud as their groans and moans.

"Oh my god."

My eyes snap to Susan. It probably wasn't intentional. She said it quietly, but it was enough for one head to rise.

It makes eye contact.

Oh, fuck!

It climbs to its feet.

A screech permeates the loading dock. Chills rake up my spine, and my body goes cold.

The sound isn't as terrifying as the other bloody eyes that all glance up in perfect synchronization. So much so that it almost seemed choreographed.

The first one is already up, moving slowly compared to the screechers behind it.

My feet keep moving forward before I can think it through. I extend my arm, attempting to pull her back.

I manage a few more steps before she breaks out into a run. The closest screecher zombie is almost on top of her.

A hand clasps my arm, halting my attempt to grab her. Screaming, I lash out to hit my attacker before realizing it's only Ren.

"Run! You can't help her."

I try to shove him off, resisting. "She's still right there!"

"You can't do anything for her, Dahl. Please!" He's pulling me so hard that I almost slip, but somehow, I manage to keep my footing.

"She's still alive," I cry. *I can do this. I can save her.*

More and more zombies are rising to their feet.

They're shoving and tripping over each other. Hungry and determined to break out of the mass of bodies.

"Dahl," he chokes.

I try to pull away, but he attempts to grab my waist. I scream or cry. I don't even know. All I see is Susan. So close... yet so far away.

A screech echoes from inside the trailer. "Angel...." This time, his voice is like a whisper. "Baby... please."

The endearments don't faze me. All I notice is how close the zombies are getting despite them tripping over each other. I know he's right. She never had a chance, but how can I accept that? She's right there! Alive...

His grip tightens. "We need to go," he pleads while dragging me back.

His strength overpowers my weakening attempt to help Susan.

Choking back a sob, I give in. My heart aches while I turn to run. *To abandon her.*

I move as fast as my body allows me to. Ren doesn't let my hand go even though I know he can outrun me. My vision blurs from tears as he leads me.

Susan's guttural scream pierces my ears.

I flinch when it cuts off, replaced by wet gurgling.

More shrieks and screeches assault the space around us. I don't look back, afraid of how close they're gaining on us.

Juan has already made it to the parking lot and hops into the driver's seat of my car while we run through the exit.

"Don't look back, keep running!" Ren shouts, slightly breathless, as we make it into the lot.

Tires squeal as Juan pulls the car in front of us. The passenger door flies open as he slams on the brakes.

We waste no time, barely jumping in before the car takes off.

Ren grabs me by the waist, hauling me in before slamming the door over the folded seat.

It's only seconds before zombies ram into us, shaking the whole car. One slips and drags before it catches under the tire. I'm thrown to the side by the violent jerk of the vehicle.

More zombies are coming from behind the building. "Where did they all come from?" I scream, fear clawing at my chest.

Up ahead, the other cars from our group are driving out one of the exits.

Before we can follow, more screechers fill the space between us and our friends.

"*Mierda*," Juan curses. He makes a sharp left, trying to clear the growing horde.

He lets out a string of curses while maneuvering sharp turns, but he finally finds a clear pathway, although it's quickly shrinking.

"Hold on to something!" he says as he slams on the gas. The old engine pushes itself as he puts force on the pedal. Ren grabs my hand again just as we run over a zombie that jumps in front of us. The back of the car gains air, throwing me onto Ren.

"Shit." Trying to right myself to put my seatbelt on, we get thrown again, and this time, he barrels into me.

Juan finally clears out of the lot, but the noise attracts more zombies to the area.

Instead of heading towards the freeway, the way our group most likely has gone, we head in the opposite direction, towards a residential area.

The horde finally falls behind as we speed away.

We all seem to release a collective breath. How we managed to get away is beyond me. Glancing back, I can see the horde getting further behind us as we drive away at a questionable speed.

It isn't until we slow down that I let my mind process what happened.

How the hell can we keep surviving like this... when will our luck run out?

My body is shaking again, the memory of Susan and the horde becoming too much. My chest tightens as tears slip down my cheeks. My breathing becomes slightly erratic, but even as I try to calm myself, it still feels like I'm breathing through a straw.

Ren squeezes my trembling hand. Brow's furrowing, he scoots over and faces me.

His hands come up to cup my face. "Are you okay?" he whispers. His voice is strained, and concern blankets his features. "Breathe," he says. He takes in a deep breath, wanting me to mimic him. I follow his lead until my own becomes less uneven.

He uses his thumb to brush the tears from under my eye. "Are you okay?" he asks again.

Whispering back, I say, "Yeah. I think so."

He's silent for a long time as if lost in thought. It isn't until his breath catches when he speaks. "What were you thinking?" he whispers even softer, resting his forehead against mine. "Do you realize how close you were to dying? How close we were to losing you?"

The pain behind his words leaves me stunned. It's like the loss would be *his*. Swallowing, I whisper, "I'm sorry. I—" I choke back a sob. "I thought I could help her."

His breath hitches again as he inhales. Tilting his head slightly, he leans in, hesitantly brushing his lips against mine. He doesn't let go of my face but instead pulls me closer.

His kiss is soft and ends as fast as it began, but that doesn't diminish the impact it has on my swelling heart. His mouth hovers over mine like he can't get himself to pull away. Something about this feels different than the first kiss we shared. It's heavier. Its depth is an unspoken confession. It has my eyes only welling further with the overwhelming emotions.

"I knew your kindness would be your downfall." He doesn't release me but lifts his head to look me in the eyes. "You need to be kinder to yourself instead, angel. Otherwise, you'll die in vain."

Before I can respond, Juan interrupts, breaking the little bubble we've found ourselves in.

"Where the fuck did they all come from? There was no way there were that many there the whole time, right? We were in that store for a while. Not one heard us," Juan says, eyes nervously flicking to the mirror and back to the road a few times.

We all stay silent a moment before Ren speaks up. He lets me go and faces the front. "I don't know. Probably. There had to have been a lot of people hiding to keep their attention, but who knows what happened." His hand grabs mine to intertwine our fingers.

"Maybe someone op—" Juan is cut off.

Tires screech as he turns the wheel too hard.

The world is suddenly spinning before we're lifted off our axis.

Everything seems to happen all at once but also spans the longest moment of my life.

I'm jerked forward and up into the locked seatbelt. I'm weightless for a split second before slamming into the seat over and over again. My hand is torn from Ren's.

The sound of crunching metal drowns out our cries.

My heart is in my throat as we get tossed around like a carnival ride.

Glass shatters, raining down around us. The pain isn't comprehensible as my mind tries to grasp what's happening.

My head hits something solid as I'm jolted back into the benched seat again.

Finally, it stops. I'm on my side, still strapped in.

Only the loud, continuous horn and the ringing in my ears exist.

A soft groan comes from the front. I blink a few times, making out Juan trying to undo his seat belt to climb out.

The car has landed on the passenger side and there's a zombie inches from the now broken windshield. It's partially crushed under debris, desperately clawing at the hood of the car to get to us. It's completely unfazed by its broken body.

In the back of my mind, I know the loud horn will only attract more. We need to leave as soon as possible... but I can't seem to move my body. My arms feel like lead as I try to blink back the slowly invading darkness. The seat belt digs into my stomach as gravity presses me into the door of the car.

"Ren," I croak. When he doesn't respond, my panic surges. "Ren. Are you okay?"

I tilt my head and try to focus on what I can see. Instead of being belted into his seat as I expected, he's lying between me and the front seat, his back facing me. I can't see his face, but he's not moving. Smoke rapidly fills the space, and Juan's curses fade as he climbs out of the car.

No!

"Ren!" I exclaim. *Oh, God. Please be okay.* "Ren. Please wake up." I strain to lift my arms but manage to shake him gently.

He doesn't make a sound or move. All I can hear is the sound of the horn and the ringing in my ears.

"Ren. Please," I cry as I fight my bleary vision.

Tears continue to fall while I take in his unconscious form. *No. Please... No.* My heart breaks at the possibility that he isn't okay.

He has to be. He's been this never-ending strength. He's the impossible boulder in the landslide.

He can't leave us.

My sob is as violent as the crash.

While I try to move again, a telling screech sounds in the distance.

No. No. No.

I try to fight the ache in my head and the darkening of my eyes. It's taking everything I have to keep them open.

Metal scrapes and the door above me opens. "You guys okay?" Juan asks hoarsely.

His hands reach in, but I don't pay him attention while focusing on Ren. Another screech sounds. Closer. *Too close.*

"Ren." My voice is weak. I can barely hear it. "Please..." *Wake up.* "Please."

I blink frantically, but my vision won't focus.

It's like I'm underwater. The sounds and other voices outside are muffled and warped.

Voices? Who else is out there?

Hands reach down to grab me, but it's all lost on me as the darkness threatens to take me.

The last thing I can manage is another soft plea for Ren.

Please don't leave me...

Please...

Note to My Readers

I can't believe it's the end of book one! Now that we are here, I wanted to say thank you for picking up my debut and giving it a chance. I hope you loved Ren and Dahlia as much as I do, and I can't wait for you to see what happens next. If you didn't love it or maybe you absolutely hated it, that's okay. I still appreciate you taking the time to read it. And hey, if you got this far, you still most likely finished it. So, thank you. I wouldn't be here if it wasn't for you all being willing to support independent authors.

So, happy reading, and I can't wait to see you around for book two of the Amongst Desolation Series.

WHAT'S NEXT

Want to know what's next?

Follow me on social media and stay tuned for updates!

https://linktr.ee/ajsomers

ACKNOWLEDGMENTS

This process hasn't been easy, and I want to thank those who have been a constant support system for me. I apologize in advance, it's a bit long and messy, but it felt right to write them out like small letters instead of meshed paragraphs.

Mr. Somers and Berlin,

I know it wasn't always smooth sailing through this, but you were willing to take on more so I could follow my dreams. You understood how much this book and becoming an author meant to me and gave me the opportunity to shift more of my focus and finances into this book. Even when you went back to school and were running on fumes through most of it. I love you so much and I couldn't have done this without you. And Berlin. Well, you're still just a child, but you are the reason I started writing again in the first place. I hope I can make you proud and be the best example and mother that I can be. Your silliness and unconditional love has been the reason I get up and strive to be more.

Olive W.,

We met in the beginning of this journey when we swapped our early drafts. First, thank you so much for being willing to read such an early draft of my book. You have no idea how thankful I am to have you alongside me during this time. You put up with my ADHD hot-mess-of-a-brain, and are always willing to bounce ideas off each other, or just chat about life. Your support has meant the world to me. I am so thankful to have met you and can't wait to see you thrive in the author world.

Sally L.,

You have been nothing but genuine and supportive since we became friends. You are always willing to answer questions about publishing and writing, and you never complain. Even when I blowup your chats. (I'm sorry!) I am incredibly thankful for your friendship and even more so that you were willing to help me format this novel. Thank you so much. You have been the best friend, and I can't wait to see where you go in your own author journey.

Lauren S.,

Although you didn't have a hand in the book process itself, I just wanted to thank you for always being a supportive friend. Getting closer to publishing, things got stressful, and you never stopped standing by me and letting me lean on you. I love you so much and I am so grateful for you. Also, thank you for being willing to take B. so I could write. You have no idea how much that means to me.

Lauren N.,

Thank you for being the friend/sister version of my "Little dream amidst the nightmares." During this process, you have been there for me on multiple occasions. Even when my mind is in a dark spot, you let me lean on you and word vomit what was on the circus chaos of my mind. Your encouragement means the world and I love you so much.

•••

I wish I could continue to write longer messages of gratitude, because there's so many people who've been so supportive, but if I did name everyone and write long letters, I would be about twenty pages deep. So, a few other quick thank yous because you all have been amazing.

Sara, words cannot describe how much I appreciate you. Thank you for alpha reading for me and always being so helpful when I need to ask questions.

Alicia, you have been nothing but supportive and you taking the time to beta read and continue to answer beta-related questions and hype me up, means the world to me.

Crystal, thank you so much for your friendship and always being the best hype-woman. I low-key strive to have a book you fall in love with some day.

Millie, words cannot describe how much I appreciate you. You have been a hype-woman, beta reader, and even helped me with some more character-building questions.

Shawna J., I can't thank you enough for beta reading for me. I swear, the way you went through my manuscript, I would have thought you did that for a living. Your feedback and comments were amazing, and some had me laughing out loud. Thank you so much.

Claire F., thank you so much for taking the time to beta read for me even though you are writing your own books and are basically super-mom/teacher. Your feedback was incredibly helpful, and I appreciate you so much!

●●●

Lastly, I wanted to thank those who helped me work on this book on a professional/developmental level.

Sarah, I am so happy I got to work with you on developmental edits. You were amazing and I hope to work together again soon. (Developmental edits - Edits and Revisions)

Lindsey, you were incredible, and I appreciate the added comments to help make my novel the best it could be. I hope we can work together again soon as well. (Line edits - Lindsey Clarke Editorial)

Ashe, my cover turned out stunning. I am such a huge fan of your art, and I'm so thankful you were able to do my cover. I can't wait to work on the next two covers. And thank you for reading and connecting me with Devon! (Cover @spookgeist)

Devon, words cannot express how much I appreciate you. Thank you for being willing to read and give me insight into the culture and language aspect of the novel. I couldn't have done it without you.

Rosie, thank you so much for taking the time to read for me and give me any insight needed. I appreciate it so much.

Anson, thank you so much for being willing to help answer cultural and language questions. You never complained and let me pick your brain throughout the entire process. It was all incredibly helpful.

Dalvin, thank you so much for answering all of my questions, and even going as far as asking an officer when you weren't sure about something. Everything you gave me will help with Ren's character throughout the entire series. I can't express enough how much I appreciate your help.

Andrew, I only asked one or two questions, but I just wanted to say thank you for being willing to answer them. I hope to portray my characters and certain situations as authentically as I can, and you helping me allows me to do so.

Sally L., I already mentioned above but thanks again for formatting this beauty!

THE WRITER BEHIND THE PAGE

AJ is a Neurodivergent/Disabled romance author from Orange County, California. When she isn't writing or reading, she most likely has her hands in other creative hobbies, or is spending time with her husband, daughters, and her scaly and fur babies. She's also an avid coffee drinker and lover of suspenseful stories and games. Prior to having her daughter, AJ was a certified (volunteer) Sexual Assault advocate in OC. Mental health and SA advocacy is incredibly important to her. With her books, she hopes to inspire others, and to show them they are not alone. She hopes her readers can resonate with her characters and see that everybody experiences mental illnesses and trauma very differently.

Resources

Never forget that YOU matter. This world would be a lot duller without you in it.

Should you ever have thoughts/ideations of suicide, I highly encourage you to call or text '988' or if that is not available where you reside, visit https://988lifeline.org/

•••

Just know, that I see you. I hear you. I believe you.

If you are from OC, California, I highly recommend calling the 24/7 (Confidential) hotline should you ever need someone to talk to about your own SA experience, or a loved one's experience, or need resources/have questions regarding SA.

OC California-

(949) 831-9110 or (714) 957-2737

Or visit https://waymakersoc.org/

If you are in another location in the US, RAINN also has a 24/7 hotline (confidential)

(800) 656 4673

or visit https://rainn.org/

•••

I know it may be hard to reach out for help when you need it. It may feel intimidating or embarrassing, but I promise you, it is okay to put yourself first above all else. Your mental health matters. YOU matter.

If none of these options are available to you, please do not be afraid to confide in a loved one to ask for help.

Put yourself first.